Honor's Quest

KRISTEN
HEITZMANN

♦♦♦♦♦♦♦♦♦♦♦♦♦♦♦♦♦♦♦♦♦♦♦♦♦♦♦

Honor's Quest

BETHANY HOUSE PUBLISHERS
MINNEAPOLIS, MINNESOTA 55438

Honor's Quest

Cover illustration by Joe Nordstrom
Bethany House Publishers staff artist.

Published by Bethany House Publishers
A Ministry of Bethany Fellowship International
11400 Hampshire Avenue South
Minneapolis, Minnesota 55438
www.bethanyhouse.com

Printed in the United States of America
2 in 1 ISBN 0-7394-0594-2

To Devin
As you grow into manhood
may you become the man of honor
God created you to be

. . . whatever is true, whatever is noble,
whatever is right, whatever is pure,
whatever is admirable—
if anything is excellent or praiseworthy—
think about those things

PHILIPPIANS 4:8

ROCKY MOUNTAIN LEGACY

Honor's Pledge
Honor's Price
Honor's Quest
Honor's Disguise

KRISTEN HEITZMANN was raised on five acres of ponderosa pine at the base of the Rocky Mountains in Colorado, where she still lives with her husband and four children. A music minister and artist, Kristen delights in sharing the traditions of our heritage, both through one-on-one interaction and now through her bestselling series, ROCKY MOUNTAIN LEGACY.

Part One

One

Ragged scraps of cloud hung beneath the edge of blue nubby mountains like gauze torn from a blanket of gray. The keen December air held an expectant breath as Abbie stepped out and drew it into her lungs. She watched a black-capped chickadee puff itself on the bare cottonwood beside the ice-edged stream, then took the bucket and headed for the pump.

Monte's plan for indoor plumbing was only talk now, with the financial struggles that seemed to mount daily. Her heart ached that her own foolishness had put them in jeopardy. Monte blamed it on a kind heart and a stubborn streak, but she knew it was just plain ignorance.

Abbie hung the bucket and gripped the pump handle. The cold of the metal penetrated her beige kid glove. She'd thought all her schooling, her voracious reading, and the woodcraft Blake had taught her would set her up fine for life. Marriage to Montgomery Farrel had proved her wrong.

She worked the handle until the water gushed, then kept it smoothly coming. When the rush nearly reached the brim, she released the handle and lifted the bucket from the hook. She didn't need indoor plumbing and spigots that ran hot and cold. She'd bathe in a mountain stream if only Monte wouldn't worry.

He tried to hide it, except in those honest moments when they held each other in the dark. Then he admitted his fears. Had he not lived through ruin enough with the war that destroyed his father's southern plantation?

He had established himself so solidly here in the Colorado

Territory. But his brother-in-law had turned things upside down, and, man of honor that he was, Monte vouched for Kendal's debts. Abbie wished she'd known and understood.

But she hadn't. She had foolishly sacrificed valuable stock certificates held in her name. That she had thought to help Kendal, that the venture turned out fraudulent, that those certificates were now held by a self-satisfied banker, were all due to her ignorance.

Monte's sister, Frances, was right. There was more to being a lady than she would ever know. Abbie held the bucket with both hands and started for the house. She was too headstrong, too impetuous, too—

A hand snaked from the shrubs and clamped her mouth as a cold knife touched her throat. Her heart thundered in her chest and she felt her pulse against the blade's edge. She tensed to swing the bucket into her assailant, but with a swift glance at the hand on her mouth, she went immediately still.

Taut brown fingers trapped her breath with her voice. One move and the Indian knife would not only open her throat, but relieve her of her hair, as well. She forced her nerves to calm and stood straight.

Any show of fear could endanger her. She thought of all the tales she had scorned, all her brave declarations that the Indians were not to be feared but respected. Now with her life at the tip of an Indian blade, she resisted the surging terror.

She waited. Almost imperceptibly, the hand loosened; the knife left her throat. Still, she did not move or turn.

The man's breath warmed her ear as he spoke very low. "Wise One."

Abbie spun, sloshing water down her skirt. Its icy jolt was nothing compared to her sudden relief. "Gray Wolf!"

He snatched her into the cedars and gripped her mouth again. What was he doing? Why would he threaten her with a knife after once saving her life? Had he lost his mind?

"No speak." His face was hard and firm. He looked every inch Comanche. Though their worlds touched at strange, unexpected times, she could not assume she knew him.

She nodded.

Gray Wolf raised his head, listening. A second later, Abbie heard the approaching hooves. They were far but moving fast and coming their way. Gray Wolf stiffened. It seemed his every sinew tensed, as a buck ready to spring, and she realized it was fear driving his actions. Did he think she would betray him?

He flinched when she touched his arm. She pointed to the door, then started for it. She could scarcely hear him follow but felt him there. She pulled open the door to the back room. The kettle was steaming on the small stove for her bath. She left the door open behind her and set the bucket on the floor beside the tub, then removed the kettle from the heat.

The light dimmed as Gray Wolf filled the doorway, then stepped inside. She walked slowly to the door and closed and latched it behind him. His scent filled the small enclosure, an aroma of sweat and something musky from the small pelts that hung at his belt beneath the black woolen coat. He stood like a caged animal.

"It's all right," she whispered, then walked to the door connecting to the kitchen. She pressed her ear to the wood. Pearl's humming was interrupted. Abbie caught Monte's voice but not his words.

"She's havin' her bath, Mastuh Monte."

His steps approached the door. Abbie motioned Gray Wolf into the corner. He pressed in among the brooms and carpet beaters.

Monte tapped the door. "Abbie?"

She reached into the tub and sloshed the water. "What is it, Monte?"

"There's a posse here looking for an Indian brave."

"What on earth for?"

"I don't have the details, Abbie. Have you latched the door behind you? They found his horse in our pasture."

"The door is latched." Abbie prayed he'd ask no more. She wouldn't lie to him, but she wasn't sure how he'd take her hiding

Gray Wolf from the law, and she owed Gray Wolf a debt greater than Monte's honor.

"I don't want you out there until this is settled. Have you water enough?"

She smiled. "Yes, plenty."

"Marshal Davis and the men are searching the grounds."

"I won't go out, Monte." Nor, she realized, would they come in. Not if they thought she was bathing. She relaxed as his steps faded and Pearl took up her humming again. The smell of grits and hot cakes sizzling in pork fat seeped into the room. Gray Wolf had not moved.

Abbie crept to his corner. "Gray Wolf, why are they looking for you?"

"White man's lies."

"What have you done?"

"My brothers are dead."

Abbie pictured the young braves who had hunted with Gray Wolf. The same men who, with Gray Wolf, had slain Buck Hollister and the other outlaws and rescued her. They had given her life and freedom. Could she now do less for Gray Wolf, whatever his crime?

She heard voices outside and spun as the door latch was shaken. It held firmly, and the voices passed on. She turned back. "You'll be safe here, for now at least. Do you understand?"

He nodded once.

"Turn to the wall . . . please."

He stared at her a moment, then obeyed, arms crossed at his chest, back straight. She poured the hot water from the kettle into the bath with the cold from the bucket, then doused her head and scrubbed her hair clean. Once she caught him glancing over his shoulder, but he didn't repeat it.

She toweled her hair and twisted its thick length at the nape of her neck, then pinned it there. She approached Gray Wolf. "I'm finished now. I'll bring you food." She went through the door to the kitchen.

Pearl turned from the stove. "Breakfast is ready, Mizz Abbie.

I fed de marshal's men, but they's plenty more."

"Thank you, Pearl."

Monte stood when she entered the dining room. His white pleated shirt, gray vest, and trousers were immaculate, and his dark hair waved back from his face and fell in unruly curls to the back of his collar. His brown eyes were as warm as boiled molasses as he pulled the chair and seated her, then kissed the crown of her head. "Mmm. You smell sweet."

"I should. It's the honeysuckle rinse you bought me."

He brushed her shoulders with his hand as he sat. She thrilled at his touch and wished nothing distracted her from his company. But Gray Wolf waited, and she hadn't any idea how to broach his presence to Monte. Pearl brought the hot cakes and grits and a bowl of stewed apples.

Monte blessed the food, then glanced at Abbie. "Bit of excitement this morning. You heard nothing when you were at the pump?"

Abbie dropped her eyes to the hot cakes and cut. "How well does one hear Indian braves, Monte? You know the skill with which they move."

"It's not a good sign that he left his horse in our pasture. How far can he go on foot?"

"A good distance if he has a mind to. Did they find any sign of him?"

"No. But that doesn't mean he isn't hiding near." Monte reached for the small, cut glass pitcher that held the pure maple syrup, freighted west from the Vermont forests.

Abbie could hardly taste the sweetness she usually savored. "What is he accused of?"

"Murder."

"Of course."

Monte raised a dark eyebrow at her tone. "Meaning?"

"What's the whole story?"

"Four men are dead. The Dillon brothers, Mag French, and his son Travis. It seems they were liquored up; maybe they meant to have some fun. Ethan Thomas heard the commotion out behind his place and saw the brave escape on horseback. The description matches the horse found in our pasture."

Abbie bristled. "Four men to one. That hardly sounds like murder."

"There were three other braves."

"What happened to them?"

"Killed." Monte wiped syrup from his lips with the fine linen napkin.

Abbie controlled the anger in her voice. "You said four men dead. Did the marshal forget to count the braves?"

Monte set down his fork. "Forgive me, Abbie. I spoke without thinking. I'm only repeating what the marshal said."

"I know that. But don't you see, Monte? Just as you took it for granted and didn't look past the loss of settlers' lives, so will others. What chance has that brave?"

"He'll receive a trial, same as any man."

"The same as any man? Can you really believe that?"

"Abbie . . ."

"You know what Mag French and his son were like. The Dillons were little better. Who exactly do you think started the fight?" She was losing control of her emotions.

"It doesn't matter who started it. The fact is—"

"They'll hang him."

Monte made a sound of exasperation. "Abbie, there has to be some order."

"If it were Mag French who escaped with four braves dead, would they hang him?"

Monte folded the linen napkin and laid it beside his plate. He released a long breath. "Likely not."

"So much for order."

Monte narrowed his eyes. "Abbie . . ."

"It's Gray Wolf, Monte. It's Gray Wolf they're hunting."

He rested his hands on the table edge and stared. Abbie held his eyes steadily. He must understand. She couldn't bear to defy him.

"Where is he?" Monte's voice was low.

"In the back room."

"He was with you while you washed?"

"I wasn't in the tub, Monte. I . . ."

"Deceived me." His tone was flat, and she sensed his impending anger.

"Only until the posse left. I couldn't risk . . ."

"Trusting me."

"No, I . . ." Abbie stammered.

Monte pushed away from the table and stood.

Abbie sprang to her feet. "Please. Hear me out. I didn't want to compromise you. Could you have looked Marshal Davis in the eye and told him Gray Wolf was not here?"

He turned. "Could you?"

"I owe him my life. Would you not have lied to a Yankee soldier to protect those in your care?"

"Gray Wolf is in your care?"

"Would I be here today but for him?"

He rubbed a hand over his eyes. "Abbie . . ."

"He is not guilty of murder."

Monte paced across the room and back. "Even if that's so, what do you propose we do?"

"Give him a horse and food. Let him make his way back."

"They have the ranch surrounded."

For a moment she felt what Gray Wolf must feel. His enemies closing in, his safety in the hands of one who could so easily betray him. What chance would he have? "Then let me get him through."

"No."

"Please, Monte."

He leaned his head back, then slowly lowered it. "How?"

"I can head for Pa's in the wagon."

"That's crazy, Abbie."

"They won't suspect if it's me alone."

"They'll think I've lost my mind letting you out. Besides, Gray Wolf won't agree to it."

"I think he will."

Monte ran his hand through his hair. "Abbie, it's not right."

"Is it any less right than what Mag French did to Gray Wolf's brothers? He defended himself, Monte. But will anyone believe that?"

He crossed to her. "I'll take him, then."

"He won't trust you. He came to me, and it's my debt to repay. Besides, I have a better chance." She smiled. "Being a lady and all."

He took her shoulders and drew her close. "I won't have it."

"I'm safe with him." *As safe as anyone could be with a brave like Gray Wolf.*

"You don't know that."

She wrapped her arms around his waist, sensing him weaken.

He closed her in a tight embrace. "He's Comanche, Abbie."

"I know." She stretched up and kissed him. "I'll feed him first. You choose the horse."

"That hurts."

"He'll treat it right."

"Hah."

"At any rate, it's necessary." She pulled away. "Tie the horse to the back. I'll say I'm taking it to Pa's, and I'll cut through his homestead to make it true."

"You think of everything. God help me if it's ever me you try your wiles on."

She swirled her skirts in her wake.

"Abbie."

She glanced back over her shoulder.

"No one else is to know."

She nodded.

Gray Wolf ate ravenously. Abbie watched him as she filled a bag with foodstuffs. He ate as though it were his last meal. She prayed it would not be so. She had secreted the cold beef and oatmeal muffins from the kitchen with Pearl none the wiser. Monte's honor depended on her secrecy.

Though she had no doubt that God understood what she did, men were another matter. And whereas she might be forgiven as sentimental and emotional, Monte would not be. A tap on the door told her he had the wagon ready. Gray Wolf looked up from his plate.

"Gray Wolf, I'm going to hide you in the wagon and drive you past the men looking for you. Do you understand?"

He pushed the last piece of muffin into his mouth and stood. He was not tall, but every inch of him was lean and muscular. His chest muscles bulged in the buckskin shirt as he drew himself up. "You hide me."

"Yes. Under the tarp in the bed of the wagon. Monte has loaded it with other things to help with the disguise. He has a horse for you, as well."

"Why you do this?"

"Did you want to kill those men?"

"Yes."

"I mean before they set on you, did you plan to hurt them?"

He stood stoically without speaking.

"The law doesn't always reflect the truth, but truth still matters."

"We were to hunt. White man's settlements drive away the game. Comanche go hungry. Mountains hold the secret places. We came to hunt. We came in peace."

"Then I will get you through to go back to your people."

"My people are no more."

Abbie stared at him. "There must be . . ."

"Those on government land. They are not my people. They do not live free. They live . . . white man's ways."

She felt his emotion like a force—pride, regret, anger. She felt her own shame. "I am sorry, Gray Wolf."

"You." He touched her forehead as he had once before. "Wise one."

She felt the sting of tears. There was nothing more she could do. He had to make his own way. Maybe he would. Or maybe he would end up on the reservation. At least he would be alive. "We must go now."

She cracked the door open and saw Monte standing at the

head of the wagon. The horse tied to the back was young and strong, if not of the finest lineage. She bit her lip in gratitude. Monte would not count that loss lightly if only for the horse's sake. But perhaps Gray Wolf would be more careful than was usual for his people. He could not so easily replace the beast as in years past.

She opened the door and stepped out. "All clear?" she murmured and dropped the sack of food into the back.

Monte joined her. "I believe so." He helped her raise the tarp and Gray Wolf slipped beneath. "I certainly hope you know what you're doing."

"Thank you, Monte . . . for understanding."

"It's honor, Abbie. You owe a debt."

She smiled up at him. That, he understood. *Honor.* Was there ever such a taskmaster beneath God himself?

He kissed her briefly. "Be careful. If you're caught, act featherbrained . . . if you can." His mouth quirked.

Abbie giggled. "I'll give such a performance, Carolina Diamond would be green."

Monte lifted her to the seat. "Abbie, this is not a lark."

She saw his concern and looked suitably subdued. He pressed her hand but said no more. Abbie took up the reins. She was hardly past her yard and into the open country between Monte's ranch and her pa's when two men stepped out from the scrub oaks, one of them large and lumbering.

She reined in. "Marshal Davis."

He removed his hat and held it to his chest. "Mornin', Mrs. Farrel."

"Almost noon. Any sign of your fugitive?"

"No, ma'am." He glanced at the wagon bed. "Is your business pressing? I don't feel too safe with you traveling alone. I'm surprised Mr. Farrel . . ."

"I'm heading to my pa's. It's not far."

"It's a good step yet."

"I've things to deliver that won't keep. Pa's birthday is tomorrow next." It was, but how that had come to her only the good Lord knew.

"I still wouldn't—"

"Mr. Farrel was satisfied with your search, and I have my pistol." Of anyone, Marshal Davis should know she could shoot. She shuddered at the memory of his questions the morning after she had killed the young rustler.

He hesitated. "I'd send an escort, but..."

"There's no need, though I thank you for the thought."

"Yes, ma'am." He replaced his hat. He looked more bearish than ever when he lumbered back to the bushes.

Abbie slapped the reins. He hadn't even asked about the extra horse. But she'd tip the corner of Pa's homestead anyway, just for good measure. She brought the wagon up the foothills as far as she could manage on the rough terrain.

Though this wasn't the native home of the Comanches, Gray Wolf knew these hills. He'd hunted them with his brothers when hard times forced them north. He'd come to know the mountains and surrounding hills as he'd known the plains. She reined in and climbed down.

Gray Wolf raised the tarp. He leaped down from the wagon bed and stood poised on the balls of his feet. The breath of wind caught his crow black hair as he gripped his knife and scoured the scrub oaks and ponderosas.

She made no move until she saw his muscles slacken. Then she went to the horse and untied its rope. It was unsaddled, and Monte had not included a saddle in the wagon bed. No matter. Gray Wolf would ride bareback.

He took the rope and looked hard at her, his eyes burning with sudden intensity. He reached out and took her arm, his grip firm and insistent. "Wise One, come."

Abbie's heart jumped to her throat. She shook her head. "No."

"Gray Wolf squaw." He held himself up, straight and powerful, and his grip tightened.

She met his eyes and the fear left her. He'd been the leader of his clan, respected and feared. Now he was alone. Her heart squeezed in pity for him, but she didn't show it.

She raised her chin. "I'm honored, Gray Wolf, but I have a husband already. My husband gave you this horse." She'd remind him of his debt. "In thanks for your saving my life." That made them even.

He stood silent, then released her arm and stepped back. She thought he would speak, but always what passed between them in silence was stronger. He took the leather thong strung with animal claws from his neck. She was certain it was strong medicine, but he held it out to her.

She took it from his hand. "Thank you."

With a swift motion he swung to the horse's back and kicked in his heels. The animal leaped upward through the trees, its muscled flanks rippling and its breath white. She watched until he was out of sight, then clutched the animal claws in her palm. *Godspeed, Gray Wolf. May your paths lead to peace.*

She turned the wagon down the mountain and headed back. She saw no sign of Marshal Davis as she drove. He must have changed his position. It was too much to hope they'd called off the search, but she was glad now to have it concentrated on her property. Gray Wolf would vanish into the mountains.

Perhaps one day she would see him again, but likely not. She thought of him riding alone and sighed. Not that she would ever consider going with him. She might know how to track and fish with a spear and other things that hardly behooved a lady, but her world and Gray Wolf's would never blend. And she was already married to the man she loved.

She would certainly not mention Gray Wolf's offer to Monte. How he would scowl! She glanced back over her shoulder and smiled. Then again, maybe she would.

Two

Abbie looked down at the elegant pink stone, white-gabled, pillared house. Her home. The house, yard, and outbuildings had a settled graciousness that both welcomed and unnerved her. It was Monte's grace, Monte's heritage she saw. Her spirit was in the land, the wide open range ahead, and the wild, rugged mountains behind her.

As she neared the house, she saw Sterling Davis ride away. He was not part of the searchers, she was certain. He worked with Pa and ran the telegraph. He must have brought news, urgent news if it came by telegraph.

She quickened her pace, left the horse and wagon at the stable, and hurried inside. She stopped at the door to the library. Monte stood in the center of the Aubusson rug, his face ashen. He held the telegram but stared at the wall.

She rushed in. "Monte, what is it?"

He turned. His dark eyes looked deep and hollow. His voice seemed to come from a great depth. "It's Frances. She . . . died of pneumonia."

She felt the breath leave her. "Oh, Monte." She gripped his hands. They were cold, especially the burn-scarred palms. The telegram fluttered to the floor as she caught them to her chest.

His tone stayed flat. "We must go for Jeanette. Frances asked . . . that we take the child."

Abbie pressed in close to him. She couldn't bear the hard restraint she heard in his voice. "Of course. Oh, Monte, I'm so sorry."

He stroked her head but seemed miles away. He was blaming himself, though there was nothing he could have done. His sister, Frances, had been in his charge so long—through the war when they were young and afterward, when his father returned broken and maimed. After her grief this last year, the loss of her home and Kendal's death, Monte had tried to keep her with them, but she had refused.

Abbie tucked her head beneath his chin and reached around his back. She felt his tense muscles under her palms and knew he exerted great control over the emotion surging through him. Her own tears sprang loose and dampened his shirt. She hurt as much for his loss as for Frances's passing.

His voice was thick. "Will you pack? I have things to attend to before we can go, and I want to catch the morning train."

"Yes, of course." She drew away, but he pulled her close again and pressed his lips to her forehead. She raised her face and he kissed her, cupped her cheek briefly, then released her.

As she went up the stairs, she thought of little Jeanette. How was she faring with her mama gone? She had her mammy and her grandmother, Kendal's mother, but it was a mama the child needed.

Abbie's heart ached, remembering the little girl bundled in her arms as she took her down the hillside on the toboggan. She heard Jeanette's laugh, felt again the tiny mittened hands in hers. She longed to be there already, to wrap the child in her arms and hold her close.

Oh, Frances. She'd been so thin, worn by fear and anger and grief. Yet she'd seemed strong, more able to cope than before Kendal's death. Had it been a ruse? Had she mimicked strength to make her escape? Had she known Monte would never let her go unless he believed she would cope?

Abbie took out the carpetbags and satchels and pulled them open. Charleston. She was going to Monte's home. She needed only black, but it must be the very best. She had the black silk from Kendal's funeral, and the chintz, and the linen day dress.

She laid out Monte's frock coats, waistcoats, trousers, and

shirts. He looked so somber in black, but she supposed they all must. She debated between his chesterfield velvet collared overcoat and the inverness with the deep cape. What was she thinking? What did it matter what they wore, when Frances . . .

Frances. All the unkind things she'd thought of Monte's sister haunted her now. Frances had been so proper, so condemning. And yet inside she'd had the same longings, fears, hopes . . . *Dear Lord, Frances rests with you now. I pray she's united with Kendal and their struggles are over.*

Zena tapped the door and came in, her assistance automatic, her dark hands swift and efficient. She packed the Saratoga trunk, and Abbie worked beside her. She couldn't be idle when her heart was so full it might burst. She felt a stabbing ache for Monte.

Frances was all he'd had left of his birth family. She thought of Mama and Pa and Sadie and Grant. She had so many to love, and he had lost all. She closed the carpetbag. "Will you finish here, Zena? I'm going to tell Mama we're leaving."

"Yessum. I's sorry 'bout Mizz Stevens."

Abbie pressed her hand. She wasn't surprised Zena knew already. James and Pearl and Zena knew all their business and handled it as though it were their own. "See that Pearl has something hot for Monte as soon as he returns."

"Yessum."

For the second time that day, Abbie rode to Pa's ranch. She caught sight of Mama in the yard hanging linen on the line. It would freeze before it dried if the sun didn't show itself. She tied Zephyr to the hitching post and glanced at the buggy outside the barn. It was newer than Pa's and too fancy for—

"Hello, Abbie."

The voice came from the house, and Abbie closed her eyes and counted to ten . . . slowly. Didn't she have enough to deal with just now?

"Abbie, did you see our new buggy?"

Not even the chance that Grant was there, too, made facing Marcy Wilson . . . Martin any easier. Abbie turned. Marcy stood in the back doorway, one hand to her hip, the other on her newly bulging belly.

The fact that Marcy was carrying her brother's child did nothing to soften Abbie's feelings for her sister-in-law, and it only heightened her present loss. Frances at her worst was a rose to the stinging nettle, Marcy.

"Grant sent all the way to Denver for it to get the color I wanted."

Abbie glanced obligingly at the buggy again. The claret-colored side panels were attractive, and she could only imagine what Grant had paid for Marcy's selection. "It's a very nice buggy, Marcy. If you'll excuse me . . ."

"Ma's out back."

Abbie cringed. She couldn't help it, hearing her own mama referred to as Marcy's. "I know. I saw her."

"I can't take the cold. Doc says my condition makes my skin sensitive."

Abbie nodded dully. She didn't want to think of Marcy's condition or see the gloating look she wore when speaking of it. Her own failure to conceive Monte's child was starting to gnaw at her, and she could handle only one ache at a time. She turned her back on Marcy.

The moment she heard the door close behind Marcy's tender skin, she lifted her skirts and ran for the clothesline. Mama was at the far end with wooden clothespins in her mouth and a fresh, cleaned pillow slip in her hands. "Mama!" Abbie stopped just short of throwing her arms around her neck.

"Gracious, Abbie." Mama dropped the slip and took her hands. "What is it?"

"Frances. Pneumonia took her. Mama, Monte's in a bad way."

"Oh, dear."

"I know he feels responsible."

"He mustn't."

"But you know how it is."

"Yes, I know." Mama gave her shoulders a hug. "I'm sorry, Abbie. What can we do?"

Abbie shook her head. "We're leaving in the morning. Frances asked that we take Jeanette. I don't understand it, the way she feared for the child to be raised here. But I am glad. Just thinking of that little motherless girl . . ." She stepped back. "I wish I had her right now."

Mama smiled. "Soon enough. It will be hard on her. Losing her pa and now her mama so soon."

"I don't understand it sometimes."

"It's not our part to understand, Abbie. Only to accept."

"I know that." But knowing didn't make it happen. She knew that from experience, from her own pain when Monte married Sharlyn, when Buck Hollister killed Blake, when Sharlyn died of scarlet fever.

Yet what else could one do? Life and death were in God's hands, and refusing to accept that was next to stupidity. Some things were too sublime for mortals.

"Ma! Oh, Ma-a." Marcy stepped delicately across the yard with her hooded cape held close to her cheeks.

And then again, some things were only too mortal. "Mama, I have to run. Please give Pa my love."

Thankfully Mama refrained from comment at her disdain for Grant's wife. Abbie squeezed her and cut across the garden away from Marcy's path. Right now facing Marcy again was more than she could stomach.

♦♦♦♦♦♦♦

In the dim that preceded the dawn, Monte crossed the yard to where Cole Jasper stood awaiting his instructions. Ordinarily he had no qualms leaving the ranch in Cole's charge, but this time wasn't ordinary. After the losses Captain Jake Gifford had caused them, compounded by the loss of Abbie's stock certificates and the expense of this trip, the ranch was in a precarious position. One wrong move, one more setback . . .

He looked into Cole's hard, manly face. He'd learned well enough this last year to trust Cole. His loyalty and stubborn cussedness had saved Monte's life when Captain Gifford had him beaten and left to die. But until now, Monte hadn't revealed how desperate their circumstances were. This last he'd withheld through his own pride.

Cole tossed the butt of his cigarette and ground it with the heel of his boot as Monte stopped before him. His green eyes held their usual mix of respect and insolence. Monte could be thankful for that now.

If Cole Jasper had followed his orders to let him handle things alone, the coyotes would have feasted on his flesh. But Cole had let him take it as far as he could, then personally settled with Captain Gifford. Remarkably, it didn't rankle to consider Cole an equal.

Monte drew himself up. "We'll be on our way shortly. Before we go, there are some things you should know." Briefly but frankly he explained the situation. He saw Cole's surprise at both his honesty and the information. "So you see why it's critical you run things as tightly as possible. I hate to turn away hands, but . . ."

"Dunbar's hirin' on, and Ephart last I heard. If I cut loose a few, they won't be hurtin'."

Monte frowned, but Cole's response showed he understood the situation. "I trust your abilities, Cole. Make whatever decisions you deem necessary. I don't intend to prolong this trip, but there will be matters to attend to."

"I'll keep things in line here. I'm sorry about yer sister."

The words were sincere, though gruffly spoken. Monte forced away the painful rush and nodded. As long as he focused on the business at hand, he could hold the ache at bay. But the long hours on the train would be agony.

He turned as James brought their bags to the porch and the stable boy, Will, helped him load the trunk into the wagon. Abbie came to the door and stepped out. In black she seemed more slender still, her waist tiny in the corset to which she reluctantly submitted.

Her brown curls escaped the black ribboned bonnet and cascaded down her back. Hardly a matronly style, though her incredible blue eyes were somber enough. In spite of his heartache he felt his breath catch. Would he ever not feel that at just the sight of her? He hoped not.

He turned back to Cole and caught a similar reaction. The old jealousy flared, but he subdued it. How could he fault Cole for being as helpless in Abbie's presence as he was himself? "We'll be on our way, then."

As Abbie approached, Cole took off his hat and ran a hand through his unruly blond curls. "Have a safe trip. My condolences, Abbie."

"Thank you, Cole."

Monte lifted her into the wagon and climbed up. He felt the burn scars on his palms as he took up the reins. His hands were stiff but no longer so tender. He was thankful for even the limited use of them.

He had already instructed James and Pearl and bid them farewell. Now he nodded to Cole, who tipped his hat in salute. Abbie pressed close to his side as they drove. Will rode in the bed to keep hold of the trunk and bags and return the wagon. With nothing else to consider, the grief crowded in.

Abbie put a hand to his arm, as though sensing his pain. She would, she who was cleaved to him. He gave her a weak smile, and she returned it with tears sparkling in her eyes. He squeezed her in his arm. "If you cry, Abbie, you'll be my undoing."

"I won't, then." She raised her chin and blinked the tears away.

Too soon they reached town and separated. Monte and Will unloaded the luggage, and the porter saw it onto the train. Monte took Abbie's arm and helped her into a first-class carriage. No matter how precarious their circumstances, he would not have Abbie's first trip by train any less than the best.

For himself, it mattered little. Everything he felt was subdued. Nourishment had no flavor, life no zest. Even holding Abbie last night had not ignited his flame. He felt washed again in the waves of failure. How had he thought Frances could stand alone? How had he not seen she would perish in her sorrow? Why had he not insisted she stay? Why, why, why?

Monte's thoughts blended with the clatter of the wheels as the miles passed by. He became aware of Abbie's gaze and shook himself free of the cloud. "I'm sorry we haven't better circumstances for our adventuring."

She reached for his hands and kissed them.

"Abbie . . ." He smiled. "Mind yourself. Try to recall the proprieties expected of a gentleman and his lady."

"I was thinking more of my husband."

His heart quickened a moment, then stilled. "It would behoove you to recall the lessons my . . . sister . . . so painstakingly presented you."

Abbie sat back and sighed. "I do recall them, Monte, but like a foreign language. Frances was right in her assessment of me. I'm afraid I'll fail you in Charleston. As hard as I try, I'm bound to say or do something that will show everyone just how ill-bred I am."

Monte quirked an eyebrow. "Ill-bred? Never. As Kendal said, you're the new breed of lady. Be yourself, Abbie. Only leave me my decorum." He managed to warm his smile before turning again to the window.

He should entertain her, engage her in conversation to wile away the hours. But those few words had drained him. *Abbie understands,* he thought grimly. She understood too well.

They changed trains in Denver and continued on. Abbie urged him to eat and he made a good show of it in the dining car, though what he ate he couldn't recall. He thought of Frances's thin shoulders. She had wasted away from fear and grief for Kendal. She hadn't the fortitude to withstand a sickness. If he had kept her with them, built her strength . . .

A voice inside said she would not have thrived. She longed for the streets and shore of Charleston. She longed for her home, her people. She could not make the break as he had. She was bound to the South. If only Kendal had seen that!

If only he, himself, had seen it. He would have sent them both away, back to the place Frances belonged. The West was too rough, too unmade for her. Hadn't she said as much again and again? He should have known. He should have known. He leaned his head back and closed his eyes.

Abbie dozed across from him. He could hear her soft breath. Her presence was a comfort, though also, in a way, a torment. How could he hope to merit her love when he so frequently failed in his duty?

That she loved him he knew without doubt, and the miracle of that still shook him. But Frances had loved him, also. Too much, maybe. And depended on him. Why had she thought at the last to forsake his care? Why had she gone? Why had he let her go?

Sleep would not come, but lethargy settled in his bones. How could he make this right? Where was honor in the face of death? He thought of Jeanette. Yes, he could do right by his sister's child. Is that why Frances had asked it of him? Did she know his honor would require some service, some atoning?

Monte opened his eyes and watched Abbie sleep. He had thought by now to have her with child. He knew the lack burdened her. Having Jeanette would be good for Abbie. She mothered so naturally.

But he ached to see his own seed growing inside her, to raise up his prodigy to own the land, to carry on his work and his name. He sighed and sank back into a fitful rest. Jeanette would be a start, and he silently thanked Frances for asking.

Three

Abbie stared out the polished wood-framed window of the train at the live oak trees with the queer dangling masses of grayish green that hung and waved in ghostly tatters. When she'd wakened that morning, the landscape had seemed foreign, wholly new. Now it seemed eerie, unreal.

"We're in the Lowcountry, nearing Charleston."

She turned to Monte, surprised. He'd spoken so little, she was amazed he'd noticed her curiosity.

"That's Spanish moss draping the trees."

"I've never seen anything like it."

"There is nothing like it. There's no place like the Lowcountry."

Abbie pointed out the window. "What grows there?"

"Rice or indigo."

She looked at the distant, swampy fields and shook her head slowly. "I can't picture you here."

"I'm not actually from here, not from the Lowcountry, at least. Our plantation was inland. Chandler's is a half day's ride and ours some five miles beyond that. Frances moved to Charleston when she married Kendal. He was in commerce there, while we merely used the port to ship our crops."

"What did you raise, Monte?"

"Cotton and tobacco. Cotton we sold to England, tobacco had a native market."

"Tobacco. But you don't smoke or chew or snuff it."

"I never developed a taste. That was a sore point with my father."

"I'm glad you don't. Pa thinks it's unhealthy for the lungs, and spitting is—"

"Don't say that down here, Abbie. Tobacco's the lifeblood of many a planter." His voice had taken on a stronger slur as they neared their destination, but not the strange twang she heard some speaking.

"Why do they sound that way, Monte?"

"That's the Geechee speech. They come from the true lowlands along the Geechee River."

"What are those trees in the marsh there?"

"Cypress."

"Is the land always so wet?"

"The low fields drain and fill with the tides. Charleston is a peninsula, flanked by two tidal rivers and surrounded by islands."

Abbie felt him withdraw again. He seemed lost in his memories. She'd never seen him among his own people, in his own country. What was he feeling coming back? How would it be for her to approach the Rocky Mountains after making her home elsewhere for four years?

He seemed . . . more refined, more cultured; his speech more accented, his tone softer, smoother. In his black frock coat, black quilted waistcoat, and white pleated shirt, he was magnificent. And he held himself with an elegance and calm she'd never manage asleep.

It touched her deep inside, how different their worlds were. This was Monte's place. It seeped into his bones, into his blood. With every breath he took on this journey, he became more the South Carolina gentleman and less the Colorado rancher.

The train pulled into a station so large it seemed a small city. Abbie stepped out into the cavernous depths filled with people and soldiers. Though the uniforms were like those the western cavalry wore, these men carried themselves differently. There was an awkward watchfulness in some, insolence in others, but nowhere the easy carriage of the men who patrolled the territory back home.

She glanced at Monte. If he noticed the Union soldiers, he made no sign. His face was set in that unreadable mask that concealed his thoughts and rebuffed intrusion. He led her through the station and out to the street.

The porter followed with their bags, and Monte instructed him to load them onto the hack waiting at the curb. He didn't lift a hand, but stood by while the driver helped the man load the trunk. Then he helped her into the seat.

Monte gave him the address. "We'll go straight to Kendal's mother. She's expecting us, and the train was remarkably near schedule."

Though December, the evening air was almost warm and bore a heavy tang. It felt damp when she drew it into her lungs with each quickening breath. "Where are we, Monte?"

"This is King Street. The heart of commerce in Charleston."

Abbie stared out at the stores they passed: dry goods, hardware, tobacconists, haberdashers, wines, medicines, and on the corner a store selling just books. She could scarcely take it in. They left King Street for a residential area, but it was no less wondrous.

She'd never seen so many tall, elegant houses, colorfully painted and graced with lacy wrought iron balconies. They were closely packed and lined with iron fences and walled gardens, many with palm and magnolia trees, climbing vines, and flower beds, some still blooming.

She watched a lamplighter start his rounds in the dimming dusk. A dog barked and she heard it answered distantly. Abbie felt overwhelmed by the age and languor of the place, so different from the raw birth pangs of Rocky Bluffs. She knew what the Union said of Charleston, the hot seat of rebellion, and she sensed its stubborn, rebellious spirit.

For the first time she wondered if another place could be as awe-inspiring as the Colorado Territory. A pure white bird with sharp tapered wings soared overhead, and another, gray and short tailed, settled to the street as they passed. Abbie looked back over her shoulder at them.

"Sea gulls." Monte's expression softened. "You look all of fourteen gaping like that."

Abbie ignored his jibe. "Sea gulls, Monte! Where's the sea?"

He pointed. "The harbor's through there, but you can't see it from here. We'll walk the promenade tomorrow." He squeezed her hand, then once more reverted to silence.

People strolled the walks in the balmy evening, and Abbie took it all in: the sight, the sound, the smell. This was Monte's land. If not the city itself, still the people, the air, the ground. How she wished it were not Frances's death that brought them here. How she wished . . . but her wishing could be nothing to Monte's.

She tucked her hand into his, and he held it without speaking. It was enough that they were together. His loss would never pass, but the intensity of the ache would fade with time. She knew that. Thoughts of her childhood companion, Blake, no longer stabbed her as they had. And the regrets for her part in his death had dimmed as Monte's would—with time.

But for now, the pain was fresh and raw. Her remorse could hardly match his, but she ached for Frances leaving this world so soon after returning to these streets she'd missed so badly. She sighed.

The carriage stopped, and Abbie stared up at the pillared house. The portico alone soared far above her, and above it a white and rusting lacework balcony. Though the house was incredibly elegant, its rose-colored paint was chipping and pock holes marked its walls. Signs of war? Still?

Monte helped her down and led her up the steps. As they went inside, she pictured Kendal here. It echoed his flamboyant elegance. Here were people who lived by appearances, though she noticed the age and wear of the furniture and wall coverings.

She remembered Frances's remark, *"If Kendal were not a gentleman, he would be a rogue."* In this dim, stuffy place, she'd be tempted herself to rebel. She followed Monte meekly into the vaulted drawing room where they were announced.

Not a shaft of daylight found its way through the heavy brocades at the windows. Gas lamps along the walls provided weak light as she walked across the carpet, flourished with reds and golds, though the gold fringed edges were frayed. A gilt-framed portrait of a long, narrow-nosed man filled the wall above the green marble fireplace. Only his bushy eyebrows made him interesting, though he obviously found himself so.

The sable-gowned woman on the emerald velvet settee beneath him might have been carved of marble, the way she sat so straight and still. Her white hair beneath the black cap framed her face, but her skin was amazingly smooth and translucent. Her eyes bore into Abbie without a glance for Monte.

Though certain her dress and coiffure were satisfactory, Abbie felt like a bad apple with a smooth, rosy skin. She'd been caught staring, and who knew what else the woman had read of her thoughts. She tried not to squirm, and her sympathy for Kendal increased. Had he, too, never measured up?

Kendal's mother at last turned to Monte. "Montgomery Farrel, time has been good to you."

Monte bent and kissed her hand. "As to you, madam."

She scoffed. "I am no longer in the spring of my years, nor even the autumn. But I'll accept your compliment as I have few enough flung my way these days. So this is your wife."

"Mrs. Stevens, may I present to you Abigail Martin Farrel."

Abbie didn't correct the "Abigail" and curtsied. "I'm very pleased to meet you."

"I see you chose her on looks."

To Abbie's surprise, Monte smiled. "That definitely played its part, madam."

Mrs. Stevens snorted. "I like a man who tells the truth." Then she sobered. "I'm an old woman. No one should live to see her offspring in the grave."

Abbie felt a pang and saw its shadow pass over Monte's countenance.

"You're here for the child, and it's a good thing. I haven't the energy to see to her as she needs." Something flickered in her eyes, and Abbie wondered at it. Did Mrs. Stevens resent Frances's request? Or was it something else?

"But first, you've traveled a long way and been nourished poorly, no doubt. Your wife needs meat on her bones regardless."

Abbie wondered if she would remain "your wife" for the duration of their stay.

"You'll stay for supper."

"Thank you." Monte bowed.

"I'll have it laid directly. You'll want to freshen up from your trip." She raised her hand and a servant led them away.

Abbie couldn't help feeling dismissed. Mrs. Stevens had the grace of an angel, the imperiousness of a queen, and the warmth of a reptile. But that was unfair. She was grieving as were the rest of them, and her sharpness could be due to her pain.

Abbie washed and primped meticulously, but in the long, narrow dining room, she felt Mrs. Stevens' eyes like needles. She sat at the table, trying to remember the tedious rituals Frances had taught her. *The body should be held tolerably upright, though not stiff as a poker. Appear comfortable, natural, at ease, but never lounge. It is vulgar to take fish or soup twice . . . be careful to touch neither your knife nor your fork before finishing your soup. . . .*

She caught Monte's eye and saw a flicker of amusement. He would enjoy her discomfiture, the knave. All this was easy for him. His impeccable manners were so natural he lived and breathed them without thinking. He was genteel to his core. Abbie was a poor imitator.

Her temper flared, and she relaxed in her chair. "This chicken is delicious, Mrs. Stevens. I must have your recipe."

"Cook doesn't use a recipe."

Undaunted, Abbie laid her knife across her plate. "Mama cooks that way, too. She always thought it best to feel your way through. A touch of this, a pinch of that, the feel of the dough, the aroma in the steam. It's much better that way. Personally, I haven't a cookbook to my name, but then Pearl won't let me near the kitchen anyway."

The corners of Mrs. Stevens' mouth twitched, though she merely applied herself to her meal. Abbie guessed she was being compared to Frances, and failing miserably. Well, fiddlesticks. But she caught a glimmer in Monte's eyes and her heart sank. Was he ashamed of her?

The delicate chicken caught in her throat, and she choked, stifled it, then tried to wash it down with the pale wine in the fragile stemmed glass. Abbie didn't care for the taste of wine, and Monte seemed content without it—especially after Kendal's decline with spirits. Today, though, Abbie hadn't dared refuse when the servant poured it in her goblet.

She refrained from further comment but thought of meals at Mama and Pa's table. She and Grant and Sadie had been boisterous, encouraged by Pa to engage with him in discussions and even on occasion to argue their points. And argue they had, though good-temperedly as a rule.

Mama had expected decent manners, no talking with their mouths full, no grabbing, no elbows on the table. But beyond that they'd enjoyed their meals tremendously, though nothing this fancy touched their plates. Still, she'd take biscuits and beans with camaraderie over this stiffness any day.

She sent Monte a defiant glance but found him lost in his thoughts. He'd spoken so little these last two days. She felt them drifting apart now when they most needed each other's strength. Grief isolated. Maybe Mrs. Stevens felt the same.

Abbie dabbed her mouth. "It was a joy to know your son, Mrs. Stevens. His high spirits were always a pleasure. And he could certainly tell a tale and appreciate a good one himself."

Mrs. Stevens went very pale, and for a horrible moment Abbie thought she'd be sent from the room. When the elderly woman looked up, her eyes were bright with tears. "And what tales did he enjoy, pray tell?" Her hand trembled, but a spot of color came to each cheek. "I would love to hear what gave him pleasure when he was away from me at the end."

Abbie drew a shaky breath and recalled the afternoon he'd found her in the library and wheedled from her the tale of her escape from Buck Hollister and his gang of outlaws. He'd been enthralled, amused, and bemused. She folded the fine linen in her lap and laid her hands atop it.

"As you know, law and order in the territories is not what you have here, Mrs. Stevens. There are men more ruthless than decency can describe. We had in the Colorado Territory one such man named Buck Hollister."

She felt Monte stir, but she was in it now. "He was a man of such nefarious character . . ." Abbie wove her tale, all the while watching the expressions play fleetingly over the woman's face. She purposely played up her fear in the grasp of the men who murdered Blake and her helplessness in Gray Wolf's camp. She finished with her realization that God had His hand in all things, even those beyond their understanding.

Mrs. Stevens stared at her long and pointedly, then turned to Monte. "I feel your wife has more than beauty to recommend her. But I pity you keeping her in hand."

He smiled. "Kendal recognized in Abbie the spirit that is winning the West. I'm afraid Frances was made of softer stuff."

"We are ill-equipped for life's woes. Strength comes through pain, but that pain either hardens or breaks."

Monte looked pensive, then nodded. "And I lacked the wisdom to see which way it would go."

Mrs. Stevens pursed her lips together. "Frances was at peace in her passing. If she regretted her choices, she never said." She turned and fixed Abbie in her gaze. "Tell me the truth about Kendal. Was the trouble that ended his life of his own making?"

Abbie felt her chest constrict. Telling the truth would dishonor the woman's son. Yet his mother was obviously not content with whatever Frances had told her. She recalled Kendal's drunkenness, his deceit, and his advances.

She felt the blood flame to her cheeks, but the words clogged her throat. "He . . . was misguided in his choice of companions and misled by his desire to regain his losses."

Mrs. Stevens smiled dimly. "You've learned too well the subtlety that is not natural to you, my dear. Was he in love with you, then?"

Abbie flushed deeper. "No. He loved his wife, though for a time he lost sight of it." She glanced at Monte. She had never actually described all of Kendal's behavior toward her. The day on the snowy hill when he pressed his advances and she slapped him soundly, the kiss on the road when he made the irrevocable choice to continue his wrongdoing. "At the last, he paid for his mistakes with the highest honor."

"Frances said he died saving you." Her tone was bitter but not condemning.

Abbie could give her nothing but plain honesty. "Yes. He took the bullet meant for me."

Mrs. Stevens stared at her hands, then turned to Monte. "Forgive my overshadowing your loss. I know how dear Frances was to you, and she was a daughter to me, though I . . . sensed the disquiet between her and my son." She cleared the emotion from her throat before continuing.

"Their child, I fear, has tendencies toward the worst in both of them. You'll not find the task an easy one, though Mammy handles her tantrums to some degree. Yet, I think your wife will see the task through. You've not conceived children of your own?"

Monte sent a protective glance Abbie's way but answered simply, "Not yet."

"Perhaps it's better that way. At least for a time." She stood slowly, gaining her balance with her hands tightly on the table as her servant hurried to move the chair.

"I think it best you stay with me these next days. Jeanette will become accustomed to you on familiar ground, and your departure will be less trying. Jonah will show you to your rooms. Good night." Holding her cane, she walked away.

Abbie felt like a mouse played with by the cat—discarded, limp, and shaken, but amazingly intact. She glanced at Monte. His dark, handsome features were brooding, but he raised his eyes to her.

"Well, then, that's settled." He stood and tucked her hand in his arm, and they followed Jonah to their rooms. Abbie couldn't help wondering if his name weren't truly prophetic.

She walked into the well-appointed room chosen for her and stood in the center feeling small and altogether homesick. Another servant returned with Jonah carrying her trunk. When they left as silently as they came, she opened the carpetbag and took out her nightgown. She could hear Monte in the adjoining room. She suddenly felt tired.

She removed her clothes and hung them carefully in the maple wardrobe. Its cedar lining sent a pungent aroma into the room when she opened and closed the doors. She put on her white batiste lace-edged nightgown and let down her hair.

She shook it out and ran her fingers through the tangles. They loosed and fell thickly down her back. She turned when Monte tapped the door between their rooms and entered. His face was strained as he crossed to her and took her hands in his.

"I'm sorry, Monte. I didn't know how else to answer."

"You did fine." He stroked the hair back from her cheek, then kissed her softly. "And I was hardly ignorant of Kendal's . . . attraction. Don't think any more of it." He kissed her again, and there was warmth in it.

Abbie clung to him, feeling their love lessen the pain of loss, at least for the moment. His hands were strong on her back, and she pressed her palms to his chest and returned his kiss. His need was in his eyes and in his lips and in his hands.

He spoke hoarsely. "Whether we conceive a child is in God's hands. But it'll not be for lack of effort this night if we don't."

In spite of the august surroundings, he wakened her desire, and she surrendered to his love.

Four

The tall, elegant walls fairly shook with the shrill cries. Monte was stunned by Jeanette's vehemence as she hurled herself at Mammy's skirts, pounding with her fists. She was Frances all over again. Mammy stood stoically and let the child wear herself out, then took her in hand and led her from the room.

Mrs. Stevens sighed. "Well, you've seen it firsthand now. Are you still of a mind to have the child?"

He turned from the window. "We're of a mind to honor Frances's request, and even were that not so, we would hardly shirk at a little show of temper." He laid his hand on Abbie's shoulder where she sat across from Mrs. Stevens.

"And you?"

Monte knew Abbie's mind was more set than his. Hadn't she spent years ministering to the orphans at the mission? She answered softly, "Jeanette is my niece and I love her. We all have our failings, and those in one so young are hardly set in stone."

"Hmph. My experience says otherwise. Once they find their temper, they're not likely to lose it."

"Nevertheless, one can be trained to channel the behavior more acceptably."

"Perhaps. And your western territory may be wide enough to contain her. Well, then, I'll see that Mammy's and the child's things are prepared for travel, and you'll leave at week's end." Mrs. Stevens rose and left them, as was her wont after pronouncing their fate.

Abbie stood and gripped Monte's hand. "Monte, I must speak with you."

He quirked an eyebrow. "So speak."

"I have nothing personally against Mammy, and I'm sure she's done her best, but I want to take Jeanette alone."

"What?"

"I want to mother her myself, as Mama did me. I don't want other arms rocking her to sleep, other hands dressing her and plaiting her hair."

"Abbie . . ."

"Jeanette needs a mama, not a bevy of servants who give in to her every whim."

"You don't understand—"

"Yes, I do. I want a child, not a charge."

"If we have children of our own . . ."

"I'll still refuse a nanny or mammy or nurse or whatever you want to call it. I'll raise and nurture my own children, and I'll raise Jeanette as though she were my own." She clutched his hand to her chest. "Please, Monte."

Their intimacy last night had eased his sorrow and left him susceptible. He groaned. "Don't use your eyes like that. I can't stand against it."

She bent one knee up on the chair seat and leaned into him.

His blood kindled. "You're a minx and you know it." He cupped her chin in his hands. "And you use it as mercilessly as—" He caught movement beyond her dark curls and looked up. "Chandler."

Abbie spun, and Monte caught her from losing her balance against the chair.

"Mrs. Stevens' man let me in, but I've interrupted a tender moment, I see." Chandler came forward and bowed over Abbie's hand, then caught Monte's between both of his. "It's good to see you, Monte, though I'm so terribly sorry about Frances. Milton did everything he could, but . . . she hadn't the will. She was already declining before the illness."

Chandler's words burned into Monte's pain, confirming his

suspicions. She hadn't the will to live. She was declining already. How had he been such a fool? He forced a response. "Milton doctored her?"

Chandler nodded. "Doctor Graby had an outbreak of measles at the Myers' Plantation. But no one could have attended her more carefully than Milton. He never left her side. He knew how close you were and deeply grieves his failure."

Monte pictured Milton Rochester—next to Chandler, his closest friend. He knew Milton to be competent and conscientious, but for a moment the need to share the blame overwhelmed him. Milton was his own age. What could he know of urging to life one whose hope was shattered?

Monte turned away. He heard Abbie murmur to Chandler, but it took all his resolve to combat the emotions surging inside. Why had Graby left her to Milton? Why had Frances forsaken life? He felt Chandler's hand on his arm and contained his despair.

"Don't try to find blame, Monte, nor take it on yourself. It won't change anything. It can't bring her back."

Monte drew himself up. Chandler knew him too well, read his thoughts as though they were his own. He nodded stiffly.

Chandler released the grip on his arm. "How long will you be with Mrs. Stevens?"

"Through the week."

"Maimie and I would have you extend your trip and spend the following week with us. One week at least, a fortnight even better. Maimie is desperate to see Abbie, and I've not had a moment's peace."

Monte glanced at Abbie and read her hopeful gaze. He sighed. It was inevitable. Even the mournful circumstances of this trip would not preclude the required visits. Though his heart was not in it, Abbie and Maimie and Chandler, and countless others, must have the opportunity. "What of Jeanette?"

"She'll be with us." Abbie spoke without hesitation. "It'll be good to spend time with her here in the same city and climate but out of this house. It could lessen the impact of the trip and the changes."

"She's welcome, of course," Chandler added. "How old is she now?"

Monte turned. "Two, but very precocious."

"She's nearly three." Abbie smiled. "But she has, indeed, developed a vocabulary. And we worried so when she seemed slow to speak."

"Very well, Chandler. We'll accept your offer with pleasure." Monte bowed.

"Very good. And now I'll leave you, as I've business to attend to. Again, my deepest sympathy."

When Chandler had gone, Monte turned to Abbie. "I'm going to visit the grave. Will you come?" His throat was tight, but he needed to see these things through.

"Yes, Monte." Her eyes were somber as her tone.

"We'll have to walk. Only the *nouveau riche* have carriages."

"I can walk."

"We can take the horsecar from downtown."

He led her down the streets and to the graveyard, where too many lay beneath the earth, casualties of war, disease, misfortune. The peaceful dead, the violent dead, the hopeless dead. *Oh, Frances.*

His steps faltered as he stared across the rows of headstones at the Stevens family plot. The monument to Kendal's father loomed over the newly carved stone near the edge. The pristine stone was white as her skin, sharp as her tongue . . . and final.

He walked forward and gripped the iron railing, then opened the gate and went in. Abbie was not at his side, though when they had separated he didn't know. He stood over the bare earth and read the headstone.

In loving memory of Frances Marie Stevens.

His eyes blurred at the dates. So young. Twenty-four. He swallowed the tears clogging his throat and felt Abbie's hand on his back.

She said nothing but her touch was comforting. He reached around to press her to his side. "Was there some way to prevent this?"

"No," she said softly.

Lord, what could I have done?

Heaven was silent. As with Sharlyn, death had plucked a fragile bloom before the petals had faded and withered. As with Sharlyn, he was helpless to prevent it, but acceptance was slow in coming. He laid the hothouse gardenias and zinnias on the mound and straightened. When he turned, he saw Milton Rochester outside the railing.

"Mrs. Stevens said I'd find you here."

His friend's face was bleak, the small black eyes and compact features pressed tighter than usual. Monte's anger flared, then passed. He held out his hand and Milton gripped it.

"It's dreadful to lose a patient, but horror when it's one dear to you and yours." He shook his head. "I tried everything medicine had to offer."

"I'm sure you did your best for her." Monte's chest tightened with the words.

"I'm sorry, Monte." Milton's gaze held, then flickered to Abbie.

"Forgive me. Milton Rochester, may I present my wife, Abbie."

Milton bowed over her hand. "A rare pleasure. Chandler spoke of your beauty, but I thought he exaggerated. I see now that every word was true."

"I'm pleased to meet you, Doctor Rochester."

"Milton, please." He stepped back as Monte swung the gate open and followed Abbie out. "Have you plans for the day?"

"I'm taking Abbie along the promenade. She's never seen the ocean."

"Never seen it! Well, it's a sight on a day this fair."

Monte smiled. It would be a sight for Abbie regardless. He recalled their first outing when he'd described the ocean for her mind's eye and brought her to tears. Oh yes, it would be a sight for Abbie. He tucked her hand into his arm. "Will you join us, Milton?"

"If it's not imposing."

"Of course not. We've too many years between us to miss the

opportunity now." Monte glanced back once more at the grave. His step faltered.

"It was peaceful, Monte. I don't think she suffered."

Monte nodded, felt his throat tighten, then drew a long breath. "I'm thankful for that."

♦♦♦♦♦♦♦

Abbie leaned on the iron pipe rail that lined the promenade and stared with wonder at the sparkling expanse of water fed by the tidewaters that rushed into the bay from either side of the city. The ocean was more green than blue in the main body and deep, churning brown beneath the dock at her feet. The massive pilings, encrusted with salt and barnacles, stood solidly amid the surging, slapping waves.

The breeze flapped the rolled sails of the ships at port. Gulls circled and cried and perched on their skeletal masts and crossbeams as they rocked and swayed. Abbie breathed the sour, salty tang and gazed past the low tree-covered islands across the water to the blending line of water and sky.

She felt Monte's gaze and turned to find both his and Milton's eyes on her. She squeezed her hands at her chest. "It's incredible. Oh, Monte, I'd love to climb aboard ship and head out there where the water is all around, the gulls diving, and the wind full in the sails."

He smiled. "With the wind today, you'd learn soon enough if you had the stomach for it."

"What do you mean?"

"Have you heard of seasickness?"

She pushed back the hair whipping her eyes and looked out at the rising waves. "It would be worth it."

She saw the amusement flicker in Monte's eyes as he took her elbow, and they started on down the wide promenade. Milton pointed out the different boats and told them who owned them, who captained them, and all he knew of their previous successes or failures.

"You sound like a seaman yourself," Abbie said.

"A hobby only. My heart is in medicine. Always has been. Even with its limitations." Abbie saw him glance regretfully at Monte, and his narrow shoulders sagged. She felt the strain between the two men. It was unlike Monte to place blame erroneously, but he said nothing to ease Milton's distress.

"Will you lunch with us, Milton?" Monte asked.

"No, I'm afraid I can't spare any more time. I'm sharing Doctor Graby's rounds."

Monte nodded. "Then we'll take our leave."

Abbie walked briskly beside him as he led her down a narrow way to a small teahouse in sight of the wharf but far enough away to be free of the rough traffic of sailors. Monte seated her and took the chair across. He ordered coffee and sweet rolls, then returned his attention. "Well, Abbie, you've seen the ocean. How does it compare to your plains?"

"I can't compare them. They're too different. But it's wonderful, as wonderful as you described. Do you remember?"

"I was thinking of it as I watched you take your first look. One day I'll take you across the sea to all the places you've imagined."

She smiled and gripped his hand. "I'm glad we came first to your home, Monte. Will you take me to see your plantation?"

"It's no longer mine, Abbie."

She felt a swell of remorse. "I'm sorry. I didn't mean . . . I just thought . . ."

"It's all right. I'll show you the plantation, if you like, when we go to Chandler's."

"Is it very painful to come back?"

He sighed. "Painful? Yes and no. Things change, I know that. Would I trade what I have now for what was before? No. Yet . . . I could wish that the difficulty, the hardship, and even the suffering that I see around me were not so. Everywhere are the signs of destruction, poverty, struggle."

He sipped his coffee and shrugged. "But with it, or perhaps because of it, there is the bravery, the unconquerable spirit of the South, especially South Carolina. That, Abbie, will never be equaled nor destroyed. No matter how long the soldiers remain, how strict the curfews or the restrictions, they'll never break our spirit."

Abbie felt alienated by his use of "our." It reflected the closed expressions she saw all around her.

He laughed low. "I guarantee you, the life of every Yankee in Charleston is one of frustration."

"Why?"

"They can occupy the houses, walk the streets, even give the orders, but they'll never belong and they know it. They can't break into the circle, and the knowledge gnaws at them. They're like dogs at the gate, whimpering for one glance from the people inside. And they'll never get it. Never."

Abbie was astonished by his fervor, though his voice was low and his drawl pronounced. Her heart sank. She, too, was an outsider. Perhaps she was admitted through the gate by marriage, but she would never belong. She suddenly ached to be home on the rough, dry ranch, in the scrubby hills that clung to the feet of the towering mountains.

Monte read her distress and pressed her hand. "It's just the way it is, Abbie."

"The belle who doesn't fit the mold. I'm not even a belle. How could Mrs. Stevens tell from the first moment?"

Monte smiled, spread his hands. "Abbie . . ."

"I did everything Frances told me. I—"

He caught her hand between his. "You can't change who you are. And I wouldn't have you change. I could have had any southern lady I wanted. I chose you."

She knew that was true. Monte with his fine looks and finer ways. She sighed. "I guess that counts for something, but I feel . . . more like the dog at the gate."

He threw back his head and laughed. It was the first he had laughed since the terrible news, and she was not the least concerned that it was at her expense.

"You shouldn't paint those pictures if you don't want me to take them seriously."

He bowed over her hand. "I should know better indeed. Forgive me."

For a moment she felt close to his heart, then his grief settled again, and he released her hand. "We should go."

"Yes. I want to spend time with Jeanette." Even if it meant being closed inside Mrs. Stevens' dreary walls. At least they would spend Christmas with Chandler and Maimie.

♦♦♦♦♦♦♦

Abbie found the child in the upstairs room that served as the nursery. She was dressed in white with peppermint red stripes and ruffles and ruffles of lace. It was difficult to tell where the lace left off and the child began. Mammy bustled around when she entered, picking up the discarded dolls from the floor.

"Thank you, Mammy, that will be all." Abbie waited for the woman to leave. It felt uncomfortable to speak to another person that way, but she'd seen that it was expected and didn't want to stand out more than she already did.

Jeanette eyed her from her perch at the child-sized table. "Do you want tea?" She held up the miniature handpainted teapot, confident in her abilities as a southern lady. Just shy of three, Jeanette probably already contained the elements of decorum she herself lacked, Abbie thought grimly.

Abbie smiled and took her place on the other small chair. "Yes, thank you."

"That's 'Manda's chair, but you may use it."

"Amanda?"

Jeanette pointed to the French porcelain doll in the corner of the window seat.

"Ah. It's kind of her to allow me."

"*I* say you may, not 'Manda. She can't say in my room. Only I can."

Abbie bit her tongue. Now was not the time to instruct. First she must have Jeanette's trust. "Jeanette . . ."

"I'm Jenny." Her face looked fierce a moment. "Mama calls me Jenny. Grandma calls me Jeanette, and I don't like Grandma."

"Jenny's a lovely name." And she understood the child's difficulty with her grandma, though it was disrespectful to say so.

"I have ap'rcot crumpets and tea."

"Very nice indeed. I'm privileged to be your guest." She took the cup of imaginary tea Jeanette handed her. "Do you remember when we took the toboggan down the big hill at Uncle Monte's ranch?"

"Papa spoiled it. He made us go home."

The child had a more remarkable memory than she expected. But if thoughts of Kendal upset her, she didn't show it. "Uncle Monte and I are going to take you back to the ranch with us. Would you like that?"

Jeanette handed her a tiny fluted plate. "Have a crumpet."

Abbie took the plate and mimicked eating. Jeanette's eyes stayed on her as she delicately dabbed her lips with the scrap of linen. "The best I ever had."

" 'Manda can't have any."

"Why not?"

"She sassed Grandma."

"Oh dear."

"It doesn't matter. Mammy will sneak her some. And then she'll cry and cry to get some more."

Abbie nodded slowly. "I see. That isn't very honest, is it?"

Jeanette looked at her pointedly, her little chin coming up in exact replication of Frances. Suddenly she knocked over her chair as she jumped up and ran to the window. She shook the doll and cast her to the seat, then rushed to the cupboard and threw all the doll's clothes on the floor. Then she threw herself with them and set up a wailing to rally the town.

The door flew open and Mammy descended like a great dark hen.

Abbie stood up. "I'll handle this, Mammy. You may go."

The woman sent her a dark look, shook her head, and puffed her lips, reminiscent of Pearl. Well, Abbie was used to such disapproval and more determined than ever that Jeanette not grow up as self-centered as Monte's sister. Three years of indulgence was enough.

When the door closed behind Mammy, Abbie took her place at the little table again. Though Jeanette's caterwauling set her teeth on edge, she made a great show of pouring herself another cup of invisible tea and helping herself to another excellent crumpet. She didn't speak as she ate and sipped but admired the view from the window.

After a full five minutes, Jeanette stopped screaming and watched her from the floor. Abbie turned her attention to the doll. "What a great many things you can see from that window, Amanda. It must be very interesting in your seat." It didn't matter that the doll lay head down with her pinafore over her face.

Jeanette raised up on one elbow to study the window. She stood and walked slowly over, then climbed up on the walnut shelf and kneeled against the panes. "They took Mama away in an ugly black carriage."

"Yes."

"She can't come back."

Abbie climbed into the seat with the child. "Yes, I know."

Jeanette turned on her and beat her fists against her legs. "I don't like you! I want you to go away! Go away! I want Mammy! Mammy . . ." She wailed again.

Abbie caught her little fists and pulled her into her lap. She curled the child against her chest and held her while she cried. There was grief in this outburst, and that she would not ignore. The hollering became sobs, and Abbie rocked as she stroked the dark, damp curls. So much hurt for one so little.

Dear Lord, comfort your little one. And give me wisdom. Abbie kept rocking as the child stilled. "Shall I tell you a story?"

Very slightly, Jeanette's head nodded against her.

"Once upon a time, there was a little girl named Red Riding Hood. She was called that because . . ."

Abbie kept her voice soft while she continued to recite the story and stroked Jeanette's soft head and small, curved back. "And the wolf gobbled up the granny in one swallow."

The child looked up with wide eyes.

"Then the wolf put on the granny's nightcap and climbed into the bed." She felt Jeanette press close against her. "Red Riding Hood knocked on the door . . ." As she spoke, Abbie smoothed the child's tangles and felt the dampness dry on her cheeks. " 'My, Granny, what big eyes you have.' 'The better to see you with,' the wolf said."

Jeanette took Abbie's fingers in her little fist.

" 'My, Granny, what big ears you have.' 'The better to hear you with,' the wolf said." Abbie covered the little hand with hers. " 'My, Granny what big teeth you have.' 'The better to eat you with!' And the wolf jumped from the bed and swallowed Red Riding Hood in one gulp."

Jeanette pulled away and stared up. Her little mouth made a perfect O.

"Now a woodsman passing by had heard Red Riding Hood's cries." Abbie caught the two little hands and held them firmly. "He came into the house, saw the wolf, and split him open. Out jumped Red Riding Hood and her granny safe and sound."

Jeanette smiled. It was radiant, and Abbie was struck again by her likeness to Frances, and for that matter, Monte. They all favored his mother's side.

"You see, Jenny, the wolf is death, and Jesus is the woodsman. He conquered death, and when we pass through it He brings us to new life." She turned at the tap on the door, and Monte entered.

He raised an eyebrow at the two of them curled in the window seat, and she knew the nature of his inquiry. Likely as not, he'd heard the commotion and come, albeit reluctantly, to her rescue. She smiled. "Jenny, go give Uncle Monte a hug."

Five

Abbie tucked her knees up under her skirts and settled onto the apple green spread at the end of Maimie's bed. The rose-and-green chintz curtains were pulled into puffs at either side of the tall, narrow windows to let in the December daylight, and the tasseled ties fascinated Jenny, who cupped and petted one with her small hands.

It was a cheerful room, so like Maimie, and Abbie drew up her knees contentedly. She'd spent most of the last three weeks there, as Maimie was in the final months of her pregnancy. After the stillbirth of her first child, the doctor was taking no chances and had ordered her to bed.

Abbie was just as glad after what she'd endured with Mrs. Stevens—an extended week of her very proper lady friends and callers coming to gape, and later gossip, about her. She more than suspected Mrs. Stevens drew great pleasure in watching her writhe, though she never gave any indication, maintaining her carved marble poise. Abbie was thankful Maimie's condition precluded callers. She'd had quite enough of that.

She glanced down as Jenny now dug her fingers into the button box. She had found the box filled with multicolored and faceted buttons at the bazaar and presented it this Christmas morning to the child, remembering the fun she had when Mama let her rummage in her buttons.

When Jenny raised her hands and scattered them across the floor, she bit back the reprimand. Their battle of wills was still tenuous, and she chose her conflicts carefully. When she turned back, she found Maimie's heart-shaped face and frank brown eyes steadily on her. Abbie shrugged slightly.

Maimie smiled. "You'll do fine."

Abbie sighed. "It's . . . harder when there's been so little discipline."

"Yes, but you have the instincts. And so does Monte, only . . . perhaps it's not fair, but . . ." Maimie shook her head.

"I know. I think it's his grief that keeps him separate."

"Forgive me, Abbie, but I don't think it's grief alone."

"What, then?"

"Guilt. I saw it when Sharlyn died. He blames himself for Frances."

Abbie fingered the quilted spread. "She depended on him so. He took the responsibility seriously."

"Too seriously."

"Maybe. But what else could he do? Even with Kendal—I shouldn't speak ill of the dead and I know he did his best—but Monte saw his failure. How could he not continue his responsibility?"

Maimie laid a hand on her belly beneath the coverlet. "He did all he could for her. But there comes a time where he must release it, Abbie. Frances is gone, and I fear . . ."

"What, Maimie?"

"I fear that as long as he holds himself responsible for her death, he'll not take Jeanette to his heart."

Abbie glanced down at the child as she scrambled under the bed for the errant buttons and climbed out victorious. Maimie had spoken her own fears. Though Monte was gentle with Jenny, he made no attempts of his own to kindle a relationship. Indeed, he spent most of his time away with Chandler on the plantation.

He was out with Chandler and two others right now for the traditional dove and quail hunt. But if it wasn't that, it would be something else. In Maimie's company, Abbie didn't fret, but she felt his distance.

Nor would he speak of his loss. When she mentioned Frances, he grew quiet and pensive. Unlike Abbie, delving into memories to ease the loss, he seemed determined to bury it, ignore it, and hide it in work.

That he enjoyed his work with Chandler, she couldn't deny. And it was good for him to have an outlet. He was tender and close with her at night when they were alone. He loved her with a need she'd not felt in him before. But during the day he was cool and distant, as though daring grief to touch him.

Abbie sighed. They'd extended their stay a third week already, and though she loved her time with Maimie, she wondered at his reluctance to go home. What if he wanted to stay for good? She had heard the tone in his voice when he showed her his land, the house he grew up in, the soil that bore the crops that had sustained his family for generations.

They'd spent less than an hour looking at his old plantation, but he seemed to age in that time. At twenty-seven, he bore too much on himself. She shook away the clouds. "I'm worried, also, but he has to find his own way out. It will take time. It always does."

Maimie rubbed her hand over her stomach, mothering already without thought. Abbie felt a pang. Would she never know that joy? And then she felt remorseful. God had given her Jenny. "Monte will grow close to Jenny once we're home and he's settled into his own."

"I hate to think of you going. If only it weren't so far."

"The train helps. I have to admit, as much as I hated it coming through, it has made travel easier."

Maimie laughed. "Monte wrote of your despair at the coming of the train. Chandler and I laughed so."

"Well, it seemed so . . . civilized. So settled. I like the land wild."

"I know. That's what Kendal loved about you."

Abbie shook her head. "Poor Kendal. He was so lost."

"Not entirely."

"No. At the end, he found his way."

"And Frances?"

"When she left us, I believe she had put her trust in the Lord. She was in His hands."

"Then help Monte to see that. Life and death are not in our control. But if our souls are in order . . ."

Abbie felt Jenny's hand on her knee and turned. The child held up the string of buttons and Abbie smiled. "It's lovely, Jenny. Well done."

Jenny scrambled up beside her and hung it over her head. "For you."

"Thank you." She gave her a hug. "Now, then, it's time for your nap."

Instantly Jenny's lip protruded and her eyes took on stormy depths.

Abbie held her gaze firmly and the child relented. She took her by the hand and stood. "Come. I'll tuck you in."

◆◆◆◆◆◆◆

In the glow of the lamps that evening, Monte stood between Abbie and Chandler as the guests arrived. Though Maimie could not participate, Chandler had insisted on this soirée. The family had dined at three, and now the guests arrived for sweets and liqueur.

As he and Abbie had not been there for the funeral, this enabled people to offer their condolences as well as share the festivities. He was hardly in the mood, but Chandler was right. It was expected.

Beside him, Abbie was obviously dazzled by the finery and array, though she could hardly not notice the shabby condition of the garments and slippers. Even so, the gowns had been exquisite in their day. The gentlemen's swallowtail coats were impeccably clean and tailored if well worn, and those with jewels bore heirlooms, though many who had possessed such no longer did. Courtesy of Yankee and, more painfully, Confederate marauders.

The Yankees he could forgive. But much of Charleston's destruction, especially that of the planters' homes in the outlying area, had come at the hands of the southern forces. The white trash farmers bore a hatred for the ruling planter class deeper than anything the Yankees felt. They were quick to take advantage in the lawless days before military rule set in, and their vicious pillaging scarred more deeply than any other.

Of course, Abbie knew none of that. He glanced at his wife. She looked fresh as a mountain rose, even in black. Her eyes had that sapphire glint surrounded by lashes that drooped at the sides and quickened his pulse, but her color seemed pale and her step uncertain. That was not like her at all, and he chided himself for leaving her so much to Maimie.

Had he missed something with his lack of attendance? Did she mourn more deeply than he thought? But there had been no love lost between his wife and sister, though he could hardly blame Abbie for that. She had done her best.

He turned and greeted the Blackwells from Columbia. Edward Blackwell had overseen several of Monte's father's business ventures. "How do you do, Edward. Fine to see you, sir."

"And you, Monte."

"May I present . . ." Each time he presented Abbie, he felt more fortunate. He was a lucky man. More than lucky. God had blessed him beyond his deserving. And yet with that emotion came the companion fear. What if something happened to Abbie? What if he were unequal to keeping her safe, well, whole?

Perhaps his fears were unfounded, ridiculous even. Hadn't she proved herself strong and brave and well nigh invincible? But he could no more control the feeling churning inside than he could the events of this life. He could only mask them and put on the face of courage.

He accepted Edward's condolences and turned to the next couple. He would be glad to leave the line, but as Chandler's guest of honor his responsibility was clear. He felt Abbie sway beside him and turned in alarm. Never had he known her to grow faint, not even in the face of death and horror and despair.

She was as strong and hale as a yearling thoroughbred. But as he caught her arm, he read the confusion in her eyes. "If you'll excuse me," he murmured to Chandler and led Abbie away from the entry into the parlor. He helped her to sit. "Abbie, what is it?"

"I don't know. I feel . . . I must be catching something."

He felt a wave of fear and pushed it away as irrational. "I'll take you to bed."

"I don't want to miss Chandler's party in our honor. I feel stronger now. If only this fool corset weren't so tight. I swear when we go home, I'll never wear one again."

"Don't put those thoughts in my mind, Abbie. I won't be fit for polite society." He bent and kissed her. "Are you certain you're all right?"

"Yes, I feel fine. A little squeamish, but everything I've eaten lately has been so different. Something must not agree with me."

He laid the back of his hand on her forehead. "There's no fever."

"No. I'm sure it's nothing." She stood up and collapsed against him.

Monte caught her with alarm as she fainted in his arms. Gently he laid her on the settee, then rushed to the hall. Milton stood in a cluster of gentlemen, and Monte hesitated only a second before gripping his arm. "Pardon me." He bowed to Milton's companions. "But I must borrow Milton immediately."

Milton turned in surprise. "Monte?"

He tugged him from the room. "It's Abbie. She's fainted."

"Oh, well . . ."

"No, you don't understand. Abbie's never had a faint moment in her life." He rushed Milton to the library, fighting to control his concern.

She stirred when Milton dropped beside her and slapped her hand. Monte felt his chest constrict. Surely nothing serious was wrong, surely . . . Milton held the salts to her nose, and her eyes fluttered open.

Abbie startled. "Good heavens . . ."

"That's right. Take it easy, now. Monte, will you leave us a moment? And send a man for my bag. It's in the cloakroom."

Monte frowned at Milton's clipped orders. He didn't want to

leave Abbie, not . . . in Milton's hands. Wasn't that what he was thinking? Goodness, it wasn't Milton's fault. When would he accept that? He forced his legs to obey and went for the bag himself.

Milton took it and ordered him out again. Monte stood outside the door, staring at the knotted oak panels.

"Monte?" Chandler touched his arm. "I could only just break away. Is Abbie all right?"

"I don't know. Milton's with her." He said it more gruffly than he intended. "He ordered me out."

"And well he might. Come, have a brandy, a cup of syllabub."

"No, I'll wait."

"Monte, she's in good hands."

Chandler tugged his arm and Monte followed. Brandy would be good, but he declined as he did the frothy cream concoction. He wanted nothing dimming his reactions or thoughts when Milton returned. He ran his hand over his face and glanced at Chandler.

"Relax, man. Abbie's as hearty as they come."

"Then explain her fainting."

"I'll leave that to Milton." He nodded, and Monte turned.

"Is she—"

"She's fine," Milton assured him.

"Then what was wrong with her?"

Milton smiled. "Nothing that won't be right in nine months. Or more precisely, eight, I'd guess."

Monte stared at his friend's smile. Was the man daft to be amused by his wife's illness? Was he as incompetent as he'd feared? What was this nine months, eight months. . . ?

Chandler clapped him on the back. "That *is* good news, man."

Monte turned. An extended convalescence good news?

Chandler laughed. "Abbie's with child, Monte. Your offspring."

Abbie with child. He felt staggered. How had the thought not occurred to him? Because he avoided that thought, studiously, lest he dwell on the disappointment. And because his thoughts had been preoccupied by death. *With child.* His child. He spun and strode to the parlor.

Abbie looked up when he entered, and her pale cheeks flushed.

He dropped to his knees before her and took her hands in his. "Abbie . . ."

"It's nothing I ate."

He pulled her hands to his chest and found himself without words.

She slipped her hands around his neck. "Oh, Monte . . ."

"My darling." He kissed her forehead, her eyes, her mouth. "What did Milton say? Is everything all right?"

"Yes, fine. It's normal to feel queasy and dizzy and tired. It'll pass soon enough."

"You'll have the best care. I'll find the finest doctor in Charleston. . . ."

"In Charleston? He'll have a dreadful long trip, then."

"What do you mean?"

She caught her fingers in the hair at the back of his neck. "You're surely not thinking of staying here."

"Only until the baby comes. I'll not risk—"

"No, Monte. This child will be born on the Lucky Star. He'll be a true Colorado baby."

"But, Abbie . . ." Monte groaned with the vision of Sharlyn wasted with fever, his tiny cloth-wrapped son lifeless in his hands.

Abbie gripped his head between her palms. "I'm not Sharlyn, Monte. I'm strong and healthy, and Mama's there and Doctor Barrow. Everything will be fine. But I have to do this in our own home, Monte, with the Colorado granite under my feet."

Monte shook his head. "I'll discuss it with Milton. If he feels it's safe . . ."

"Monte, I know what I want."

He smiled wryly. "You always have."

♦♦♦♦♦♦♦

Though Monte's breath was deep and slow beside her, Abbie couldn't rest. She felt miserable, more miserable than she would let him know. It took all she had to keep her supper down, and her head swam every time she moved. She was bone tired, but her mind raced.

She was carrying his child. At last she held his baby inside her. "Sweet Lord," she murmured again and again. "How good you are to me." Her emotions swung between ecstasy and concern. Jenny must not suffer by this. She must see that the child's needs were kept as important as her own. She must not allow Monte to continue his overindulgence of her to the neglect of Jenny. She must encourage his relationship with the child. She must . . .

The night wore on. Her body cried for sleep, and when Monte stirred and pulled her close, she let his warmth lull her. She carried his child. *Oh, thank you, Lord.*

Six

Abbie handed Jenny into Monte's arms and followed him from the train, stepping carefully over the tobacco slime on the floors surrounding the spittoons at either end of the cars. Behind her, the porter carried their bags to the luggage car where he collected her trunk and the two that held Jenny's things. Abbie climbed out and breathed in the keen mountain air. Her lungs exulted in its freshness, though the March sky had the tone of light that belongs to lingering winter.

Her breath misted, and Monte turned. "Are you cold? I wired James to send the carriage."

"I'm fine, but let me get Jenny's bonnet." She straightened the bonnet and tucked the soft curls into the child's collar. After Charleston's muggy warmth, the chill would be especially sharp to the small girl, though tomorrow might be as fair and warm as one could wish on a spring day.

Abbie could see that Jenny's eyes were still puffed from fussing all day and much of the night. Maybe she'd been wrong to leave Mammy behind. Maybe she truly wasn't up to raising the child without those sturdy hands taking the brunt of Jenny's temper.

But that had been her compromise. She would stay with Chandler and Maimie through January, February, and most of March—until Milton declared her hale—if Monte would agree to leave Mammy behind. Perhaps it hadn't been fair to trade on his protectiveness. She felt a pang of conscience, but only for a moment.

They had been there for the birth of Chandler's son, Nathan.

Maimie had labored two days and reached the point of exhaustion. Abbie recalled the long hours at her side, bathing her brow, but the joy of her healthy son had renewed her, and Abbie felt more determined than ever that her child be born on the ranch.

She glanced at her husband. With gentle words she'd broken through his fears, and now they were home. Did he feel any of the surging joy that rose in her? She caught sight of James, his dark face and grizzled head, his shoulders hunched as he brought the carriage up. Will jumped down from the seat beside him. He'd grown out of his pants again, and his brown hair hung in his eyes, but his grin was broad.

She smiled back as he took the carpetbags and tossed them into the carriage. He would be a big man when he grew into his legs. Unlike many in his position, stable boy from the time he was small, Will could read and write—thanks to their school sessions outside the stable with their backs to the wall. He gave her a hand into the carriage while Monte tucked Jenny under the warm lap robe.

Abbie's heart swelled as they drove. The land around was brown and dry, with pale green yuccas spotting the prairie between the patches of snow. Snow streaked the sides of the mountain slopes beneath the dark blue pines. She glanced back over her shoulder at Pikes Peak, crowned in white and huddled beneath ponderous gray clouds.

She turned back and caught sight of the ranch. The cottonwoods around the house and along the creek behind made a skeletal streak across the rough brown land clumped with twiggy scrub oak and olive green juniper spears. The Lucky Star. Unconsciously she put her hand to her belly. *We're home, baby.*

She caught Monte's eyes on her and smiled. His returning smile was so full of warmth and joy she could hardly keep from throwing her arms around his neck. But Will was altogether too impressionable, even if James would have ignored it.

She was surprised by how tired she felt climbing the stairs to the porch. Though the queasy stomach had all but passed and removing the corset had stopped the dizziness, she couldn't avoid the weariness that made her far less active than she wanted to be. She hoped it would pass, but if it didn't it was a small price to pay for the miracle that would come. The miracle that was returning joy to Monte's eyes.

♦♦♦♦♦♦♦

Sirocco was testy as Monte rode him across the open range among the herd. He'd likely not been exercised as much as he needed in their absence. But now that he was back, the stallion would see some use. He reined in beside Cole.

Astride his large palomino, Cole took one last draw on the cigarette, then rubbed it out on his boot heel and tossed the stub. "So you're back."

Monte gazed out across the backs of the herd to Breck Thompson and John Mason bringing in a pair of strays. The cattle breath steamed the air as the animals grazed and stood chewing their cud. "Everything looks good."

"Got a couple hundred cows with calf. They'll be droppin' anytime."

"How many men have we?"

"Those two plus Matt, Curtis, and Skeeter. And Charlie, of course. I didn't think you'd want to cut loose a good cook with roundup close." Cole rested his hand on the pommel. "When the time comes, we'll need to take on some, but for now . . ." He shrugged. "We got what we need."

Monte nodded. "I hope running it lean will give us the edge. Beef prices are up. If they stay that way until autumn, we'll ship the four-year-olds out with the full weight steers. I've some other ideas to discuss with you, but I want to study on them first."

Cole nodded. "Padriac Beard sent a man after beef for the fort. I told him next week we'd deliver."

Monte frowned. Lieutenant Beard had been more than willing to truck with the scoundrel Gifford. He'd accepted stolen Lucky Star cattle re-branded with the double diamond, but Beard wasn't fooled. He knew well what he was doing, aligning with a fellow Yankee against the southern rebel.

Cole must have read his expression. "Their money's as good as any. The men are hard up for meat and willing to pay extra for Lucky Star stock. I let 'em know the hardships caused by Cap'n Gifford drove the price up." He pulled a crooked grin. "The man all but groveled."

Monte eyed Cole, his slow smile meeting his foreman's. Cole required no thanks or congratulations, but as their eyes met they shared the triumph. One small step back on track. "Good" was all he said.

Monte rode back to the house, left Sirocco to Will, and found Abbie in the parlor with Jenny, as Abbie insisted they call her. He flinched at the sight of the child so like Frances. Looking at her brought him back to days when Frances and he had trifled away the time riding their father's land. He recalled swinging her on the long oak swing in the hot, lazy days before the war.

Abbie glanced up from the book she read to Jenny. "All in order?"

"Cole's managed admirably. I want a word with Joshua. Would you like to see your folks?"

Her face brightened. "Yes. I'll just bundle us up. Want to go for a ride, Jenny?"

"May 'Manda come?"

"Of course. We couldn't leave Amanda."

"And Chalky and Spark?"

"No. We'll let the kittens stay here."

Monte frowned at the two scraggly kittens in the box beside the settee. "Where did they come from?"

"Will found them in the barn out of season. It's a new mother, and she seems to have all but abandoned them. He thought Jenny would enjoy caring for them."

"The barn seems an appropriate place."

"I want them in my room." Jenny stood, her face ready for battle.

"Well, we don't have animals in the house, Jeanette." He saw Abbie wince and corrected himself. "Jenny. The cats belong in the barn."

She screwed up her face, but he turned to Abbie. "I'll fetch the buggy. Wrap warmly." He escaped as Jenny warmed her lungs on Abbie's ears.

♦♦♦♦♦♦♦

Abbie kept Jenny snuggled between herself and Monte. The clouds had devoured the mountains to the roots, and they entered the fog at the foothills of Pa's homestead. Her heart sank when she eyed the claret buggy also parked in the yard, then soared as Pa and Grant came from the barn—next to Monte, her two favorite men, even if Grant had dismal taste in women.

Grant lifted her down, and she reached back for Jenny. "Jenny, you remember Uncle Grant." She spoke cheerfully, though in truth the child had possibly seen him once or twice and likely never spoken at all. But she hoped to keep Jenny from feeling overwhelmed by all the new places and people.

Jenny pressed her face to Abbie's neck and eyed Grant warily. Abbie caught sight of seven-year-old Tucker coming out of the barn swinging a stick. She waved and he hurried over.

"Jenny, this is Tucker."

Tucker dug the end of the stick into the ground and eyed Jenny. "Wanna see the chickens?"

To Abbie's surprise, Jenny detached and scurried after him.

"I'll keep an eye on her," Pa said. "Mama's inside. Go in out of the cold."

She pushed open the door and went through the front room to the kitchen. Mama looked up from the stove, her face rosy and moist from the steam. "Abbie."

Abbie rushed in and caught Mama's hands between hers. "Oh, Mama, I have news."

Mama's eyes teared. "You're expecting."

"Mama! How did you know?" Abbie pressed the rough, worn hands between hers.

"I see it in your face. You've never looked lovelier." She turned. "Wouldn't you say, Marcy?"

Abbie silently groaned as Mama turned her to face Grant's

wife. She hadn't seen her at the table, so eager was she to greet Mama. Marcy's smile was thick as sorghum.

"Certainly, Ma. Of course, she's still awfully thin. Have you been ill, Abbie? Perhaps the travel . . ."

"I'm perfectly fine." Abbie tied on an apron.

Mama turned back to the pot. "Have you told Pa?"

Abbie glanced out the window. "No. But by all the back-slapping outside, I'd guess Monte has."

Mama smiled. "I *am* happy. Monte's been so patient."

"I'd stand and congratulate you, but my back aches so." Marcy waved a hand. "The doctor says I have delicate bones."

"Well, don't strain yourself." Abbie took the pot of boiled potatoes from the stove to the board. "Shall I peel?"

"Thank you, Abbie."

While Marcy carried on about her house and the new addition for the baby, Abbie rubbed the skins from the potatoes. She tried to think charitably and bit back the rude remarks that came too readily to her tongue. She prayed that the penance of Marcy's presence would count for something.

"We've had to move the bed to the ground floor since I can't use the stairs. Grant carries me if I really need to get up there."

Abbie felt a recurrence of morning sickness.

"He's so attentive. I hope you find Monte half as considerate when things get difficult for you, Abbie."

"I don't expect any difficulty." Abbie dropped the potatoes into the bowl, atop the chunk of butter. She shot Marcy a glance in time to catch the sour expression that hastily faded when Mama turned.

Marcy shrugged. "Of course, you can't say. Especially with it taking so long to get with child. Why, there could be any number of problems. Doctor Barrow might even order bed rest for you."

"Nonsense. I'm as healthy as ever." Abbie gently stirred the potatoes to coat the butter, then pulled a branch of parsley from the bunch tied to the ceiling beam and crumbled it over them. And one thing was certain; she'd never confess a single pain to Marcy.

The men crowded in, Pa with Jenny on his shoulder. He swung her to the floor, and she ran to grab Abbie's skirts. Abbie stroked her head. Let the child get acquainted, and she'd likely forget her shyness. Look how well Tucker was doing. If a little transplanted orphan could thrive on good, loving care, surely Jenny could, as well.

They gathered at the table and Pa offered thanks. Abbie felt a surging joy at being once again with those she loved most in the whole world. She'd even try to like Marcy. There must be something to like if Grant doted on her as she said. She'd just missed it for so many years now, she wasn't sure where to look.

And speaking of looks, the ones Marcy gave Monte were enough to turn her stomach. If she was playing some game with Grant's emotions, trying to make him jealous, she'd better be careful. And if she was seriously mooning over Monte still . . . Abbie forced a smile when Marcy passed the rolls.

After supper she pulled her coat tight and carried the scraps to the compost heap. The moon made a dull glow in the cloud canopy. Monte was heading to the barn to harness the horse as she started back. Inside, she passed Mama drying the last of the pots and went in search of Jenny.

Tucker had been sent to wash and get ready for bed, so she couldn't be with him. Marcy sat alone in the front room, and Abbie guessed Grant was likewise hitching up his buggy. She stooped so Marcy wouldn't have to strain her delicate neck, in case the doctor had warned her of that, too. "Have you seen Jenny?"

"She went out with Monte. I tried to keep her, but she's so flighty."

Abbie bristled. "She's hardly flighty. She's very young and she's suffered much." In the dim light, she saw the glint in Marcy's eyes.

"Well, time will tell. At least now—if you carry through—you won't have only your borrowed child."

If Abbie had been just a little younger and hadn't her family to think of, she'd have slapped Marcy soundly.

"Good-bye, Mama," she called as she buttoned up her coat and walked out. Monte was just leading Toby from the barn.

"I'd have come in for you. Have you been out here long?"

"I only just stepped out. I was escaping something venomous."

"Patience, Abbie." He lifted her in beside Jenny, already tucked into the lap robes.

The child was drowsy and laid her head in Abbie's lap. Abbie stroked her curls as Monte drove. She fought her anger at Marcy's words. *Borrowed child.* Marcy knew that would cut deep. She didn't dare say "foundling," but her intent was the same. And then Monte all but making excuses for her. Abbie seethed.

Monte nudged her with his elbow. "Come, Abbie. Let it go, whatever it was."

"I don't understand you . . . or Grant."

"What don't you understand?"

"How can you be taken in by her? Did you see how she looked at you? I've never seen anyone flirt so brazenly. Makes me wish Grant would take his hand to her."

"That's hardly likely in her condition, and I didn't—"

"Of course, you didn't. You're used to women adoring you. But you enjoyed every moment."

He grinned crookedly. "I believe you're jealous of Miss Marcy."

"Jealous! Of all the ridiculous notions." She pushed his soothing hand from her knee. "The day I'm jealous of that she-snake . . ."

"Well, she's certainly jealous of you."

Abbie put up her chin and turned away. Didn't he know there was such a thing as simple spite?

He spoke softly. "You beat her out in her pursuit of me. Soundly, I might add. And, no, I wasn't blind to her attentions. Grant adores you and no doubt defends you against her railings. And now she has not even her coming child to set her above."

Abbie stared at him.

He tipped his head. "It puts me in mind of Rachel and Leah. I always felt a little sorry for Leah."

"Rachel and Leah loved the same man."

Monte was quiet.

Was he suggesting. . . ? Surely Marcy wasn't still in love with Monte. Hadn't she all but thrown herself at Grant's feet? And the way she went on. "Grant does this . . . Grant does that." Abbie shook her head. And as for Marcy's opinion . . . she'd never received anything but scorn and ridicule from Marcy.

Monte was wrong. Her motivations were spite and meanness, but there was no convincing Monte. His innate gallantry would never see it. She drew a long breath. The air smelled of snow. That was good. The land was dry.

♦♦♦♦♦♦♦

The snow didn't come in the night, and the clouds dimmed the morning, still masking the mountains completely as Abbie crossed the yard to the stable. She slipped inside, found Zephyr in her stall, and spread the saddle blanket across her back. As she reached for the saddle on the rack, a voice surprised her.

"I'll get that."

She jumped and spun. "Cole! Don't you know better than to sneak up on someone?"

"My apologies." He pulled off his hat and held it to his chest, but there was a glint in his green eyes and a wry twist to his smile. "But I wasn't sneakin' up. I was already here when you snuck in." His rascal smile broadened.

Abbie frowned as he replaced his hat and swung the saddle to the mare's back. He brushed close, and she smelled tobacco and sage and horses. He always smelled of the outside.

He reached under and fitted the cinch strap, pulling it tight. Then he gently kneed Zephyr's belly to release the trapped air and tightened the strap again. "So how'd you fare in fine, uppity Charleston?"

"All right." She bristled at his dubious glance. "Why shouldn't I?"

"Don't get yer hackles up. I just figured a place like that might not be to yer liking."

"A place like that? You've been to Charleston?"

"Not Charleston, but others like it."

She set her chin and challenged him. "What others? I thought you came up from Texas."

"I did. That don't mean I never spent a day outside it."

She reached up and stroked Zephyr's muzzle. "Charleston was lovely, in spite of the war damage."

"I wasn't meanin' the buildings and streets." Again his eyes mocked as he pressed the bit between Zephyr's teeth.

"What were you meaning?" She didn't want to hear it, but couldn't let it go.

He slid the bridle over the mare's ears. "The folks. The ladies and gents."

"And why wouldn't I fare well with the people of Charleston?"

The corner of his mouth twitched. "Forget I said anything, Abbie. Where're you off to?"

"Do I answer to you?" She snapped without thinking and saw his mouth tighten. She had treated him as high-handedly as Charlestonians treated their servants. Well, he deserved it. He . . .

Cole stepped back and handed her the reins without reproof.

Her conscience stung. "I'm sorry, Cole. It's just . . . I wish it weren't so obvious."

"What?"

"My social deficiency."

He grinned crookedly.

She drew herself up, all pangs of conscience forgotten. "You needn't laugh at me."

"I ain't laughin'. And it ain't you who's deficient. It's the rest of them stiff old cats."

Abbie bit back the smile at his apt description of Mrs. Stevens' friends. She smarted still from the guarded, all-knowing glances they'd sent one another, glances that said Monte had married beneath him, poor boy. She led Zephyr to the stable door and scanned the yard.

"What's goin' on, Abbie? What are you sneakin' off from?"

"I'm not sneaking."

"Heck you ain't."

She turned on him. "Well, if you must know, I'm going for a ride."

"I figured that much."

"That's all there is to it."

"Then why're you jumpin' and peekin' around like you're guilty?"

"I'm not guilty. Doctor Rochester said it was perfectly fine to ride for a few months yet, but Monte . . ." She stopped. She shouldn't complain to Cole about Monte, and the look on Cole's face would have silenced her anyway.

He pulled a paper from his pocket and a pouch of tobacco. "So you're expectin'."

"Yes," she said softly. It didn't matter that a proper gentleman would not have mentioned his guess. In a way, Cole was entitled to know.

He sprinkled the tobacco onto the paper, rolled it, and licked the edge. "Mr. Farrel's right, Abbie. This is wild country, and it's fixin' to snow."

"I know that as well as you."

He struck a match on the wall and held it a moment, then blew it out without lighting the cigarette. "Sorry."

His thoughtfulness touched her. "That's all right, Cole. I'm past the sensitive stomach."

"Ain't right to smoke in front of a lady, 'specially the boss's wife." He gave her a hand to mount. "Take 'er easy out there."

Abbie swung up. "Thank you, Cole." She smiled down at him and felt doubly guilty knowing he wouldn't go to Monte. But she had to get out, feel the wind in her face, feel Zephyr's spirit as she carried her over the land. A buggy ride to town or to Mama's just wasn't the same. Anyway, she'd confess it if Monte asked.

She urged Zephyr to an easy lope, confident the mare's smooth stride would not jar the baby within. She understood Monte's concern, but Zephyr was far less skittish than she'd been. They understood each other now. Zephyr anticipated her commands, and she sensed the mare's moods.

She'd sensed Cole's, too. Did her news distress him? She remembered how she'd felt when Sharlyn told her she was carrying Monte's child, proof of their marital devotion. The ache tightened her chest. Cole had behaved better than she had.

Maybe he'd put his feelings for her behind him. Maybe he no longer cared as he once had. She hoped that was so. Though he swore he'd never be so inclined again, she suspected Cole could love a woman well. If only he hadn't chosen her.

Abbie sighed and slowed Zephyr's pace. The cold penetrated her woolen coat and she breathed its keen bite. For all his teasing and scolding, Cole was still a good man. If she hadn't given her heart to Monte from the first, she might have cared for him more deeply than she did.

But God had made her for Monte. She would never love another. Abbie brought the horse around. At least she and Cole remained friends . . . even though he provoked her like no one else. He seemed to think that, after Monte, he was in charge of her. The truly annoying thing was that Monte thought so, too.

She supposed that was only right. Cole had proved himself worthy of that trust. Hadn't he risked his life to save her from the rustler, Jip Crocker? Still, he didn't have to be so exasperating. She wished he didn't understand her so well. Sometimes he saw more clearly even than Monte.

And she didn't understand him at all. What did she know about him, about his life before he signed on with Monte? What did Monte know? Likely little more than she did. Monte judged a man by the character he showed, not by his past or pedigree. In that, he was unlike his Charleston associates.

She frowned. How had Cole known she'd failed in Charleston? Not that it took much to reckon it. And why did she care? She'd always disdained the refinement she now coveted. Did she really covet it?

Would it matter to her if not for Monte? If he were a man like Pa, well educated and intelligent but simple and respected for his good sense and good humor instead of his position and standing.

If that were the case, she wouldn't care if she could properly simper over tea.

But Monte was a gentleman. Everything about him bespoke his genteel roots, more so now after seeing him in the company of others like him. It was no wonder Cole suspected her inadequacy. It must have been glaring to all.

Not all. Maimie and Chandler took her as she was. She warmed at the thought. And Monte did, too. He loved her with all her flaws. She put a hand to her belly. *Oh, baby, you'll be the best of both of us.*

That thought convicted her of her disobedience to Monte's wishes. How could he expect her not to ride? But he did, and that was what mattered. She turned Zephyr around.

The first flakes fell in large white clumps when she neared the yard. It would be a wet snow—the spring snows always were—and from the look of the clouds, a heavy one. She turned Zephyr over to Will at the stable and hurried to the house. Already snow clung to her hair, and her cheeks were red from the gusting wind.

Startled, Monte looked up from his desk when she rushed into the study.

"I'm sorry, Monte. I disobeyed and took Zephyr out. As you can see, no harm came to me or the baby, but I realize it was wrong to disregard your request and I've come to confess." She stooped down beside him and rested her hands on his thigh.

"Good heavens, Abbie. I'm not Father Dominic." But his eyes flickered with amusement. He took her hands in his. "You're cold."

"It's snowing."

He frowned. "Then you're lucky you made it back before it started in earnest. Abbie . . ."

"Please don't scold. I had to go. I've been too long from the land. I had to see it spread out around me, taste the wind and smell the sage. I . . . what are you laughing at?"

"Nothing, my wild mountain wife." He pressed his lips to her fingers. "But I will have your promise it won't happen again."

"If the urge comes on me so much I can't bear it, I'll find you first and beg."

He groaned.

"Besides, the snow will keep us inside a day or so at least."

"A day or so? Abbie, you've more than yourself to think of now. This baby . . ."

". . . will be as strong and healthy as the Colorado land itself."

His eyes burned. "That is my fervent prayer. And that's why I've asked you not to ride or go far afoot."

Abbie softened. "I know, Monte. I understand your concern."

"Good. I trust it will keep you honest."

Seven

Monte stared out at the swirling mass of white. The first day of snow had been bad enough, but this day he'd watched at the window for it to relent until the daylight vanished and the night deepened. Only the lamplight through the glass illumined the flakes, which were falling more densely than he'd ever seen.

The cold, too, was unusual for March. The bitter wind felt as though it came straight from the polar ice caps and drove the snow in gusts. He thought of the cattle out on the open range. The horses and those cows with calf had been gathered into the fenced pasture, but all were without shelter.

With their long legs and powerful build, the Longhorns were better suited to handling such weather than other breeds, but even they would be hard pressed in this storm. This infernal, unpredictable western weather. He turned from the window when Abbie touched his elbow.

Her eyes were alight as she gazed on the scene. "Isn't it lovely? It's like a Russian fairy tale."

He swallowed his concerns and smiled. "Yes. You're up late. I thought you retired long ago."

"I did." She lifted the silk lapels of her wrap as proof. "But you never came up."

He glanced at his desk. "I've had business to catch up on."

"You work too hard."

He chuckled. "Hardly."

"Come up now." She reached her arms to his neck, and her eyes held the blue depths he could drown in.

His pulse quickened, and he took her in his arms. He had barely tasted her lips when a pounding at the front door drove them apart. "What now?" He hurried from the room and met James in the hall. "I'll get it, James."

"Yessuh."

Monte pulled the door open to Cole, who stood hat in hand. Snow clung to his coat and jeans and mustache.

"What is it, Cole?"

"Snow's driftin' up four feet already, Mr. Farrel. The calves in the west pasture are gonna be in trouble."

"What are you suggesting?"

"We gotta get them out to a cleared space."

What cleared space? Monte looked at the blizzarding snow in the halo of light. "Is it possible?"

"Won't be easy, but they'll drown if we don't."

"Drown?"

"Breathe the snow into their lungs. Some are likely buried already. And if they can't move they'll freeze."

Dear God. "Very well, let me get my coat. Have you roused the others?"

"I'm on my way." Cole glanced at Abbie.

She responded immediately. "What can I do?"

Monte opened his mouth to send her up to bed, but Cole spoke for him. "Get somethin' hot goin' for the men to drink. The wind's nasty, and we'll need to be fortified." He turned and hustled down the steps.

Monte closed the door. Cole was wise. Abbie would have never agreed to rest quietly while they were out. It was good to assign her a task that kept her in the house.

"Strong coffee, Abbie. As much as you can make." He pulled on his long coat and fastened the buttons, then found his gloves and hat and started for the door.

"Monte." She took a muffler from the hook and wrapped it around his neck. "Please be careful."

"It's the cattle at risk, Abbie. Don't worry." He kissed her forehead and went out. The snow flew in his eyes and nostrils as he crossed the yard to the stable. He could see none of the outbuildings and only several feet ahead of him, but he knew the way blind. He stepped inside and found Will, bundled up himself, with Sirocco and another already saddled.

"Can I help, sir?"

Monte eyed him. He stood almost at height with him, had a huskier build, and his young voice had cracked with coming manhood. Monte guessed for this night they could use all the hands they could get. "We'll need extra horses. Ride up with us and you can rope a remuda, as many horses to the man as you can manage."

"Yes, sir." Will grinned broadly.

Oh, to be young and worry free. Monte took Sirocco's reins and led him out. He mounted as Cole and the others came from the bunkhouse with their own steeds. In minutes they were coated with snow, and hats did little to keep the wind from blowing it into their eyes and mouths.

Cole rode up next to him. "Better stay together until we get the pasture in sight. Then we'll have the fence to guide us."

Maybe, Monte thought. The way the snow was drifting, the fences could be buried. The horses fought, chest deep in some places, toward the pasture that held the new calves. Surely the cows would provide some protection against the wind and snow for their young.

He heard Cole hollering, but the wind snatched away the words. Monte kept his head down and urged Sirocco on. The stallion was trembling with exertion, puffing at the snow in its face. Beside him he heard Breck swear and understood the sentiment. He tried to see the others, but in the dark and storm they were lost to view.

Cole's powerful palomino burst through, and he reigned in before him. "We're off course, Mr. Farrel. Turn north." He pressed past to give word to the others.

How in heaven's name Cole could tell anything about their position was beyond him, but Monte pulled Sirocco to the right and started on.

"Is that the fence line, Mr. Farrel?" John Mason asked beside him.

Monte followed his outstretched arm and squinted through the storm. "Can't tell, John. Just keep on." Next to Will, John Mason was the youngest of them out there, but he'd grown up some since signing on with Gifford and learning from hard experience the value of loyalty. And where was Will, anyway?

Monte wrenched around to look for the boy. This was hard enough on the rest of them with more years and strength. "Have you seen Will?"

"No, sir." John held an arm to his eyes against the cutting blast of wind.

Monte wheeled and followed the trench back that Sirocco had just cut. He passed Curtis and Breck and found Cole coming back. "Did you see Will?"

Cole nodded. "He's with Charlie."

So even the chuck wagon cook had come to help. It cheered him, the loyalty of his men. He swung Sirocco again and followed the path already cut by Cole's horse, Scotch. It seemed they'd been out there for hours, but all sense of time was wiped away by the storm. It was worse than Cole had indicated. No moon penetrated the cloud cover except to give a dull illumination to the whirling flakes stinging their eyes.

Cole pulled up and jumped from Scotch's back into the snow that rose to his chest as he shouldered into the drift and dug through with his arms. "Found the fence, Mr. Farrel."

Monte stared along the crested ridge only slightly higher than the mounding snow beyond it. Where were the animals?

"No time to find the gate." Cole took wire cutters from his saddlebag and snipped the wire, then dug down for the next and the last. "We'll cut through here." He mounted Scotch and brought him through the gap.

Monte followed and heard Breck calling the others through. Sirocco staggered against the chest-high snow, and Monte scoured the dark land for sign of the other horses. He strained his eyes toward a darker mass ahead and heard a frantic whinny.

He hollered to Cole and leaped down, thrashing with his arms from side to side and pushing his weight to clear a way to the horses huddled there.

He stumbled and fell to his knees against something solid, then groped with his gloves until he uncovered the swatch of frozen, matted fur. He sat back on his heels and felt Cole stoop beside him. Cole dug into the larger mound to his left and found a dusky hide. Cow and calf had perished together.

Monte stared through the swirling madness. He could make out a few horned heads above the surface of the snow, and his throat tightened. "Have we a chance?"

"For some of 'em, maybe. If we work quick." Cole stood. "Get the men to walk abreast and trample the snow to the gap in the fence. I'll see what I can locate."

"Get to the horses, Cole."

"I reckon they'll manage a mite better than the cattle at this point. I don't think we'll salvage any calves."

Monte shook his head and turned back. He passed Cole's orders and fought beside the men to cut the swath through the snow. Sirocco was spent and made no move when he left him standing behind. Shoulder to shoulder with Breck, Monte dug through the drifts with his body, feet, and hands, but even as they pressed and trampled, snow piled again behind them.

Still they made steady progress to the fence, then dropped, exhausted and oblivious to their soaked and freezing condition. The wind had long since numbed his face, and Monte was thankful for the muffler Abbie had wrapped about his neck. His chest heaved with exertion, and he rolled to his side against the wall of snow they'd created.

He raised his head as two figures loomed up outside the fence line. Two riders on horseback, one with a lantern that barely penetrated the storm, the other slim and . . . He leaped to his feet as Abbie slid down from Zephyr's back. His angry frustration warmed him. "Abbie!"

"I brought coffee" was all she said.

Monte glanced at her companion on the other horse. James

held the lantern, looking abashed. He was not to blame. The servant had no chance against Abbie's wheedling.

Monte grabbed her shoulders and turned her. She was bundled into her coat and, he noticed with annoyance, his trousers. Her head was tied in a scarf but covered thickly with clumps of snow. The hair at her forehead was matted with ice and her lashes likewise.

"What are you doing here? You could have been lost in the blizzard!"

"I followed your tracks." She reached for the large canteens that hung over blankets on the mare's sides.

His exasperation left him speechless.

"Here." She produced a tin cup from the saddlebag and poured. "Drink this."

He took the coffee and sipped, letting the steam thaw his nose and cheeks. She poured cups for the others, and he couldn't help notice their relief and adoration. He released a slow breath. Why was he surprised? Abbie home, warm and safe, while others toiled in danger was not a picture he could conjure with even his best imagination.

Monte watched her hand a steaming cup to Cole, who had just ridden over and dismounted. He didn't look the least surprised. Had Cole anticipated her extending his orders? Probably.

Monte drained the cup. The heat and bite of the coffee brought life to his system, as it would the others. He joined Cole and his wife. "Well?"

"There's a few still fightin'. We can get through, but it'll take all of us."

Monte turned. "Abbie, you and James get back to the house. Thank you for the coffee, but please, don't come back again. We'll have more when we're through here."

"I can help bring the animals. Zephyr's fresh still—"

"No." He bristled when Abbie looked to Cole.

"Git back to the house, Abbie. You heard yer husband." Cole nodded his head toward the house, but his tone was less convincing than it might have been. Monte wondered if Cole would have agreed had the order not already been given.

Abbie raised her chin. "You said yourself it would take all of you. Well, James and I are two more."

Monte took her arm and marched her toward the fence. "Now is not the time. Every minute counts, and we have a job to do."

"I can help, Monte."

"If I have to escort you personally, that's one less man to bring in the stock." He sent James a scathing glance. "Take her in hand." He turned on his heel and heard James's plea behind him.

"Come on, now, Mizz Abbie. You got no cause to be out here."

Monte refused to look back and give her hope. Cole had sent Will on to rope fresh horses, not that any would be fresh in this, but at least they hadn't worked as hard yet. With the other men, Monte stripped the saddle from his tired mount, resaddled, and went after the band of cattle huddled at the south fence. His stomach sank when he saw that they stood on the bodies of others less fortunate.

Cole barked orders, and like his men, Monte followed them. He had no experience to match Cole's and knew well enough to do as he was told. The wind took his hat, and he scrambled through the drifts after it. He was nearing exhaustion and guessed the others were, as well, but they continued to dig out the survivors and prod them toward the trench.

Some of the cattle seemed dazed, others dropped and could not be roused, but some gained new strength and pressed through the trench and beyond, following the tracks the men had made from the yard to the pasture. Monte dug with his hand to free one long-horned cow and found a calf huddled beneath in a pocket of air created by the mother's legs.

He eased the calf loose and both made their way along the trench. He leaned against the snow wall and fought the trembling of his limbs. How much longer could they sustain the exertion? He turned and saw Will collapse.

Monte made his way through to the boy and pulled him up from the drifts. "Get on a horse and go back to the house."

"I'm sorry, Mr. Farrel. I can manage still."

"No, you can't. Nor can the rest of us. We've done what we can here. Now go." He turned and helped Matt free a steer entangled in the stiff, frozen legs of three others, then ordered him likewise back to the house. Matt was too weary to argue. He nodded and fished his hat from the snow.

Monte turned into the buffeting wind and almost sat back in the drift, so shaky were his legs. He pushed forward to Cole. "I'm sending the men home. We've done what we can."

"I reckon so." Cole slapped the flank of the horse he'd extricated. He rubbed his face with his arm. "Dawn's comin' on."

Monte peered up at the swirling darkness. Cole's sense was keener than his to detect that, but he was weary enough to believe they'd worked through the night. "You coming?"

"I'll make one more sweep."

"Don't linger."

"Nope."

Monte released the mount he was riding into Breck's care, resaddled Sirocco, and rode him back. The track was well trampled by the animals following in line, and he found they'd gathered in the yard between the house and outbuildings where the structures had kept the snow from accumulating as deeply. It looked odd to see them huddled about the walls of the great house, but he shook his head and rode past. He tended Sirocco, then went inside.

The warmth hit him so powerfully he almost collapsed, but forced himself to the kitchen where Abbie flitted like a ministering angel between Matt and John and Will, already there. Pearl ladled cups of hot soup into bowls for them, and they ate it at the rough table on stools.

Monte took his gratefully and let it warm his hands before lifting the spoon to his lips. The life returning to his fire-scarred palms was painful, but the hearty beef and vegetable stock renewed him. He sent Pearl his thanks with a look.

Abbie put a plate of hot biscuits on the table. "Help yourselves, gentlemen. There's more coming."

Seeing her working side by side with Pearl brought a smile to his lips. No one but Abbie could have invaded Pearl's domain and remained intact. She'd had an upward road of it, but Pearl had at last taken her to heart. He watched the men flush when she ministered to their weary souls with hot food and a smile. Dressed now in a blue cotton skirt and white shirtwaist, she was a welcome sight.

Curtis and Breck staggered in with Cole behind them.

"Drop your wet things on the floor there, then come and get warm." Abbie poured fresh cups of coffee as Pearl ladled more soup. The wind whistled at the window, but the glass steamed from the warmth in the room. Even James and Zena crowded into the doorway.

His household. His people. Monte ached for the stock he'd lost this night. There were certain to be more when they searched the open range. But gathered here was his family, all but Jenny, who no doubt slept blissfully upstairs with Abbie's stories driving her dreams. He looked at his wife and she met his gaze. In the dawning light he felt a surge of love for her. *Thank you, Lord, for this woman and all those gathered here.*

Eight

Abbie stood in the entry when Monte came inside, stamping the slush and mud from his knee-high boots. The sunlight through the open door was bright, but his expression bleak. Her heart sank. "Is it as bad as all that?"

"Worse. We've lost eight hundred head that we know of. Others have wandered so far, driven by the storm, that it will take weeks to search them out, if we ever find them at all." He sagged against the wall.

Abbie went to him and took his hands. "What will we do? How can we bury so many?" She'd driven past the west pasture on the way to Mama's and seen the carcasses half covered in snow.

"We can't bury them. The ground is frozen. Once things dry, they'll be burned."

She heard the desolation in his voice and had no words that would not be empty solace.

He shook his head. "We've lost steers that were marketable at full size. And Longhorns are such slow growers; four years for the calf to mature, eight to ten to reach full weight. How can I put in that kind of time again?" He shook his head. "I was counting on this year's beef herd to pull us out."

She tightened her grip on his hands. The sunshine through the window behind him seemed mockingly bright. "Surely there will be some to market. And with that you can buy—"

"I can buy nothing," he snapped, then bowed his head. "Forgive me." He brushed her fingers with his lips and pulled away. "I'll be in my study. Would you send Pearl with coffee?"

Abbie watched his back until the door closed behind him. He hadn't even removed his muddy boots. Zena hurried over with a cloth to wipe his tracks from the wood floor. Abbie went to the kitchen and gave Pearl his request. She would have brought it herself, but his dismissal was clear. She wandered upstairs and found Jenny dressing Amanda, or rather undressing her. The doll's things lay strewn across the floor.

Jenny looked up. "May we sled now?"

It was on her lips to refuse outright. She certainly shouldn't risk a toboggan ride herself. What happened the last time was evidence of that. Maybe Will . . . The distraction would keep worry at bay. Abbie held out her hand. "Come. We'll see what we can do." Downstairs, she bundled the child, took her by the hand, and headed for the stable.

Will met them, toboggan in hand. "I saw you comin'. I guess this is what you're after?"

Abbie smiled. "It's impertinent to assume you know a lady's mind, Will."

"Ain't I right?"

"*Aren't* you right?"

"Aren't I, then?"

"Yes, you are. Jenny would love a slide or two."

"You too?" He grinned.

"Yes, I would. But I won't since . . ."

He blushed. "I forgot about the baby."

"How did you know?"

He kicked his boot in the snow. "Heard the men talkin'. Come on, then."

He carried the toboggan he'd made from barrel slats to the hill behind the stable, and she followed. Had Cole told the men, or had Monte? It wasn't unlikely Monte had alerted them to be especially watchful of her. She felt the joy of his care like a great downy quilt about her heart.

Abbie looked down the slope and remembered the disastrous ride with Kendal. Had he intentionally swerved the sled off into the trees and around the turn of the hill, tumbling her off in order to make his advances? She frowned. How was it two men from the South could be so different? Monte with his devotion to honor, and Kendal . . .

Will settled Jenny onto the front, then gave the sled a shove and jumped on behind. Jenny's laughter was musical. The sun dazzled Abbie's eyes as she watched them go. Overhead a chickadee warbled, and looking up, Abbie felt spring touch her heart. Even though the snow lay deep on the north slopes, elsewhere the sun was quickly turning it to rushing torrents down gullies that lay bone dry most of the year.

Thoughts of their losses depressed her spirit, but wasn't the spring proof that God would bring them through? Surely if they lived simply, cut back on their expenses . . . she wouldn't need anything new. Monte had given her gowns enough to last for years.

And they could dine just as well on plain fare as on the sumptuous meals Pearl turned out. What other expenses were there? Payroll for the men, and wages for James and Pearl and Zena. That was the worst of it, she guessed. Household expenses, coal for the stoves and braziers, oil for the lamps, repairs and upkeep, feed for the horses.

Unless they still owed money on Kendal's fraud. Monte was determined to cover that and retrieve her stock certificates . . . at the escalated price Mr. Driscoll was asking. She wasn't supposed to know that, but she'd come across the discarded response to Monte's inquiry. From the condition of the paper, she could imagine Monte's rage when he received it.

Then there were the previous debts he had vouched for in Kendal's collapse and those he took on to support Frances until her death. She had no idea what that amounted to, but the burden obviously hung heavy on him. *Oh, Monte, must your honor extend to everyone else's shortcomings?*

Will tugged the sled up the hill with one hand and Jenny with the other. Their cheeks were red, their eyes bright. From her perch at the top, Abbie tried to look as cheerful as they.

Monte tethered Sirocco and crossed the walk to the bank. Everything in him cried out against what he was about to do. But what choice had he?

The blizzard had destroyed him. They could eke along, as were his fellow ranchers Dunbar and Ephart, but Monte knew from experience that catastrophe brought collapse. He'd seen enough plantations go down because they'd hung too long by a thread.

Though he knew the risk of taking a loan, it was better to run strong and get back on top. Even if it meant groveling to Mr. Driscoll. He still stung from his last encounter when he tried to reacquire Abbie's holdings. But he would swallow his pride to save his land, especially now with a child coming to inherit it all and Jenny to think of, as well.

He rang the bell on the counter, though he was certain Driscoll had seen him coming. Elam Blanchard, the clerk, hustled out from Driscoll's office. "Yes, Mr. Farrel?"

"I'd like to see Mr. Driscoll."

"One moment, please." He scurried back in.

Monte looked around at the small paned windows, the fine wood trim, the brass cagework. A small spider wove a web across the corner of the ceiling where the sunrays caught in the delicate threads. A cloud passed over and the web disappeared.

Minutes passed. Driscoll was toying with him. He refused to turn when the door opened behind him. Two could play at that game.

"Mr. Farrel?"

He turned.

"Mr. Driscoll will see you now." The clerk opened the half gate and let him pass through to the inner sanctum of Driscoll's office.

Mr. Driscoll stood up behind the desk, smug in his brocade waistcoat and ankle-length gaiters. His fox-colored side whiskers bunched when he smiled. "Good afternoon, Mr. Farrel. Cigar?" He held open the brass tin.

"No, thank you." Monte waited while Driscoll lit up. He hoped it was Chandler's leaf. "I sent notice of my request. I've come to see if you've had time to consider it."

"Well, now, Mr. Farrel, I have had a chance to look over your situation. An unfortunate business, your losses these last few years."

Not unfortunate for you. "I would prefer we limit our dealing to the present."

Driscoll leaned back in the tight leather spring chair. "In banking decisions, Mr. Farrel, past history is an integral part of the puzzle. And whereas I can't fault your business sense, nor your diligence, there is some question as to your judgment."

Monte bristled. "The Lucky Star is prime land, my stock the finest in the area. The financial losses last year were due to circumstances that no longer exist. They had nothing to do with the good standing of the ranch."

"Nonetheless, you've shown a propensity to overextend, albeit for humanitarian reasons. It's still not good business. Covering other men's debts to your own detriment may earn you treasure in heaven, but this bank deals in earthly gold." He laughed at his own joke, then cleared his throat. "And then the blizzard. Well, you're not the only one to have suffered losses. Surely all the ranchers could claim just a need as yours, yet . . ."

Monte drew a long breath. "Are you refusing my loan?"

"Refusing? No. I just want you to understand why I'll need collateral."

Monte felt the muscles tighten in his jaw. He'd expected this but it rankled nonetheless. "I mentioned certain stock certificates."

"Unfortunately, the stock certificates you mentioned don't interest me."

Monte gripped the arm of the chair. "They're perfectly good mining stocks."

"Mining is precarious, especially now with so many playing out and the uncertainty of the government's coin policy."

"The mines I've invested in are solid." Though trying to sell his shares now with the current lag would mean more losses.

Driscoll shrugged. "No, I'm afraid the only collateral I can accept is the deed to the Lucky Star."

Monte fought to control the surging fury. He forced himself to calm. "The Lucky Star is worth far and above the amount I requested."

"So it is. And when you've paid back the loan, you'll have your deed."

"This is usury."

"If you think you can do better elsewhere . . ." Driscoll spread his hands.

Monte felt his pulse throb in his temple. By the time he established relations with a Denver bank and brought his suit to them, with no guarantee they'd be any more flexible than Driscoll, he'd have defaulted on his payroll and starved his family.

He thought of Abbie and the child within her. He thought of Cole and the men who had fought with him through the drifts to rescue the animals they'd saved. He thought of the land, his father's dream, and groaned silently. Then he looked at Driscoll, smug behind the desk.

He stood up. "Thank you, Mr. Driscoll, but I cannot accept those terms." He turned.

"Think about it, Mr. Farrel," Driscoll called. "You'll be back."

Nine

"Jenny?" Abbie looked under the white ruffled bed and in the wardrobe. She'd already searched the other rooms but with no success. Pearl hadn't seen the child, nor had Zena. Abbie had left Jenny to nap after the birthday party she'd thrown her. April twenty-third, and Jenny was three going on thirteen.

Abbie cringed when she thought how imperiously Jenny had treated Clara Franklin's little Dell and Melissa's daughter, Suzanna. Then, true to form, she'd thrown a rousing tantrum over one of her gifts, and Clara and Melissa had left, thanking God Jenny wasn't their responsibility. Abbie went from the last guest room into the library. "Jenny?"

Nothing. She glanced into the drawing room and the parlor, then searched the cloakroom, growing crosser by the minute. She checked under the coats hanging nearly to the floor, then put one on and went outside. Standing on the porch, she shielded her eyes and gazed out over the yard.

The barn where the kittens were was the likeliest place. She crossed the yard and pulled open the broad wooden door. The April chinook blew hard and whistled through the cracks. The barn was warm, though the sun was now sinking in the west. She breathed the smell of hay. "Jenny, are you in here?"

No answer. Abbie's concern and irritation grew. Where could she be? She went out from the barn to the bunkhouse. Breck and Matt Weston had dismounted and penned their horses in the east corral. Breck greeted her with a tip of his hat on his way back around the side. "Can I help you, Mrs. Farrel?"

"Have you seen Jenny? I can't seem to locate her."

"We just came in from the range, ma'am."

"Where's Cole?"

"I don't know. Matt and I were runnin' down strays."

Abbie peeked into the bunkhouse but it was empty. She turned with a sigh. She wished Monte was back from the Dunbar ranch. But he'd said it would likely be dark before he returned. She headed for the stable. That was not a safe place for a small, curious girl. Surely Will would return her to the house . . . if he was in there. Lately he'd spent more and more time out with the men.

The wind caught the door when she pulled it open, but she held tight and stepped inside. She stopped short at the sight of Jenny perched high on Cole's palomino, Scotch, with his big sheepskin coat about her. Cole had his back to her, but Jenny looked over, smiled, and gripped the pommel. Cole turned.

He looked stubbornly defensive, and Abbie thought better of teasing him. She joined them at the stall. "Jenny, I've looked all over for you."

Cole slid the bridle from Scotch's teeth. "I found her in the yard."

"Don't you think she's a little small for Scotch?"

"Nope."

"No?"

"Not if I'm leadin' him. Don't want her growin' up prissy like her ma, do you?" He reached up and swung Jenny from Scotch's back to the stall railing. "Sit there, now, while I take his saddle off." He loosened the cinch, sliding the belt through the double metal rings.

Abbie reached out. "Come down from there, Jenny."

"No. Cole said I can watch."

"That's Mr. Jasper to you, young lady," Abbie instructed.

"Cole's fine by me." He unbuckled the belly strap and turned on her. "Abbie, I'll bring the young'un up soon as I'm done here with Scotch."

"I think she should come now."

He crossed his arms and leaned his shoulder on the stall. "How come?" His green eyes went over her. They were the color of the sea in the Charleston harbor, and they held a touch of the ocean's stormy peril.

"She needs to know she can't just wander off on her own."

He turned back to the saddle. "Well, she ain't wandering, she's helpin' me."

Abbie stared. Of all people, Cole was the last one to whom she'd expect Jenny to attach. And who'd have suspected Cole would have a soft spot for little girls in his obstreperous heart? She could see she was defeated, and the shine in Jenny's eyes was too rare to squelch. She could scold her later, when Cole wasn't there to gainsay every word.

"Bring her straight in. The night's coming on."

"Yes, ma'am."

She hated it when Cole used that roguish tone. She spun, swirling her skirts behind and stalking out of the stable. Her eyes must have held fire, because Monte looked concerned when she nearly collided with him outside the door.

He had Sirocco by the reins, but reached an arm to her. "Abbie?"

"Cole has Jenny. Will you see that he brings her in as soon as he finishes?" She flounced past. There, let Cole explain himself to Monte.

◆◆◆◆◆◆◆

Monte rolled his eyes to the library ceiling. Jeanette's screams coming through the floor made him want to scream himself. What demons possessed the child? He could hear Abbie's voice raised over the din, but steady and firm, not angry. How did she maintain her calm? What Jenny needed was a thrashing.

And he ought to administer it, but he didn't dare. It was Frances all over again. He drew a long, shaky breath. He had indulged his sister in everything, letting her pouting and tantrums sway his better judgment. And he had done everything in his power to protect her from the consequences of her actions.

He had raised her to become the weak, self-indulgent woman she'd been. Never mind that he'd loved her, that it was his father's place to raise her, not his, that the war had created extraordinary circumstances. Frances was his charge, and he'd failed her. How could he now take responsibility for her child?

He'd imagined some cathartic experience. The chance to undo his wrong by loving Jenny. But it was impossible. She was impossible. Only Abbie seemed able to break through, yet he knew it took its toll on her. He read the weariness in her eyes after a battle. It wasn't fair to leave it to her, but then, she'd refused to bring Mammy.

He sighed. Maybe Abbie was right. Maybe Selena's child-rearing was superior. Hadn't she produced Abbie?

Then let Abbie handle it. The pounding on the ceiling signaled the tantrum had moved to the floor-kicking stage. Monte took up his hat and went out.

◆◆◆◆◆◆◆

Abbie pulled open the sash to let the morning light into Jenny's room. The child rubbed her sleepy eyes and sat up in the bed. She looked exhausted, and Abbie knew the fits of temper that preceded her sleep nearly every night were wearing on her. But as much as she hoped for Jenny's love and trust, she must establish authority or Jenny would never break the pattern that had ruined Frances.

"Good morning, Jenny." Abbie bent and kissed her cheek. She expected no act of affection in return. Jenny's clinging to her skirts and burying her face against her neck were nothing more than self-protective gestures. At best, Jenny suffered her company as long as she was entertaining enough.

Jenny slipped out of bed and stood in her bare feet. "I want Zena to dress me."

"She will, dear, as soon as you've had your bath."

Jenny bunched her fists at her sides. "I don't want a bath. I want to help Cole with Scotch."

"Yes, well, Cole is working now. He's with the herd."

"I want to see the cows. Cole said he'd show me. He promised."

Abbie squatted down before the child. "And maybe he will. But right now, you need your bath." She took her hand but Jenny yanked it away.

"I won't. I want to see the cows." Jenny crossed her arms and stuck out her lip stubbornly. She looked for all the world like an Arabian knights's genie from a bottle, but Abbie knew she'd be granting no wishes.

Abbie sat back on her heels. "Do you know what happens to little girls who won't wash?"

Jenny's stance wavered.

"They develop a scent. They smell. And out here when people smell they attract wild animals, coyotes and wildcats and bears." She watched Jenny's eyes widen.

"And wolfs?"

"Perhaps. And another thing, Jenny. God likes us to be clean."

Jenny put her hand in Abbie's. Abbie smiled. She knew well which part of her message had affected the change. But hopefully some bit of the second part had sunk in, as well. She had a pang of conscience thinking how many times Mama must have clung to that hope with her. She led Jenny down to the back room and drew her bath.

Zena put her head in the door. "You wants me to bathe her, Mizz Abbie?"

"No thanks. I can manage."

The child was so beautifully formed it thrilled Abbie to see her as God had made her, without all the ruffles and layers. She sponged the warm water down Jenny's back and sudsed the fine dark hair, then rinsed her clean and dried her. "There now." She wrapped her in a towel and carried her upstairs, then allowed Zena to dress her and fix her hair.

Abbie longed to do it herself, but Zena deserved more than housework to fill her days, and she could see she delighted in the task. When Jenny came out dressed in the blue woolen habit and boots, Abbie laughed.

Zena wrung her hands. "She say she ridin' with Mistuh Jazzper."

Abbie took Jenny's hand. "Thank you, Zena." She went downstairs, pulled on her own coat, and led Jenny to the stable. "Saddle Zephyr for me, please, Will." Monte couldn't fault her this ride.

She and Jenny waited in the sunshine until Will brought out the stormy gray mare. Yes, it meant riding against Monte's wishes, but she could hardly take the buggy to the herd on the open range. With only a slight pang of conscience, Abbie mounted, and Will handed Jenny up. She settled the child into the saddle before her and urged Zephyr with her knees. She would teach Cole not to make promises he didn't mean to keep.

The herd came into sight, scattered over the greening range in clumps. She caught sight of Cole riding the edge, swinging his hat to bring in a stray. Even without Scotch and at that distance she would know it was he. Only Cole rode a horse as though he'd been born on it. She urged Zephyr down the gentle slope.

She'd never taken the mare in among the cattle, but no doubt Cole would spot her long before she neared them. Sure enough, he spurred Scotch and met her at the base of the slope. He tipped his hat, revealing the unruly blond hair, but didn't remove it. He was working and didn't take kindly to interruptions.

Abbie smiled smugly. It would make her point that much stronger. "Good morning, Cole. Jenny said you promised to show her the herd."

Cole looked from her face to Jenny's and back. His scowl pulled into a crooked grin. "That's right."

Abbie stared, unbelieving, as Cole pulled Jenny from Zephyr's back and tucked her in before him. Jenny's eyes danced, and Abbie felt her mouth fall open on words that vanished before they came.

"Did ya have other business, Abbie?"

"No, I . . ." She hadn't intended to leave the child.

Cole tipped his hat again and headed off.

Her anger flared. He'd read her purpose and thwarted her intentionally. What on earth would he do with a little girl in his saddle? She pressed her knees to go after him, but he spurred

Scotch and took off with Jenny firmly in his arm. She could hear Jenny's laughter all the way.

She turned Zephyr crossly and started back. If he thought she'd wait and watch his shenanigans, he had another thing coming. He could just bring Jenny back to the house himself. She took Zephyr out on the range as far as she dared before her exasperation eased. The last thing Jenny needed was Cole encouraging her.

Her stomach made a serious complaint, and she looked up at the sun high in the sky. She felt crankier than ever by the time she got back, washed, and met Monte in the dining room for lunch. She'd been so caught up in Jenny's scheme she'd forgotten to have breakfast. With a start, she realized Jenny hadn't eaten, either.

She exulted in wicked delight at the thought of Cole with a hungry, whining child. She hadn't long to savor it, though. She'd hardly taken her place when James admitted Cole with Jenny in hand.

"She washed at the pump."

Abbie caught Monte's surprise when Cole lifted Jenny to the chair, then turned to go.

"She must be starved," Abbie threw at him.

He glanced back over his shoulder. "Nah. She had jerky from my pack."

Abbie seethed. Of course. Cole Jasper was never caught short, never without a solution . . . or a retort.

Monte quirked an eyebrow. "What was that all about?"

Abbie glanced at Jenny taking it all in. "Maybe it would be best to discuss it later." Thankfully Monte didn't push it. He obviously had his own thoughts to contend with. She bit into the salt-cured ham they'd brought back with them from Charleston. Somehow it lost its flavor when she thought of Cole feeding the child on jerky from his pack.

She should have known he would figure out something. Cole Jasper never had a moment's indecision, nor was there any difficulty he couldn't master. For some reason that both annoyed and comforted her.

After lunch, Abbie read to Jenny and tucked her in for her nap. Jenny made no argument. Her morning with Cole must have worn her out, for she was asleep within moments. Abbie sat beside her, watching her chest rise and fall. She was worn out herself. She lay down beside the child and stroked her chubby fingers. For all her tyrannical tendencies, Jenny had her sweet moments—and not just when she was sleeping. If only she could reach inside where Jenny's affections lay.

At this moment it overwhelmed her to consider the task of training Jenny, especially with so much to undo: Frances's disinterest, Mammy's overindulgence, Kendal's desertion. No wonder the child fought every step of the way. But Abbie would not give up. She would persevere until she convinced the child she was not only there to stay, but that she loved her.

Ten

Abbie stood on the boardwalk outside the newspaper office in the sparkling May sunshine that illuminated the new leaves and settled like warm honey on her face and hands. Together with Pa she watched the unusual procession stop in the street; two wagons with canvas covers, three boys with sticks to herd the motley sheep that followed the wagons, and an assortment of blue-eyed, red-headed men, women, and children on foot. A likewise fiery-headed man leaped down, and Abbie saw his Roman collar. "He's a priest, Pa."

She was jostled by Eleanor Bailey and her sister Ruth pushing forward among the gathering crowd. "It's the Irish." Eleanor nudged her sister.

"Stinkin' Irish," someone murmured, but Abbie didn't catch who.

Pa stepped down from the walk and met the priest in the street, hand extended. "Welcome, Father. I'm Joshua Martin, but my mother was an O'Neil, and my wife's name was McKenna."

"Both goodly names." The priest pumped his hand. His eyes crinkled at the sides when he smiled. "I'm Father O'Brien, and this is my flock from County Meath. We've traveled all the way from New York City."

"That's a good long stretch."

Abbie couldn't hold back any longer. She hurried down to meet him.

"This is my daughter Abbie."

"And as fair a daughter as a man could wish. If lookin' can

tell, you'll have a grandchild soon to dandle on your knee."

"That's right." Pa beamed. "That'll make four."

"A lucky man, indeed."

Abbie glanced over the huddled forms in the wagons. "How have you come all the way from New York City, Father?"

"We've come as you see us, with all our earthly treasure. Irish are not appreciated in New York. But I've heard this is God's country in the West. We've come to homestead. We're farmers all."

Abbie couldn't help but notice the worried faces on most of the women. They looked haggard and weary, as well they might, but there was a cheeriness, too, a seeming irrepressible good humor.

Pa patted the neck of the lead ox. "Where are you headed?"

"Where the Lord leads us. Is there a church to worship in?" Father O'Brien scanned the street to the white frame church near the end.

Pa shook his head. "That one's Reverend Shields'. He's the Methodist minister."

"But there's the mission, Pa."

Father O'Brien turned. "The mission, lass?"

"Father Dominic and the Franciscan brothers built a mission east of town to minister to the Indians. Until last year it served as an orphanage, as well, but Father Dominic passed on and the brothers were called back east. It's been empty, but it's not in disrepair. At least it wasn't last time I rode out." She glanced up and saw the wondering, hopeful glance of a young woman with pale blue eyes and curling red hair.

"Well, then. That sounds a good place to start. Can you direct me?"

"I'll do one better. I'll ride out with you." Pa hooked his thumbs in his suspenders. "There's lots of empty country around the mission. I'd guess you could file to homestead out there."

"We'll have a look, then. Sounds as though the dear Lord's diggin' a furrow."

Wes McConnel joined them from the smithy in his leather apron, and when Pa introduced him, Father O'Brien clamped his hand with gusto. "A pleasure it is to find countrymen farin' well. This is a goodly land, I think, for all its barren looks."

"It's a good land, Father." Abbie smiled. "The best."

"I'd not be knowin' that yet, lass. It's a bonny green place we've left, and our hearts are heavy with the leavin'. But we'll see, now, won't we?"

She nodded. "Yes, you'll see. Pa, may I ride out with you?"

"We'll take your buggy. You folks need supplies or anything before we start?"

"We'll water the horses, but we've naught left to purchase supplies. The good people back home took a collection, and it's gotten us this far. Now we'll live by our wits."

"If there's anything you need . . ."

"We're not askin' charity, friend. But if you've a mind to barter, I'd not say no to a pint, nor would the lads."

Abbie hid her smile behind her hand.

Wes McConnel laughed, his lined and sooty face as delighted as a boy's. "Then come on. We'll slake our thirst at the saloon." No wonder he'd bred a son like Blake.

"Have you no decent Irish pub, then?"

" 'Fraid not. But the beer's just as good."

"It's the company I'm missin'."

"Well, you've two Irishmen in Joshua and me. We'll make merry enough for you."

Abbie watched the three of them and five younger men head off, but Pa would keep his head and usher them out again in short order. Else he'd answer to Mama for it. She turned to the women. They seemed not at all chagrined that the men had left them marooned in the street, and they leaned on the wagons laughing and chatting.

She stepped close. "I'm sorry to interrupt, but hadn't you better clear the street?"

The woman she'd noticed first turned to her. "And where would we go, then?"

"Well," Abbie waved her arm, "just down to the end there."

"Will you walk with us, Abbie Martin?"

"Yes, I will. But I don't know your name yet."

"Nora. Nora Flynn." She climbed up onto the lead wagon the Father had driven and nickered to the horse. A dark-haired woman who looked nearly Mama's age drove the second wagon, and Abbie walked among the sheep and children to the end of town.

Nora jumped down beside her. "That's Mary Donnelly in the other wagon, and my sister Glenna, there. She's married to Alan O'Rourke."

The tall, red-haired Glenna smiled and shifted the rosy baby on her hip. "And when's your baby due?"

Abbie rested her hand on her belly. "September."

Nora took the arm of a demure woman with broad teeth and auburn hair. "This is Peggy McSweeney. She has the big dark husband, Connor, and she bears babies the like that'll grow as big as their da." The women laughed. "I'll not introduce the little ones. You'd never keep 'em straight thrown together like this. But that's my youngest sister, Maggie, in the braids. She's fourteen this day."

"Happy birthday." Abbie sent a smile to the bony girl with red braids. She pushed a curious sheep away from her skirts and laughed. What a wonderful, fun group this was. She guessed Nora was unmarried, since she hadn't mentioned a husband of her own. But she seemed of an age with her, and Abbie felt a quickening of friendship.

"Peggy's mother, Moira, is in the wagon restin' from fever, so we'll not disturb her."

Pa and Wes and Father O'Brien came out of the saloon three blocks down, followed by the other Irishmen. Abbie identified Connor McSweeney at once. His dark head was fully above all the others, and he had shoulders like an ox.

"That's my brother, Doyle, behind Father O'Brien, Nolan and Kyle Donnelly, and Alan O'Rourke beside them. Glenna made the catch lots of girls were hopin' for. Isn't Alan handsome?"

Abbie looked at the ruddy man she indicated. His thick auburn hair and easy smile were attractive indeed.

"I was more than half in love with him myself, but he never

had eyes for any but Glenna since we were small."

Abbie thought of Blake, of the closeness they'd shared growing up and his devotion to her. Her heart ached to think how he'd have enjoyed meeting these folk from County Meath.

"What did I say?"

Abbie turned, surprised.

"I must have touched somethin' unknowing."

Had Nora read her so clearly? "You reminded me of a dear friend I lost."

"It's sorry I am to bring that sadness to your eyes. You have a sparkle otherwise. I saw it the first moment."

Abbie sighed. "It's been two years since Blake was killed. But sometimes I feel it fresh. He would have liked you all immensely. He was Wes McConnel's son."

"And he was fine, I'm sure."

"Yes. He was fine."

"So where's your husband, Abbie Martin?"

"It's Abbie Farrel."

"Och, of course. How silly of me."

"He's with the cowboys and ranchers at roundup." She read Nora's lack of comprehension. "Every spring, the ranchers band together to gather the cattle from the open range, separate out the herds, and brand the new calves. They do it again in the fall for any late calves and to put together a beef herd to ship to market."

"Yes." Abbie thought of how hard Monte worked these days.

"I'd like to meet him."

Her heart swelled. And she'd like nothing more than to introduce her fine husband. "Once you've settled in and he's back, I'll have you over."

Abbie climbed into the buggy Pa drove with Father O'Brien. The small children were bundled into the wagons, and they all started out along the track to the mission. The sheep and herders would follow more slowly, but the rutted track was easy to see, with the winter grass low and matted and the new green grass springing through.

The second day of May was as pretty a spring day as Abbie could hope for. A meadowlark sang from somewhere nearby, and overhead white puffs of clouds hung from the sapphire sky. The breeze was neither warm nor cool, just the touch of air on her cheeks.

Snow clung still to the crevices of the mountains, but the earth was soft and the breeze smelled fresh. It was hard to think that the blizzard had come just over a month before. How was Monte faring? Was he finding the lost cattle that had wandered so far in the storm? Cole would know what to do. There was no one who knew cattle better; of that she was convinced.

As they neared the adobe buildings encircled by trees, she pointed. "There, Father O'Brien, is the chapel and garden. Beyond that, the house that also served as school for the orphans."

"Ah yes. And where are the orphans now?"

"With families in the area. Wes McConnel has Jeremy, and Mama and Pa are raising little Tucker. I believe they're all well situated, but I can't say I don't miss going to the mission and finding all their cheerful faces. I schooled there with Blake McConnel when we were young, then taught the children with Father Dominic. It'll be good to have children there again, though I don't suppose any will actually live at the mission house."

"All in good time, lass. The good Lord will show us what's to be done and if the land will yield."

"I'm sure it's different than where you've been, but things can be raised here."

Pa reined in, and Father O'Brien climbed down from the buggy. He bent and dug his fingers into the hard, dry earth. "It puts me in mind of Adam's fall from the garden. Like the moist but stony soil of Erin, this land will be worked with the sweat of our brows."

Abbie couldn't argue. It was land that gave grudgingly to those who would tame it, more suited to grazing than farming. The sheep would thrive. Pa's small flock was evidence of that. But whether the ground would bear what they planted depended on the rain and what irrigation they could dig from the creek that flowed in the gully.

Father O'Brien walked to the door of the chapel and stepped inside. She knew what he would see: cool dark walls, wooden benches, the carved crucifix of the Savior that always reminded her of the first priest martyred by the Indians he'd come to serve. They'd lashed him to a tree and burned him after extensive torture.

But Father O'Brien knew nothing of that. He'd see only the Lord Jesus in His final sacrifice. And he'd sense the devotion, the commitment, the peaceful purpose of those who had served inside those walls before him. She saw it in his face when he came out.

"Glory be. The Lord has planted us."

As Pa drove her back to the ranch, Abbie turned to him. "What did Father O'Brien barter for the beer?"

"Stories."

"Stories?" Abbie asked, confused.

"The man can spin a yarn as long as the territory."

Eleven

The next day, Abbie put the two chickens into the crate and waved her thanks to Mama. She set the crate onto the buggy seat beside the rose bush wrapped in burlap. Nora would be pleased. She nickered to Toby and started for the mission.

The ride was long and bumpy and, as much as she hated to admit it, uncomfortable in her condition. It had surprised her how openly the Irish women had discussed her pregnancy without the least embarrassment. Even Father O'Brien. They seemed to have an uninhibited enjoyment of life, even after trekking across the country with next to nothing to their names.

She reined Toby in outside the long, low mission house, and Nora came to the door. Her hair was loose over her shoulders like a coiled red mane, her skin fair with a scatter of freckles over the bridge of her nose. Her wide-set eyes and bone structure were like Mama's, though Mama's coloring was anything but Irish, thanks to a single gypsy ancestor who'd passed on the brown eyes and hair.

"Good mornin' to ye, Abbie Farrel."

Abbie smiled at the way she pronounced "morning." It was a strange but pleasant accent, somehow warm and real, and she realized Mama's own speech had hints of it still. Strange how she'd never really considered Mama's Irish background until these visitors arrived. Their very Irishness seemed to bring it out in the rest of them.

"Good morning, Nora. Come see what I have for a housewarming."

Nora came out with a red-haired cherub at her heels. "This un's Danny, Glenna's second."

Abbie climbed down and ruffled Danny's thatch of hair. Then she reached for the crate of chickens and held the pair out to Nora. "A chicken and a rooster, to start your own flock."

"Och, imagine. Can you spare them, then?"

"They're from Mama. She has only Pa and little Tucker and herself to feed. She's been sending extra eggs to the hotel for two years now. Even after Pearl took three layers and a cock."

"Pearl?"

"Our cook."

"Your cook, Abbie? Have you servants, then?"

Abbie cringed. She hadn't meant to show Nora up. "They came out with Monte, my husband, from the South. After the war, they had nowhere else to go except to try to make their own way. The poverty and destruction were horrible."

She shuddered at the memory of the utter filth and hopelessness she'd seen the Charleston Negroes living in. "Even though they were freed, they stayed with Monte."

Nora's eyes widened. "Your husband's a slave owner?"

Abbie drew herself up. "Of course not. Slavery is abolished, and even were that not so, Monte treats them as part of the family."

"I'm sorry, Abbie. It's surprised I am, not judgin' you. And I'm thankful for the chickens. They're a bonny pair."

Abbie turned. "I've something else for you." She took down the rosebush. "You'll have to plant it near the creek, but it blooms red and smells sweet."

"You're too kind." Nora set down the crate and gingerly took the plant.

"Just welcoming you." Abbie swung her arm. "Now that we're neighbors. Monte's ranch, the Lucky Star, is just down that way some miles, beyond the low bluff. It's the same creek that flows past our house."

"Then I'll think of that when I'm at the water and wonder if you're drawin' it same as us." Nora smiled.

"We've a well that pumps it up from underground, but I spend a lot of time at the creek. There's a spot I'll show you that's lovely. Monte took me there on my first visit. It's very special to me."

"It would be a joy to see it and to meet your Monte. I see ye love him mightily. Come an' have a cup of tea."

Abbie followed her in, past the pallets and blankets laid out on the floor of the long room and into the large kitchen where Brother Thomas had once rolled the mounds of bread dough and steamed the vegetables he and the children raised in the garden out back. She looked through the window at the handful of tots playing out by the garden wall. It was good to see children there again.

She took the cup Nora handed her. "Where's everyone else?"

"Out lookin' at the land. They'll be choosin' their plots an' breakin' ground."

"What about you?"

"I'll live here at the big house and do for Father O'Brien, since I've no husband."

Abbie heard something in her tone but couldn't identify the emotion. Surely Nora wasn't ashamed to be unmarried. She was lovely and hale and would no doubt be swarmed with offers.

"I'm keepin' the little ones while the others are out."

"I'm sure it's wonderful to have such close ties; your sister and brother and their families all here together."

"Aye."

Again her tone was reserved.

Abbie sipped her tea. It was strong and hot in the crockery cup. On the stove a huge pot of potatoes simmered, but she saw nothing else cooking or in readiness.

"I wonder, Abbie, would your husband have a milkin' cow we could work for?"

Abbie pictured the rangy Longhorns. The eastern Shorthorns Monte had tried to crossbreed had died of Texas fever, carried, Cole said, by a tick that the Longhorns were immune to. The Longhorns were hardly tamed to milk. But Pearl had a pair of milk cows, and Monte had gotten Belle to replace Buttercup, who had died in the fire.

She looked into Nora's pale, hopeful eyes. "I'm certain he can get you one. He knows the market."

"We've no funds, though."

"We'll figure something out." A thought jumped to mind. "My pa runs the newspaper. Maybe Father O'Brien would sell him stories to print. He's always looking for something new."

Nora assessed her quietly. "I don't think folks would care to hear our stories, Abbie. Not unless it's in their blood like you and your da and Wes McConnel."

"I don't think that's so. People aren't divided here so much as other places. Out here we need each other, and our differences are . . . overlooked." *At least to some degree*, Abbie thought to herself.

"If that's so, then it's like nowhere else I've been." A shadow passed over her eyes, and this time Abbie recognized it. Bitterness, grief, and anger. But it passed as quickly as it came.

Abbie heard a horse outside and turned. "Are you expecting someone?"

"Who would I be expectin'?"

Abbie stood with Nora and walked to the door. She pulled it open.

Davy McConnel swung down from his horse and sauntered over with the same nonchalant stroll she remembered in Blake. He pulled off his hat and tossed back the brown hair that hung in his eyes. "Howdy."

"Nora, this is Wes McConnel's son, Davy. Davy, Nora Flynn."

Davy smiled. "Pa thought you might have some work fixin' up the place. I came to offer my help."

Nora crossed her arms and leaned her hip on the door frame. "And what help can ye be?"

"Anything you need." He looked up. "Check yer roof, breakin' ground . . . anything."

"I suppose you've come hungry, too."

Nora's manner surprised Abbie. Why was she so prickly and defensive?

"Nope. Ma stuffed me before I set out. She said the last thing you all needed was another mouth to feed."

"She's right at that." Nora straightened. "The others'll be troopin' in soon. You can ask Father O'Brien what he's needin'. For m'self, I have no use for you."

Abbie met Davy's eyes as Nora turned from the door and disappeared into the house.

"Well, that was a fine welcome." Davy scratched his head and replaced his hat. "Guess I'll have a look around and see for myself what's to be done."

"She must be tired and overwrought. They've come so far and not had an easy time of it, I gather."

Davy shrugged. "Might be the McConnel men just aren't lucky with ladies." He sauntered around the side of the house.

Abbie's cheeks burned. Had he meant that to cut her as it did? *Blake.* Here, where they'd spent so many childhood hours, she always felt him near. But Davy was right. She'd been bad luck for Blake. He'd loved her as she couldn't love him. He wasn't content being like a brother to her. And that's why he left.

She sagged against the jamb. Davy had his own heartache from it all. It was his two brothers, Mack and Blake, who were killed by the outlaws. And he knew well enough Blake had gone as much for her as to find gold in the mountains. Was she bad luck for Monte, too?

She went inside. Nora sat in the kitchen with Danny on her knee and a fresh cup, smiling brightly as though nothing were amiss. Abbie stopped in the doorway, but she motioned her to sit.

"I suppose I'd better get home."

"Finish your cup before you go."

Abbie sat. "There's a chance the men'll come back today."

"From their roundup?"

"Yes. It's been longer than usual already. The blizzard scattered the cattle, and I suppose the men are riding farther afield to find them."

"Did they break through the walls, then?"

Break through the walls? Abbie tried to picture what Nora

meant. "Most of the range isn't fenced. It's just open country. Monte's one of the only ranchers so far to fence some of his pasture land, but he uses that mostly for the horses."

"Then how do you know whose cows are whose?"

"By the brand and the earmark. Monte's cattle have a star brand and a single notch on the left ear. This year they started roundup at the Farringer range down to the south, so they'll end on Monte's. We're the farthest north in the district."

"And the cattle all run together?"

"They mostly stay near their home ranges, but those encompass miles of open land. And the blizzard scattered and confused those that survived."

"You've mentioned this blizzard. Surely it's been months since winter."

"Out here snow can come all the way into June, and the next day'll be as warm and shining as summer. But the blizzard we had last March was devastating. We lost nearly a thousand cattle, including all but one of the new calves, and thirteen horses."

Nora's eyes widened. "That's a staggerin' blow for sure, but have you so many to lose?"

"I don't know what we have left." Abbie stared into her cup. "Monte's concerned."

"It's a rich man ye've married, Abbie."

Abbie nodded slowly. "We have much to be thankful for." She heard Davy hammering at the back of the house. Nora tensed but said nothing, and Abbie finished her tea and stood. "I'll come again if I may."

"Of course you may. You're welcome anytime."

Then why wasn't Davy? Abbie climbed into the buggy and turned Toby for home. Next time she'd bring Jenny with her. It would do the child good to have others her age to play with. The encounter on her birthday had shown Abbie the need. If Jenny was to behave, she must learn she was not the only child who mattered.

♦♦♦♦♦♦♦

Monte turned from his stance at the study window and smiled when Abbie rushed over. He folded her hand in his. "And why was my wife not here to welcome me home?" He said it playfully but meant it nonetheless.

"I brought a pair of chickens from Mama to the new folks at the mission."

He raised an eyebrow and she explained at length, with every detail down to the sheep. Her face fairly shone with the excitement of it all.

"And Nora wondered if you might find them a milk cow, only they've no money to purchase it."

His heart squeezed and he released her hand. "Nor have we, Abbie. We've scarcely seven hundred head surviving, and . . . our funds are depleted." He felt stripped and barren.

She stared into his face. "Seven hundred?"

"There are carcasses all the way to Walsenburg." He couldn't tell if she truly understood what that meant. Many of those surviving were not of marketable weight, and it would be years before he built up the herd to what it was—if they held on long enough to accomplish it.

"Oh, Monte!"

He turned back to the window. "I'm not sure what to do, Abbie. For the first time in my life, I'm not sure where to turn."

"Turn to the Lord, Monte. He's never failed us before."

He smiled dimly, then stared once again out the window. He knew God was in control. God had given him Abbie, brought him victory over Captain Gifford, sustained him through loss and sorrow. He had surrendered his will to the Almighty, serving Him as honorably as he could. But he was not a man to wait only on the Lord and do nothing himself.

Yet he was caught now between indecision and inability. What he would do, which was build up the herd with fresh stock, he could not for lack of funds. What he would never do, turn over the deed to Driscoll and the bank, would give them the funds he needed.

But at what risk? His child's inheritance? His land? The land was the difference between bond and free. Land had separated the planter from the poor white farmer in the South. Land . . . and honor. The swamp farmers and poor whites had turned against the landowners, grasping what they'd never earned, destroying what they coveted.

He would not forget their betrayal easily, nor would he surrender to their kind, in the person of Driscoll, his ranch, his home, his freedom. He could refuse to pay Kendal's debts. He could disavow responsibility. But even so, they had already drained his reserves. Driscoll was right. It had not been good business to step in where Kendal failed. It had been honor.

And by honor he would continue. He could live no other way. He glanced down at his wife, silent beside him. "Don't be troubled, Abbie. We'll find a way through, God willing."

"I know we will, Monte."

Twelve

Oh, for heaven's sake, Marcy." Abbie put her hands to her hips. "It won't hurt you to gather lettuce from your tiny little garden. You're not doing yourself or your baby any good acting so helpless." It was only at Mama's insistence that Abbie was there in Marcy's kitchen instead of out enjoying the fine May afternoon.

She would have preferred to be at Nora's, where the laughter always matched the hard work, where stories flew as fast as their fingers over the tasks at hand. She longed to drop by Clara's and hear her chatter. She yearned to be home with Monte and Jenny. Anywhere but here with Marcy's whining.

No doubt Mama would frown at her exasperation, but truly Marcy took it too far. She reached out and tugged her to her feet. "A little exercise certainly won't hurt."

"But I can't go out in the sun. Doctor Barrow—"

Abbie slapped a straw hat over Marcy's shining blond curls. "You won't even know it's there." She propelled her toward the door. "And it's not fair to expect Grant to do all his work and yours, as well. The least he can expect is supper when he comes home."

Marcy sent her a scathing look and waddled over the small patch of garden to the rows of early lettuce that glowed in the golden sun rays. "I certainly hope you don't expect any sympathy when you get this big and awkward. Because I'll remember—" She drew in her breath sharply and pressed her hands to her cheeks.

"What is it now?" Abbie's annoyance with Marcy's theatricals made her voice sharp. Marcy doubled over and gripped the fence, and Abbie felt a jolt of fear. "Marcy?"

"Something broke. It's gushing down my legs and—" She broke off with a cry.

Good Lord, the baby. Abbie put an arm around Marcy's shoulders. "Can you walk?"

Marcy straightened, then cried out again and clutched Abbie's arm until the circulation stopped. "I don't think so! I—"

"You can't have the baby out here in the garden."

"Have the baby?" Marcy looked at her with stark terror.

What did she think was happening? Had she no sense at all? "Here, lean on me."

"No! This wouldn't have happened if you hadn't forced me out here." She bent double again and wailed.

Abbie looked quickly at the next house over. No help there; it was Howard Murphy's place, and he'd be at the saloon with the other single men who roomed with him. If only Grant were here. But he was coming in on the evening train, and the Lord only knew when it would actually arrive.

He should have known better than to accept that legal case in Denver, even if it was a favor to the judge. But, then, the judge was Marcy's father. Abbie girded herself for battle. "We're going inside. There's nothing else for it." She took Marcy by the shoulders and propelled her gently but firmly toward the house.

"You're hateful, Abbie Farrel. You did this on purpose." Her hat slipped sideways, and she yanked it from her head and tossed it to the ground. "You've always—Ohhh!"

"Stand here until it passes." In spite of her steady tone, Abbie was concerned. The pains were far too close, and there was a good deal of blood in the wetness on the ground where Marcy had stood. "Okay, now. Slowly." She took Marcy's weight against her. *Please Lord, don't let her faint.*

She got her to the back stoop before the next pain made her scream. If she could just get her inside. Thank God the bed had been moved down. In truth there was no way Marcy could have gone upstairs in this condition.

Marcy cried out. "How could you? You think you're so smart. I told you . . ." She gasped.

"Just a little farther now. You're almost there." Abbie pushed the door open and eased her inside. She glanced at the trail of blood on the stoop, but said nothing. No sense making Marcy any more scared than she already was. She got her to the side of the bed and sat her down. "Can you strip off your things?"

"Of course I can."

"Then do so while I get Doctor Barrow."

She was glad Marcy didn't argue. She rushed from the house and down the rutted lane. Thank goodness Grant and Marcy lived near town, but it was still a good mile to the main street. She ran, though her own increasing bulk made it difficult. She passed McConnel's smithy and Pa's newspaper office. A handful of men parted before the saloon to let her pass.

"Everything all right, Mrs. Farrel?"

She scarcely looked to identify the speaker, but knew Ethan Thomas's voice. "It's fine." She said it as much for herself as for him. "But I need the doctor."

He caught her arm. "You stand here, ma'am. I'll run for the doc."

Abbie stopped, held her side, and leaned against the wall. "Tell him Mrs. Martin's having her baby." She drew long breaths, more winded than she had any right to be.

"Here ya are, Abbie." Wes McConnel brought her a glass of cider from the bar. As she drank it, she watched for the doctor and Ethan to come out. *Oh, please be there.* Down beyond the hotel, she looked at the station, but it would be some time before the train arrived.

Come on, she begged inwardly. It seemed interminable, but at last the doctor stepped out with Ethan behind him. They climbed into Doctor Barrow's buggy and drove up. Ethan jumped down and Wes gave Abbie a hand in.

Doctor Barrow took up the reins. "She's at home?"

"Yes."

He slapped the reins lightly. "Well, these things take time. Likely there's no hurry."

"It doesn't seem normal. The pains are very close, and she's bleeding more than I'd expect."

He frowned, then increased the horse's pace. When they reached the house, Abbie directed the doctor to Marcy, then went to the kitchen. She started the water heating on the stove and searched the cupboard for clean cloths. The water warmed reluctantly. Everything seemed to take longer than usual, each moment hanging on the last.

Come on, come on. When the water boiled, she joined the doctor and Marcy in the dining room that now held the bed. Marcy was drenched with sweat. Her gown clung to her, and her face was taut. She bared her teeth as she thrashed.

Abbie felt a stab of fear. What if she had pushed Marcy too far? What would Grant say if anything happened to her? *Please, Lord.* She watched Doctor Barrow remove his cuff links and roll his sleeves.

He scrubbed his arms in the basin and wiped them dry. "Get to her head and soothe her while I see where we are." Doctor Barrow spoke without turning, then delved beneath the blankets.

Marcy screamed, and Abbie wet the cloth from the pitcher and smoothed it over her brow. Marcy opened her eyes and panted, "Grant?"

"He's not here yet."

Doctor Barrow sat back, and Abbie looked with panic at his bloody hand. Mamie's delivery had not been like this. Fear clutched her heart.

The doctor stood and plunged his hand into the basin. "I was afraid of this. The baby's breech."

Abbie's thoughts raced. Breech. That meant turned wrong, not positioned to be birthed as it should. At least that wasn't her fault. She couldn't be blamed for the baby's position.

What was she thinking? How could she think of herself when Marcy's life and her baby's were at risk? What would Doctor Barrow do?

He checked Marcy's pulse and felt her abdomen. "It might yet turn on its own." He applied pressure and Marcy wailed. Abbie soothed her brow, willing her strength. Her pains were too close, too sharp, her fear too intense. Abbie could almost smell it.

Doctor Barrow watched and waited while Marcy labored in pain and fear, but seemingly to no avail. The clock ticked and the hands moved. With frightening regularity the pains came on Marcy, but they seemed to do nothing. Abbie soothed, but Marcy's screams increased. If only she wouldn't fight it. On and on it went.

None of the pain and effort seemed to accomplish anything. When fresh blood gushed, Doctor Barrow stood abruptly. "The placenta may have ruptured. I'll have to take the child now." He twisted a cloth. "Give her this to bite down on."

Abbie's heart sank, but she took the cloth and eased it between Marcy's teeth. Marcy's eyelids drew back from the whites of her eyes. She tried to fight, then gripped the bedding until her knuckles turned white. She screamed through the gag. Abbie held her shoulders down against more strength than she thought Marcy possessed.

"There, now," she soothed. "He's turning the baby so it can come out. You'll be fine. You'll be just fine." *Oh, God, she will be fine, won't she?*

How could it take so long to turn the baby? She kept her eyes on Marcy's face and refrained from pleading with the doctor to hurry. Her job was to keep Marcy calm, and Marcy's frantic gaze was riveted on hers, as though she could draw strength from Abbie's firm demeanor.

"There, now." She held Marcy's eyes with more compassion than she'd ever felt for her. She shared her woman's agony and ached for her.

Marcy screamed again and gripped Abbie's arms to the bone.

"That's right. Hold on to me. It's almost over." What did she know? For all she knew it could be days still, just like Maimie. No. Marcy would be dead by then. This birth was too violent to be sustained. *Oh, sweet Lord . . . help her. Bring the baby soon.*

"Mrs. Farrel." It was more a bark than a beckon. "The baby's tangled in the cord. Come hold the head while I loose it."

Hold the head? Abbie's heart raced as she reached down to secure the tiny bluish head protruding from Marcy's body. *Oh, Lord in heaven.* She closed her eyes when he reached inside. Marcy seemed beyond caring. Abbie moved one hand, then the other as the doctor worked the cord free from the baby's neck. Marcy wailed, and with a sudden rush the baby girl came free into Abbie's hands.

Doctor Barrow turned the infant and smacked her backside. The baby cried.

Oh, thank you, Jesus. Abbie's own breath came in gasps as she held the baby while Doctor Barrow tied off and cut the cord. The infant was small and gangly, but she cried with all the power she had.

"Wash and wrap her," Doctor Barrow ordered. "I'm not through here."

Abbie took the baby just as Marcy thrashed again. From Doctor Barrow's expression, she was not out of danger yet. Abbie bathed the crying baby in tepid water, then diapered and dressed her in the gown she found in the dresser upstairs. Her crying stopped when she bundled her tightly into the blanket she'd left warming near the stove.

She carried her back to Marcy. Doctor Barrow was washing the blood from his arms at the elbow. Marcy lay still and quiet, and Abbie's chest constricted.

"She's sleeping."

Her breath released audibly.

"I hate for you to see that with your own turn coming soon, but I'm awfully glad you were with her. We'd have lost them both. Even now..." He cleared his throat. "She's lost a good deal of blood, though the worst of the hemorrhaging has passed."

Grant burst through the door and stood panting. He'd obviously gotten the word and run all the way from the station.

"Congratulations, young man. You have a daughter."

Abbie remembered she was holding the baby and brought her

to him. Grant stood dumbfounded, then slowly reached out and took his child into his arms.

Abbie smiled at the awe in her brother's eyes. "Have you a name for her?"

His throat worked. "Emily. Emily Elizabeth."

She squeezed his hand and left the room. Marcy and the baby were in his care now, and the doctor would no doubt fill Grant in. She was as fatigued as she could remember being. Her arms and shoulders ached, and she was famished. They never had made Grant's supper.

She rubbed the back of her neck and went outside. It was dark and Monte would be worried. She wished she hadn't unhitched Toby but reattached him wearily, then climbed into the buggy and started home. She had barely made it from the stable to the lane when Monte rode up on Sirocco. His face was stern, and she recognized his concern.

Sirocco stamped and snorted as he reined in and dismounted. "Abbie."

"Marcy had her baby. A daughter."

His expression lightened. "That's marvelous." He looked toward the house, then tied the stallion behind the buggy and climbed in beside her. She gratefully handed him the reins and leaned against his shoulder. She was asleep before the lights of town faded from view.

Monte felt Abbie's weight against him as he drove. Her breathing was deep and her body limp, signs of exhaustion. Would she never realize her limits? Did she not understand the terror he felt when she failed to arrive on time or pushed herself beyond her strength?

Did she not know how much he wanted this child, how deeply he feared burying another son or daughter? Would Abbie never settle into the wifely mold? He sighed. He had not married her because she fit any mold. Precisely the opposite. A smile pulled the corners of his mouth.

His youthful rejection of the rigid strictures of his southern upbringing had landed him a woman as unlike his first wife as the Colorado Territory from South Carolina. While part of him struggled to tame her, the rest exulted in her strength and audacity. She would bear him a child the like of whom he'd never seen.

♦♦♦♦♦♦♦

Abbie slept clean past noon the next day. She was appalled to see how high the sun was when she opened her eyes, but Monte sat on the end of the bed and laughed.

"I hope this teaches you." He handed her a cup of tea.

"Goodness, Monte. Why didn't you rouse me?"

"I wanted you to realize that you have limits."

"As if I didn't know that." Abbie sat up and sipped the tea.

He stuffed a pillow behind her.

"I'm not an invalid, Monte. I don't need you to pamper and attend me as Grant does Marcy."

"Is that what this is all about?" Monte's tone was suddenly stern.

"What?"

"Are you trying to prove to Miss Marcy that you're stronger than she?"

Abbie bristled. "I resent that. I've no need to prove anything to Marcy."

He clasped her free hand. "Then do me a favor and refrain from heroics just long enough to bring our child into the world."

"What are you talking about? What heroics?"

"I spoke with Doctor Barrow this morning."

As though that told her all. "And?"

"He said without your help he could not have turned or untangled the infant. He also said you ran the mile to town and stayed on your feet through all the grizzly hours without once quailing at the sight of blood. I let him know you weren't given to faints."

"Thank you, Monte. It's all a bunch of nonsense to think any of that was beyond a woman's natural inclination. Of course I had to hurry, and I'm not so large yet that I can't run."

"Even if it means sleeping fifteen hours straight." His amusement was tempered with concern.

"Well, I haven't an answer for that." Abbie closed her eyes and savored the tea.

"I have. You overtaxed yourself."

She sighed, snuggling back into the pillows at her back and resting the cup and saucer against her chest. "Thankfully, Marcy's baby is delivered. You've no idea what an ordeal she endured. She was utterly spent by the end."

"It's a miracle they both survived. Doctor Barrow said a breech birth doesn't always turn out that way. Your quick action made it possible."

"There, now. You can't scold me further."

"I'm not scolding." His voice was gentle.

"What, then?"

"Appealing. With all my heart. Don't strain yourself."

"If it makes you feel better, I'll spend the day in bed. Jenny can join me and we'll have stories and tea and . . . what?" She caught the contradiction in his expression.

"Cole took her out this morning to see the new foals. With his help, one of the mares birthed twins last night. I needn't tell you how unusual that is."

"Oh, Monte! And they're healthy and strong?"

"And pretty. She'll enjoy it."

"Did Cole take her on Scotch?"

Monte nodded. "And she looked for all the world like Cleopatra astride an elephant and in complete charge of everything."

Abbie could well picture it. And Cole encouraged her naughtiness. "Is she back?"

"She wasn't when I came up, but I'm sure she's safe with Cole."

Abbie set the cup down on the bed stand, tossed back the covers, and swung her legs to the floor.

"What happened to your promise?"

"I can't stay in bed wondering where she is. Anyway, I'm perfectly well rested, and I want to see the foals. Colts or fillies?"

"Fillies, and I should have known better."

Abbie caught his face between her hands and kissed him. "*You* may escort me."

He helped her stand and pulled her close, resting a hand on her stomach between them. "Will nothing induce you to stay?"

"Not as long as Jenny's twisting Cole around her finger and spoiling whatever headway I've made these last months."

"Really, Abbie."

"Really."

He released her. "I'll await you downstairs. But I insist you eat before we go."

"You needn't insist. I'm starved."

♦♦♦♦♦♦♦

The foals were pretty indeed, cinnamon brown with white blazes, and they tumbled skittishly about the mare when the buggy drew up to the fence. But Cole and Jenny were not at the pasture. Abbie turned. "What do you say now, Mr. Farrel?"

"I'm sure they're somewhere close." He turned the buggy and drove back to the yard.

Abbie rested her hand in his and climbed down, but she didn't go toward the stairs. He shook his head when she headed off, but he didn't stop her. Nor did he join the search. He went up the stairs and inside as she rounded the corner, passed the stable, and headed for the bunkhouse. Jenny's laughter carried on the breeze.

Abbie rounded the south wall of the bunkhouse and saw them. Cole, squatting, elbows on thighs, untangling the small loop of rope from his neck and shoulder. He handed it to Jenny who stood before him in skirt and petticoats. Laughing, she tossed it onto his head again.

Abbie leaned into the shadow of the wall and watched. Jenny's back was to her, but she could imagine the light in her eyes to match the laughter. Cole made a to-do about her snagging him, then gave her another try. This time the rope caught him in the face, but he picked it up from where it fell and adjusted it in her hand. "There. Now, try again."

Instead, she dropped the rope and stretched her arms around his neck. Abbie could see Cole's expression as he hesitantly closed his arms around her and patted her small back. Feeling ashamed to witness the tender moment without their knowing, she moved back from the corner. A twig snapped under her foot, and Cole looked up.

Abbie stepped away from the wall. "Hello, Cole, Jenny."

Cole stood and gathered up the rope. "No need to eavesdrop, Abbie. If you want the child, just come an' take 'er."

"I didn't mean to eavesdrop. It's just . . . she was enjoying herself so. I love to hear her laugh."

Jenny clapped her hands together. "Cole taught me to rope."

"A fine skill for a lady." Abbie caught Cole's frown and stooped down to brush the dust from Jenny's skirt. "Auntie Abbie has a few such skills of her own."

Cole snorted. "Such as?"

"Oh . . . spearing fish, tracking animals, climbing trees."

He eyed her. "I don't reckon you practice them much."

Abbie stood. "No. Not lately."

"I always believed a girl had as much right to knowin' things as a boy."

"Then would you say a boy ought to learn to sew and cook and clean?"

Cole rubbed his jaw, and Abbie saw the sunlight catch in the blond stubble beside his mustache. "I reckon if a body has a mind to learn somethin', he ought to learn it regardless."

"And if he hasn't a mind to?"

Cole hooked his thumbs into his belt. "Some things ought to be learned anyway. But oftentimes before you realize that, the opportunity's gone." He bent and chucked Jenny under the chin. "Run along, now. I got work to do."

Jenny caught his rough hand and kissed his knuckle, then skipped over and took the hand Abbie extended. Abbie had never seen her so free with her affection. As they walked back to the house, she watched the sunlight play in Jenny's curls. "Jenny, what is it about Cole that you like so much?"

"I like how he smells."

Abbie bit her lip against the surprised smile and looked across the yard. What did Cole smell of? Tobacco and horses and the wind off the range; strong, manly scents. No wonder Jenny snuggled close. Did she even remember her pa? Did Cole somehow conjure feelings of comfort and familiarity?

She pictured the child in his rough embrace, only it hadn't been rough. It was amazingly gentle. That's what had made her step away. She'd glimpsed a side of Cole he didn't often show.

Jenny suddenly tugged her hand free and pointed. "Look. A bunny." She scurried after the cottontail that disappeared under the porch, but the rabbit disappeared out the far side with Jenny none the wiser.

Abbie stooped and lifted her to her feet. "The bunny's gone, Jenny. Come inside and wash now."

Thirteen

Abbie stayed dutifully close to home the next two weeks, but on the Sunday following, she took Jenny and drove out to the mission chapel. Monte declined, saying his day of rest would be better spent in peaceful solitude. It was no doubt in reaction to the earsplitting tantrum Jenny had thrown the night before.

Though lessening in frequency, the incidents had increased in volume and duration. Abbie prayed for wisdom, but it seemed long-suffering was the answer she received. Jenny was no further along the road of self-control than a wild thing. As she stood in the yard with Ma and Pa, the McConnels, and Pat Riley from the lumber yard, Abbie watched her dealing imperiously with the Irish children, Meghan and Danny and Katie Lynn.

They had rushed out together to play in the yard in the sunshine after Mass. Now Jenny was prancing like a princess and demanding their adoration. Meghan seemed willing enough and Danny, as well, but Katie Lynn gave her a push. Before Abbie could reach them, Jenny had two fistfuls of Katie's red hair and Katie had slapped her across the face.

Both girls were yammering to wake the dead. Abbie hooked an arm around each and demanded they retreat. Jenny refused to let loose Katie's hair, and Abbie pried her fingers off, then clamped a hand around the small wrists and dragged her back. Glenna took hold of Katie.

"Your Jenny has a temper to match Katie's own. Sometimes it's best to let them fight it out and see what comes of such."

"I'm very sorry."

" 'Twas Katie that pushed. It's not often someone stands up to her."

Abbie glanced up to see Nora watching, then took Jenny firmly in hand, and joined her friend in the shade.

"You've your hands full, Abbie Farrel."

"She's had a lot to contend with in her short years. Too much loss."

"Aye. Loss is a debilitatin' thing for a wee lass. Or not so wee." Abbie glanced up, but Nora turned her gaze to Father O'Brien. "A grand homily he spoke this mornin', eh?"

"Yes. I've always related too well to the prodigal son. It seems that his fault was not so much truly wickedness as impulsiveness."

Nora smiled. "Are you impulsive, Abbie?"

"Only to a fault."

Nora laughed. "Aye, and you remind me of someone." The laughter died in her eyes and faded from her lips. She took a stick and shooed the chicken from the chapel doorway. "I'll be about Father's meal, now. 'Twas good seein' you."

"And you, Nora. Will you come to tea tomorrow?"

"Can my own feet take me there?"

"I'll send James to fetch you."

"I wouldn't feel right. I'll borrow Mary's wagon."

"Just follow the track and take the right fork."

"I'll do that. Good day, Abbie."

Abbie watched her retreat inside. What secrets did Nora Flynn harbor behind her smile? She glanced up and saw Davy McConnel watching, as well. He stood in the yard beside his mother, Mary, and sister, Mariah. But his attention was on the door through which Nora had passed.

She knew from Wes that Davy had come out every day and worked on repairs to the mission chapel and house. But it seemed by his expression he'd still not received a welcome. Why did Nora disdain him? He was a fine man, strong and hearty if not outright handsome. He had Blake's contagious smile, though she doubted Nora had yet encouraged it.

Abbie shook her head and stooped down to Jenny. "How would you like to go see baby Emily?" Abbie had promised Mama before Mass to check in on Marcy.

"May I show her my critters?"

"What critters?"

Jenny ran to the little bag she had left lying on the step, snatched it up, and ran back. "The critters Cole made me." She shook the bag.

Abbie heard the wood pieces clatter together and smiled. "Certainly. I'd like to see them, too."

Thinking of visiting Marcy brought none of her usual animosity. Maybe experiencing the trauma together had melted the boundaries of her dislike. At any rate, seeing the baby would provide a distraction for Jenny.

Pa hoisted Jenny into the buggy, then gave Abbie a hand. "Tell Grant I have a matter to discuss with him."

"All right." Abbie took up the reins.

Jenny was quiet as they drove. She fingered the bag at her side and took in everything around her: the squirrel that skittered up the ponderosa and chattered from the branch, the magpie calling from its tip. But she seemed to shrink into herself as they neared town.

"What's the matter, Jenny?"

She spoke without raising her head. "I don't like Aunt Marcy."

Abbie could hardly correct her honesty when it so closely paralleled her own feelings. "Why not?"

"She doesn't like me."

"That's not true, Jenny."

"Do we have to stay long?"

"No. We'll see the baby and ask if there's anything Aunt Marcy needs." Abbie reined the horse to a stop before the green frame house. She noticed Jenny tucked the bag of animals into the corner of the seat.

"Don't you want to bring them in?"

Jenny shook her head.

"May I see them?"

Jenny pulled the bag out, loosed the drawstring, and dumped the carved wooden creatures into her lap. Abbie recognized Cole's workmanship, another facet of his personality that seemed incongruous. It was amazing how he captured the nature of each animal with the fine strokes of his knife. She examined a Longhorn steer, an antelope, and a running horse, then a chicken and a bear and a rabbit.

"When did he give you these?"

Jenny shrugged. "I don't 'member."

Abbie slipped them back into the bag. "Why don't you bring in the bag. You don't have to take the animals out."

Jenny pulled the string and clamped the bag in her little fist. They knocked and Marcy's mother opened the door to them. Abbie was not at all surprised or put off by the haughty look she gave them. She was used to it. Like Marcy and her husband, the judge, Darla Wilson saw most of the world from the end of her nose.

"Good morning, Mrs. Wilson. We've come to pay Marcy a call."

"Come in, Mrs. Farrel. I'll see if she's up to callers."

Abbie waited in the front room as Marcy's mama ascended the stairs. Grant must have moved their bed back to the bedroom. A few minutes later Darla Wilson returned. "You may come up."

Abbie was surprised. Surely Marcy wasn't still bedridden. She bit her tongue and headed up, Jenny in hand. Marcy was indeed ensconced in pillows and covers on the large bed. She held the baby in her arms, but her face reflected none of the radiance Abbie would have expected.

As soon as Darla Wilson left the room, Marcy put up her chin. "Have you come to gloat, then?"

Abbie stopped short. "Gloat?"

"I know what you're thinking, Abbie Farrel. How I disappointed Grant producing a baby girl. And how dreadful a time I had. Of course, that was thanks to you, bringing on the labor before I was ready."

Abbie felt her ire burn. All her natural animosity returned, but for Jenny's sake she masked it. "I don't know what you're talking about. Grant's thrilled with Emily, besotted. He's not foolish enough to expect a son. He's as happy as can be. And as for the rest . . ." She swallowed her pride. "I'm very sorry if what I did brought on your labor. Truly I am, but it has worked out for the best."

"Oh yes." Marcy tossed her blond ringlets. "You got to be the center of attention . . . again! I'm so sick of Grant and Doctor Barrow telling me you saved my life." She screwed up her face. " 'Abbie ran all the way. How lucky it was that Abbie was there. Abbie didn't flinch even with all that blood.' " Marcy's lip protruded. "It was my blood, my suffering, but no one can talk of anything but you."

Abbie forced herself forward to the end of the bed with Jenny clinging to her skirts. "You were incredible, Marcy. I've never known anyone to suffer like that so bravely."

Marcy's color left her cheeks. "Are you mocking me?"

Abbie shook her head. "Not one bit. You brought that baby with the worst of circumstances, and did it . . . heroically."

Marcy sank back into the pillows. She seemed at a loss, and for a moment Abbie saw something flicker in her eyes. Then she turned up her nose. "Of course Grant wouldn't say so."

"He didn't see it. He doesn't know. No man could understand, not even Doctor Barrow." Abbie stroked the post of the footboard. "They do their part, but have no inkling what it's like for us."

Again Marcy seemed at a loss, and Abbie felt chagrined that she had never made the effort before to reach out as she was now. Was it possible Marcy was vulnerable? Marcy with all her haughty airs?

"May we see the baby?"

Marcy looked down as though only realizing the infant was there in her arms. She held her out and Abbie took her. She sat at the edge of the bed and held the baby for Jenny to see. Three weeks of feedings had filled in her cheeks. Emily had Marcy's blue eyes, at least so far. Her dark hair had fallen out and a pale fuzz covered her skull in the loose-fitting bonnet.

"She's beautiful. How could you think for one minute Grant is disappointed?"

Marcy looked toward the window. She was quiet so long Abbie thought she'd ignore her question. Then she sighed. "I know how Pa felt about me. Especially when Ma never produced a boy."

For the first time, Abbie glimpsed inside Marcy. She'd never even wondered what made her so mean, so faultfinding. "I promise you Grant is as happy for this baby girl as he'd be for a son. You have nothing to be ashamed of."

For the fleetest moment, Marcy's eyes held gratitude, then they hardened again. "I never said I was ashamed."

Abbie glanced at Jenny laying out the little animals along the edge of the bed. Of course Emily was too small to notice, but Marcy glanced over.

"What's all that?"

"Animals Cole carved for Jenny."

"Cole Jasper, your foreman?" The haughty tone was back in her voice.

"Yes. He has quite a talent."

"What has he to do with your niece?"

Abbie smiled down at Jenny. "They're fond of each other."

"I certainly hope you won't foster that," Marcy sneered.

"I've no need to. They've developed it on their own," Abbie answered honestly.

Emily mewed, and Abbie handed her back to Marcy.

"Well, if you've any hope of making a lady of the child, rough men like Cole Jasper—"

"Marcy." Abbie eyed her squarely. "I'll not have you say a word against him. He's a fine man. He's saved Monte's life and mine at his own risk."

"That's all fine and good, as long as he knows his place."

Abbie's temper flared.

"Don't be so innocent, Abbie. He's only using the child to get to you. You know how he feels about you. Everyone knows he proposed marriage."

Abbie sprang to her feet, scattering the little animals. She saw the look of triumph in Marcy's eyes and realized she'd been baited. How had she thought to change a pattern that had been cast between them from childhood. Jenny scrambled to gather the wooden animals into the bag, and Abbie contained her fury.

"You have a lovely daughter, Marcy. I hope your recovery is swift." She took Jenny by the hand and walked out. *And I hope your whining and nastiness don't drive Grant stark raving mad.*

Fourteen

The noon sun bathed the wood floor of the entry, and Abbie smelled the linseed oil Zena had rubbed into the tight, fitted planks. She took a long, slow breath. She had slept poorly, thinking of Marcy's words. How was it she could have such heartfelt sympathy for Marcy one moment and such scathing contempt the next?

Each time she tried to break through she was rebuffed. She and Marcy were oil and water. They'd never mix. Marcy had always possessed a sharp tongue and aimed it her way. Abbie didn't hold her solely to blame, though. She'd fired plenty of shots at Marcy, as well, and she knew they'd hit bull's eye. How could anyone undo that kind of bad blood?

Maybe it was foolish to think they could find common ground. Especially when Marcy held such a poor opinion of the people Abbie cared for. Cole, in particular. Marcy's attitude toward him was nothing short of contemptuous, though why it should be, she couldn't say. Just plain snobbery, she supposed.

She heard wheels in the yard and hurried to the door. It was early for tea, but maybe Nora had expected the trip to be longer. Her heart jumped at the thought of seeing her friend, someone who shared a laugh and a chat without malice.

She opened the door in surprise to Reverend Shields, then smiled. "Good day, Reverend."

He removed his hat and nodded. "Mrs. Farrel. Is your husband home?"

"Yes. I believe he's in the study. May I take your hat?"

"Thank you. I hope I'm not intruding."

"Not at all. I'm having a friend for tea. Won't you join us, as well?"

"I'd like that very much, if it's not too much trouble."

"It's no trouble at all." Abbie tapped and opened the door to the study. "Monte, Reverend Shields is here to see you."

Monte looked up from his desk. "Come in, Winthrop."

Abbie left them, closing the door softly behind her. She went to the kitchen and found Pearl. "Reverend Shields will also join us for tea, Pearl."

"I already seen him, Mizz Abbie. I's warmin' a pie."

Abbie smiled. "He loves your pie."

"Don' you say that. Don' you gimme the big head." But her cheek dimpled with the suppressed smile.

Abbie wandered upstairs. Waiting for Nora now, the time seemed to hang. She glanced in the nursery at Jenny. The child was dressed in sky blue satin with ribbons to match tied into her dark ringlet curls. She looked exquisite, too pretty to touch. She looked like Frances, and Abbie felt a pang.

Zena looked up from the ring of marbles between them. "Is you needin' Mizz Jenny now?"

Jenny frowned, and Abbie felt as though she'd been caught longing for something she shouldn't have. But that was ridiculous. Jenny was hers to love. Why couldn't it be as easy as it seemed to be for Cole Jasper? She shook her head. "No. I'll call when tea is served."

She walked back down. She was eager but at the same time anxious about this visit. What if Nora was overwhelmed or offended by the discrepancy in their circumstances? Maybe she shouldn't have asked her so soon. Maybe they hadn't yet become close enough. But how could she continue to receive Nora's hospitality without returning the invitation?

She looked out the window, but except for Will watering the minister's horse, the yard was empty. What did Reverend Shields want with Monte? No doubt he was collecting for some cause or other.

The fire she'd lit in him when they placed the orphans had kindled to a blaze, and there was always some need. He came to her when a matter required personal attention, and to Monte when it was financial. She sighed. This time he might leave disappointed.

She heard a horse and wagon and looked out to see Nora. The wagon stopped at the end of the drive, and Abbie knew her friend was getting the full effect of the majestic pink-and-white house, the grounds, and the outbuildings with the mountain peaks behind. She half expected the wagon to turn around, but after a few moments, Nora came on.

Abbie sighed her relief. She hurried down to greet her. It would not do for Nora to be shown in by James who, bless his heart, maintained the formal manners and attitude he'd learned in the South. She opened the door and went down the stairs as Will handed Nora down from the wagon.

Abbie reached out her hands and grasped Nora's. "Welcome. I'm so glad to have you. I see you found your way."

"No trouble at all." Nora's eyes went up the house. "But I don't know as I'd've come if I'd known it was this grand."

"It's a fine house Monte built, but it's a home like your own."

"Not exactly like." Nora grinned.

"Will you come in?"

"I'd like to see that special spot you told me of first, if you don't mind. Maybe it'll build me courage."

Abbie slipped her arm through Nora's. "I'd love to show you."

They walked along the creek under the cottonwoods to the circular pool where Monte had first taken her. The chokecherries had finished blooming, and green berries clustered on the branches. The Queen Anne's lace stood white beneath. Wild lupine and fairy trumpets colored the grass, and the creek gurgled over the rocky bottom.

She watched Nora view the wild beauty. What did she think of when her eyes settled on the clear, cold water?

"It's a lovely spot, Abbie. I can see why it's special to you."

"And Monte. It is his favorite place on the whole ranch. But then, I doubt he'll ever truly love the wide, empty prairie as I do."

"I admit I've no love lost on this barren land meself."

Abbie smiled. "That doesn't surprise me. One day I'll take you to Pa's homestead where I was raised. We'll go up into the hills and you'll see the beauty of the mountains up close."

"The mountains are fearsome tall."

"We'll just climb the feet."

Nora shook her head and gave a little laugh. "These are not the bonny green hills of Erin, of that you can be sure."

Abbie started back toward the house. Monte and Reverend Shields would be eager for tea. As they came around to the front, Nora eyed the buggy in the yard. "Have you other company?"

"That's Reverend Shields' buggy. He came to see Monte about some matter or other."

"And your husband received him?"

"Of course he . . ." Abbie paused at the look in Nora's eyes. "Reverend Shields is our friend. He's the Methodist minister. Monte was raised Methodist."

Nora's eyes widened, then hardened. "You married a Protestant . . . and a landlord."

"My husband knows and honors the same God."

Nora's glance went over the house. "Forgive me, Abbie, but I'll not go inside. I won't set foot in a manor house, not even for you. Ye're welcome at the mission anytime."

She turned on her heel, climbed into the wagon, and slapped the reins without another word. Abbie stood, stunned. How could Nora judge Monte and Winthrop Shields without even setting eyes on them? How could she refuse to come into her home? Abbie sank to the lowest stair. She felt worse than she had from any insult Marcy had ever thrown her way. The door opened behind her, and Monte stepped out.

"Abbie, I requested Pearl lay the tea. Are you . . ."

She looked up to him.

"What is it?"

"Nora won't come into the house of a Protestant landlord."

He looked out at the wagon disappearing down the track. "I'm . . . sorry."

Abbie stood up and turned. "There's no need to apologize." She climbed the stairs to him. "Whatever Nora Flynn might think, I know God draws no distinctions. He sees the heart and knows its surrender." She glanced back over her shoulder. "Or the lack."

She took Monte's hand. "Come, let's not keep Reverend Shields waiting." She was sorry for whatever bitterness was stirred in Nora's cup, but she would not allow division in her heart. If Nora could not accept her husband, she was not accepting her.

♦♦♦♦♦♦♦

When Sunday came again she found Nora friendly, but by the looks of all the women, she knew word had passed that she was the wife of a Protestant "landlord." Though why that word seemed to connote such contempt, Abbie hadn't a clue. She allowed Jenny to play in the yard and chatted with Nora and Glenna about baby Delia's new tooth.

Glenna hurried away to retrieve Danny from the dirt when he'd tumbled, and Davy McConnel approached. He removed his hat. "Mornin', Abbie. Miss Flynn, I wondered if you'd care to walk a bit."

She scarcely smiled, but nodded. "The name's Nora, and I'll take a stroll, Davy McConnel."

Abbie caught the look of triumph that passed over Davy's features. Maybe compared to Monte, Davy McConnel didn't seem such a burden to Nora after all. Or maybe she was not eager to be alone with her any more than she had to. Abbie's heart sank. She had counted Nora a friend. Not since Sharlyn died had she had any but Clara to truly call friend.

She gathered Jenny up and took her home.

♦♦♦♦♦♦♦

Cole sat astride Scotch in the mild June heat. He'd been riding the fence of the pasture where they'd contained what remained of the herd. He looked for damage and repaired what he found: loose wire and broken or leaning posts demolished by the weight of the snow or washed out from the melting runoff. But just now he couldn't keep his mind on the stretch of fence beside him.

He looked again at Abbie walking the prairie. She seemed to be deep in thought. Her hair blew back from her face in the warm wind, and she covered the ground as naturally as any lithe pronghorn. Lithe she was, except for the bulge where the baby grew inside her. That's what had her on foot instead of riding her spirited mare. Mr. Farrel was taking no chances.

Cole could hardly blame him, though he knew Abbie chafed. She was not the compliant doll his first wife had been, nor anywhere near as fragile. She reminded him of a Comanche squaw he'd come upon in Texas, giving birth out on the plain with nothing but the wind to help her. He'd ridden away with a sense of having witnessed something that shamed him in its simple endurance.

Abbie had that same courage, that brave stubborn quality that made her a survivor and kept her close to his thoughts no matter how hard he tried. Montgomery Farrel was a lucky man. Cole dismounted and strode to a post where the wire hung loose. He took a nail from the bag at his hip, pulled the wire into place, and hammered it in.

Abbie stopped at the noise and looked up. He returned her wave with a brief salute. Front on, he couldn't help but look at her belly. It wasn't the loss of her figure that bothered him, nor even—he hoped—that it was another man's child. It was the thought that she might change, become like the married hens who cackled around the house and became plump and complacent.

He didn't want Abbie to lose her spark. That was what set her apart. That—and her wit, and her smile, and her eyes—and countless other details he didn't want to think on. He stood when she approached, then took off his hat. He rubbed the sweat from his brow with the back of his sleeve. "Nice day fer a walk."

"It's a beautiful day, though I'd rather ride."

"You've gone a fair piece."

She shrugged but didn't complain about Mr. Farrel's protectiveness. She had grown up some there, keeping to herself things she might have told him before, things that made it hard to keep his head straight.

She touched the post. "Damage from the blizzard?"

He looked along the fence. "That and the dry. Makes the wood crack and the nails slip out. Just a matter of puttin' 'em back in."

She nodded. "Need a hand?"

He grinned. "You're desperate, ain't ya?"

"I am not desperate." She put her hands to her hips. "Just because someone offers help—"

"I know what stir crazy feels like. Here, hold that wire and keep yer fingers free of the post."

She held the wire while he hammered. He couldn't help noticing how the tips of her fingers tapered down to her fine pale nails. But her hands were strong, not the limp, useless hands of some ladies. He remembered the feel of them in his and frowned. "I can get the rest."

"I don't mind." She walked to the next post and pulled up the wire.

With the least effort, he could get used to working beside her. "Look, Abbie, I work better alone."

She dropped the wire. "Suit yourself." She started down the slope.

"Abbie . . ."

She paused.

"Don't go far."

She tossed her head and increased her stride. She'd probably head for Kansas just to spite him. He banged the nail into the wood with such force the post split. He swore under his breath.

Fifteen

Cole eyed the new men he'd signed on to drive the herd. Ben Smythe looked like he'd barely passed peach fuzz, and Jeff sat on a horse like an eastern sissy. But with the railroad through, men with any real experience driving cattle were hard to come by. They'd moved on up to Montana or stayed in Texas. With Mr. Farrel tight on payroll, this was the best he could do.

He glanced at Breck and Matt Weston. At least he'd have two decent cowboys, and John Mason would serve as wrangler. He already had the remuda ready, eight horses for each man. He'd need to know each horse by sight and keep track that none strayed along the way.

Charlie sat in the chuckwagon, and he was an old hand at it. Cole left it to him to pack the bedrolls, supplies, water, wood, and tools. Skeeter would see to things on the ranch while they were gone. Skeeter was steady enough to leave in charge. Breck would have been his preference, but he needed him for the drive.

Cole drew himself up in the saddle. Fact was, a real cattle drive sounded mighty good just about now. They'd catch the branch of the Santa Fe Trail coming from Bent's Fort and follow it out to Dodge City, Kansas. He could almost hear the clamor of that city already. Yes, indeed.

Since the railroad had come through, they'd driven the cattle to the stockyards east of town and freighted them to the markets. It had been too long since he'd actually taken a herd across country to the cow towns in Kansas or beyond. That Mr. Farrel hadn't the funds for freighting the herd was downright advantageous, not that he'd tell Farrel so.

But now that Charlie had pulled up the wagon, he and the men were ready to hit the trail. He looked over the herd, spread over the land east of the yard. Six hundred and ninety of their own and twice that again gathered from Dunbar, Ephart, and Hodge, with some two hundred head between Farringer and Bates.

He turned when Mr. Farrel came out of the house dressed in chaps, a denim shirt, vest, and a red kerchief. Cole frowned down young Ben's surprised hoot. Mr. Farrel might look the southern gentleman, but he had steel in his hide. Cole had learned that well enough. Only trouble was he knew next to nothing about cattle.

Cole followed him to the stable. "What are you doin', Mr. Farrel?"

"I know we're shorthanded. I'll fill the gap."

"With all due respect..."

"I know your opinion, Cole. I don't pretend to be proficient, but surely there's work I can do."

Cole leaned on the stall while Mr. Farrel saddled his Arabian stallion. His choice of horse alone showed his lack of knowledge. That high-stepping, long-necked blue blood was no cutting horse and no swimmer, either, by the looks of his breadbasket. He might have a nice smooth stride, but he was skittish and high spirited.

Mr. Farrell tightened the cinch and turned. "I've instructed Will to add horses to the remuda. I'll be covered."

Had Monte read his thoughts? Cole half grinned. Time was when he could have taken twice as many head with seasoned men, but the country was filling up, and folks were testy about cattle driving through their land. Even along the old trails nesters had fenced in claims and farmers were planting crops. They didn't take kindly to Texas Longhorns spreading the fever among their stock, and it could get ugly.

Mr. Farrel was a decent horseman and a good shot, even with his hands scarred up from the fire. But that wasn't his concern.

"Mr. Farrel, I'm not real sure how the men..."

"You're the trail boss, Cole. I'm not here to make trouble, just to get the job done. Besides, I want to see for myself what comes to market."

"You lookin' to buy?"

"We'll see what we fetch for the herd."

Cole took off his hat and scratched his fingers through his hair, then shrugged. "I'm ridin' point, and I got the other four ridin' swing and flank. You'll have to ride drag and eat dust all the way."

Mr. Farrel nodded. "I'll manage wherever you put me."

Cole could hardly stop him. Though Mr. Farrel seemed willing to subordinate, Cole knew where his pay came from. He went out and took up Scotch's reins. Abbie stood on the porch. Her belly protruded in her skirts, but the rest of her was slender as always.

How did she feel about her husband going along? She gave nothing away as Mr. Farrel led the stallion to the steps. She leaned down, and he kissed her cheek. They'd no doubt said their passionate good-byes inside.

Cole kicked the dirt with his boot. "Mount up." He swung into the saddle, whistled, and they started. They met Curtis with the herd, then drifted them awhile before lining them out.

Riding point, he chose the path and set the pace. He'd push it hard the first few days to trail break the herd, get them away from the home range, and make them lay down at night. Then they'd take it on gently. This was all second nature. He could hardly remember a time he hadn't known what he knew.

He glanced over his shoulder to see the herd stringing out four or five abreast behind the lead steer. Already the natural leader had taken his place. Cole would keep just ahead of the stronger, rangier cattle while the weak and lazy ones dragged behind.

Mr. Farrel's job was to keep the stragglers moving. Cole couldn't see him through the brown dust cloud, but he figured he was there gutting through it. He'd never mistake Mr. Farrel's fine manners for weakness again.

◆◆◆◆◆◆◆

Monte adjusted the kerchief over his mouth and nose. He felt worse for Sirocco than himself, though the stallion kept his pace without complaint. The Arabian was not a cowhorse. It was a mistake to bring him. Monte hoped it was not the first of a string of mistakes.

Cole hadn't exaggerated about the dust, but by weaving to the edges of the herd he could find respite from the choking cloud. It was no worse than the slow suffocation he felt most days now. His attempt to find financing with the Denver banks had proved as futile as he expected.

Too many ranchers were in his predicament. No one would loan without collateral. As much as he disdained the man, at least he had an established relationship with Driscoll. He might be a hard man, but he was honest. And he'd banked all he had on that honesty when he had at last turned over the Lucky Star deed as collateral on the loan.

He didn't want to think about it. He hadn't slept for two nights afterward. But what choice had he? The mining stocks had fallen to a fraction of his investment. He needed the horses and could ill afford the ones they'd lost in the blizzard. In his defense, Driscoll had been considerate and professional. He had allowed provision for prepayment against the principal of the loan. And Monte hoped with this drive to put some of that behind him.

He looked up to see Cole circling back, whistling and waving his hat to keep the cattle at a trot. Monte guessed it was as much to show the men to keep the pace. He passed around between Monte and the chuck wagon, which trailed far enough back to be out of the dust, then headed on up the line.

They pushed hard until the sun was high overhead, then Cole again circled and gave word to spread the cattle out to graze. They would change horses and eat, then move on. Monte urged the stragglers off the dusty trail onto the range alongside, and the fractious animals bawled and balked, then began to feed. He slid from the saddle and slapped the dust from his pants with his hat, then put Sirocco in John's hands and joined the others at the chuck wagon.

By the time they had the cattle settled, Charlie had set up, started a fire, and had coffee on. Though the June heat beat down, Monte swigged the coffee from the tin cup to wash the dirt from his throat. Even his teeth were gritty. But he sat cross-legged on the ground with the others and took the plate of beef and beans Charlie offered.

"Ain't what you're used to, Mr. Farrel, but it's better than some blokes get."

"Thank you, Charlie. Hunger makes for good seasoning." He caught Cole's eye and nodded.

Cole dropped beside him. "Think I'll have you ride flank this stretch, Mr. Farrel. Young Ben can be dragman and keep an eye on the fat Bessies."

"Whatever you say, Cole."

"So are you gonna tell me what you've in mind for the market?"

"I want a look at some faster growing, beefier breeds."

Cole squinted at the herd scattered over the prairie. "You won't find any as hearty as the Longhorn, nor as suited to the range."

"I don't suppose I will. But I don't have the luxury of eight to ten years for a marketable steer. I need an animal I can turn over quickly, a good breeder with more meat than hide."

Monte ran the johnnycake through the bean sauce on his plate. "Times are changing, Cole. I think the days of the open range are ending. The trouble with Gifford and the blizzard showed us that. I've a mind to fence what we can and risk winter feeding of a better breed."

Cole rubbed his jaw. "I've thought on that myself, though it goes against the grain. I've had a lot of years ridin' herd on Longhorns. Don't know as I'm suited for any other breed."

"I won't make the change without your go-ahead."

"I figured you had it in mind when you said take 'em all."

"Well, as we've hardly any calves after the blizzard kill, it seemed now was the time."

"Cain't rightly argue that." Cole scraped the rest of his beans into his mouth and followed it with the final chunk of johnny-cake. "We'll have us a look in Dodge."

"I'll trust your judgment."

"Ain't likely we'll get much by way of numbers."

"Whatever we get will be a start."

♦♦♦♦♦♦♦

With her hand resting on her belly, Abbie watched until the dust died down in the distance. Monte had said it could take a good three weeks to drive the cattle into Dodge City, Kansas, and the same back if they got new animals, and provided they had good weather and no delays. Cole wouldn't rush the stock or they'd lose meat and not bring as good a price.

That Monte was going himself showed just how desperate this drive was. The entire herd. *Oh, Lord.* Had she known how badly her misjudgment would hurt Monte, she'd have spit in Kendal's face . . . and Mr. Driscoll's, as well.

Monte had only confided in her his latest dealing because she so vehemently argued against his going on the drive. How could he have thought to seek a loan from that man after . . . Her chest ached. He must be desperate indeed to have considered it. Thank God he turned Driscoll down.

She turned as Jenny pressed into her legs. "Is Uncle Monte gone?"

"Yes."

"And Cole?"

"Cole too." Abbie felt the child tremble.

"Why can't we go?"

Abbie squatted down till her belly pressed her thighs. "It's a very long way and hard, hard work."

Jenny's hands came to Abbie's shoulders. The brown of her eyes seemed to deepen. "Are they coming back?"

Abbie stroked a hand over the smooth, soft cheek. "Yes, Jenny.

They'll be back." She pulled the child close.

Jenny wrapped her arms around her neck. "Promise?"

"I promise." Abbie said it with more cheer than she felt. How many times had people disappeared from Jenny's life? Her father and mama, her mammy. Monte was just starting to break through, and the child adored Cole. Abbie hadn't thought how their leaving would frighten Jenny.

"Let's do something special. Where shall we go?"

"The mission. I want to play with Katie."

It surprised Abbie how close Jenny and Katie had become. For such an inauspicious start, they had developed a deep devotion. "All right. Run up and have Zena change your shoes and stockings. I'll get the buggy."

She and Jenny drove out beneath a sky hazy with wisps of white strung across its expanse. But the sun was warm, and for once there was no wind.

Glenna's homestead was a single wood-frame room with a loft. The door Alan had built was split so that the bottom half could keep the children in while the top allowed the breeze. Abbie knocked on the bottom half, and Glenna turned from the fireplace where she was scraping out the ashes.

She smiled. "Come in, Abbie. Have ye brought Jenny along?"

"I have."

Katie dropped the board she was holding to receive the ashes, sending dust everywhere, and scrambled up.

"Katie Lynn! Oh, never mind. Run along."

The girls scampered out with Danny tagging behind. Baby Delia tried to gain the door on all fours, but Abbie caught her and set her safely on her bottom.

"I'll help you there." Abbie stooped to retrieve the board Katie dropped and held it in place.

"You'll soil your hands and your skirt."

Abbie swallowed Glenna's unintended insult. "It works better with two of us." She held the edges of the board while Glenna piled the ashes on.

"There, now. I'll just run it to the field where Alan's workin', then make us a cup."

"I'll start the fire."

Glenna raised her brows but said nothing. Abbie had a fresh blaze of scrub oak and cedar going when she returned. Glenna poured water from the bucket into the heavy iron pot and swung it over the fire. "I have to confess I thought I'd find ye still scrapin' for a spark. Nora said you have all your work done for ye."

Abbie felt her face flush. She could almost hear Nora saying it with her singsong voice. *"Aye, and she lives in a fine manor house the like of which I won't enter."* She sat on the three-legged stool by the hearth. "We have servants who help, but that doesn't mean I do nothing. I spent two years in a tent house smaller than this helping Mama cook over a fire pit outside. That was in the mining camp at Auraria."

She flicked a flake of ash from her skirt. "Then we moved to the homestead and lived in a soddy until Pa built the frame house my folks live in still. I've worked every day of my life in the house, in the garden, and at the mission teaching the children."

Glenna sat across from her. "Ye canna blame Nora. She sees everything with a dark eye now."

"Why?"

"I should let her share the grief in her own time. It's enough you know it's not only you that feels her wrath."

"Do you mean Davy?"

"Aye, and others. She puts on a cheery face, but she canna change her heart. It's not your Monte she hates, but others like him."

"How does she even know what he's like? She never laid eyes on him."

"Aye, she did. She saw him in town two weeks ago. Father O'Brien was talkin' with your da, and he introduced your Monte around. She said he was a handsome man with a lordly air." She poured and handed her a cup of tea.

"My husband is a gentleman. Why does that make him an enemy?"

"Because in Ireland the gentlemen are the enemy."

Abbie dropped her forehead to her fingertips. "I don't understand."

"You wouldn't unless you'd lived it."

Abbie sipped. So Nora had met Monte and said nothing of it. What made a woman so bitter she could hate without cause a man like Monte?

Glenna stood. "I'd better take a look at the children. They've been quiet too long."

Abbie followed Glenna out. She saw Katie and Danny parading behind Jenny along the edge of the field where Alan worked the plow, their arms outstretched, feet skipping. Jenny loved nothing better than follow-the-leader, especially when she was the leader. But true to form, Katie stepped out of line and declared herself leader, then hopped down the slope with her hands on her head.

Jenny frowned, but Danny was already making awkward hops after his sister, and she did not want to be last in line. Abbie smiled into her cup. Poor Jenny. She was more like Auntie Abbie than her own mama. She leaned against the wall and finished the tea, then looked across the land at the chapel and mission house.

Should she go tell Nora hello? Somehow she was drawn to the fiery-haired woman in spite of her ill feelings for Monte. Maybe when Nora came to trust her, she could make her see that wealth and breeding did not always corrupt. Whatever her experience in Ireland, things were different here.

"Would you mind if I left Jenny for a bit and ran over to see Nora?"

"I was hopin' you'd ask that."

Abbie pulled herself into the buggy. She was getting ponderous when it came to wagons and buggies. She'd be glad when the next two and a half months were past and the baby delivered. A wave of anticipation washed over her with a rush. Monte's child. How could anything bother her when she carried Monte's child?

The sun was hot, and sweat moistened her upper lip as she stopped the buggy outside the mission house and found Nora peeling potatoes on the step. At her feet the chickens pecked at the peels.

"Hello, Abbie."

"Fine day for sitting outside."

"If I stayed in the kitchen I'd not need to boil the potatoes. They'd just roast beside me."

"Father Thomas always opened the front and back doors to make a draft. But even so he worked up a sweat."

"It's the dry heat. There's never a mist. Either the rain pours down like a flood, or the wind carries dust. There's no softness here."

Abbie remembered Frances's impressions. No fervent defense of the territory's charms would change another's homesick longings. Abbie eased herself to the step beside Nora. "Hand me the long knife. I'll slice as you peel."

Nora took the knife from the step and presented it handle forward. She made no comment, and Abbie wondered if Nora's words about her not working had been more slander than actual belief. Either way, Abbie put it aside. She would not bear a grudge where she could help it.

How strange to have spent the last year proving she was refined, only to have Nora find her too much so. She almost laughed. Would she never be what others expected? Was that her thorn from the Lord?

She took the spud Nora handed her. "Jenny's playing with Katie. It's amazing how they've worked out their animosity."

"Children heal quickly."

"That's true. And I think we underestimate the power of those friendships. Blake and I . . ."

"Yes?"

"We were constant companions, and, well, we were very close."

"Would you have married him if he'd not been killed?"

"No. I loved Monte."

Monte's name hung in the air. Nora shooed a chicken who pecked at her foot. "I've enough potatoes now. I'll set them to boil." She stood with the bowl. "Will ya have a cup of tea?"

"No thanks. I had one at Glenna's. And I should take Jenny home. Monte and Cole have taken the herd to Kansas, every last cow, steer, and calf, along with some of the Dunbars' stock, as well. They'll be gone some while, and I promised Monte I'd not wander far or late."

"Thank you for coming."

Nora's eyes warmed for a moment, and Abbie almost felt the closeness they'd shared before Nora learned about Monte. Then it was gone, and Nora turned inside.

Monte rolled into the blanket on the hard ground. Not for any money would he admit how bone weary he felt. With sundown, they'd circled the herd, closing them in tighter and tighter until they lay down and settled. Now Breck and Matt took the first watch, riding slowly around the herd singing low and mournfully. It might comfort the cattle, but it only made Monte think how he could be home with Abbie.

Even his eyelids felt crusted with dust. Whatever Cole saw to be so cheerful about was beyond him. The work was grueling and, at its best, unsatisfying. But . . . this was his hope: to unload the herd profitably and choose a new breed. Perhaps Cole could have handled it, but with so much resting on this success, he'd needed to be present. If only the ground weren't so hard.

He woke to Cole's shaking him, surprised by the fatigue that kept him from springing awake as he might have. He felt the honor, however, as the others received Cole's boot, something more than a gentle nudge and less than a kick in the hindquarters. He could swear Cole enjoyed it, too.

"Here you are, Mr. Farrel."

Monte sat up and took the cup of coffee Charlie offered.

"I'll whip up some tucker 'fore you've had time to say howdy to yer stomach."

"Quit jawin', Charlie, and git at it." Cole drew down the brim of his black Stetson and stalked off.

Charlie winked at Cole's back. "He wakes meaner than a

spring grizzly. Leastwise he means us to think so."

Monte stood and stretched the kinks from his limbs. Oh yes, he felt each one, bone and sinew, another reason to have stayed with Abbie. Didn't he pay the men to do this? That thought was as sore as he. Would he have the means to pay them much longer?

After packing in Charlie's "tucker" with the best of them, he mounted. Awaiting Cole's orders kept him humble. He'd like to say he'd ride on ahead and meet them in Dodge, but his own pride wouldn't allow it.

There was challenge in Cole's eyes. Good-humored, but challenge nonetheless. And he wasn't about to let some cocky Texan have the best of a true South Carolina rebel.

"I'll have you ride swing today, Mr. Farrel. We'll see what you do with the front side of a herd. Just in case you need to make a run for it, why don't you leave yer fancy stallion with Will and take a real horse."

"When it comes to running, I'd wager Sirocco against any horse here, your Scotch included."

Cole grinned a rascal's grin. "I reckon that depends. Give them a track and you'd be right. But if that long-legged pedigree has ever outrun a frenzied herd, I'll eat my hat." He swung around and started them off, men and beasts alike.

Monte stroked Sirocco's neck. "Never mind, you fine son of the desert. Cows aren't all they're cracked up to be."

Astride a solid bay named Blackjack, Monte managed his side of the herd as they drifted the cattle the first two hours of daylight, then lined them out and drove. Cole must have bones of steel, the way he set the pace and circled tirelessly—ruthlessly, Monte's backside answered.

He noticed a cow weaving outward to the side of the line and increased his pace to shoo her back. She rubbed her head against the steer beside and slightly forward of her. He shouldered her in, but she butted him back. Monte slapped the rope on Blackjack's flank and the horse shot forward.

Whatever had gotten into the cow, he'd need to contain her if he didn't want her irritating her companions into bolting. He drew alongside, and the cow raised her head and gave a long bawling *maaaoo*. Monte swung the end of the rope in a circular motion as he'd seen the others do. She took notice of him with her head turned, then butted through the gap behind the steer.

"Go on, now. Back in line." He swung the rope again, this time catching the ground enough to kick up dust and make it snap.

Her dun hide flinched, and again she moaned, but she wouldn't turn back. She came close enough for him to prod her with his boot in the stirrup. His horse held steady as Monte swatted the rope on the cow's flank. "Go on, now."

He smelled the dust kicked up by Cole's mount. The man must have eyes in the back of his head. Monte turned, expecting Cole's scowl or at least his insolent half grin. What he saw was downright amusement. Monte spread his hands, annoyed. "She's turned stubborn. You'll have to rope her in."

"That ain't stubborn. She's givin' you the big-eyed howdy."

"The what?"

"You must have a way with the ladies. You've charmed her into season."

Monte frowned. "Well, tell her I'm married." The last thing he needed was this joked around the fire. And Cole was just ornery enough to do it.

Cole laughed. "Yes, sir, but I cain't promise she'll listen. Females got a mind of their own. Sometimes they'll pick out the rangiest bull when a full-blooded specimen is there for the takin'."

Monte got the point directly. Cole had come a long way if he could tease him about Abbie. He drew up in the saddle. "I'll ride point while you sweet-talk her."

"That's fine by me, long as you keep us headin' to Kansas." Cole grinned.

"I think I know that much."

"I reckon you do."

Monte heard his laughter as he urged Blackjack ahead. The cow bawled. Charmed her, indeed. That man had gall.

Sixteen

From two miles out, Dodge City lived up to its reputation as a noisy, rowdy cow town. Cole felt his pulse increase. Yessiree, Dodge was one rollicking place. He checked the loads in the gun at his hip. Not that he expected trouble of that sort. The law in Dodge was up to whatever shenanigans any of his tribe could dish out.

But if the cattle got spooked, it'd take more than hat waving and whips to get 'em back in line. And he knew well enough the sheriff in Dodge would not take kindly to their running a herd through the streets. It would take all Mr. Farrel's fine words to ease that one.

He glanced at Mr. Farrel beside him. He'd weathered the trip admirably, and even proved useful. After nearly four weeks in the saddle, he hardly looked the gentleman rancher at all. Cole grinned. "Well, Mr. Farrel, we're bringin' 'em in."

"We are indeed."

"We'll reach the stockyards before we hit town, corral the herd, and have us a drink."

"I don't think that word has ever held quite the same meaning."

"Likely forty pounds of dust has made it down yer gullet."

"At the least."

Cole laughed. "Well, sir, Dodge is the place to wet yer whistle."

"The sooner we dispense with these boneheaded bovines, the better."

Cole whistled and gave the signal for the men to draw the herd in tighter. They were in sight of the acres of fencing that made up the stockyards west of town. It had been a relatively uneventful drive, and he wanted to keep it that way. No panic or scattering, no stampeding through town, just a nice, easy finish to a long, dry ride.

When the herd was contained, the men took off with new energy. The half month's pay he'd put in their pockets would not stay there long. Cole clapped Mr. Farrel on the shoulder. "Much as I hate to say it, you're not such a bad cowboy after all."

"Much as I hate to say it, if I never see the bony backside of a steer again, it'll be too soon."

Cole laughed. It felt good. He felt good. There was nothing like reaching the end of the trail, bringing the herd in, and gettin' clapped on the back for a job well done. The sun was sinking into the thick Kansas sky, and flies swarmed their heads as they corralled the herd and left them.

They rode into town and went into the first decent-looking saloon on the street. No good taking a man like Mr. Farrel into some of these places, not with Abbie waiting at home. And he certainly wouldn't be looking for a faro game or poker table. They took a stool at the bar and Cole ordered them both a tall, frothy mug. Nothing chased the dust from the trail better, whether Mr. Farrel took to it or not.

Mr. Farrel cupped the mug and shook his head. "I don't know how you do it."

"Do what?"

"Hold up in the saddle. You must have a steel hide to keep it up at your age."

"I ain't as old as you think I am."

Mr. Farrel sucked the foam from his mug. "How old are you, Cole?"

"Thirty-two."

Mr. Farrel put the mug down hard.

Cole chuckled. "Yeah, I know. You thought I was old enough to be Abbie's pa."

"I don't believe you."

"I've been on the backside of a herd since I was twelve years old, while you was bein' dressed and fed by all them servants."

Mr. Farrel winced. "You don't mince your words, do you."

"Ain't no point." He drank deep. "We know where we stand. But I will hand it to you, you and yer mount both. You're tougher than you look."

"And you're not as hard as you appear. You're a good man, Cole."

"Well, don't let it out. I gotta keep an edge on the men somehow."

Mr. Farrel raised his mug, and Cole met it with his. He shared the smile, then drained his glass. With all the dust he'd eaten, it would likely make mud in his innards.

After a wash and a shave he left Mr. Farrel soaking at the bathhouse and went to find them a room. The others could fend for themselves. They'd no doubt spend the night clean through gambling away their earnings and drinking just enough to make the losing painless.

He settled on a relatively quiet hostelry with better than average food and clean rooms. Likely Mr. Farrel was used to staying in finer establishments than Dodge boasted, but at least this place shouldn't have drunks shooting it up.

♦♦♦♦♦♦♦

Monte felt as though he could soak for days and never clean off all the grime of the trail. The next time Abbie said stay home, he'd listen. He closed his eyes and sank deeper into the steaming tub. *Abbie.* Was there ever a finer thought to fill a man's mind? He jolted suddenly.

Was it possible Cole was only four years his senior? He seemed so rugged and . . . seasoned and experienced. In his thoughts he'd added years to Cole's age, guessed him at least sixteen years older than Abbie. Had he known only a decade separated them, he'd have worried more than he had, when Cole set his eye on her.

Did Abbie know? Did she care? What foolishness was this? He'd put aside his jealousy of Cole. He trusted him completely and, moreover, he liked him. Monte ran a soapy hand over his face.

But the truth was, no female had ever kindled the flames of jealousy as Abbie had, through no fault of her own. And as his respect for Cole Jasper grew, he realized how lucky he was that Abbie had not accepted Cole's proposal. He was a man who could have made her forget her first love.

The bath attendant came in with a fresh bucket of hot water. Monte took it full on the head and exulted in the luxury. What pleasure there was in cleanliness. But before he shriveled up completely, he ought to get out. He toweled himself dry and put on the clothes he'd kept tightly wrapped in the chuck wagon. Though slightly wrinkled, they were remarkably free of dust.

He was surprised to find Cole outside the door likewise washed and shaved, except for the thick mustache he'd grown back after disguising himself to rescue Abbie from the rustler. Monte felt a twinge. He took a long look at the man.

His skin was creased beside the eyes, his jaw sharp, and his cheeks slightly hollowed and wind-burned. His eyes held years of experience, but his physique was strong and straight. He was a swaggishly handsome man. Why didn't he choose himself a wife and get on with it?

"Got us a room. You mind sharing?"

"I don't mind. The less we spend on incidentals, the better."

"Well, it ain't the cheapest, but trust me, it's worth it."

Monte wanted to ask how Cole knew, but refrained. It was just different experiences. Cole would be just as lost in Charleston, or any fine city for that matter. He wouldn't know the first thing about situations that were second nature to Monte. But somehow, he didn't think Cole would care. What made a man so singular of purpose, so . . . self-confident?

He didn't think Cole looked to heaven. He'd never gotten that impression. Cole's confidence was in himself, his abilities. Monte shook his head. Hadn't he had that same confidence when things were going well, when he had all he needed and more? Was his worth based on his achievements, to come and go on the tides of fortune?

What did Cole have? A hard bunk on a ranch that belonged to another. Long days' work and no companions but the men he bullied. No one to love, no one to love him, yet he seemed doggedly self-contained. Maybe a man like Cole didn't need God. But no. No such man ever lived, whether an ornery cuss like Cole ever admitted it or not.

Moths swarmed the streetlamp at the corner where they turned. The town was as well kept as Cole described. The lawmen didn't allow horseplay of the sort that shot out lights and wreaked havoc in the streets. They went inside the gray two-story hostelry and climbed the stairs.

Cole stepped aside at the door, and Monte entered the room first. He eyed the water stain beneath the single narrow window and the sawdust trailed onto the rough plank floor. The linen looked fresh, though. The room was not fancy but suitable.

"Choose yer cot, cuz once my head hits, I ain't movin'."

Monte put his bag on the far cot, and Cole sprawled on the other. Within minutes, he slept. Monte stripped to his long johns and stretched out. The cot felt like heaven after the ground, but he was surprisingly wakeful.

Would they accomplish what they needed? Could he sell the herd for enough to start a new breed? Could he pay back the loan? He passed a hand over his eyes. *Lord, it's in your hands.* He turned to his side and welcomed the fitful sleep that followed.

◆◆◆◆◆◆◆

Monte woke to the dawning light and rose immediately. He was eager to see to business. Cole still breathed deeply in the same position in which he'd landed. Monte washed at the basin, dressed, and stepped up to Cole's cot. He put a hand to his shoulder. With a snarl, Cole had a gun barrel to his chest before he'd half shaken him.

"Good grief, Cole! Do you always wake up like that?"

Cole holstered the gun. He swung his legs over to the floor

and sat up, then ran a hand through the blond waves and shook his head. "I guess somethin' stays alert when I'm in a strange place."

Alert? Reflexes like that were not bred of alacrity. They spoke of downright self-preservation. Had Cole once cause to fear for his life? "Well, the morning's drawing on, and I want to be about our business."

Cole reached for his hat. "Soon's I have a cup of coffee and a smoke, I'll be ready."

"I was considering breakfast myself."

"I'll meet you downstairs."

♦♦♦♦♦♦♦

With steak and eggs and home fries weighting their bellies, Monte and Cole set out for the market. Beef buyers were thick, but finding someone to take a herd, half of which was not at marketable weight, was another thing. Monte was glad for Cole's connections. If anyone could do it, Cole Jasper could.

Monte spent his time looking for purchase possibilities. He was fairly settled on Herefords, but he wanted Cole's go-ahead. After all, Cole was the one who would be working the herd, and the expertise he packed into his four extra years was worth hearing.

Cole came toward him with a definite swagger to his step. "We're in luck. Couple of guys are headin' up Montana way to start them a ranch. They've been waitin' on a herd up from Texas, but I convinced 'em to take ours instead."

"How did you do that?"

"Seein' how ours traveled half the distance on good grazing alongside the Arkansas, and as how they're accustomed to wintering in the snow." He spread his hands. "Got a decent price for 'em if you're of a mind."

Monte nodded. "Let's have a talk with the gentlemen."

As they wound through the stockyard maze, Cole lowered the brim of his hat against the glare and swarming flies. "How'd you fare?"

"What do you think of Herefords, Cole?"

"I knew you were gonna say that."

Monte quirked an eyebrow.

"I reckon they're the best choice, much as I hate the stodgy Bessies."

"Then we're settled. Now all that remains is the financing. You get us the best dollar on our herd, and I'll get us the best herd for the dollar." They shook hands and grinned. They might be two very different men, but they'd found a common ground that suited Monte fine. He could do worse than Cole Jasper for his head man—and friend.

♦♦♦♦♦♦♦

Monte rode beside Cole as they brought in the three hundred Herefords and two Guernsey milk cows. The sale of his herd and the loan money had gone far enough. He felt more optimistic than he had in a long, long time.

With the Herefords he would start a new herd. With the Guernseys he hoped to make peace with Abbie's Irish friend . . . for Abbie's sake. She had said nothing directly, but he'd seen her hurt and knew she was torn.

Nora Flynn had made no effort to hide her contempt when they'd met in town. It was an unusual feeling to be so disdained. But even if his offering did no good, the children needed milk. The Lord had looked out for them unloading the Longhorns with the Montana ranchers, and he would share the blessing.

They drove the Herefords into the north pasture where they would contain them until a fence could be run around the majority of his land, all but the acres that would be planted for feed. Those acres would need irrigation come spring, and digging the trenches would keep the men busy until the ground froze; that, and branding and marking the new animals.

The men had already headed for the bunkhouse when Monte slid from the bay's back and made his weary way up the stairs and in the door. James took his hat, and Monte brushed the dust from his clothes. "Is Abbie in?"

"Yessuh. She in the—"

But the library door had already been flung open and Abbie rushed down the hall. He caught her in his arms. "Abbie . . . good heavens!" He clasped his hands around her belly. "Has it only been six weeks?"

She drew herself up. "I ought to shake you, Montgomery Farrel. I feel as big as a horse."

Monte laughed. "Oh, Abbie, how I've missed you." He kissed her. James turned away, but he'd have kissed her anyway, even with all the world watching.

She caught his hands between hers. "Tell me everything."

"I will. In detail. But first let me wash. I can't stand the dust one more minute."

"I'll heat your water, and you can tell me while you wash." Her words heated his blood as he watched her down the hall. Was a woman always more beautiful with child than any other time? She was due to deliver in three weeks, but still her step was spry, if her gait somewhat awkward. He was home, and tonight he'd feel Abbie in his arms, even if he could no more than hold her.

♦♦♦♦♦♦♦

Abbie exulted in the strength of Monte's arms around her. Eight weeks on the trail had toughened him. His scarred palms were callused, his lips dry and chapped. But the tenderness of his embrace had not diminished. He was home, and her heart could not be more full.

Though he teased, she could see the delight in his eyes when he beheld the growth of the baby. Soon their child would be born. She imagined his pride when he took the baby in his arms for the first time. She could hardly contain the joy.

And how kind he'd been to remember the milk cow and bring not one but two. How like him that was. She had not said another word after he explained their plight, but he had sacrificed to help where he saw the need. She would take the cows to Nora the very next day and tell her Monte had provided them. What a good man he was.

Stretching over, she kissed his lips, and he smiled in his sleep. "Mmmm."

"I love you, Monte."

He tightened his grasp and murmured, "And I love you."

◆◆◆◆◆◆◆

Abbie had invited Monte to take the cows himself, but he declined. Of course he wouldn't put Nora on the spot; he was too much the gentleman. Nora could make up her mind without his presence forcing the issue. So Abbie took Jenny along and pulled the Guernsey milk cows behind the buggy.

They made slow progress, but as she now felt every jolt and jar, she could not have traveled much faster. The sun had baked the crown of her head through the straw hat by the time the mission came in sight, but by the look of the clouds encroaching, the ride back would be cool if not wet. She pulled up outside the mission house and ponderously climbed down.

Jenny had already scampered to the ground and run in search of the playmates almost certain to be in Nora's care. Abbie untied the cows and led them to the step. She knocked loudly on the door, knowing the sound must likely carry to the kitchen or the yard behind.

Father O'Brien opened the door and stared at the two mild-eyed cows before him.

Abbie smiled. "Father O'Brien, these milk cows are a gift from my husband. He brought them back from Dodge City, Kansas, with his new herd." She glanced past his shoulder at Nora staring darkly. "They'll provide good milk for the children."

"And a mighty blessin' indeed." Father O'Brien stepped out and looked the animals over. He ran a hand along their flanks. "A peaceable pair, they seem."

"They're very gentle. I milked them myself this morning, but they'll be ready again come evening. The production is a little low from the drive, but I'm certain it will build up in no time." She glanced again at Nora, who now stood in the doorway, and Father O'Brien turned.

"What do say you, Nora darlin'? Is this not a blessin' from God to have milk for the little 'uns?"

"It is a boon, Father. We thank you, Abbie."

Abbie drew herself up. "It was Monte's doing. My part was only telling him the need." She watched the emotions fight inside Nora, but she would not back down. This was Monte's kindness, and he deserved the gratitude.

Nora looked to Father O'Brien but saw that he'd not speak for her. "You'll give him our thanks, then," she finally said.

"I will. Or you're welcome to give it yourself." She saw the flicker of remorse in Nora's eyes. Thunder rumbled, and she glanced around for Jenny. "I'd better go if I'm to outrun the storm." She caught Jenny by the hand as she'd come running at the next flash of lightning. "Good-bye," she called, tossing Jenny up to the seat.

"God bless ya, Abbie." Father O'Brien waved as he led the cows to the shed.

Yes, Father. You have . . . with a wonderful, caring husband, a child to come, small Jenny beside me, and maybe, just maybe, a repentant friend.

Seventeen

Monte rode beside Cole in the mellow September evening, one week after bringing home the herd. How good it felt to be master of his property. The shaggy brown-and-white Herefords dotted the range that had been fenced to contain them. The fences would be extended as the herd grew. He had already filed for government land he'd previously used free. It would strap them, but with times changing, he must lay his claim early.

As he rode back toward his spread from the Dunbar ranch, he shielded his eyes against the westering glare and stared across the range at a large animal moving unnaturally. He pointed. "What do you make of that, Cole? Our Durham bull?"

Cole squinted beside him. "If it is, he busted a fence."

Monte frowned. "I have plans for that bull. Let's bring him in." He nudged Sirocco and circled wide to the east of the bull's path. Something in how the animal moved bothered him. It was too erratic, too . . .

"Looks like he's got into some loco weed," Cole said.

"Loco weed?"

"Lupine or such. Look how he's frothin'."

Monte frowned. This Durham bull was his hope for building the new herd. With Gifford having butchered his other, he was not about to lose this one, too. "I'll circle in and get his attention while you rope him."

"I cain't hold him alone."

"Once your rope's on, I'll throw mine." *And pray*. "Between us we'll bring him in."

"Mr. Farrel!"

Monte ignored him as the bull started loping. He urged Sirocco over. The bull made a zigzagging path, but he intercepted him. He swung his hat and got a good look at the bull square on when it stopped. Its eyes were crazed. Cole was right. The animal looked loco indeed. Poisoned, but hopefully not past repair.

He had its attention. The great head swayed from side to side, then dodged up and down in swift, jerking motions. Foam flecked its mouth and chest. Sirocco shied. Monte held him steady and reached for the rope that hung at the side of the saddle. It snagged, and he worked it free, keeping his eyes on the bull. Sirocco was tense and skittish.

Monte considered how best to handle it, then swung down from the saddle. The stallion was as unaccustomed to this as he, and he wouldn't risk the horse. He'd be better on his feet. He heard Cole holler, but his whole attention was on the raving beast. Its muscles rippled as the head lowered.

Time suspended and his nerves tensed as Monte looked straight into its face and realized his mistake. *Dear God.* Sirocco bolted and the bull charged.

Cole galloped hard. What possessed Farrel to dismount? He shouted and fired, but the shot grazed off the bull's flank and the animal continued its plunge. It hit Farrel full force, caught him up on its head and shook him like a doll. Cole screamed with all the breath in him.

The bull dropped Farrel and spun, tons of muscle and rage. Its hide twitched as it lowered its head and charged. As one, Cole and Scotch swerved. Cole fired into its skull, once, twice, again. The animal staggered to the side and collapsed even as its weight carried it forward.

Cole jumped down and ran to where Farrel lay, blood frothing from his mouth. Desperate, Cole steeled himself and tore open the blood-soaked shirt. He winced as the fabric pulled away from the torn, mangled flesh of the man's abdomen. His rib bones were bared, snapped off and jagged, and inside—

Cole felt his gorge rise. *No!*

Monte opened his eyes. "Cole." It was more wheeze than voice.

"Yes, sir." Cole kept his terror from showing, but the man knew. He had to know.

"Look after Abbie . . . and my child." The blood gurgled in his throat.

There was no point protesting, nor time. "You know I will." His word was all the comfort he could give.

Monte nodded and closed his eyes. "The Lord is my shep—"

Blood bubbled from his nose and lips, then stopped. With a pain like a hammer and anvil in his chest, Cole reached a slow hand to his hat and pulled it from his head. The feeling of loss overwhelmed him. This shouldn't be happening, not here, not now, not like this. Montgomery Farrel was too fine a man to end like this. It wasn't right.

But, then, when was death ever right? He'd seen too much of it to have any rosy impression of peace and joy. Already the blood congealed on Mr. Farrel's chest.

Montgomery Farrel was the closest thing to a friend he'd had. He wasn't sure when that had happened or how it came about, he only knew that Mr. Farrel had brought out the best in him, and the camaraderie they'd shared these last months wasn't near long enough.

He swallowed hard against the knot in his throat. *What of Abbie?* Hadn't she had enough to bear? Cole groaned, gripped his hair with both hands, and pressed his eyes shut. Guilt weighed heavier than grief. Abbie had trusted him, and he'd failed her.

He looked down at the silent face in his lap. He would give anything to be lying in Mr. Farrel's place rather than taking the news to Abbie. How in heaven's name was he going to tell her?

♦♦♦♦♦♦♦

Abbie took one look at James and rushed for the door. She stared down the stairs to the wagon, her heart pounding her ribs. Cole stood between her and the wagon bed, circling his hat in his hands. Why didn't he speak? Why didn't he say something? He must know he was scaring her to death.

"Is it Monte? Is he hurt? Is it bad, Cole?" Her feet wouldn't move as they should. She started for the stairs, but they felt weak and shaky.

"I'm sorry, Abbie. I'm real sorry."

Why was he sorry? Why wouldn't the fool tell her what she needed to know? Why wasn't he running for the doctor? She pushed past him to the wagon. A blanket covered the form in the back . . . covered it entirely.

The breath left her lungs. She reached for the blanket but Cole caught her wrist.

"Let me." His voice was both tender and despairing. He pulled the blanket and freed Monte's face.

Monte's dark lashes lay against the shadows beneath his eyes. His lips were parted but moved not at all. His stillness was not that of sleep or even injured, damaged repose. He was too quiet, too pale. He was dead.

No numbing denial blocked the pain as it had with Blake. Her mind knew with excruciating clarity that Monte was dead. With a high, keening wail she slumped against the wagon side and clutched the child within her. Cole reached out to her, but she shook him free and pulled herself up.

She turned and searched his face. A burning rage filled her. How many times had she trusted him to keep Monte safe? He was the one who knew, his was the experience. How could he let this happen? She yanked the blanket down and stared at Monte's crushed chest. She touched the torn, crusted skin of his abdomen. He was cold. Where was his warmth? She felt his hand, scarred and callused. No gentle caress, no strong grasp, only cold, lifeless fingers.

The horror broke over her like a flood, took her under, dragged her low. She was suffocating. Arms held her, and she heard Pearl's voice in her ear, but the words were lost. Her head pounded again and again. *Monte's dead. Monte's dead. Monte's dead.*

♦♦♦♦♦♦♦

Hours passed, or were they years? Mama came, and Pa. With Pearl they laid out the body, but she sent them away. Her own voice sounded harsh in her ears as she resisted their comfort. No one would touch him. No one but she.

Alone, she washed the blood and gore from his flesh. She dressed him in the gray trousers and white shirt, the black coat he'd worn on their wedding day. Every moment that passed drew him farther and farther away. She felt herself dying with him. Her heart scarcely beat, her breath was no more than a whisper of air through parted lips.

Father O'Brien and Reverend Shields came, and other faces passed through the rooms, too. Doctor Barrow . . . Grant . . . Clara. They were like specters with no real form or substance. The doctor had her drink something warm and thick, and weariness overcame her.

♦♦♦♦♦♦♦

When she opened her eyes, the sun was bright. She dragged herself from the bed and felt Pearl's arms supporting her. "There, Mizz Abbie. Go slow now, lessen you faint."

Faint? She wasn't given to faints. Hadn't Monte said as much? Hadn't Monte—her legs gave way and she clutched the bedpost.

"It's the medicine the doctor gave you. He wanted you to sleep through till . . ."

Abbie forced her eyes to focus on Pearl's face. "Till what?"

"They's gettin' the ground ready."

Abbie closed her eyes. A terrible heaviness weighed her down. She could hardly stand against it, but Monte would not go into the ground without her. Doctor Barrow had no right to order it. Who was he to separate her from the man she loved? Had not death already done that?

She wanted to scream, scream away the deadly shell that closed around her heart. "My clothes."

"Mizz Abbie, the doctor . . ."

"My clothes, Pearl." She stood while Pearl pulled the petticoats and the black linen dress over her head. Someone must have let the waist out in the night. Zena or Pearl or Mama.

The hill was covered with people. They looked like black crows perched beside the headstones on the hill as Abbie approached on James's arm. His elderly hand trembled as he wept, but she stood tearless. The pain went far, far deeper than tears. It was a cavernous hole that would never be filled. More and more of her would fall in until there was nothing left but the pain. The grave gaped, but it was nothing compared to the hole inside.

Reverend Shields spoke. " 'Yea, though I walk through the valley of the shadow of death, I will fear no evil . . .' "

Her mind felt detached. Around her people cried. Friends and neighbors, acquaintances, those from town, others from much farther, all came to honor Monte. She saw Marcy on Grant's arm, red-faced with weeping. She saw Pa's eyes swim, and Mama's. Little Tucker stood solemn between them.

Where was Jenny? There beside Zena, safe and cared for. Across the crowd she saw Cole, hat in hand, head bowed. He looked . . . diminished. She turned away and let her gaze come at last to the coffin. Not the pine box that had held Blake but a fine mahogany coffin from the undertaker. Who had made the arrangements?

"We know that this life is but a shade, a passing moment in the span of eternity. Montgomery Farrel knew and loved the ways of the Lord God Almighty. He trusted his soul to the eternal destiny laid out for him from the beginning of time. He was a man of vision, of compassion, integrity, and honor."

Honor. "*The backbone of all that is just and right and good.*" Abbie could almost hear him. "*Honor is doing what you must even when your heart is not in it.*" He had lived that. Monte had personified honor in every deed, every thought, every decision he made.

"He was a man of subtle temperament, slow to anger and generous with mirth. A man of good humor."

Abbie pictured the smile playing on Monte's lips, the raised eyebrow, the amusement in his eyes. She felt the blackness threaten. The pit of pain ate at her soul. Yes, Monte was surrendered to God. Yes, he walked even now the heavenly streets. But why, why, why?

" 'The LORD gave, and the LORD hath taken away; blessed be the name of the LORD.' " Reverend Shields closed his Bible, and four men took up the ropes. Abbie swayed as they lowered the coffin into the hole. She tightened her grip on James and caught Doctor Barrow's frown. Let him frown. Didn't he know it didn't matter? Nothing mattered.

She reached for the handful of earth, felt it filter through her fingers, heard it strike the wood. He was gone. Monte was no more. Pearl took her other elbow, and between the two old servants she made her way down the slope. Her feet moved of their own volition, propelled perhaps by James and Pearl, perhaps by some muscular function not connected to her mind.

She gained the house, went to her room, and locked the door. She refused, over Pearl's mournful pleas, to admit Doctor Barrow. She refused to admit anyone, not Reverend Shields, not Clara, not Grant nor Pa, not even Mama. She was alone in her grief. No loving arms, no grieving eyes would sustain her. She wanted no one, needed no one, trusted no one. She was alone.

♦♦♦♦♦♦♦

Over the side of the stall, Cole watched Pearl descend on him.

"Mistuh Jazzper, I's worried. It's been three days now."

Cole heaved the saddle over the rack. What was three days to a loss like Abbie's? He didn't want to interfere with her grief. God knew she'd had enough to break any lady. She had a right to hurt.

"It's the baby, Mistuh Jazzper."

He rested his hands on the saddle. What did Pearl want with him? Abbie's shocked, condemning look when he'd brought Mr. Farrel home had told him well enough she wanted no part of him. And nothing she could say or think was worse than what he told himself. He had no business letting Mr. Farrel—

"She can't carry that baby with no food and water."

Cole jolted. "No food and water?"

"She been locked in her room three days. She won' let no one in, not even her own mama."

Cole felt like a jackrabbit in a snare, and he'd as soon bite off his own limb as face Abbie. But what was he to do? He stared at the tooled curve of the saddle, then turned. "A'right."

He strode to the house, his stride more confident than his spirit. Zena stood in the hall, wringing her hands. He felt about the same, but he'd make a good show of it for their sakes. He headed up the stairs and tapped the door. "Abbie?"

He hadn't expected an answer. He tried the knob.

"It's locked." Zena twisted her apron. "She done locked herself in."

He hadn't realized they'd all followed him up, even James. The three dark faces implored him, but what could he do? "Open up, Abbie."

Nothing. He stepped back and kicked the door open. Pearl and Zena jumped, but inside, Abbie never flinched. She sat like she was carved in wood. Her face was to the window, but her eyes were blank, hollow, and dark-circled. Shock and dehydration. He'd seen it before in a woman whose husband was shot full of Apache arrows and scalped.

He closed the door behind him. No sense making her a spectacle. He pulled out the chair from her dressing table and straddled it. Guilt and despair churned inside him as the hands on the clock circled the face. She sat there still and mute.

He watched her without a clue what to say. *Sorry about your husband, Abbie. He was the first real friend I had, and I let him die.* He felt her grief invade him. He'd done this to her. He'd failed her. He saw her throat move.

"Why are you here?" Her voice was like wind on dry leaves.

"Cuz I'm the only one ornerier than you."

"Go away."

If she had said it with more life he'd have left, but instead he stood and walked to the window. He stopped in her gaze but couldn't attract it. "I know you want to be alone, but you ain't alone. You got a young'un inside that needs mothering and folks outside needin' you, too."

She said nothing.

How could he break through? The last thing he wanted was to hurt her more, to force the pain to the surface. "I reckon you got a right to hurt, but you don't wanna risk Mr. Farrel's child."

Her eyes flared and met his. That's what he was looking for. If she could fight back . . .

"You gotta think what he'd want, Abbie."

"Don't *you* talk about him."

She said "you" like he was the foulest rattler that slithered the earth. He swallowed the ache and pushed. "I cain't believe he'd want you quittin' like this." He saw her knuckles go white. "He knew you had courage. He'd expect you to carry on."

She stood up sharply, gripping the headboard. "How dare you. You! It's your fault he's dead! You should have helped him, stopped him."

"Don't you think I tried? That bull thrashed him before I—" He staggered back as she flew at him.

Her fists beat his chest. "I trusted you! I hate you! I hate you. I wish it were you the bull—"

"You think I don't know that?" He caught her wrists. "Haven't I wished the same thing?"

"I don't care what you wish! I can't stand the sight of you. I can't—" She cried out, gripped her side, and doubled over.

"Abbie?" He held her arms.

"Don't touch me!" She staggered back to the bed, both hands to her belly.

Cole didn't look twice. He pulled open the door. "Go on in, Pearl. I'll git the doc." If her fury brought on the baby, so be it. He'd take her wrath over them dead eyes any day.

♦♦♦♦♦♦♦

Abbie fought the waves, crying out and slapping the hands that soothed her. She screamed inside at the injustice. She couldn't have the baby without Monte. She couldn't. She wouldn't! Even as the pains increased, she refused her body's need.

"Don't fight it."

But she would fight! The pain seized her, pressing, crushing. Another hand came to her forehead, with a familiar lavender scent. She opened her eyes. *Mama.* Sobs choked her throat.

"I'm here now, Abbie. It's going to be all right."

No. No, it would never be all right. The pain again. She didn't scream. She wouldn't scream. She wouldn't let them know how it hurt. *Oh, Mama.* The faces faded in and out. Someone put a damp cloth to her lips and she sucked. How long since water had touched her throat?

The pain seared through her again and her body convulsed. Where was Monte? *Monte? Why didn't he come?*

"She's wandering," someone murmured.

"Not long now." The reply was terse. She knew that voice. Doctor Barrow. He'd been with Sharlyn when Monte's son died. *Monte's son. Monte's baby. She'd lose the baby. She knew it. Cole had said . . .*

She convulsed again. Her body was tearing apart, acting without any direction from her mind. She groaned with the terrible tightening that stopped her breath and pushed against it without thought. It passed, and with it her strength. She shook all over.

She was dying. She would die. *Yes.* The thought washed over her. *Yes, she would die. She was tired, so tired. Monte . . .*

But the baby. The pain came so hard she ground her teeth and pushed with everything she had—and felt the release. The baby . . . her baby . . . the cry so weak, then stronger, lusty . . . She opened her eyes. Doctor Barrow held him struggling while Mama wrapped him. He stopped crying, and Abbie's heart plummeted.

Give him to me. No one responded, and she realized she'd made no sound. She tried harder, forcing her voice from the depths of her chest. "I want him."

The room swam. Abbie fought it. She noticed Marcy in the corner, Mama bringing her baby to Marcy . . . "No!"

Mama turned.

"I want him . . ." She tried to rise and her head spun, but Mama brought the baby to her. Abbie couldn't lift her arms, so Mama laid him at her side.

She spoke softly. "Marcy has milk . . ."

"No."

Mama bent beside her. "Abbie . . . you're too weak."

"I'm not."

"You have no milk."

Couldn't Mama see her heart was breaking?

Doctor Barrow laid a hand on Mama's arm. "Feeding can wait. She'll not stay awake long."

Abbie panicked. Not stay awake? If she slept, she'd find the baby gone. She clutched him to her side and fought the exhaustion. How could her body betray her? How could . . . she jolted awake, then drifted. No! She must . . . not . . . sleep. . . .

◆◆◆◆◆◆◆

Abbie woke screaming and thrashing in the face of Buck Hollister's sneer as his men, Conrad, Wilkins, and Briggs, made off with her child. Doctor Barrow caught her shoulders as she clawed him and stared through the darkness, desperate for a glimpse of the baby.

"Calm down, Mrs. Farrel."

"Where is he!"

"Quiet now. Your child's just fine."

A sudden weakness washed over her. "Where is he?"

"In the next room with Mrs. Martin. Sleep and fluids are what you need. The more you get of each, the sooner you'll take charge of your son." He handed her a glass of water.

Abbie drank. Her throat was raw and dry. Her body felt like a hollow husk. It no longer had the baby inside, and she felt thin and weak. She sank back to the pillows and closed her eyes. Yes, she needed sleep. As she drifted off her mind wandered. *Mrs. Martin . . . which Mrs. Martin? Mama . . . or . . . Marcy . . .*

Eighteen

Abbie forced herself to drink both the milk and the water on her breakfast tray. Under Pearl's watchful eye, she thrust spoonful after spoonful of buttered grits and eggs down her throat. Then washed it down with tea. Surely, surely her milk would come in.

"That's good, Mizz Abbie." Pearl beamed.

"Bring me my son."

"Yessum. But Doctor Barrow, he said—"

"I don't care what Doctor Barrow said. I want my son. I've spent the whole night without him, and I want him now."

Pearl puffed her cheeks. "Yessum." She muttered her way out the door with the tray.

Abbie sat up in bed. If she didn't need to guard every ounce of strength, she'd go for the baby herself. Why had she been so careless? How could she risk herself and her son as she had? No matter. She would stuff herself until she could nourish her child. He was all she had and no one . . .

She glanced up at Marcy with the tiny bundle in her arms. Fear and fury raced through her veins. She saw tears in Marcy's eyes. What right had she to cry? What right had any of them? It was her loss. Hers and her son's. Wordlessly, Abbie reached for the baby.

Marcy eased him into her arms. "Oh, Abbie, he's the most beautiful baby boy I ever saw."

Abbie studied her baby's face. Raw pain ripped her heart. He was so like Monte, dark and fine featured. His limbs and fingers were long and slender. How could she bear it? How could she bear never seeing Monte's joy? Were the angels in heaven singing? Were they rejoicing that this child had come into the world whole and strong, though all around him grieved?

"Abbie, I know you won't believe me, but I'm so very sorry. Monte—"

"Don't. Don't speak his name. I don't want Elliot to hear and know what he's missing."

Marcy swiped at a tear. Her confusion was evident. Abbie didn't care. She didn't care what Marcy or anyone else thought. Elliot Montgomery Farrel would not be marred by the grief that accompanied his birth. He was perfect. The most perfect child ever born, and nothing would spoil that.

"Tell Pa to fetch Father O'Brien. I want my baby baptized."

"Now?"

"Yes, now, Marcy. Right now. This very minute."

She put up her chin. "You needn't snap. Pa's gone home, and it's pouring rain."

Abbie clenched her teeth against the words she wanted to shriek. "Well, send someone. I don't care who." Abbie held the baby close as Marcy left the room. He slept soundly in her arms to the steady pattering of rain, and she dozed in and out of consciousness. She woke at the tap on the door.

Father O'Brien came into the room more solemn faced than she thought possible. His blue eyes held none of their usual Irish twinkle. Even his flaming hair seemed quenched and drab. Of course, it was wet from the rain outside. He set his bag on the table.

Marcy stood in the doorway with Emily in her arms and Grant and Mama beside her. Pearl and James and Zena crowded the hall behind them. Abbie fought the disappointment. It was not as she'd envisioned it, not the joyous welcome into God's kingdom on earth that her son deserved.

Oh, Monte.

Father O'Brien draped his stole over his neck. "Who'll you be havin' for godparents, Abbie?"

She hadn't thought of that. She looked across the room, the cottony numbness starting in her head again. "Grant?" Her voice was pale.

"We'd be honored." He took Emily and put her into Mama's arms, then urged Marcy forward. She looked uncertain, uncomfortable, vulnerable.

"Grant and Marcy will be Elliot's godparents."

"And what name have ya given the child beyond Elliot?"

Abbie swallowed the knot in her throat. "Elliot Montgomery Farrel." Monte had chosen Elliot after his grandfather, and she had added Montgomery.

"A fine, strong name, and one to wear proudly."

Abbie watched dry eyed as Father O'Brien blessed her son with salt and oil and water, then handed him to Grant to bless with the sign of the cross on his forehead, and to Marcy, then back to her. *Elliot Montgomery Farrel. Elliot, meaning faithful to God.*

"Thank you, Father." Her head was starting to spin with weariness.

"I've someone downstairs who wants to see you, but she's not thinkin' you'll admit her."

Abbie watched the reposed features of her son, his tiny lips suckling in his sleep. "Nora?"

"Aye. And she'd've stayed outside in the rain if I'd let her."

"Of course I'll see her." The heaviness settled in her chest. She heard Nora enter and forced her eyes briefly to leave her child. She noticed the others had left, and Nora stood alone before her.

Nora gripped her hands together. "It's sorry that I am, Abbie. Your Monte was a good man, and I'm ashamed I let my grief color my thoughts and actions. He didn't deserve my ire, and I wish I'd come to know him."

Abbie felt the tears form a hard knot in her throat.

"I don't blame you if you turn your back," Nora continued, "but I'm hopin' you'll forgive me. You've been a better friend than I."

Abbie stroked the baby's soft head with her finger.

Nora came forward and sat on the edge of the bed. "I know

how hard it is. My Jaime was a comely man, his hair like jet and his eyes the blue of twilit sky. But he had a fire inside by the name of freedom, and it burned him fierce."

Abbie's head felt leaden as she sat.

"It's the way of the landlords, you see. They don't want us on the land, and if once we can't pay . . ." She spread her hands. "Eviction isn't only humiliatin', it's . . . inhuman. They came to take down the house. That's how they make certain no one will live there again. They pull it down with the ropes until no stones are left standin'."

Abbie listened.

"When they came, no one was at home to warn them that my grandmother slept inside. She was blind and feeble, but alive nonetheless. They had the ropes on the beams before we came in sight. My mother ran. She gained the door callin' out, but they gave word anyway for the horses to pull. Both she and my grandmother were caught in the rubble."

Abbie's lips parted but no words came.

Nora's voice was barely above a whisper. "Jaime, he took a stick to a soldier on the nearest horse." Her voice broke. "What harm could he do, I ask you?" She pressed her hands together until the knuckles turned white. "The soldier hit him with the butt of the rifle. Then they tied him to the wheel of the wagon and whipped the flesh off his back. It took him four hours to die, and he never once knew I held him."

Abbie met Nora's eyes and saw the raw pain. It quickened her own, but she pressed it down.

"I hoped the tellin' would help you understand why I . . . judged your husband poorly. It's no excuse, but it's all I have." She dropped her face to her hands. "And I'm so dreadful sorry for your hurt."

So that was the secret of Nora's grief. And it was dreadful. She had a right to feel bitter, to shut her heart. There was only so much the heart could bear. Abbie clutched Elliot to her chest. She didn't want to dry and wither as Nora had, but already she felt it beginning. Her voice came thinly. "Thank you for telling me."

Nora nodded. "I'll go now. Maybe . . . when you're stronger, you'll have a cup with me."

Abbie swallowed the ache. "I will."

She watched Nora walk out, straight and unbending, wrapped in her grief but refusing to give in to it. Oh yes, they were akin to each other. More so than she had guessed.

She looked down at Elliot, ran her eyes over every tiny feature. He was part of her and part of Monte. He was all she had of the love that had made her whole and alive. She felt the chasm gaping and clung to the warmth of the baby.

Elliot stirred and screwed up his face. He made a small mewing wail, sucked in his breath, and wailed again. Abbie felt a burning in her chest and a rush. She closed her eyes and released a slow breath, then put the baby to her breast.

◆◆◆◆◆◆◆

"You's gwonna spoil that baby. He's got 'im a cradle to sleep in. If you don' put 'im down, he won' never sleep on his own."

Abbie stroked Elliot's cheek. It was no longer hollow after six days of feeding. He was small but strong and alert.

"Let Pearl take 'im, give 'im a nice bath an' . . ."

"No."

"I know you's missin' Mastuh Monte, but—"

"I don't want to hear another word. I told you I don't want his name spoken."

Pearl hung her head. "Ain' right, Mizz Abbie."

"Right, Pearl? What's right about any of this? The only right thing is this baby, and I won't have him growing up knowing what he's missing."

Pearl muttered and shook her head.

"But you're right. It's time I was up."

"Now that ain' what I . . ."

Abbie handed Elliot into her arms and slid out from the covers. "Send Zena. I'll need a corset to get into my clothes."

"Lawd, Mizz Abbie. You ain' goin' out?"

"Unless you'd rather show Mr. Jasper up here to my bedroom . . . again."

Pearl puffed her lips but went for Zena. In less than a breath the young woman was there to help, and Abbie suspected she'd been listening at the door. The corset brought her waist almost to where it had been before Elliot. Abbie supposed that was because he was taking as much from her as she could manage to get in.

She didn't care. She'd give every ounce of strength she had to keep him healthy. It was a miracle he'd received no harm from her foolishness. Doctor Barrow said that's how it worked. She was the one at risk, for the baby took what he needed from her body's reserves.

But that was over now. She would get her strength back. She always did. And she had a ranch to run and decisions to make. She raised her arms for Zena to pull the black crepe dress on. She sat while Zena stroked the brush through her hair. How strange that it now seemed natural to sit there like a dressmaker's doll with other hands doing for her what she could easily do for herself. How much she'd changed as Monte's wife.

Monte. Would she ever not feel weak at the very thought of him? She knew Pearl disapproved of her decision. Didn't they understand she'd die if they spoke of him? How could she go on, raise her son, take each new breath if the pain sucked away her life? The only way was to cover the pit, pretend it was not there waiting to devour her.

Monte would understand. God would understand. Her hand trembled as she reached for the honeysuckle scent and dabbed it to her throat. She remembered Monte dropping his head to breathe it against her skin. It would be easier to simply die, but Cole was right. Monte would expect her to go on. She would not fail him.

She pushed away from the dressing table and stood. Her hair hung loose down her back. Zena hadn't yet twisted it up. It didn't matter. She had a task that wouldn't wait. She swept downstairs. "James, fetch Mr. Jasper. I'll meet him in the study."

She went into the room, Monte's room. For a moment her heart failed her. She could almost see him behind the desk, raising his head to greet her, putting aside his business to stand and take her hands. *Oh, God, I'll die of the pain.*

She turned when Cole tapped the doorframe with a knuckle. A hard knot settled in her stomach, and she walked behind the desk. A barrier, any barrier is what she wanted between them. She could hardly refrain from throwing herself in his face like a wildcat. The very sight of him incensed her.

She cleared her throat. "Mr. Jasper, I'd like you to find employment on another ranch. If you'll tell me what I owe you . . ."

His green eyes held her. "You don't owe me nothin'."

She looked away. "I'd like to square your wages, but I don't know what you were paid." She pulled open the drawer to the desk and searched for a ledger. There. She took out the leather-bound book and opened it across the desk. She flipped the pages to payroll and found Cole's name at the top. Monte had been generous . . . of course. Her chest squeezed and she looked up. Cole was gone.

Cole crossed the yard. His heart felt like a stone in his chest. What did he expect, that she would turn to him in her grief? She'd lost the only man that mattered to her, and she blamed him for that. She sure didn't need him around to remind her, no matter what Mr. Farrel had charged. How could he keep his promise with things as they were?

You'll just have to understand, Mr. Farrel. It's better this way, Cole thought.

He strode to the bunkhouse and gathered his things. It didn't take long. He slung the roll over his back.

Breck stood in the doorway. "Goin' somewhere?"

"Unless Mrs. Farrel says different, you're in charge here."

"How come?"

"I'm movin' on."

"Where to?"

"The next herd, I guess." Cole looked out across the yard, his glance landing briefly on the house, then away.

"Cole . . ."

"Look after her, will ya, Breck? She's a mighty brave lady, but she's not so strong as she thinks."

"I'll look after her, but Cole . . ."

"Let it go, Breck. I been here too long a'ready. A man might put down roots if he stays too long in one place. And roots is one thing I never wanted."

Breck stepped back to let him pass. Cole stopped and breathed the autumn air. "Sure is a fine day fer hittin' the road."

"Will you keep in touch?"

"Cain't write, but I might send word somehow time and again."

"Look after yerself."

Cole nodded, then headed to the stable for Scotch. He and that old horse had covered a lot of miles. He had a hankering to sleep under the stars again. Too bad the nights were so cold.

♦♦♦♦♦♦♦

Abbie pushed past Pearl standing in the hall with the coffee tray she'd expected her to call for. "Ain' right, Mizz Abbie. Ain' right you cuttin' him loose. Mistuh Jazzper, he's a good man. He done his best by you an' Mastuh Monte."

Abbie spun, her fury flaming inside. "Take yourself to the kitchen where you belong. If you won't honor my request and refrain from speaking . . . of him . . . then you and James may find employment elsewhere, as well." She trembled. She would have to guard her strength.

Turning, Abbie went upstairs to feed Elliot, then took her coat and bonnet and stalked out to the stable. Will stood, sober and unspeaking, and she guessed he'd parted with Cole. In his own way, Cole had looked after the boy these last years, and she guessed Will was not happy.

"Saddle Zephyr for me, Will." No more buggy riding now that Elliot was born. She took the reins Will handed her and mounted. Zephyr tossed her head, and Abbie turned her, then cantered from the yard. The way to Mama's seemed long and difficult, and an ache filled her lower back by the time she reached the house.

She slumped down from the mare's back and clung to the saddle before straightening and going to the door. It opened at her knock, and she looked down at Tucker. He grinned.

"What are you doing out of school, young man?"

"Mama said I can stay with Jenny."

"I see. Well, I hate to disappoint you, but I've come for Jenny. So you have no excuse now."

His face fell, and he kicked the toe of his boot on the floor. "Can't you teach me again? I don't like Mr. Ernst. He's not fun like you were."

"Well, sometimes you have to do things that aren't fun. Learning is its own reward." She saw that her words meant nothing to him. "Where's Jenny?"

"In the kitchen." He dragged his feet down the hall.

Abbie found Mama and Jenny by the stove stirring the crabapples for jam. "I've come for Jenny."

Mama looked up with wide eyes. "Abbie, you shouldn't be up yet."

"I'm perfectly hale." She stooped to receive the tentative hug Jenny offered, then clung longer than she intended.

Jenny wiggled free. "We're making jam. Want to help?"

"Not today. I have to get back to Elliot."

Jenny pouted. "I want to make jam."

"Well, you can't."

"Abbie." Mama took her arm and led her to a chair.

Abbie sank down weakly.

"Let Jenny stay awhile. Have these weeks with the baby; get your strength back."

Abbie rested her head on her hands. Maybe Mama was right. She certainly had nothing to give. Elliot took what he needed, and his warmth in her arms gave her strength. But what good would she be to Jenny?

She nodded slowly. "Do you want to stay, Jenny?"

The child nodded vigorously. It hurt, but Abbie smiled. Children were so honest. Brutally so. But she did feel relieved to let Mama handle her responsibility awhile longer. Jenny was in good hands, and she . . . she was so tired.

It took all her strength to keep in the saddle back home and then walk to the house. She staggered up the stairs to find Elliot wailing in Zena's arms. She sank to the bed and fed him, then slept through lunch and tea.

♦♦♦♦♦♦♦

The next morning was overcast, and Abbie received without interest the breakfast tray Pearl brought. She felt dull and lethargic, and riding Zephyr had caused her to hemorrhage. If she cared to avoid Doctor Barrow, and she did with all her heart, she must be wiser.

She ate and fed Elliot, then dressed and sat by the window with a book. She scarcely noticed which one, and the words passed beneath her eyes without touching her mind. She saw Monte's Bible on the stand beside the bed, but she could not touch it. It would open the pit, and she would fall.

A horse in the yard caught her ear, and she glanced down and frowned. Mr. Driscoll. What did he want? She stood, waited a moment for the dizziness to pass, then went downstairs. James met her at the foot of the stairs, and Mr. Driscoll stood inside the front door. She would have had him stay outside.

"Mizz Abbie, Mr. Driscoll's here to see you."

"Thank you, James." Abbie stood in the hall. This would be concluded swiftly enough she needn't ask him to sit. "Yes?"

"Mrs. Farrel, may I extend my deepest sympathy on the loss of your husband."

She said nothing. Next to calling him a liar, what could she say?

He cleared his throat. "I've come to make you an offer . . . for the ranch."

"I beg your pardon?"

"I figured you'll be selling, and I—"

"I've no intention whatever of selling the Lucky Star. You may go."

"But, ma'am, surely you realize a woman of your tender years knows nothing about—"

His audacity, to come there as though invited, to presume to advise her. His greed showed in his face. "Get off my land, Mr. Driscoll. If you set foot here again, I'll have my men shoot you."

He went white, then red. "You will sell, Mrs. Farrel. Sooner or later. I already hold the deed." He gripped the doorknob and let himself out.

Abbie leaned against the banister. Was it true? Had Monte turned over the ranch deed to Mr. Driscoll? It wasn't possible. But the loan. How had he secured the loan? Had he given in to Horace Driscoll after refusing once? She recalled him pacing in the night, groaning in his sleep. She knew he was worried, but could it have been as bad as that? She rushed to the study, emptied drawer after drawer.

No, Monte. Not the ranch. Not Elliot's land. She sank to the chair and clutched her head in her hands. *Oh, God, how could he?* She braced herself against the chair back. Grant would look into it. He would advise her. Driscoll was right. She knew nothing of running the ranch. But she would learn. It was all here in Monte's books.

She would gird herself with knowledge and fight Driscoll and anyone else who thought to take advantage of her. She would preserve Monte's heritage for his son. One day Elliot Montgomery Farrel would be master of the Lucky Star, and it was her part to keep it running until then.

Part Two

Nineteen

F*or he's a jolly good fellow, for he's a jolly good fellow, for he's a jolly good fe-l-low . . . that nobody can deny.* As Abbie set the cake on the table before her son, Elliot's blue eyes radiated excitement. He extinguished the four candles with one wet puff.

"You didn't make a wish." Jenny tossed her dark braids over her shoulder. "And it's too late now, because you have to do it before the candles are out."

"I did too wish. I wished—"

"If you tell it, it won't come true."

Elliot looked up at her, and Abbie felt a pang. How like Monte's were some of his expressions. Already his little eyebrows quirked expressively, and he had the natural Farrel grace of motion. His dark hair and straight features were Monte's, and he would be tall one day.

Only his eyes were hers. Their blue so closely matched her own that sometimes she longed for them to go brown like Monte's. But at four years old that wasn't likely. He was a handsome child, drawing people's glances, as did Jenny.

At seven she was as precocious as she'd been at three. Though her tantrums no longer took her to the floor in sobs, she still demanded more than she gave. Yet little Elliot withstood her control. His even temper soothed her, Abbie guessed, and Jenny knew he'd not fall for her pouts. Elliot had a poise and dignity beyond his years.

She looked around the table at the children seated there. Sadie's youngsters, Matthew and Hannah, sat beside Marcy's Emily

Elizabeth and Clara's Dell and little Roger. On the other side were the Irish redheads, Katie, Danny, Colin, Meghan, with eleven-year-old Tucker at the end. Around the children stood the mothers and friends who'd come to make Elliot's day special.

Abbie looked at her sister, Sadie. She'd taken the train from Denver to be there with them. Glenna stood straight and winsome, with Nora beside her. Clara stood with Emmy and Pauline, the mission orphans she'd taken in, who now stood almost as tall as she and a good deal more slender. Clara looked to be carrying twins, though Doctor Barrow doubted it. Marcy leaned on the hutch, her golden hair pulled into a chignon at her neck, and her hand resting where her new baby grew but didn't yet show.

Mama brought the knife, and Abbie put it in Elliot's hand, then helped him cut into the warm marmalade cake. Pearl beamed when his little finger snaked out and swiped the sticky glaze. Abbie sliced the cake, then turned it over to Zena to serve.

She stepped back beside Sadie and feigned exhaustion. "Now that they're eating, we can breathe."

"He's a wonderful boy, Abbie. Monte would be so proud."

Abbie stiffened and turned away. "Pearl, bring the ice cream."

The children cheered when Pearl spooned the frozen cream onto their plates. Abbie doubted Glenna's little ones had ever tasted it, and it was rare enough in this house these days. She'd splurged and had Pearl make ice cream rather than the butter and cheese they sold in town. This one day she refused to scrimp, no matter what toll it took. Elliot would have the best day of his life.

When the children had been washed clean of marmalade and cream, Abbie ushered them all out to the yard. She bent and tied a scarf over Elliot's eyes, then motioned to Will. He was a gangly eighteen and looked even taller with the small pony in tow.

Abbie spun Elliot until he staggered, then pointed him toward the pony and let go. The children erupted in giggles and hoots as he wove forward and collided with the shaggy side of the pony. He pulled off the blindfold and crowed. Abbie had traded a good brood mare for the animal. The man had taken her for a fool, but she didn't regret it one bit.

Will hoisted Elliot to the pony's back and handed him the halter rope, though he kept hold of the headpiece. Elliot sent Abbie a brilliant smile and kicked in his small heels. The pony walked obediently in circles as he directed, but he might have just won the new Kentucky Derby the way he held himself in the saddle. Her heart swelled.

"Mrs. Farrel?"

Abbie turned. "Yes, Breck?"

He took his hat from his head. "Sorry to interrupt you, but . . ." He glanced briefly at the others.

Abbie stepped clear of the crowd and approached him. "What is it, Breck?"

"John Mason. He's come down sick."

Abbie glanced over her shoulder. He must be more than sick if Breck was bringing it to her attention. "Where is he?"

"In the bunkhouse."

"I'll meet you there in a moment." She walked back. "Mama, I have to check on something. Will you see everyone off?"

"Is anything wrong?"

"I'm not sure. John Mason's ill. I may need Doctor Barrow."

"I'll send the others home."

"I think that would be wise." Abbie hurried to the bunkhouse behind the stable. Breck stepped aside for her to enter, and she eyed John Mason thrashing on the bunk. With one look she could tell that he was burning with fever. "When did this start?"

"Some while ago, I reckon. Didn't seem so bad until today."

Abbie stooped beside the bed. "John?" His face was splotchy, and where his shirt fell open she saw rosy spots on his chest. "Go for the doctor, Breck." She rushed back to the house. She didn't bother Pearl or James or Zena. She would keep this to herself until she knew what she was up against.

She hurried into the kitchen and got a clean cloth and bowl. Out in the yard, she filled the bowl with cold water at the pump, then hurried back, sloshing as little as possible. A starling darted to the branch of a cottonwood, then parted its sharp black beak and shrilled.

Abbie passed into the stuffy bunk room. Kneeling beside John Mason, she swabbed his forehead with the cloth. He mumbled, but didn't seem to recognize her. "It's all right, John. The doctor's on his way."

She wiped her forehead with her sleeve, stood, and opened the door and windows. The August sun burned in the sky with no clouds in sight. No wonder John Mason was burning up. She hoped it was nothing serious, but he looked bad—as sick as she had ever seen someone since Sharlyn. And Sharlyn had died.

He thrashed continuously, curling up and holding his abdomen. Was it his appendix? Clara's husband Marty had an attack last year, and Doctor Barrow had taken it out. But Clara had said nothing about pink splotches. She bathed his brow again, then turned when Mama's shadow filled the door.

"I've sent everyone home but Sadie. How is he?"

"He doesn't look good."

"Let me see." Mama came close. She let out a slow breath. "I'm no doctor, but I've seen this before."

"What is it?"

"Typhoid. It swept the Auraria mining camp when you were small. Do you remember?"

Abbie frowned. It seemed she did recall a bad sickness that had kept her and Sadie and Grant from playing outside the tent. Hadn't Blake's sister. . . ? "Is that what Mariah had?"

"Yes. She recovered, but the fever . . . turned her mind."

"That's why she's the way she is."

Mama nodded.

Abbie tried to picture Mariah without her nervous tension and bewilderment. She would have been about Jenny's age when the typhoid struck. Sudden fear chilled her. She glanced down at John Mason. He wasn't much older than she, and in his distress looked younger yet. But he'd been a faithful hand, working as hard for her under Breck as he had for Monte. "I wish the doctor would hurry."

She heard a horse in the yard and went to the door, but Breck rode up alone. He swung down and removed his hat. "Doc can't come. He's got three cases of typhoid in town and a handful more scattered around. He said we best bring John Mason to him."

Abbie brushed her fingers through her hair. "Well, hitch up the wagon, then. Where are the others?"

"Matt and Curtis are on the range. We got the beef herd separated to ship out next week. Skeeter's ridin' fences—"

A thump on the wall made them both turn, and Breck rushed to the end of the bunkhouse. Abbie hurried behind him and saw Skeeter crumpled on the ground. From the smell, he'd soiled himself, and his eyes were bright with fever. Abbie gripped the edge of the wall. What horrible thing could so decimate a man?

"Get the wagon, Breck. We'll take them both."

Mama touched her arm. "Maybe I'd better take the children home with me."

Abbie felt a tremor. Could she bear to send Elliot away even for a time? She looked down at Skeeter. What choice did she have? Elliot was too fond of running down to the bunkhouse with Jenny, and she wouldn't risk . . . no, she couldn't even think of it. "I'll have Zena get them ready."

As Breck went for the wagon, she and Mama headed for the house. Sadie waited in the parlor with Matthew and Hannah, who played blindman's bluff with Jenny and Elliot. Abbie leaned close to her sister and whispered. Sadie's lips parted with concern, but Abbie squeezed her shoulder. She didn't want to alarm the children.

"You'd best stay with Mama, too. I'm sorry." And she was. Sadie's visits were too far between to miss one. Abbie hardly knew her niece and nephew. But it couldn't be helped. The children must be safeguarded, and Sadie, as well.

"Maybe I should go back to Denver." Sadie steadied Hannah, who bumped into her knee blindly, then turned, arms outstretched, and groped in the other direction.

Mama sighed. "As much as I hate to say it, you probably ought to take the first train out."

Mama spoke too softly to be overheard, but Abbie caught Elliot watching. He was altogether too perceptive.

She bent and swept him into her arms. "How would you and Jenny like to stay with Grandma and Grandpa for awhile? It would be a grand adventure for your birthday."

"How long would we stay, Aunt Abbie?" Jenny clasped her hands behind her back and swung her skirts.

"I'm not sure right now."

"I'll stay with Mama." Elliot wrapped his arms around her neck.

She closed her eyes and rubbed her cheek against his soft hair. Already the ache was starting. "Jenny will need a young man to look after her, Elliot."

"I'll look after myself. I like adventures." Jenny's taunt was more effective than Abbie's request.

"I like adventures, too." Elliot released her neck and frowned.

"You're afraid of adventures because you're little." Jenny's eyes had a teasing glint.

"I'm big. I'm four now." Elliot's cheeks flushed.

Abbie cupped his face. "And you're just the one to accompany Jenny. Your pony will go with you."

His eyes widened. "I can take Ralph?"

"Ralph?" How had the child come to that for a pony's name? "I don't think Ralph would miss the adventure for anything."

"Of course, I'll bring Snowdrop." Jenny slid her arm around Abbie's waist with her most manipulating smile.

Abbie glanced at Mama, who nodded permission to send along the small mare that Jenny rode.

Jenny beamed her triumph. "I'd better go pack at once. I'll bring Amanda and my animals." She used her grown-up tone as though packing her toys was of utmost importance.

Abbie smiled. "Pack Elliot's train." Her quick mention of the train stifled her son's longing for animals like Jenny's. For whatever reason, Elliot coveted the little animals Cole had carved for Jenny, but she hoarded them like treasure. Abbie sighed.

When Zena had the children ready, Abbie lifted Elliot into Mama's buggy. She fought the panic rising inside. It was unnatural, she knew. Four years was too long to still fear having him out of her sight. She'd been very careful not to let it show, but she suspected he sensed it. She must let him go now; his life could depend on it.

She gave Jenny a hug, though Jenny had less need of it than she, then helped her into the carriage. Will tied the mare and pony behind. Sadie waited while Matthew and Hannah climbed in, then took her place beside them. "Maybe you should leave, too, Abbie."

Abbie glanced at Breck bringing up the wagon. She could go. She could be with Elliot. She wouldn't have to be separated. Breck took off his hat and wiped his forehead with his sleeve. He waited respectfully while she decided.

"I'm needed here." She stepped back and waved with more cheer than she felt. If Elliot once suspected the pain in her heart, he'd never go. She forced herself to smile as the buggies pulled out. They were only going to Mama's. They would be with Pa. He'd keep them safe. They'd be fine. But would she?

Breck had Skeeter and John in the wagon bed, with enough padding under their heads to take care of most of the bumps. "Curtis helped me load 'em in. He's denyin' it, but he don't look too good, either."

Abbie pulled herself up to the wagon seat. "Maybe it's just the heat."

"Maybe." Breck took up the reins.

Abbie was glad for the wide brim of her hat. The sun was relentless as it sank toward the mountains. The men in the wagon bed moaned, and that sound scared her more than the rest of it. Seeing strong men like Skeeter and young men like John brought low enough to writhe was not encouraging.

They stopped the wagon in front of the clinic. Doctor Barrow came outside, looked into the bed, and nodded. "Take them to the town hall. We're setting up an infirmary."

"An infirmary?" Abbie climbed down. "Are there as many cases as that?"

Doctor Barrow took off his spectacles and wiped them on his shirt. "We found that drifter—the one you folks took in for a piece. He died just east of town. Seems he made the rounds to a number of homesteads and took a good many meals."

Abbie recalled the stranger who'd taken shelter with them for a couple days. He'd looked ill and hard on his luck. Breck had given him an odd job or two in exchange for food and a bunk. He'd even ridden out on the fall roundup and worked with the cook in the chuck wagon. "He died of typhoid?"

The doctor nodded. "And the worst of it is he camped awhile upstream on Monument Creek. Anyone who's drawn water from there . . ." He spread his hands.

"Is there a serum or . . ."

"I wish there were. Right now the best we can do is quarantine the patients."

Breck shifted in the seat. "Is there someone at the hall to help me unload these men?"

"The marshal's there with Ethan Thomas. I'll be coming myself as soon as I've gathered my things."

Abbie helped Doctor Barrow carry the crates of medicines and cloths. These would help ease the discomfort, but only the victim's constitutions would determine who lived and who . . . She stood in the door, looked at the cots and blankets set out across the floor, and fought the anger. Death was too fierce an enemy.

Breck joined her. "I'll get you home now."

"They'll need help here."

He looked back over his shoulder. "I reckon they will. But you got young'uns to think of."

"I've sent them with Mama."

"I saw. But you don't want to be exposed. You're all the parent they got."

Doctor Barrow passed by and barked gruffly. "Go on, now."

Abbie went out. She was silent all the way to the ranch. Pearl was boiling a massive pot of onions, and the whole house smelled of it.

"What are you doing, Pearl?"

"Onions keep the sickness away."

Abbie ran her hand over her forehead. One hour in that oniony steam would keep anything away. She sank to the chair. "It's typhoid, Pearl."

"I know. I got me a look at them in the wagon. John Mason, he in a bad way."

"They both are."

"You was wise to send the chillen away."

Wise, yes. But her heart ached. Elliot had filled her days since Monte . . . She rested her forehead on her palm. The house seemed oppressively quiet—no pattering feet, no chattering voices. She would even welcome a spat. She straightened. "I'm going to bathe. Will you boil water?"

"Yessum. And you takes this onion in with you."

Abbie glanced from Pearl to the onion and back. "I will not bathe with an onion." She raised a hand when Pearl opened her broad mouth to argue. "I don't care what it does, I'll not have it." She went to the back room and slid the large tub to the center of the floor.

Going out to the pump for water was a pleasure, and she thanked God that they drew water from the well and not the stream.

♦♦♦♦♦♦♦

Abbie tossed and twisted. She listened for his voice, for the sound of his soft breathing. She groped in the darkness. He had to be there, he had to; if she could just . . . *Oh, Monte, I've lost your son. I tried to keep him safe . . . I tried . . .* She threw the covers off and sat up in bed, shaking.

She'd go mad. Three nights of dreams that left her panicked; she couldn't take anymore. She had to bring Elliot back. . . . What was she saying? What was she thinking? Would she risk him to stop her nightmares? What if he caught it? What if his mind turned as Mariah's had? What if he . . . No!

She dropped her face to her hands. With both Skeeter and John Mason coming down sick, who knew how badly contaminated the ranch was? At least at Mama's he was safe, he and Jenny both, she reminded herself, feeling a twinge of guilt that her fear for Jenny was not equal to what she felt for Elliot.

She would go and see them tomorrow. She would hold Elliot as long as he allowed her. She would . . . What if she carried it there? Doctor Barrow said typhoid was transmitted through contaminated water or food . . . or contact. She had doctored John Mason, who even now clung to life by a thread. How could she be certain she was not infected?

She lay back in the bed. She could not go to Elliot, and she felt as though part of herself was tearing away. It was like losing Monte all over again. Why, why, why? She heard Mama's soft voice. "*You must not allow yourself to become unnaturally attached to the child.*" How could she not? He was all she had . . . of Monte.

She closed her eyes. *Why, God? Why must I be separated from my son, too? Was it not enough to take Monte? Are you never satisfied?*

She shuddered with the blasphemous thoughts and recalled Reverend Shields' words. " '*The* LORD *gave, and the* LORD *hath taken away; blessed be the name of the* LORD.' " At the time she had hardly heard him speak, but somehow the words had been blazoned on her heart.

They had driven everything she'd done these last four years. She'd filled her days trying to appease the God who could take from her anything He liked. Part of her knew that was not the way of a loving God, but the pain inside said otherwise.

It was easier now to drive the hurt away. She had Elliot and Jenny . . . and the ranch. She had not missed a single payment on the loan in four years. That was thanks in part to Grant's arranging for lower payments over more time. She felt a supreme satisfaction every time she handed over the payment to Mr. Driscoll's greedy hand. She would pay back every cent without fail.

She drew a long, slow breath. She'd talk to Pa in town tomorrow. He would tell her how the children were faring. He would tell her if Elliot missed her as she did him. Oh, Elliot. For his sake she hoped not, but the message would be a thorned rose if Pa said no. She stared into the darkness until her eyes closed on their own.

Twenty

Abbie opened the door the next morning to Breck standing hat in hand. "Oh no, Breck. Not someone else."

"I'm real sorry, Mrs. Farrel. John Mason passed on in the night."

It was as though he'd kicked her. John Mason? The young, blushing cowboy . . . gone? Had he breathed out his last moments while she fretted over separation from her son? Why had she not dropped to her knees and prayed for him? Was she so absorbed in her own pain that she had not even thought of his suffering?

"And Skeeter?"

"He's bad."

"Have Will saddle Zephyr."

"Mrs. Farrel, you ain't thinkin' . . ."

"I am going to the infirmary."

"It ain't no good, Mrs. Farrel. Doc's got people workin' round the clock. Ain't nothin' no one can do that ain't bein' done."

Abbie dropped her hands to her sides. "I can't just stay here and wait for the men to die." But she knew Breck was right. She had a responsibility to Pearl and James and Zena, to the other men still working, and most of all to the children. She looked past the outbuildings to the land resting in the summer heat. What was she to do? Carry on? "What about the herd?"

"Matt and Curtis and I'll get 'em to the train and send 'em off. They're scheduled to go tomorrow."

"Can you manage shorthanded?"

"Ain't that many head. Five hundred steers. We can manage."

Five hundred thirteen to be exact. Not that many, but enough to bring the money she desperately needed. Beef prices were down, but if she could pay only interest on the loan today and make up the principal with the sale, she'd have some breathing room at last. If Mr. Driscoll balked . . . She wouldn't think about that. She had considered asking Pa or Grant to help, but times had been thin for Pa, and Grant was hard put to keep Marcy as she demanded. Abbie doubted either could cover for her without hardship.

"I won't go to the infirmary, but I must see Mr. Driscoll. Please have Will ready Zephyr."

"Yes, ma'am." He replaced his hat.

She watched him cross the yard and thanked God under her breath that he at least was spared from the typhoid. She could not have done it these last years without Breck. She wondered sometimes why he stayed on with her when he could earn more at the other ranches, especially whenever someone new set up headquarters. They offered top dollar to seasoned hands who'd help them get up and running.

But Breck and the others had stayed. Even John Mason. *Father forgive me for failing him, and please help the others.*

She tied on her hat as Will led Zephyr to the steps. "Thank you, Will. Please ask Breck—"

"Will!" Breck staggered around the side of the stable dragging a man by the shoulders. "Give me a hand here."

Abbie ran with Will. The man Breck held was Curtis. He struggled to his feet, thrust himself away from Breck and ran behind the stable. The sounds of his intestinal distress reached them in the yard.

Abbie cringed. "Get the wagon, Will. Fill it with blankets."

She heard Curtis arguing with Breck. "I ain't goin' to no infirmary. It's comin' too fast an' furious."

"You got no choice. It don't matter if you mess yourself. You gotta see what Doc can do."

"Doc can't do nothin'. Look at John Mason."

"You gotta go anyway. Anyone who's got it is quarantined.

Think of Mrs. Farrel." Breck came around the side with Curtis slumped against him. The stench was foul.

Abbie stared with dismay at Curtis Potts. His eyes were haunted, his strong face screwed with pain. He collapsed in the wagon bed that Will backed toward them, then curled like a baby and groaned. That left Breck and Matt. *Dear God, preserve them.*

"Keep Zephyr, Will. I'll ride in the wagon with Breck."

Breck stepped between her and the wagon. "No, ma'am. You take yer own horse."

She shook her head. Breck was starting to sound like Cole. The thought felt sour inside her. "I'll thank you to remember who's in charge here."

"I know who's in charge, but I got my orders."

"Your orders?" She stared at him, and he flinched. "Whose orders?"

"Look, ma'am, I didn't mean—"

"Oh yes, you did. Who's giving you orders, Breck?"

"It ain't like that."

She swallowed against the sudden dryness in her throat. "Suppose you tell me what it is like?"

He circled his hat in his hands. "It's just . . . Cole said look after you. He sends up extra money to . . ."

Abbie's breath came in a sharp burst. *Cole!* So that was why the men had stayed. Cole bribed them. All this time she thought they respected her, accepted working for her, had loyalty, integrity . . . She took hold of the pommel and mounted, then turned Zephyr's head and pressed with her knees.

The wind whipped her hair into her face, but she urged Zephyr to more speed. *How dare he?* The audacity . . . She felt like a dry well. She'd accomplished nothing. Extra money. How had Breck used it? To keep the men, surely, but how else? Had he shored up her deficiencies?

How could Cole have extra money? What could he do to earn enough to send some away? How? . . . Angry tears threatened, but she forced them away. Zephyr tired, and Abbie reined in to a walk. She felt more betrayed than she had since . . .

Oh, God, you knew. You let me creep on thinking I could stand. When all the while Cole Jasper . . .

She drew a long, shaky breath. She had to compose herself to face Oscar Driscoll. She would do it. She would not allow Breck's confession to make her stumble. She would stand if it took losing every man in her employ. She'd run the ranch alone if that's what it took. She pulled up before the bank, dismounted, and smoothed her hair. Then drawing herself up, she went inside.

Mr. Driscoll met her himself at the counter. "Mrs. Farrel. It's always a pleasure when you grace this establishment."

"Thank you, Mr. Driscoll. May I see you in your office?"

"Of course." He pushed open the gate, then followed her into the small, but plush space behind the clerk's cage. He motioned her to sit. "I'm sorry I've nothing to offer you."

He always said that, and she wondered if it hadn't a double meaning. "That's quite all right. I've a request to make." She was certain she didn't imagine the glint in his eyes. She took out the interest payment and set it on his desk. "May I pay only the interest on the loan this month? I've a beef herd ready to ship that will bring in the rest by next month."

He cleared his throat and took his chair behind the desk. "Well, I must say I'm not surprised. I understand you've had several men succumb to the typhoid."

News traveled fast. But then she supposed Mr. Driscoll made it his business to know others' misfortune, anything he might turn to his advantage. "As I said, the sale of the beef—"

"Yes, yes, yes. Well, of course. How could I refuse your request under such circumstances as those you're facing? However, there is something you should know. Have you been yet to the railroad office?"

"No, why?"

"Well, it seems no trains will be coming along this spur as long as the town is quarantined."

"The town is quarantined?"

"So far as the railroad is concerned. They'll take no one in or out, and they'll not carry any livestock from the area at all."

Abbie sank back in her chair. "But . . ."

"I'm sorry, Mrs. Farrel. You look pale. May I offer . . . a spot of sherry?"

Abbie gripped the arms of the chair and straightened. "No, thank you. Forgive me, but I'll verify this news, then decide what's to be done. Thank you for granting my request."

"Uh, yes, but under the circumstances . . ."

"You'll have payment from the sale."

"But how will you make the sale if you cannot transport the cattle?"

She smiled tightly. "I'll find a way."

Once outside, Abbie felt her stomach knot. How? What way? Oscar Driscoll had known about the railroad when he granted her request. Had he only agreed because he thought there could be no sale and she would default on the loan?

He had been fair thus far, but she knew he only waited for her to slip once. He was honest, but not compassionate. Hadn't he capitalized on her ignorance in the dealing with Kendal, then held Monte responsible? Didn't he hold her to the letter of his agreement with her late husband regardless of her difficulty? She was certain he had only agreed so readily now because he believed she couldn't make the sale.

She looked down the street and saw their wagon outside the infirmary. So Breck had arrived with Curtis. Only just. He came back out with Ethan Thomas and together they hauled Curtis inside. She forced away thoughts of Breck's betrayal. After all, what grounds had he to refuse Cole's money? Cole was the one to blame. Cole Jasper. Did he think he could pay for Monte's death?

Abbie shrank away from the memory. She'd spent four years purging the scene from her mind. Monte in the wagon, Cole . . . The look on his face had told her everything. She'd rather die than look in that face again and see his pity.

Well, she couldn't undo any of it now. She had a more critical problem—five hundred head of cattle to drive to Kansas. Breck would have to find men, but where? All who'd been on the roundup were at risk of typhoid contagion.

She walked the length of the street to the infirmary. Had Breck heard yet of the railroad's ban? She climbed the steps and looked in the door. The room was filled with the sick, and there were women and children among them now.

Abbie saw Reverend Shields beside a cot and across the room was Father O'Brien. Had it spread to the Irish homesteaders? No, it was Ferdy Gaines he sat beside, speaking low. Was he offering the comfort of the afterlife? Reverend Shields leaned forward and closed the eyes of the man beside him. She couldn't tell whom it was. The stench and overwhelming misery caught in her throat.

"Mrs. Farrel." Breck took her arm, pushed the door open, and tugged her out with him. He cleared his throat. "I apologize for earlier." His voice sounded weary.

She didn't want to discuss what he'd told her. "Breck, we have a problem."

"I reckon you mean the railroad." He let go of her arm at the foot of the steps.

"We need to make that sale. I've no choice in that. We'll have to drive the cattle ourselves, but we'll need men."

"Mrs. Farrel . . ." Breck sagged against the wagon, and she noticed the sweat beading his forehead.

"Breck? No . . ."

"Get Cole. He'll help ya. He's madder'n a hornet that I told ya, but . . ." He gripped the side of the wagon and winced.

"What are you talking about?" She caught his arm. "Let me help you inside."

"I can make it alone. Cole—"

"Don't be ridiculous. Where would I ever find him? He's left the state for all I know."

Breck doubled over. "He's back . . . at the Red Slipper right now." He stumbled to the pillar and caught hold, then climbed the stairs and went in.

Abbie stared after him. Had every one of her men been infected? All because of the drifter. What was his name anyway? A man passing through, bringing death in his wake. *Oh, Lord.*

Should she even think of the cattle, of the ranch, of anything but the suffering of those inside?

She pictured Mr. Driscoll's face. He didn't care who suffered. He'd expect payment even if every one of her men died. If she missed next month's payment with this month's principal added on, he'd take the ranch. She had to get the herd to Kansas, but how? Cole? She shook her head. No. She'd drag them there herself before she turned to him.

Abbie suddenly felt the immensity of the task. She couldn't save the ranch. She'd fought and scraped and kept her head up, no matter what. Even when they lost forty of the cattle to disease, even when a brush fire had taken a dozen more, she'd fought back. She'd built up the herd little by little. And now after four years, she had enough to make a good sale.

"Why, Lord?"

The sky held gray rumbling clouds but no answer. She glanced down the street. The Red Slipper stood just past the hotel and Peterson's hardware. Beyond that, the bank. She closed her eyes, imagining Driscoll's look of feigned dismay. "*So very sorry to evict you. . . .*" What had Nora said? Evictions are not humiliating, they're inhuman.

No. Mr. Driscoll would not pull down the walls. He coveted the house and property for himself. Where would she go? Back with Mama? To Grant and Marcy? She shuddered. They'd made a tentative peace, but not enough to live under the same roof. Mr. Driscoll thought she should consider any number of bachelors or widowers. What business did a young lady have running a ranch? Especially a ranch he wanted.

Her anger quickened. Well, he wouldn't have it. And if she had to abase herself to Cole Jasper to save the Lucky Star . . . She groaned silently, then trudged forward. The sand on the boardwalk gritted under her shoes as she approached the swinging doors. The banjo and piano could be heard in the street.

Didn't they know people were dying? Who could frolic inside a place like that when men and women lay dying down the road? Apparently Cole Jasper could. She pushed the doors open and went in. The smell of whiskey and tobacco caught in her nostrils, and her heel slipped on a hawk of brown spittle in the sawdust.

She searched the smoky haze and saw Cole standing at the bar with Lil Brandon hanging on his arm. Abbie knew the woman's name, though she didn't recall how. She'd come in with the train and made herself popular with the men. She fairly purred at Cole's side now, and he seemed none too reluctant.

The sight of him made her blood burn. It churned the memories until she nearly choked. She couldn't do it. She turned back, but . . . if not Cole, who? Slowly she approached the bar. Lil saw her first, and no wonder. Cole was busy admiring the fingers Lil laid over his. He was certainly living up to her expectations.

"You lost, lady?" Lil twanged.

Cole turned. She could read nothing in his face but a hint of surprise. He looked harder but no older. The same unruly blond curls, roughly cropped, with the thick mustache and a couple days' growth of whiskers on his tanned chin, a dusty kerchief, flannel shirt . . . He held her steadily with his green eyes but said nothing.

She summoned up her courage. "I'm looking to hire someone to drive my herd to Kansas. I have five hundred head of marketable beef."

He narrowed his eyes, then turned away. "I ain't fer hire."

Abbie felt the blood rush to her face. Did he mean to make her beg? "I'll give you ten percent of the sale . . . fifteen percent."

He looked back with a flicker of . . . anger?

She realized she still owed him the wages he'd refused to collect when she'd sent him away. "Name your price. If it's within my means—"

"I don't want your money, Mrs. Farrel." He moved his hand out from under Lil's and stood alone, contained, self-sufficient.

Abbie felt the thrust of his ire as he stared her down. Breck was wrong. It couldn't be Cole who'd sent the money. He was meaner and cockier than ever. Who did Cole Jasper think he was? She spun.

"If it's a favor you're askin', I'd consider it."

So that was it. He wanted her to grovel, cry out her need. He was striking back, and she was vulnerable. Abbie felt the fury crawl her spine like a live thing. She should keep walking, shake the dust of Cole Jasper from her shoes, and walk out the door. But then what? She thought of Elliot and Jenny.

Her throat was tight and dry as she turned back. Lil looked as though she'd swallowed lye, and Abbie guessed she didn't appreciate the interruption. Abbie forced her voice to sound frank and disinterested. "Very well, I'm asking."

Cole reached for his hat, put it on, and tipped it to Lil. Then he turned to Abbie. "After you."

Abbie couldn't get outside fast enough. His insolence burned her. She hadn't expected him to come right away, hadn't expected . . . To her dismay she realized she was shaking. Well, what did she expect? It was too much! John Mason dead, Skeeter and Curtis sick, and now Breck . . . then Cole and his money . . .

The thought put steel in her spine. If she made what she should from this sale, she'd pay back every cent he'd squirreled by her to Breck. She imagined stuffing it into his fist and showing him the door. What if he wouldn't take it? What if he expected something else? What could he possibly want from her—an apology? An easing of his conscience? Abbie whirled and unintentionally smacked into his chest, then jumped back as though scalded.

"Pardon me." Cole's tone was brazen, but he didn't smile.

"If you won't accept pay, what's in this for you?"

He hooked his thumbs into his belt. "You got a job needs doin'; I'm doin' it."

"Why?"

He looked over his shoulder, then back. "As I recall, you asked."

"I don't want you to think—I mean, this is a job only, nothing more. Normally I'd pay . . ." She stared at the ground, at his boots, at the boardwalk, across the street.

"I ain't sure what you're goin' on about, but if you're concerned at my motives, you can rest easy. I ain't lookin' to marry a widow."

Abbie felt the breath leave her chest. How could he? *Oh, Lord, I can't do this.* The hatred boiled up and overwhelmed her. She looked straight into Cole's eyes. "I'm sorry I bothered you, Cole Jasper. It was a momentary lapse in my good judgment. Please, don't let me keep you from your . . . entertainment." She spun and stalked to her horse, wishing Zephyr had wings. Halfway to the ranch, she dismounted, ran as hard as her own legs would go, then screamed and screamed to the wind.

Cole stood in the street, watching her go, then took off his hat and ran his fingers through his hair. He hadn't intended to provoke her like that, but the feel of her against his chest had churned emotions he thought long dead. One thing was certain: her opinion of him hadn't changed. He drew a heavy breath.

Mr. Farrel, I wonder if you realized what you was askin'.

He replaced his hat and crossed the street to Scotch. He'd find out from Breck what they were up against and get the job done. It wouldn't be easy. But he had made a promise. And he meant to keep his word.

♦♦♦♦♦♦♦

Abbie walked the boundary of the south range, Zephyr's reins in hand. The beef herd was separated and waiting, ready to cover her debts for some time to come, but she had no way to get them to market. Could she take them herself?

She'd watched the men on occasion. She could rope a horse but lacked the strength to haul in a steer. She could snap a whip and whistle and shout. If it were just a matter of keeping them moving . . . What was she thinking? She didn't even know where to go.

She may as well face it. She'd thrown away her chance to drive the herd to market. What now? She could beg from Pa and Grant, no matter what the cost to them. Between them they might cover the debt for a month or two. By then Breck and the others would be over the typhoid. But what if they didn't recover? What if she had to start over with men she didn't know, didn't trust?

How could she keep the ranch going? Must she lose that next? *Why, Lord? Haven't I tried? Haven't I listened and worked and served? Must I have nothing left?* No, she couldn't think like that. She had the children. It struck terror in her soul to think she'd offended God with her questions. What if He required the children, as well?

She would die. It appalled her how often she thought of that. But it was true nonetheless. If anything happened to Elliot and Jenny, she would have nothing to keep the breath in her body. Not even the land spoke to her anymore. It had become too much of a struggle.

Maybe she should let it go, take the money Mr. Driscoll offered and . . . and what? The blackness of her mood sank to her feet and they dragged in the buff-colored grasses. She smelled the sage and felt the breeze. It had an early autumn feel to it. The season was changing, and so was her life.

She felt a pain as real as any fleshly hurt. What if she let the ranch go? She could find a position teaching, enough to support herself and the children. She'd keep whatever she made on the sale for Elliot, his inheritance from . . .

Oh, Monte. You must understand. I can't do it alone. I can't do it without you. I'm not even sure I want to. What is the Lucky Star without you? Barren land too stubborn to yield anything but trouble.

Abbie kicked at a yucca—the all but indestructible plant known as the Spanish Bayonet, or soapweed to the Indians. The yuccas would be there generation after generation. *Lord, show me the way. I'm tired and confused.*

Courage.

The word seemed to emanate from her spirit. Abbie closed her eyes and stood with the breeze in her face. Courage. So she couldn't quit. Somewhere inside, she'd known it. But where she would find the strength, only God knew. *God knew.* Did she believe that? She had to. She'd go stark raving mad if she didn't.

Twenty-One

Abbie was hardly surprised when Cole knocked on the door early the next morning. He was too stubborn to let it go, but he looked as though he'd slept as badly as she. Good. She hoped his insolence choked him.

He tipped his hat up. "I cain't find Breck. Thought you might know where he's off to."

She stilled her anger. "He's in the infirmary."

Cole frowned. "He's got the typhoid?"

"That's right."

He released a sharp breath. "Who do you got for the drive?"

"What concern is that of yours?"

He leaned against the door frame, his hips slack and his mouth a stubborn line. "I told you I'd drive yer cattle. Now, who you got?"

She relented. If Cole was God's answer, she'd bear the cross. "So far Matt Weston's not come down with symptoms."

"And?"

"He's the only one."

"You tellin' me I got one cowboy to drive the herd to Kansas?"

"How many do you need?"

"Fer five hundred head? Two with experience, plus a chuck wagon and wrangler."

"You'll have them," Abbie asserted with more confidence than she felt.

He eyed her dubiously, then hooked his thumbs in his belt. "A'right. I need some money."

"I thought you said you didn't want my money." She sounded as smug as she felt.

"We need supplies."

Now she felt as foolish as she'd sounded. "Oh. Get whatever you need and tell Mr. Simms I'll square with him after the sale."

"Right. You boil up bedding fer four men, have it rolled and ready. I got my own."

"Boil it?"

"If it's been slept on with typhoid."

Abbie shuddered. When Cole left, she found Pearl in the kitchen. "Pearl, pack up whatever James will need to cook with on the trail."

"What you talkin' 'bout? James don' cook."

"We're driving the cattle to Kansas. And he's the cook."

Pearl brought her hands to her hips. "An' what you s'pose you is?"

"Wrangler, I guess. Will and Matt are the cowboys."

"Mistuh Jazzper, he not gonna like this."

"Mister Jasper's not in charge. I am." Abbie untied her apron. "Now, you gather pots and utensils and tell Zena to make bedrolls for four." She was not about to use the men's bedrolls from the bunkhouse. She had enough fresh blankets at hand in the house.

Pearl and Zena would have to see to the animals and all other details in their absence. She sent Will to help Matt ready the herd and prepare the remuda. When Cole came back with the supplies, she'd have everything laid out and ready. Then he'd hardly be able to argue.

When Abbie had seen to all that she could without further direction, she went to her room. Her heart pounded in her chest when she pulled open the wardrobe that held Monte's things. They smelled fresh in the cedar lining. She sagged against the door. She had not opened it since she'd packed them all in there. But she could hardly go on the trail in skirts and petticoats.

With trembling hands she pulled out beige trousers. Monte had been slender enough for a man, but the waist . . . She would cinch it with a belt. Abbie held the sleeve of the fine linen shirt to her cheek. *Oh, Monte.* She stripped to her chemise and pulled the shirt over, then rolled and tied the cuffs with ribbon.

She cinched the pants and pulled her boots over the rolled cuffs, then stood, strangely comforted by Monte's trappings. His scent was destroyed by the cedar smell, but the clothes had touched his skin. She viewed herself in the mirror. She looked like a boy—well, not entirely. But a vest would help with that. She used the green velvet vest from her riding habit. It was fitted and shapely, but it would do.

With a tap on the door, Zena came in and gasped.

Abbie turned. "Here." She handed her a note. "Take this to Mama's." She'd thought better of going in person. She'd never be able to leave Elliot so long if she laid eyes on him for a moment, especially if he was upset by it. Her chest constricted, but she fought it. Mama would see to him and Jenny.

"And this letter is to be delivered to Mr. Driscoll at the bank. It explains my decision and contains another month's interest payment. See that it's in his hands today."

Zena nodded mutely.

Directly after lunch, Abbie put her wide-brimmed hat on her head and tied it at the throat. Pearl puffed her lips and muttered, but she knew better than to argue. Abbie went into the yard when she heard the wagon rumbling in. Cole would have already seen the stacked items to be loaded. He gave her a slow look down, then leaped from the seat. "I see the stuff. You got the men?"

She'd fed the men and given their assignments. "Matt's on the herd. Will's roped in the remuda. He may not be experienced on a drive, but he's worked with the men and he can learn." They could all learn.

Pearl came out with another armload of things for the chuck wagon. She muttered low as she tucked them in among the foodstuffs Cole had already arranged in the wagon bed next to the firewood and tools. James stood hat in hand, looking from one to another of them as though hopeful he would receive a last minute reprieve.

Cole leaned against the wagon. "So where are the men?"

"James will cook, and I—"

"No way you're ridin' this trail."

Abbie jutted her chin. "I can catch and care for the horses, saddle and unsaddle. I can chop wood and snap a whip if I have to. You said you need a wrangler; here I am."

Cole swore.

Abbie stared, then clamped her mouth shut. If he wanted to show how rough he could be, she'd show how little she cared. "Now, then. This isn't a crack-of-dawn start, but we can cover some miles before sundown."

Cole shook his head, opened his mouth to argue, then clenched his hands and held one finger to her nose. "Get one thing straight. I'm givin' the orders."

She swallowed her retort and nodded curtly.

He shook his head again and unwound Scotch's reins from the hitching post. He was definitely not happy, and she felt little better. Spending the next two months with Cole Jasper would be like bedding down with a rattler, but she'd won, and that gave her a smug satisfaction. Abbie mounted Zephyr and circled around to where Will waited with two dozen horses. He gave her a sly grin, then sobered and joined Cole.

Cole barked orders and they started out, catching up to the herd at the eastern edge of the Lucky Star range. Matt had lowered the fence; they were ready. Cole raised his hand and whistled, and they left the ranch behind. Abbie pulled her kerchief over her mouth as she trailed the line of cattle with the spare horses. She glanced back at James driving the chuck wagon.

Her heart swelled at the sight. They would do it. They would get the cattle to market and make the sale. She felt fleeting gratitude toward Cole Jasper, then reminded herself she'd pay him off at the end. He was necessary at the moment, but she didn't have to be happy about it.

So help me, I'm a bigger fool than I thought. Cole spurred Scotch and set a brisker pace for the cattle than necessary. He'd have the trail broke by tomorrow if he kept it up, but at the moment the thought of pushing the swagger out of Abbie Farrel was incentive enough. He circled round, hollering and snapping the whip.

He ought to use it on her hide for good measure. He passed the remuda without comment, cut in front of the wagon, and started back up the other side. The Herefords hadn't the spunk and muster of the Longhorns, but they were less excitable, too. That didn't mean they wouldn't spook or stampede, but they'd be less inclined to go off at any provocation and wouldn't run so fast and far.

He pushed the pace until they were well away from the home range, cracking his whip and whistling when the cattle lagged. He was riding point with Matt, and across the backs of the animals behind him he saw Will holding his own. *Experienced.* He shook his head.

Abbie Farrel was more than any one man should have to bear. He'd have liked to strangle Breck when he learned he'd told her about the money. He'd hoped to go on providing with her none the wiser. Now he'd have a fight on his hands—as though bustin' broncs and fleecing seasoned gamblers for the extra funds wasn't punishment enough.

Just before sundown he gave word to Matt and Will to throw the herd off the trail to graze and water. Full-bellied, well-watered stock was more prone to rest easy and less likely to spook. Cole searched out a bed ground with good elevation and dry grasses, such as the herd would choose on its own if they were range cattle.

Then he marked their own campsite near a quiet bend of the creek. He'd kept everyone at it hard, as much to wear out the herd as to show Abbie she wasn't as tough as she thought. But watching her dismount, he had a pang of remorse.

She walked stiffly to the wagon, which James had brought to a halt. From the back, she took out stakes and a hammer. At Matt's direction, she strung a rope from the wagon to one stake and then to another, making a triangular corral to hold the horses for the night. This close to home they might be tempted to head for their own pastures. Will helped her get the horses to the water. A few days on the trail, and Matt and Will would be too weary to take on extra work.

Cole shook his head. He'd set a more reasonable pace tomorrow. He strode to the wagon and took the ax from Abbie's hands. "Get some water ready."

She didn't argue. He splintered the log, then set the next one in place until he had enough for a good fire. The night would be cold. That was one reason they shipped cattle in the fall instead of driving them. Water was another. By August and the start of September all the seasonal streambeds would be running low if not dry. But he didn't tell Abbie that. If she thought she could do this, who was he to stop her?

He piled the wood next to the circle of stones James had formed. "Sure hope you cook better'n I do."

"I don' cook at all, Mistuh Jazzper. Mizz Abbie, she say throw it in the pan an' get it hot. I say throw what in?"

"Sheez. What happened to Charlie?"

"His heart give out last year. Mizz Abbie, she feed de men at de house now."

Cole kicked a log back to the pile and stalked to the wagon. Abbie was stirring batter in a bowl.

"What're you doin'?"

She answered without looking. "Making cornbread."

"So you're cook and wrangler?"

"If need be."

"You won't make it one week keepin' that up."

She flashed her eyes at him. "Try me."

They sat around the fire and ate beef and cornbread and beans that tasted better than anything Charlie had ever forked up, and he'd been one of the best chuck-wagon cooks around. Cole glowered. He scraped his plate clean and set it on the stones by the fire.

"Find a saddle, men. Let's close 'em in." He remounted with Matt and Will and began circling the herd tighter and tighter. The muleys naturally hung back until the horned steers had lain down. They'd be the first up, too, a self-protective instinct amidst a crowd of sharp-horned partners.

When they had the herd bunched in and lying down, Cole nodded to Matt. "You got first watch, Matt. Wake me at midnight." He dismounted.

Abbie took the mare's reins. "What about me?"

"What about you?"

"When is my watch? I expect to do my part."

He kicked the dirt and looked out across the open land. If she didn't beat all. "A'right. I'll wake you at two."

She led the horse to the corral and unfastened the saddle. Cole watched her heave it off and carry it to the row of saddles by the wagon. She put a hand to her lower back, then straightened and made her way to the bedding she'd spread between the wagon and the fire. James was already snoring a short distance away.

He turned and dumped his own bedroll on the ground. He sat down, rolled a cigarette, and lit it. He took a long drag, blew the smoke slowly, and shook his head. *A dern fool and no doubt about it.*

Abbie lay in her blankets in too much pain to sleep. She was accustomed to riding, even riding hard, but not for so many hours at the pace Cole set. She more than suspected he'd done it on purpose. They'd changed horses twice before he made camp, and not all the Lucky Star horseflesh had as smooth a stride as Zephyr. She would harden up, she knew, but that was no consolation at the moment.

She leaned on her elbow and watched Matt slowly circling the herd. He sang softly. She couldn't catch the words, but the tune had a loneliness that echoed her own. She missed Elliot so fiercely it hurt. She gripped her ribs and buried her face in the blanket lest she moan and betray her ache.

Was he snug in his bed dreaming beautiful dreams? Did he miss her? How would she ever bear the weeks without him? It wasn't possible, but she had to do it. Without the sale, they'd lose the ranch. And now that she'd decided to do this, she had to give it everything she had. For Elliot. And Jenny.

But not to have his little arms around her, hear his laughter, watch his every expression. Not to whisper in his ear her love, not to smother him with kisses until his giggling grew to a shriek . . . Abbie clutched herself tightly and moaned. If she got through this she'd never leave him again. Never.

Maybe, maybe if they kept up this pace they'd be there in less time. Without driving a herd back home they could go much faster. The whole trip could be done in . . . five weeks, four? She'd work hard, bear any pain without complaining, if it brought her back to Elliot sooner. Maybe the railroad ban would be lifted and she could take the train home. *Oh yes.* She drifted off imagining the reunion with her son.

♦♦♦♦♦♦♦

Cole stood over Abbie. With her face cradled in her arm and her hair lying loose, she looked so sweet it stabbed somewhere deep. The night's chill didn't seem to reach her flushed cheek, and her eyes were soft with shadow. He stooped, refrained from stroking the hair back from her face, and touched her shoulder instead.

She opened her eyes. They looked foggy for a minute, then fastened on him. "My turn?"

"Look, Abbie, why don't you just sleep . . ."

She sat up and shoved the sleeve that had unrolled back up over her hand. Her fingers were clumsy as she searched out the ribbon and retied it. Then she threw the blanket off and stood up. She shivered and bent for the coat she'd laid beside her bedroll. "I just ride and sing, right?"

"And watch."

"For?"

"Wild things, uneasiness in the herd, anything sudden or loud. Look, you ain't—"

"I can do it." She raised her chin. "So go to sleep already."

"Get Will up at four."

She checked the small clock that hung at her neck and nodded.

"I got you saddled."

"Thank you." She walked stiffly to the horse, and he saw her wince when she climbed up. He could kick himself from here to Kansas.

Cole settled into his blankets but couldn't sleep. Just knowing Abbie was out there circling the herd made him restless. It went against everything he knew. When snatches of her song reached him, he would've liked to block his ears, so badly did he want to get up and relieve her. But she insisted on doing this her way.

He rolled to his side and yanked the blanket over his shoulder. But he was still awake when she bent to waken Will. This was going to be one weary trail.

Twenty-Two

In the dim light, Abbie woke so stiff she thought she'd grown paralyzed overnight. She gritted her teeth and forced her legs to slide out from the blanket. Her back ached from her tailbone to her neck, and muscles she didn't know she had cried out for recognition. She pushed herself up and felt in her shoulders and arms the effect of pulling saddles on and off all day.

She'd be lucky to lift one this morning. She caught Cole watching her from where he crouched by the fire, and smoothed away all signs of discomfort. He was ornery enough to turn back if he thought she couldn't make it. She wouldn't give him that satisfaction. He had the fire going and, by the smell, coffee boiled and bacon frying.

Shame rushed to her cheeks that he'd done her part. She saw James chopping kindling with the small hatchet. With his grizzled head and hunched back he looked too old to be out there. Why hadn't someone wakened her? Abbie tried to stand, but pain shot up her legs. She looked to see if Cole had noticed. She'd be mortified if he had to help her up, but he was pouring a steaming cup of coffee.

Steeling herself, she got to her feet. Once there, walking wasn't so bad. She extended her hands to the fire to chase the chill. Cole handed her the cup and she took it. She sipped the coffee. It was strong and bitter but the warmth felt good.

He tossed his cigarette and crushed it with his boot. "If you want the eggs to be edible, you'd best see to them. I got the bacon ready."

She went to the wagon and dug the eggs out of the flour barrel. So far none had cracked. She broke each into the bowl and whisked them. The motion sent pain shooting through her arm, but the stiffness was passing.

She forked the bacon to a plate and poured the eggs into the drippings. With a spoon she turned them until they were plump and moist, then she pulled the skillet from the coals. Will held his plate out without hesitation, and she scooped them on with a smile, then served Matt and Cole, then James and herself.

At the rate Cole shoveled it in, they'd be on the trail in no time. Good. The sooner they were done with this, the better. She refused to think of Elliot waking up without her. Had Mama told him it would be a long, long time before she was back? Or was she letting each day tell its own story?

How were Breck and Skeeter and Curtis? She eyed Matt as she scrubbed up the pan. How was it he'd escaped the typhoid? She wiped the pan dry and hung it on the wall of the wagon. A shadow fell over her washtub, and she looked up at Cole.

"Why don't you ride in the wagon today? Will can take the horses, and Matt and I will handle the herd."

"I'm perfectly capable of riding."

Cole swiped his jaw with the back of his hand, then shrugged. "Suit yerself." He walked away and hollered to the men to saddle up.

"I pack it up, Mizz Abbie." James stuffed the bedrolls into the wagon one by one.

She nodded, wiping her hands on her pants. One thing she hadn't thought to bring was an apron, but likely soon enough she wouldn't care. She roped in Starlight, the four-year-old mare, and saddled her. The minute she was up she realized what a mistake she'd made riding the saddle again, but she was not about to let Cole know.

Abbie whistled between her teeth and moved the horses down with the herd to graze. They trailed along gently for two hours while the animals ate; then Cole and Matt and Will began stringing them out, and once again Cole set a brisk pace, though not, she thought, as brisk as the day before.

If she didn't think about it, the pain in her saddle-weary areas was bearable. At least it kept her from brooding on the inner pain of separation. She should have said good-bye. Jenny especially needed that. She was so afraid of losing the people she loved, and Abbie knew that in her own way Jenny loved her.

It wasn't the warm expressive love Abbie might have wanted. It was love on Jenny's terms. Not like Elliot, who seemed to sense her mood and fill the need with nothing spoken between them. How like Monte he was, warm and affectionate. Her horse stumbled and she cried out, then bit her lip against the jarring pain. Starlight was no Zephyr.

Cole circled around, and Abbie straightened in the saddle. The position put pressure on her inner thighs where the pain was worst, but she maintained it until he was past. He didn't turn her way, but she knew he was watching. Let him think what he liked; she could do this.

At noon they spread the cattle and horses out to graze along the trail. Abbie clung to the side of the wagon while James pulled out the pans and lit the fire. She stirred up hash and corn. In the Dutch oven she soaked dried apple slices in cider and brown sugar and topped them with dumpling batter. She covered the pan and set it in the coals to simmer while the hash heated.

Her coffee was neither strong nor bitter, she noted with pride when she took a sip, and Will and Matt were effusive in their praise of her apple dumplings. Even though the sun was hot, there was an autumn tinge to the air. By evening it would be brisk, and she guessed this night would be colder than last. Well, there were extra blankets should they need them.

They rode again, changing horses once in midafternoon. Freckles, her spirited gelding, had a choppy gait, and riding him was sheer misery until they finally stopped when the sun was no more than a sliver over the distant mountains. Abbie could scarcely remember seeing a sundown that didn't silhouette the rugged peaks, which were now dwarfed by the expanse of empty land between them and her.

Abbie gripped the pommel and prepared to dismount. She willed her leg to come over the saddle and swing down, but it wouldn't obey. She closed her eyes and grit her teeth against the pain, then startled at the grasp on her waist. Cole eased her down, and though the shame of it sent fire to her cheeks, she allowed him. Otherwise she'd spend the night on the gelding's back, and as far as she was concerned, she never wanted to see that horse again.

"Take it slow." He supported her forearm and led her toward the fire ring James was building.

James had loaded the stones in and out of the wagon each time they set up camp where no stones were at hand. As she walked stiffly toward him, she hoped this would not prove too much of a strain on him. She didn't know how old he was, but he'd seemed bent and grizzled the first time she met him at Monte's door.

Cole stopped her four steps short of the blaze. "Stand here a minute."

His command was gentle, and she obeyed. The last thing she wanted was to sit on the hard ground. Besides, if she went down she'd be there for good. He came back from the wagon with a bedroll and set it behind her.

"How can I cook, sitting on that?"

"I'll cook tonight."

"You?"

"I've kept alive, ain't I?" He nudged her down.

The soft roll was immensely better than the hard saddle. She looked up to see Matt tending the horses. Across the camp, Will looked little better than she. He was no doubt every bit as saddle sore and bone tired. She sent him a weak smile, and he returned it. Well, they'd each have a few hours before their watch required them back in the saddle.

Cole's stew was tolerable if a little scorched. A touch of sage and parsley or any seasoning besides his liberal use of pepper would have helped, but she was hungry enough to enjoy it regardless. She washed it down with coffee, though she'd have preferred tea. Why hadn't she thought to bring some? She should have known Cole wouldn't stock it.

She spread out the bedroll where she sat. Since James managed the cleaning up, she may as well take the chance to sleep. In the deepening darkness, while Cole and Matt circled the herd to make them lie down, she knelt and prayed. So many people were heavy on her heart, not least the men fighting the typhoid.

She prayed they'd recover, she prayed the fever would not spread, she prayed for Nora and her friends. And she prayed for Mama and Pa and the children. Her chest squeezed. No. She would not fear for them.

Mama and Pa lived away from town, they pumped their water, and they had not taken the drifter in. Her children were safe. Elliot was safe. She opened her eyes and saw Cole had returned. He was seated cross-legged on the ground, watching from across the fire. He sipped his coffee but didn't turn away.

The intensity of his expression kindled her resentment. She lifted the blanket and slipped beneath. The fire crackled, and tiny flecks of light leaped up and vanished. Her muscles throbbed, but her eyes were heavy and she let them close in blessed oblivion.

Cole frowned. The only way he'd get through eight weeks of this was to put her out of his mind and let her fend for herself. He could do it, too, if he had a mind to. Problem was, he was so starved for just the look of her that he couldn't turn the other way. And when he looked, he'd notice how brave and tenacious she was and get to thinking of all the times she'd surprised him.

Like that time with Buck Hollister and the Comanches. Hearing her tell it the morning after she'd returned safe from capture by outlaws and rescue by Indians had sealed her in his heart. How many years ago was it now? Seven, eight? That she could hardly stand the sight of him didn't change it, except to keep him mindful of what a dern foolish thing it was.

He swirled the coffee in the bottom of his cup, then tossed it to the flames. Morning would come too soon to sit brooding now. He climbed into his blankets, but couldn't get out of his head the feel of her waist in his hands. He scowled. She'd ride in the wagon tomorrow if he had to tie her to the seat.

♦♦♦♦♦♦♦

Abbie woke to the first traces of dawn. Cole was stoking the fire. He laid a piece of log across the top. Did he never sleep? She realized with a start that she'd missed her watch. Had he tried to wake her? No. He'd meant to take her watch. He felt sorry for her.

Her ire brought her fully awake, and she sat up. Cole glanced over. She stood before he could lend a hand. The pain in her muscles was acute but not debilitating. Maybe sleeping through had helped. Maybe she was growing accustomed. She walked to the wagon and took out the pot for coffee.

She dipped it in the water barrel and brought it to the fire. "I'll thank you to wake me next time."

"It don't matter."

"I intend to do my part. Will's as sore as I am, but I imagine you woke him."

"If he takes on a man's job, he oughta do it like a man."

"Then maybe you ought to consider me a man."

From where he squatted, elbows on thighs, he glanced up and held her in his gaze. "That ain't rightly possible."

She turned and stalked to the wagon, returned to lay the greased griddle on the fire rack, then went to the wagon again without a word. With vicious strokes she stirred the batter for the hotcakes. She hoped they choked Cole Jasper.

She left the cleaning up to James and went to water the horses. Will offered to do it, but she refused. She felt battered and stiff and wanted nothing more than to be in her soft bed with Elliot in her arms, but she'd be darned if she'd give in to Cole's opinion. She had the first horse saddled when he joined her at its side.

"Ride the wagon today, Abbie."

"I will not."

"I'm not askin'."

She faced him squarely. "Let's get one thing straight. I don't need you to look after me. We both know how that turns out."

She saw him stiffen, but her vitriol was unleashed and she wanted to sink it deep. "The only back you watch is your own." She watched his jaw tighten. "And another thing. I don't want you slackening the pace. The sooner we're through with this the better."

"You tellin' me how to do my job?"

"If I have to."

"If you want yer herd delivered alive, you'll leave it to me." He took her arm and walked her sharply to the wagon. "You're ridin' here today."

"I'll ride where I please and keep the pace."

"I ain't gonna push these animals now that they're trail broke, and I ain't gonna bury you."

The pain exploded inside her. She looked at him with all the venom that coursed her veins. "Why not, Cole? It's what you do best."

Whatever effect her words had, he kept it from his face. His eyes were mirrors, flatly reflecting her venom. He let go her arm and walked away. The fury left her cold. She felt a hard knot in her stomach and a weariness deeper than her muscles. She looked up at James, who'd taken his place on the wagon seat. His old, dark face was creased with concern. Silently she climbed up beside him.

◆◆◆◆◆◆◆

Selena Martin held Elliot to her chest and rocked. That he missed Abbie was obvious, but then how could it not be so? She'd barely had him out of her sight these four years, and now it was as though she'd gone out of his life. His small sobs stilled as she rocked.

She glanced at Jenny reading by the fire. She'd put on a hard little shell and pretended she didn't care taffy that her auntie was gone. Selena knew different, but the child didn't show it. She kept up her charade with painful dignity.

Jenny talked on and on about the things she had, as though recounting the list would keep them from disappearing. She talked about her dolls and her books and her carved animals. She talked about her mare and the barn cats and even the cattle. But she didn't talk about Abbie, and she didn't cry.

Elliot cried and took comfort here against her chest. Selena sighed. She had read Abbie's note three times before she believed her daughter had actually gone on the cattle drive. Whatever possessed her? Didn't she realize the danger, the hardship, and risk to herself and the children both?

Learning from Pearl that Cole Jasper had returned and was driving the herd for Abbie had assuaged some of the worry. He was a trustworthy, capable man. Still . . . Selena stroked Elliot's cheek. She hoped Abbie knew what she was doing.

Twenty-Three

Cole stood looking out at the darkening sky. The thunderheads were heavy with rain, but that wasn't what concerned him. It was the noise that went along with them. He'd set up camp early, suspecting trouble, and it looked like trouble was indeed rolling their way.

He glanced at Matt and Will sitting by the fire in the fading light of day. It would take all three of them to keep the herd together this night, circling opposite directions so no steer could get loose without being sighted. Even so, stopping five hundred head was no easy task for three men if it came to it.

Abbie dished up plates of beans and biscuits and handed them to the men at the fire. She set Cole's on a rock and walked back to the wagon. He strode over, took it, and went back to watching the storm. It was moving their way, no denying it. He ate the food absently, then returned the plate to the stone.

"No one's sleepin' till this storm is past."

Matt scratched his hand through his tangled brown hair. "I reckoned that."

Abbie came and picked up his plate to wash.

"Abbie, I want you and James to bed down in the wagon." Her lips parted, but he stanched her argument. "It ain't no time to get maidenly. There's a storm comin' that's got this herd jittery, an' I don't want you trampled if they bolt."

"What about the rest of you?"

"We'll be on horseback till it passes."

"Then I'll ride with you. You'd have another hand if I were a man, and I doubt you'd order him to sleep with James."

Two weeks hadn't changed her tune. "If I had another hand, he'd know what to do in a stampede."

She brought up her chin. "So tell me."

"It ain't a matter of tellin'. It's a matter of knowin'. Here." He pressed a hand to his gut.

Abbie turned away and washed the plate, then loaded the supper things into the wagon. The wind gusted and flapped the canvas cover. She flipped the hair from her eyes. He couldn't tell whether her expression was submissive or resistant. She'd built up walls so high, he doubted she was in there at all.

And that suited him fine . . . as long as she stayed out of his way. He strode to Scotch and mounted. Matt sent him a questioning look. "I'll tell you when I need ya." He rode out among the grazing herd, sensed their disquiet. It was time to ring them in. He doubted they'd lie down, but at least packed together they'd be inclined to run the same direction.

He took a good look at the lead steer. He'd keep his eye on that one. If he ran, he'd have a contingent. That steer with the white eye-patch was jumpy already. He'd herd him deep inside where he'd feel the others around him. Several of the muleys clustered together away from the rest. They could make a heap of trouble if they'd a mind.

Cole rode back to the fire. "Let's put 'em to bed."

Will and Matt joined him and they circled the herd in. Any skittish ones, he pressed through, keeping the solid steers to the outer edges. As he'd guessed, they kept their feet. He heard rumbling in the sky, but that wasn't the kind of thunder that brought trouble. It was the flashes of lightning and the sudden cracks of thunder that sent a herd careening.

With the three of them, it would be all they could do to keep this a short night. Great drops of rain started and gathered speed until the water ran from his hat brim. He motioned Matt and Will to their positions, and together they circled, singing low in the scant hope they'd soothe the herd. *Ip-e-la-ago, go 'long little doggie, You'll make a beef steer by-an'-by . . .*

The rumbling came again overhead, and Cole tensed. He willed himself to relax. Nothing set the cattle on edge so quick as a nervous cowboy. Scotch held steady. That horse was like his own flesh, though he was growing too old for this kind of business. Cole schooled his mind to focus on the soothing rhythm of horse and song. The rain beat down, and Cole circled, slow and steady, slow and steady.

Abbie watched Cole position himself between the distant herd and the camp. The rain had slackened to a thin drizzle, though the sky hung heavy and ominous. Water ran from his slicker, and his head was bowed, hat pulled low. There was no glow of a cigarette. Instead she heard the wavering tones of a harmonica. She'd not heard him play before. Maybe it was how he soothed the cattle in a storm.

It had a comforting tone, she had to admit, and she recognized the tune, "Wayfaring Stranger." Where had Cole learned the Negro spiritual? She knew it from James's singing while he worked. Once again, she realized how little she knew about Cole Jasper.

And that was just fine. The less she knew the better. Once she had felt close to him, trusted him. Now she knew better. But wasn't she trusting him again? The thought nagged. She trusted his expertise with the cattle. Monte had done as much. But then, Monte had trusted Cole with his life.

The pain gnawed. She had never asked Cole exactly what happened. It was enough that he had failed. She recalled the night Cole brought Monte home beaten by Captain Gifford, felt again her fury that he'd let Monte go in alone. So what that Monte had ordered it. Cole should have known.

Yet he had risked his life to rescue her from the rustler. Time and again he'd been there when she needed him. She didn't want to think about that. She pulled the coat around her shoulders and peered out of the hole in the canvas.

James sat hunched in the other end of the wagon, as uncomfortable as she. Who did Cole think he was, ordering people to do unnatural things? Maidenly indeed. But then he might think nothing of "bedding down" with a strange woman. She recalled his hand under Lil's and frowned.

Lightning streaked the sky and thunder cracked. She could just make out Matt and Will still circling the far edge of the herd in the near darkness. In a gust of wind, she saw Cole raise his head. The harmonica stopped. The storm seemed to hold its breath. Then suddenly lightning slashed down with a queer buzz and split a tree on the low hill behind the herd.

The fireball sprang up, brilliant in the night. Abbie felt the jolt in the ground beneath the wagon. Will's horse reared, then the sudden bawling and trampling drowned out the fresh torrent from the sky. Cole wheeled and fired his gun, spurring Scotch to the side to point the herd. But the cattle kept coming. They would trample him. Again and again he tried to point in, but the force of the rushing animals withstood his effort.

Abbie sat forward and gripped the wet edge of canvas. She watched with fascination and trepidation as Scotch spun and veered sharply, then leaped up a grassy mound and charged ahead of the oncoming rush. Why didn't Cole move aside? He could get out of the way—The sudden realization choked her. He was trying to turn them away from the wagon.

He cut across and fired again and again into the ground just ahead of the steer's hooves. The front steers balked, but others piled on and the lead steers went down beneath a rush of hooves. Cole fired again, riding hard, his gun making firefly flashes.

She smelled the rain, the gun smoke, the herd. She could almost smell the fear. Cole dropped his spent shells and reloaded even as he charged toward the herd. He shot the ground before the oncoming tide. The lead cattle turned aside, and like a wave the others followed, scarcely eighty feet from the wagon.

Abbie felt the vibration of their hooves and loosed her breath. Would they stay turned? Would they scatter? Cole rode hard alongside, shooting and shouting. Matt was with him now, and they rode hard together though their voices were swallowed by the storm.

Lightning flashed and thunder cracked. The pounding of hooves continued as the herd passed out into the night. The rain fell so thickly Abbie could no longer see the rushing animals. Thunder continued in the sky.

"Mistuh Jazzper, he a good man."

Abbie turned to see the whites of James's eyes. What did he expect her to say? She sank wearily down. Yes, Cole had done his job. She shuddered to think of the cattle charging the wagon. She had a clear enough memory of Monte's crushed and trampled buggy when the Longhorns stampeded over it.

Once again Cole had risen to the task of keeping her safe. Why, why had he not done as much for Monte? She wanted to scream, to slap James for his insolence. How dare he suggest Cole was good? What good was he when Monte needed him?

Great gasping sobs seized her at the image of Monte's torn and battered abdomen, his shattered ribs and cold, lifeless flesh. But she staunchly thrust the sobs away, clenched her teeth against the tears. She hated Cole Jasper with as much passion as she'd loved Monte. And if James said one word more, she *would* slap him.

Cole pushed Scotch to stay alongside the herd until he knew all the steers had passed the camp. Each new flash of lightning and crack of thunder renewed the herd's terror and kept them running. Scotch was fagged, but Cole kept on.

If the cattle scattered, they'd lose precious time—time they didn't have. Again and again he pointed in, trying to turn the cattle, force the tide. If he could make the cattle mill, the men would keep them circling until they ran out of steam. But he couldn't do it. He didn't have men enough to stop the flow.

The ground was fast becoming a mire. The cattle would have to slow. If he just kept alongside . . . A lightning flash illumined the jut of rocks, and Cole swerved too late. Scotch screamed as his foreleg caught the edge of rock, and they went down. Cole landed hard on the jagged rocks. Pain shot through his side and head, and his leg was caught beneath the thrashing horse.

Pricks of light danced in Cole's eyes as he pulled himself loose and grabbed the horse's head in his arms. He spoke low, and the horse calmed, though he could see its eyes stayed wide with pain. Slowly he made his way over Scotch. He ran his hands down the bloody foreleg, and his stomach lurched when he felt the bone shift.

He closed his eyes and clenched his teeth, then smoothed his hands over the horse's shoulder. Why Scotch? He should have taken another horse, any other horse. He should have slowed, not pressed so hard. The last of the cattle passed at a lope. They were tiring, some limping. If he'd only held on a few minutes more.

Cole lay for a long time with his head to Scotch's neck, long enough for the herd to make some distance. Then he pulled his hat from the mud running off the rocks and stood. Scotch thrashed, then lay back. That horse would never carry him again. He felt a sick ache in his gut when he pulled the gun from its holster. He drew a long slow breath, then held the barrel to Scotch's head. "I'm sorry, old boy. You been fine." His voice broke as he pulled the trigger.

♦♦♦♦♦♦♦

Abbie stirred from her doze to see Matt riding in. The rain had stopped, though the air still hung heavy, and thunder could be heard a long way off. Dawn would come soon. Quietly, so as not to disturb James, she slipped from the wagon.

There was no stoking the coals. The whole pit was filled with rainwater. But she dug a new hole, took dry kindling from the wagon, and started a blaze in the new fire ring. The men would need something hot to chase the chill. She filled the coffeepot and set it to boil on the grate as Matt stooped beside the fire.

Will rode in and half fell from his horse. He picked himself up and staggered to the fire, where he dropped to the ground and rubbed his shoulder. He looked totally spent.

Abbie handed him a blanket. "Coffee'll be ready in a minute. Where's Cole?"

Matt drained the rain from his hat brim. "Had to put his horse down. I gotta bring him a new mount, but he said to make sure y'all were okay first."

"What happened to Scotch?"

"Broke his leg on some rocks."

Abbie handed Matt a cup of coffee. Will shook his head to the cup she offered and lay down on the wet ground. With a groan he fell asleep. Abbie pulled the blanket over his shoulders. Matt drained his cup and stood wearily. How could he go on?

Abbie straightened. "I'll bring a fresh horse to Cole if you tell me where he is."

"No need. I'll get 'im myself."

In the east the sky lightened to a dull gray. James woke and went about chopping kindling and slicing the slab of bacon. She laid the bacon in the pan to fry and mixed up oats and water to boil.

It was cooked and bubbling before Cole rode in with Matt. In the predawn dim, she could not make out his features, but he moved like he was played out . . . or worse. He dismounted and staggered. Was he injured? A guilty concern stirred inside her.

He had thrown his slicker off, and she saw blood on the side of his shirt and a gash at the back of his head. He slumped against the back of the wagon and lit a cigarette. Abbie dished a plate and carried it to him.

"No thanks." He didn't look at her. "We got work to do."

"You can't do any more without rest and food."

A drop of water fell from his mustache as he drew on the cigarette and blew the smoke out slowly. "I got cattle scattered across Kansas, injured an' lame. I ain't got time to eat."

"Take off your shirt."

He looked at her, unmoving.

"You're bleeding." She kept her voice flat and unemotional.

"Never mind."

Abbie drew herself up. "Cole Jasper, you may not care what condition you're in, but I have cattle to drive, and to do it I need you."

He snorted. "Well, when you put it so kindly . . ." He unbuttoned his shirt and pulled it off.

She saw him wince, but he undid the torn long johns underneath and pulled them down, baring a lean, muscled torso. His side was scraped and bruised, with a gash beneath his ribs that was caked with mud and crusted blood. Whatever he hit had cut through both layers of clothing and a good deal of skin. Abbie glanced up, but he was looking past her.

He tossed the cigarette and ground it out. "I could use a cup of coffee."

"James, get Cole some coffee and find me the medicine box." She took a cloth, went to the fire, and dipped it in the boiling water. By the time she was back at his side it was hot but not scalding. She touched it to his wound and felt him recoil. "I'm sorry."

"Just git it over with."

The dirt was embedded in the skin, but she rubbed as carefully as she could. Fresh blood flowed from the gash. "That'll need to be sewn." She poured a small amount of carbolic acid into the wound, and Cole hissed in his breath sharply. She boiled the needle, then threaded it with gut from the medicine box. Putting it through his flesh nearly turned her stomach, but he bore it stoically.

"Now eat your breakfast while I see to your head."

"It's just a scratch," he protested.

"It's a knot and a cut. Must you be so stubborn?"

He took up the plate and shoveled the oats into his mouth.

Again Abbie wet the cloth and washed the wound. "It's not as bad as the other. I'll just wrap it."

"Be quick about it. I gotta see to them steers."

"You can't do it now. Besides, unless you intend to do it alone, you'll have to wait. Matt and Will are dead to the world."

"I'll rouse 'em."

"No, you won't. This is one time you're taking my orders."

He caught her hand as she wrapped the bandage around his head. "If you want your herd to make it to market, they need doctorin' as much as I do. I already put down one animal. I ain't hankerin' to do others."

Abbie spoke gently. "Just a few hours' rest. Will can't do any more, and I don't think you can, either." She looked into his eyes. They were more gray than green and the whites were shot with red. "Sleep a little. The cattle will fend for themselves."

He released her hand and looked away. "A'right. Wake me in an hour." He turned away.

"Cole . . ."

He paused but didn't turn.

"I'm sorry about Scotch."

He winced when he pulled the bedroll from the wagon. He carried it close to the fire and spread it on the ground. She could have sworn his eyes closed before his head hit.

Abbie rubbed her hands over her face. While the men slept, she'd take advantage of the swollen waters in the creek bed. She took a bar of soap and her honeysuckle rinse and headed for the water. It was cold and fast, but she stripped to her undergarments and waded in, then sank down to her neck.

With a quick breath she plunged her head in, then washed. The weeks in the saddle had left her little opportunity to wash more than her face and hands each morning and night. Even this cold, unfriendly water was welcome. She scrubbed her hair and applied the rinse, then let the current drag the curls one last time.

Climbing up the bank, she squeezed out the excess water and shook her hair down her back. She shivered, then realized she was shaking with more than the cold. Her herd was scattered, her men exhausted, Cole's horse lost. Though they had plenty more in the remuda, she knew Scotch was not just another horse to him.

She recalled the time he'd loaned her Scotch when Shiloh lost a shoe, how he'd come upon her walking the lamed horse on Monte's range and sent her home on Scotch. Then he'd nursed Shiloh's leg and helped cover her dishonest behavior from Monte. Though she had confessed it to Monte herself, Cole had not betrayed her.

Abbie frowned. Seeing him without his shirt and ministering

to his injury had unsettled her more than she wanted to admit. She'd felt blessedly removed from any romantic inclinations. The nine marriage proposals she'd received in the last two years had failed to kindle the remotest desire, yet scrubbing the dirt from the cuts on the man she despised had left her shaking.

What was wrong with her? She pulled on Monte's pants, but they were so dusty and worn she hardly recognized them as his. It jolted her. What if her memory faded, as well? What if she couldn't conjure the look of him in her mind even as she couldn't recognize the pants? She dropped to her knees.

Oh, God, don't let me forget. I don't care how it hurts. Don't let me forget. She'd fallen asleep in the wagon without thinking of Elliot. How could she have gone one night without hurting for him? How could she have felt tenderly for Cole's loss of his horse, when he was the cause of all her pain?

Abbie pulled on the shirt and clenched it tightly. *Monte. There will never be anyone for me but you.* She stayed on her knees, willing the pain to subside, then rolled the shirt sleeves and stood. If it weren't for Will, she'd wake Cole now and send him off. But Will was exhausted by the hard work and long hours. Last night had nearly pushed him to breaking. She knew the look of it. She'd been there herself more than once this trip.

♦♦♦♦♦♦♦

Cole woke himself and rolled over. The sun was a good way above the horizon, though masked by clouds. It had been well over an hour since he'd dropped off before dawn. He sat up. "Aah." The place Abbie had stitched hurt worse than it had when it happened. He looked down inside his long johns at the bandage. No fresh blood.

He stood and almost whistled for Scotch, then remembered. The glazing of that horse's eyes would be with him a long time. He frowned. Why hadn't Abbie wakened him? He strode over, nudged Will with a boot, then gave Matt the same. "Git up. We got work to do."

He looked up at the clouds. The rain might hold off a short

spell yet, but they'd have wet work ahead. He watched Abbie climb from the wagon. She had his shirt in hand as she approached.

"Here. It's mended."

He took the shirt. "I'd've rather you woke me like I told you to."

"Then I guess we're even." She walked to the line of horses. "When you're dressed we can go."

He looked at the shirt and frowned. The feel of her hands was too fresh in his mind. While she'd doctored him she almost seemed to care. Obviously he was mistaken. He threw on the shirt and buttoned it, then pulled his coat over and hollered, "Move it, ya lazy dogs, 'fore I put lead in yer tails."

Will dragged himself up painfully, and Matt stretched.

Cole scowled. "This ain't a babysittin' picnic. Move it. We got injured cattle to tend." His head throbbed as he stalked to the horses and looked them over. He untied and saddled Violet, the bay mare.

He nodded to Abbie, who had Zephyr saddled and ready. "The first matter of business is to cut out the injured and see to them. Then we'll do a count and look for strays. We'll be lucky to move out by noon."

She nodded. "Then let's not waste any more time."

Now, there was a woman for you. She won't wake you when you say, then accuses you of wasting time. He mounted and spurred the mare. Abbie Farrel was far and away more trouble than any herd put together.

By the time the rain started, they'd cut out twenty-nine steers and treated their injuries the best they could. Charlie had been the one to handle that in the past, but Cole knew enough animal medicine to get by. Three cattle were dead from trampling, and most were sore footed and battered, but in spite of that, they'd come out better than they might have.

Twenty-Four

Reverend Shields read the funeral passage over the three new graves. When would it end, this scourge of the Lord? For so it seemed, like a plague of Egypt taking the strong with the weak. Forty-two graves from the typhoid in three weeks. Some came through, but clearly two out of three would leave this life.

He sighed and closed the Bible with weary hands. Had he done his job? Had he brought these souls to peace and everlasting life? He was thankful for Father O'Brien. The man had an unquenchable strength and compassion. He knelt beside the cots, bathed the disease-racked bodies, spoke of the goodness of the Lord.

Winthrop Shields felt an amazing peace to be sharing this ministry with another, even one such as Father O'Brien with his Irish Catholic ways. They'd gone round and round on their theology, but for all that, he liked the priest immensely. Between them, they might yet reap a harvest for the Lord.

He was not one to disdain deathbed conversions, and the pitiful truth was that when death's door yawned it was an easier thing to say yes to God than when all seemed right with the world. He glanced at Ethan Thomas, standing shovel in hand. As the deaths continued, fewer and fewer were willing to stick their necks out and help with the bodies, live or dead. Some who would volunteer were turned away if they had wives and children at home.

Father O'Brien had given his people strict instructions to keep to themselves until the scourge was past. It was sensible, he said, given the good Lord's willingness to pass them by. But the priest stayed day and night in the infirmary, as did Doctor Barrow and Ethan Thomas.

Ethan had lost a wife and son to cholera before coming west. He'd confided it in a rare moment of tears when young Billy Hamilton went to meet the Lord. Winthrop closed his eyes against the memory. Mrs. Hamilton, so close to bringing new life into the world, had put her firstborn into the ground with agonizing sobs. And now her husband thrashed with the fever.

Reverend Shields raised a prayer of desperation. *How long, oh, Lord, will you keep your face from us?* But did not the everlasting promise transcend this vale of tears? He made his way back to the infirmary and paused at the door. *Oh, Lord, is it wrong to long for a moment's peace, to ache for bodily rest even as my soul thirsts for you?* He climbed one stair and the next, then went inside. Doctor Barrow nearly collided with him.

Now, there was a man walking in exhaustion. Too many depended on him; too many thought he could do the impossible. On his shoulders rested the hopes of the stricken and their loved ones. He seemed to have aged years in the last month. *Give him strength, Father, to carry on. Bless him with the Healer's hands.*

Doctor Barrow gripped Father O'Brien's shoulder where he knelt beside Breck Thompson. "It's over, Father. There are others who need you."

Father O'Brien opened his eyes and slowly rose from his knees. "Sure and it's the Lord they're needin' more than my weak comfort."

Winthrop Shields looked down. Breck Thompson, Skeeter, and John Mason gone, and Curtis still fighting. Mrs. Farrel would have much to face when she returned. He shook his head. She'd not been the same person since Monte's passing. Outwardly, perhaps. Her service to others had remained fervent, but with a desperation it hurt him to see.

God wanted service out of love for Him, not fear. And was it fear that kept her alone? He knew several men had recently asked for her hand, but she had refused them all. He saw her less frequently since Father O'Brien had come and now ministered to her soul in the way she was accustomed.

But on occasion she came to his own little church and heard him preach. And she always greeted him warmly, though he saw the bleakness in her eyes. That was a woman at odds with God, no matter how well she deceived herself. Sometimes he thought it was easier for those who openly raged at the Lord. Their grieving passed. Hers, it seemed, did not.

Had they shared a spiritual like-mindedness, he would court her himself, though he doubted she'd have him. It was ludicrous to think he could succeed where so many failed. He lifted up a prayer for her. *Send her a helpmate, Lord. She needs it more than she knows.*

♦♦♦♦♦♦♦

Joshua Martin sank to his chair at the table in his warm kitchen and eyed Selena at the stove, as slender at fifty-one as she'd been at sixteen. Well, perhaps she'd settled some. Gray streaked her hair like silver veins on brown stone walls, and her hands were no longer supple and smooth. But he loved her fiercely.

Elliot suddenly appeared and jumped into his lap. Joshua squeezed the boy. He'd attended six burials that day, and it was good to feel his grandson's life and energy. One of those put in the ground that afternoon was Breck Thompson, Abbie's head man.

She'd lost three good cowhands, and Curtis hung on by his teeth. How would she keep the ranch now? He puzzled the question without finding a solution. Was it every father's wish to ease his children's burdens? Didn't it seem Abbie'd had more than her share?

If he had the funds to pay off her debts, he would do it in a breath. But though he owned his land clear and editing the newspaper had kept them fed over the years, he had nothing to call savings. He sighed.

"Are you tired, Great Uncle Josh?"

He turned to see Jenny standing at his side. She held herself too stiffly for a little girl. He reached over and tugged her braid. "Yep, I'm tired. But not too tired for a hug from my little grandniece."

She dutifully hugged his side while Elliot squeezed his neck again for good measure. Tucker leaned on the wall and grinned when Joshua sent him a helpless glance. That boy was turning out fine, and he thanked God again that Abbie had seen fit to put him in their care.

He just might be the one to carry on his work. Tucker loved working at his side on the land, but even more, he was showing an amazing propensity for words. He may be the next editor of the *Rocky Bluffs Chronicle*. But then, the boy was only eleven, and he'd had similar hopes for Grant before his son turned to law.

It had been a worthy choice, too. He clearly excelled in his profession. Even Judge Wilson admitted as much, though having his daughter wed Grant may have colored that opinion. Grant's choice of Marcy Wilson had surprised him less than some of the others. And whereas Abbie still struggled to get along with her, he had a soft spot for the girl.

All in all—he looked around the room—life was good. He had much to be thankful for. None of his loved ones had contracted the fever, though he'd lost some friends. That thought saddened him. Doctor Barrow had an impossible task, God help him. Joshua gave Jenny and Elliot another squeeze, too aware of the frailty of this life.

◆◆◆◆◆◆◆

Doctor Elias Barrow plunged his arms into the steaming bowl and scrubbed to the elbows. At last he felt he could see light at the end of the tunnel. The quarantine had kept the fever from spreading to those who had not contracted the disease directly from the water or the infected man.

Once he had learned the location of the man's camp, his orders that no one use the creek water until the contamination passed had limited the cases far better than he had hoped. And though the infirmary was still packed with sick, few new cases came in. He believed most of these left would live. They had survived the worst, and now it was a matter of returning strength to their bodies.

He would not count in his mind the numbers he had lost, though he kept a tally for his records. He could not focus on that. Medicine was a chancy calling for one who could not separate his heart from his work. He looked over the room in the near darkness of the few lamps he kept burning through the night, and dared to hope.

◆◆◆◆◆◆◆

Horace Driscoll sat at his desk and cracked his knuckles, an uncouth habit, but one he allowed himself when the bank was empty. He eyed the ledger before him with decided satisfaction. It was not that he delighted in the misfortune that was overtaking so many in the town, but after all, one had to be practical, especially in banking.

Tragedy happened. Typhoid was merely one name for it. And those like himself who escaped infection had every right, indeed the responsibility, to carry on. He had the welfare of the town as well as his own to consider.

He looked down at the page. Those hardest hit by deaths would be the first to come begging, the proverbial widows and orphans. He took no pleasure in refusing them, but refuse he must. He had the integrity of the bank to maintain and his responsibility to his stockholders in the East. That he might personally benefit was only secondary.

His gaze landed on Mrs. Farrel's account. Her property was the choicest of all. But with three of her men dead and her account delinquent for the first time . . . He scarcely contained the thought.

No one could accuse him of unfair gain. He was a fair man, competent and far sighted. But when Mrs. Farrel returned, they would speak again. And this time she would not dare expel him from her home. He owned her.

♦♦♦♦♦♦♦

Abbie listened with disbelief to Cole's information. So little? How could she get so little for the herd when they were fine beef stock? Thirteen dollars on the head when they were worth twenty or more?

"We missed the time. The market's glutted. Everyone sold off before us. I found the best price I could."

His words passed over her uselessly. All that work, all that pain, all these weeks away from Elliot and Jenny . . . for what? Could they even make it to spring on what they'd fetch? She dropped her face into her hands.

"I'm sorry, Abbie."

She stiffened. She would not break down in front of Cole. They'd get something, and that was more than she'd have if they hadn't made the drive. She drew a long breath and faced him. "Very well, sell them."

"I can winter them here and try in the spring."

She shook her head. "No, I don't expect that." Nor could she afford it with Driscoll expecting payment. "We'll make the best of what we get. It's just . . ." Her plans for paying off what Cole had sent were foiled. She would not have the satisfaction of settling the score. Nor could she afford to take the train home when they'd need every cent to keep them going until the next sale.

"How long will it take to get home?" Her voice sounded more plaintive than she wanted.

"All depends. Sooner than it took to get here. The horses can make a bit better clip. Reckon it depends on us."

Meaning her. She'd ride in the wagon the whole way if it meant getting home sooner to Elliot. "Then sell the cattle and let's go." Abbie looked down the street. It was hardly the peaceful bustling street of Rocky Bluffs. Dodge City was coarse and loud and dirty. And it smelled.

"We'll stay the night and head out in the mornin'."

"We'll head out now."

He rubbed his jaw. "Abbie, Matt an' Will deserve a night in

town. One night ain't gonna hurt."

Was he saying he wanted a night in town himself? She eyed him briefly. His expression was unreadable, but she clearly remembered his reception of Lil Brandon's attention. He likely intended to have himself a good time tonight. She turned away.

"Walk along with me to make the sale, and then we'll find us some dinner."

"No, thank you. I'll just take a room."

He took her arm and stepped off the walk, taking her briskly along with him. "You may not be hankerin' fer my company, but Dodge City ain't the place fer a lady to spend her hours alone."

Abbie caught up the skirts of the dress she'd changed into before entering town and kept pace beside him. She hadn't the energy to argue. Besides, she took a grim satisfaction thinking she just might spoil his fun, as well. Listening to Cole negotiate, she realized he'd done better for her than she could have hoped. She felt slightly chagrined walking beside him back toward the noisy street.

"There's a tolerable restaurant in that hotel yonder."

"Fine."

"Ain't fancy like some of the others, but there's less . . . activity."

She guessed she knew what he meant by activity. That he was willing to sacrifice touched her not at all. "Fine."

As they sat at the table having placed their orders, Abbie felt distinctly uneasy. For one thing, nearly every eye in the place was on her, and that was understandable since she was the only woman in the room save the one serving tables. She felt regrettably thankful for Cole's presence. "Haven't these men been taught not to stare?"

"I reckon they cain't rightly help it." He raked his eyes over her himself. "It's nice seein' you in a dress again."

She flushed with anger and wished she'd kept the pants on. So much for being thankful.

"Well, Abbie." He raised his glass to her. "Here's to a successful drive."

That his glass held tea instead of whiskey was something, she thought, and raised her own. "Not as successful as I would have liked, but I thank God it's over."

"Nearly. We still gotta get home."

The way he said *home* sent a chill up her spine. Surely he wouldn't expect to stay on. "I think we ought to discuss your wages."

To her surprise, he grinned wryly. "You cain't stand it, can you?"

"Stand what?"

"To have me do somethin' for you."

"No, I can't." She waited while the plates of steak and gravy were served, then looked at him frankly. "I want to pay you."

"I know you do."

"Well?"

"I cain't accept it."

"Why not?"

He took a bite of steak and kept his eyes on the plate. He wiped his mouth with the checkered napkin, then rested his hands on the table. "I don't reckon you want me to talk about it, but I made a promise to Mr. Farrel I mean to keep. A promise to look after you."

Abbie felt herself spiraling down. To hear Cole speak Monte's name . . . to think they had moments together before he . . . Her chest constricted, and she pushed away from the table.

Cole caught her wrist. "Don't go out, Abbie. You may despise me, but at least you know I got no intentions toward you."

She could hardly control her trembling. She stood at the brink with her loss gaping. *God help me.* They were empty words. God didn't help. He only took and took and took. She sank into her seat because her legs wouldn't hold her. The smell of the meat gagged her.

With his eyes fixed on Abbie, Cole released her wrist, then applied himself to his meal. At least he had the decency not to speak again. She fought the dark thoughts and memories, the sudden terror for Elliot. What if something had happened? What if the typhoid had spread? What if he were gone like . . . *Monte!* She screamed inside.

Cole reached over and took her hands. "I'm sorry, Abbie. It wasn't my intention to upset you."

His hands were like coals on hers. Seeing that he had finished his food, she pulled away. "I want to go now."

He put his money on the table and stood. He walked her up the stairs with a hand on her elbow, and even that touch seared her. He unlocked her door and handed her the key. "Lock it behind you. I'll be out here if you need me."

She scarcely heard him. She was thankful for the wood of the door between them, and she turned the lock viciously. A promise to Monte. To take care of her? Had Monte turned her over to his betrayer? She dropped her face to her hands.

Monte, how could you? She thought of the love she'd seen in Cole's face when he saved her from the rustler. She thought of the ache in his voice when he'd told her he couldn't leave even though she was married to Monte, that he wasn't sure Monte could take care of her.

Oh, God, had he let Monte die? Had he even caused it, in order to have her? A low wail started in her throat, but she stifled it lest Cole hear. She looked frantically at the window. A narrow balcony ran along outside with stairs to the ground. She would go. She would leave tonight. She knew the way home now.

She would get to the camp where James waited with the wagon. Together they . . . no, the wagon was too slow. She'd take a horse, several horses, with James none the wiser. She'd have a whole night's start on Cole. He wouldn't catch her. The others would come on their own.

She pushed open the window. It squeaked dreadfully, but the street was noisier than it had been earlier. Cole would hear nothing. The cold night air struck her, but she squeezed out anyway, crept along the balcony, and went down. She hurried from the alley to the street and started for the livery where she'd left Zephyr when they came in.

If she took the horses Cole and Will and Matt had ridden in, she would not have to brave the camp at all, but how could she get the horses from the livery? Cole had turned them over. Would the man let her take them? She would have to try. She stepped off the boardwalk to the shadows beside the livery.

Before she took another step, a strong arm gripped her waist and pulled her into the dark. A high, foul laugh filled her ear as the hand covered her mouth. "Well, now, what have we here?"

To her horror another voice answered. "Mighty purty. Jist our luck she's alone."

Abbie struggled and thrashed when the man came close and stroked her hair. She could see nothing of their faces, but the men were strong and their intentions obvious. She kicked back at the first one's knee, but he tightened his grip on her waist and crushed the breath from her.

The other grabbed her shoulders. "Come on, lady. We're jist havin' some fun. Give us a kiss." He leaned close enough for her to smell the whiskey on his breath.

She bit the palm across her mouth, and in the moment it was pulled away she screamed. The man shook her hard, then slapped her. She fell, and the weight of the other man came down on her. She raked her nails into his neck. He hollered and jerked back, then struck her again.

Abbie fell back, stunned, as he once again trapped her with his body. Suddenly he was yanked from her, and she heard the crack of bone against bone. He went down heavily, then scrambled up. Were the two of them fighting each other?

She pressed into the wall as the man was sent sprawling. The second one came like a ramrod, head down, and she saw that it was a third man he hit. But the third kept his feet, and her assailant took double fists to the head and stayed where he fell. The one who had caught her ran down the alley into the night. She was pulled to her feet, and she smelled the familiar scent. Cole.

He held her shoulders a long moment. "What in God's name are you doin' out here?" His anger was not cloaked in the least.

Her heart was pounding so hard she could scarcely breathe. She dropped her forehead to his vest, and he pulled her in close.

"Abbie . . ." His voice was hoarse. "Do I gotta hog-tie you?"

She didn't trust herself to speak.

"Come on." He yanked her up to the boardwalk and along its length with his hand firmly on her arm.

The street was as busy and rowdy as it had been in daylight, but she kept her eyes on the ground. How had Cole known? How had he gotten to her? She couldn't ask. It didn't matter. She wanted to cry. She wanted to hide. She wanted anyone but Cole to have come to her aid.

Outside her door he stopped and turned her. "You got anything to say . . . that I might understand?"

She shook her head mutely.

He clenched his jaw and stared down the hall. "I'll have yer word to stay put, or I'll spend the night inside the door and never mind yer reputation."

"I'll stay," she managed, then took the key from her pocket.

He let her in, then pocketed the key himself. "You use that window again, an' I'll let them eat you alive."

She closed the door behind her and fell to the bed exhausted. The shock and ache and relief overcame her, and she slept.

Cole sat outside her door, back to the wood, hat low over his brow. He'd slept in worse positions, but sleep eluded him now. He'd stepped outside for a smoke in time to see her heading off. Why would she try a thing like that? Why did she mean to leave him behind? Had he so upset her, or was it more?

He rubbed the cracked and bleeding knuckles of his right hand, then shook it out and rested it on his thigh. He understood the blame she put on him. Right or wrong, it was a normal feeling. He could tell she wanted nothing to do with him, but up to now she'd depended on his help, if reluctantly. Why all of a sudden would she try to get away from him without his knowing?

All she had to do was tell him to get, and what choice did he have? Was she afraid he'd refuse? He frowned. Was she afraid . . . of him? Why? He drew his knees up. He needed a smoke, and this time he wasn't going outside to do it. He took a paper from his pocket and rolled a cigarette, lit the end, and drew in deeply.

What had he said to upset her? That he had a promise to keep? How could that set her running? Did she think he meant more by it than just ensuring her well-being? Did she think he still hoped . . . no, better not entertain that line of thinking.

He wondered where Matt and Will were. As Matt had taken the boy in hand, he'd probably have to peel them off the floor come morning. But they'd done their job. Now it was just the trip home. Home. And then what?

He drew the tobacco into his lungs. After he got her home, he'd cut loose and go back to drifting. He'd learned better than to stay in any one place. He'd come too close to calling somewhere home. He rubbed a hand over his face and smoothed his mustache. As soon as he saw Abbie safely back, he'd hit the trail.

He rested his head back against the door. He took a drag and blew a slow stream of smoke from his lips. No sound came from the room. Did Abbie sleep? Was she lying there thinking how to be rid of him? Was she shaking still? Was she injured?

He hadn't even checked for injuries, not that she'd have let him. He rubbed the cigarette out on the wood plank floor. She'd see to herself well enough. So far he'd kept his distance. He wouldn't let her fear and trembling change that.

He hunched his shoulder against the door and tipped the hat down over his eyes. He dozed and woke and dozed again, then finally drifted off.

He almost fell in backwards when Abbie pulled the door open the next morning.

"Good heaven's, Cole. Did you spend the night on the floor there?"

"Where'd you think I'd be?" He pulled himself up and frowned. "No, don't answer that." Her smug expression was clear enough. Well, good. Let her think the worst of him. It would make cutting loose that much easier. "You ready?"

"I'd like to wash before we leave."

"Good. I would, too." He scowled at her surprised look, but refused to let her goad him.

She stopped when they reached the head of the stairs and turned. "I owe you my thanks for last night. I suppose now is as good a time as any to say so."

He tipped his hat swaggishly. "At yer service, Abbie. You're most kindly welcome."

She turned and walked down. "Where does one bathe in a cow town?"

"Well, if we'd stayed in one of the fancier hotels, we could bathe there. As it is you'll have to settle for the bathhouse."

"Lead the way."

"Yes, ma'am."

◆◆◆◆◆◆◆

Soaking in the dented tub, Abbie lathered her arms. Cole's swagger this morning was enough to make her scream. He probably thought his heroics the night before had given him the upper hand. While it had brought her to her senses, she had no intention of letting him know that.

The thoughts that had plagued her through the night still spun in her head. The feeling of safety and relief in Cole's arms . . . Surely it was nothing more than reflex after the terror of those men. She'd been foolish to think he had willingly caused Monte's death, but that didn't mean she cared for him.

She stood in the tub and poured the pitcher of rinse water over her body, then stepped out. Oh, to be clean was glorious. She refused to think of the men pawing her in the dark. Would she see them this morning, battered and bruised from Cole's beating? She shuddered and pulled on her clothes. The dress was dirty and torn at the waist but it was the only one she'd brought, so she put it back on and went out.

Cole stood in the street. His blond hair curled, and he was clean shaven with his mustache trimmed. In the sunlight, his chiseled cheekbones cut triangular shadows in his face. When he turned her way, her chest lurched. He was so handsome with his green eyes and tanned skin, his angular jaw and . . . What was she thinking? Abbie looked away when he approached.

"Well, now, if you're done . . . I thought you were gonna spend the whole day in there. Almost got us another room."

She put up her chin and started for the livery.

He caught her arm. "I got the horses over yonder. Thought you'd rather not pass that way again."

Cole's thoughtfulness stabbed her. He had no right to consider her feelings as he did. She was not his responsibility, no matter what Monte had charged. The ache heightened as she walked to Zephyr and mounted. As Cole gave her a hand, she noticed the bruised knuckles and a different pang seized her.

Matt and Will joined them at the edge of town, and they rode silently to the camp where James had stayed with the horses. He stood, grinning broadly when they rode up. The fire was burning and he had coffee on. She dismounted and set about making their meal. "We ought to have another bag of flour and cornmeal before we start back."

Cole tipped up his hat. "I planned to pick up some things once I got you out of town."

That was as close as he'd come to saying what trouble she'd caused him. "Cole . . . I do apologize for . . ."

"I'd just like to know why."

She stared at the cornmeal batter in the bowl. What could she say? Her thoughts had been crazy, born of grief and anger and desperate need. What could she tell him without betraying her own mindless fears?

"Yeah. That's what I figured." He walked away.

She almost called him back. She didn't mean to hurt him. Not anymore. But he barked something at the men and strode off.

Twenty-Five

Abbie alternated between riding in the wagon and riding horseback, but she preferred horseback. Sitting beside James in the rickety wagon over the lumpy trail made her restless, and she had toughened up so that riding was not nearly as taxing. Will's horse kept pace with hers.

"I sure do like that Mr. Twain's *Adventures of Tom Sawyer.*"

"I'm glad." Her grandfather had sent it fresh off the press the year Colorado became a state. She had given it to Will before reading it herself. "I didn't know you brought it along."

"I hadn't time to read it while we were driving the herd, but these last evenings I've made some headway. It's almost as good as the jumping-frog one."

"I'm glad you're enjoying it, Will." The last evenings around the campfire had been more restful and the men more pleasant. Except for Cole. She looked ahead to where he rode alone. He'd been singularly snappish and cross.

Why didn't he just ride off and go his own way? Surely they could make it now without him, and he obviously couldn't wait to be through with the job. Of course it was his promise that kept him. Who would have thought Cole Jasper could be as stubborn about keeping his word as . . . as Monte had been?

She shook her head, furious that she'd compared them. Monte was a man of honor, of culture, of compassion. Cole Jasper . . . She kneed the mare and caught up to him. "Can't we go any faster? Why must we poke along as though we still had five hundred steers in tow?"

Without a word, he spurred his horse. Surprised, she likewise urged the mare and heard Will and Matt with the remuda behind. They rode swiftly for the better part of an hour. She could feel her horse's chest heaving when Cole reined in. He turned and stopped beside her. "Now we'll rest the horses an' wait fer the wagon."

She looked back. The wagon was nowhere in sight. She sagged in the saddle. Of course James couldn't run the horses pulling the wagon, and the wagon would have come to pieces on this terrain. Why didn't Cole just tell her they couldn't hurry? Why did he have to be so . . . ornery!

She swung down and stalked to the creek with the mare. He was already there with his gelding, Whitesock. He eyed her where she stood, and she squarely returned his gaze.

She raised her chin. "You might have simply told me. All I needed was an explanation."

His look penetrated deep inside her. He walked away without a word. So that was it. He was still smarting that she hadn't told him why she tried to leave. Very well. If he wanted an explanation so badly . . .

Cole heard her come up behind as he walked out across the grassy plain. He kept walking, and she spoke to his back.

"In the first place, Monte had no right to charge you with my care. In the second, I never asked for your help. You had no right to send money without my knowledge to the men I thought were loyal to me. And thirdly—"

He waited.

"I hold you responsible for my husband's death."

He turned. "You think I don't know that? Not that you ever bothered to hear what happened. It might surprise you to know I done my share of grievin' fer Mr. Farrel. But I don't suppose that'd change anything you think or feel."

"Why should it?" Abbie's eyes were like ice, hard and blue.

"It shouldn't, I guess, except you're always on yer knees actin' like a Christian lady."

"As though you would know anything about God's ways."

"You got a right to be how you want. Just seems a person ought not to affect somethin' they ain't. You shouldn't pretend, if you don't believe it."

"What do you mean? Of course I believe." Her face flushed with anger.

"Like heck. You mouth the words, but they don't get no further than yer throat. Yer heart's gone bitter."

"Haven't I the right to be?"

"Maybe you have. But you ain't the only one."

Abbie's eyes narrowed dangerously. "What have you possibly suffered to compare?"

"It don't matter. The point is you're forgettin' one primary commandment. Forgive, that you might be forgiven."

"How dare you judge me."

Cole gripped her arms in frustration. "Maybe I ain't got the right. But I know a thing or two about God's ways."

"You?" She fairly spat it. "You wouldn't know God if He hit you with a bolt of lightning."

Cole stared deeply into her eyes, then released her arms. "Maybe you're right. Maybe I'm deceivin' myself. I thought I knew you, too." He turned away.

"Don't you dare walk away from me."

He stopped, then with a long breath, shook his head and started on. He heard a queer sound from her throat, and a second later she flew at him, her rage giving her strength beyond her stature. He staggered and turned, caught the arms that pummeled him.

Abbie thrashed, freed her hand, and slapped him hard. He took the blow, but caught her arm again and grabbed her close. He held her tight while she screamed and kicked against him. "I hate you! I hate you! I . . ." Her tears came in a rush, and it was worse than anything she could say against him.

Cole dropped his chin to the crown of her head. Her sobs came from a depth that made him wonder if she'd cried at all for the pain inside. He could well believe it was four years of sorrow breaking out now. He felt more helpless than he'd ever been in his life.

What did he know of God's ways? It had been a lot of years since he'd turned his thoughts that way, and they were rusty and unsure. He'd given up looking for God too young. It seemed a man ought to stand on his own. He'd only meant for Abbie to see her way, not for his own thoughts to turn to heaven. But there they were.

God. What do I do? He felt an overwhelming need to comfort but had no idea how. Automatically he stroked her back, her hair. He caught her head between his hands and turned her face up. Awash her eyes were unbelievably blue, her face flushed, her mouth . . .

Cole bent and kissed her, the aching need overwhelming his restraint. He expected another slap for it, but her arms came around his neck and her return kiss was more ardent than he could bear. He didn't dare hope her heart was in it. He pried her fingers loose and set her back. Abbie stared at him, then turned away. She dropped her face to her hands and wept.

God help him, he couldn't take it. He reached a hand to the hair that lay across her neck. Slowly he swept it aside and kissed the place where it sprang from her skin. He breathed in her scent, something sweet and flowery. "How is it you smell good even on the trail?"

"I washed." She sniffed, then tipped her head back as his lips moved across her neck to the hollow beneath her ear.

He turned her in his arms and kissed her mouth gently. Her arms wrapped his waist, and he caught her face between his hands and kissed her hard. She drove his need with her own. Her lips were soft, sweet, willing.

"Abbie . . ." Cole could hardly restrain himself. "Not like this."

She gripped his back and kissed the edge of his jaw.

He closed his eyes and pulled her tight against him. "You got a great emptiness inside, but this won't fill it. Not like this. It ain't right."

"I don't care."

"Yes, you do." He eased her away and looked down into eyes deep with emotion. Looking at her, he thought he'd die of the pain in his chest. Could a man die of loving a woman? "We need to sort this out, Abbie. And I don't think too good with you this close."

She forked her fingers into her hair, resting her forehead on her palm. "I've made a fool of myself."

"No, you ain't. I reckon that cry's been a long time comin'. And as for the rest, that was my doin'." He took her shoulders and made her look at him. "I apologize, Abbie. I had no right."

She clenched her hands, fighting the tears. "I don't know what's wrong with me. One minute I . . . can't stand the sight of you, the next . . ."

"Don't say it. We got a hundred miles to cover yet."

Her eyes met his with new fire. "Cole Jasper, you are the most infuriating man!" She started walking.

"Abbie."

She glanced over her shoulder.

"Don't go far."

Abbie wandered over the Colorado plain. The late October wind was chilly as she left Cole behind. She felt torn apart. What were these feelings she had for him? They couldn't be love. There was no one for her but Monte. God had made them one for the other. They were one. Only . . . he was gone.

That didn't change anything. Monte was her first love, the father of her child. Was she so cheap that the baring of Cole's heart could make her forget what she knew with Monte? Never.

It was only that her own heart cried out to be loved. She was twenty-six years old, and she'd had love for so short a time. Cole desired her, but more than that, he knew her. He knew her pain, her need. He'd suffered with her through the valley, and she sensed a union between them—a union of two souls who'd lived through hell and now hoped to love again. But that couldn't be . . . could it?

She closed her eyes. As always, Cole had seen through her, seen the mockery of her relationship with the Christ she professed. He had provoked her anger, but what he said was true. She shouldn't pretend what she didn't believe. But what did she believe? That if she did one thing wrong God would strike again? Elliot, maybe? Or Jenny?

What had Father Dominic said? *"There on the cross your sin is hung."* Then why did God crush her again and again? She regularly woke in cold sweats fearing to find Elliot stiff and without breath. She guarded Jenny so rigidly the child snuck away just to feel the wind in her face. She couldn't go on living in fear, but how could she stop?

"Forgive, that you might be forgiven." Forgive whom? Cole? She wanted to. Herself? God? Forgive God? The very thought seemed blasphemous. Wasn't it God's right to give and to take? Blessed be the name of the Lord. Yet . . . Abbie staggered and looked up.

She'd gone farther than she should. She turned back. The land lay empty around her. Looking out at its vastness, she dropped to her knees. *Oh, Lord, I don't know if it's right. But I forgive you for taking Monte.* Her tears flowed. *I don't understand why, but I believe your ways are above mine.* She looked into the blackness of her grief, and found that she could face it. *Please God, don't let me live in fear. Please deliver me.*

Abbie stayed on her knees until they ached, but she was hardly aware of the pain as she touched the deeper wounds inside. She remembered Monte's smile, the warmth of his eyes, his gentle, passionate touch. She remembered his hand on her as their child grew inside, his excitement that they had at last conceived. She remembered him lying stiff and cold, his chest torn open, his heart stilled. She wept until the tears were spent, then stayed silent in their wake.

She heard a footstep on the crisp grass before her and opened her eyes to Cole. He reached out and helped her to her feet. "I'm sorry, Abbie. I had no right to knock yer faith. I was wrong."

"You were right. I had lost sight of what I believe."

"I don't know enough about it to say."

"Sometimes the eyes of an unbeliever see more clearly than

those of the people God calls his own." She looked into his face. "Cole . . . tell me how Monte died."

His throat worked, and he ran the back of his hand over his jaw. "I guess you better sit." He dropped cross-legged beside her. "Abbie, I . . . you stop me if you want."

She nodded.

"First let me say yer husband was one of the finest men I ever knew. Gettin' to be a purty fair cowboy, too. But he didn't know the animals like I do. He saw that Durham bull out there walkin' crazy and thought he could bring it in. I tried to tell him otherwise, but fer all his mild manners, he could be a stubborn man."

Abbie smiled slightly.

"He was the boss. There was never any question about that even when he was so green he squeaked. Guess that was his plantation raising. But after the trouble with Gifford and the drive to Kansas, well, he'd surprised me more than once. I figured between us we just might pull it off with that bull."

Cole looked away, and Abbie sensed his sorrow. Did he truly grieve for Monte? She had seen a companionship and ease between them that had been long in coming. Now she sensed more.

Cole drew a long breath. "He moved to cut off the bull's path, and I took the other side. Then he dismounted. I don't know why. I hollered, but he just stood there waitin' to throw the rope, and the bull charged. I spurred Scotch to full gallop, fired off a shot, but there was nothin' I could do from that distance. The bull dropped Mr. Farrel and charged my way. I took it down, but it was too late."

The tears ran silently down her cheeks. *Oh, Monte. Why?* He had risked the fire for Chance, lost his life for a bull. A bull!

Cole's voice grew hoarse. "He hadn't more than a minute, but he asked me to look after you and his child. He was peaceful in that."

Abbie dropped her forehead to the hands folded on her raised knee. It hurt more than she had believed possible. After four years it was like losing him again. *Why, Monte, why? Oh, dear God.* She felt Cole's hand on her shoulder and leaned against his side. He wrapped her shoulders in his arm. They sat in silence.

The sunset rays faded and the air grew cold. Abbie stirred. "I'm sorry, Cole. I blamed you wrongly, and I apologize."

"No need."

She brushed the hair from her eyes. "I'm ready to go back now."

"I reckon that's good as it's gettin' dark. I was willin' to set here all night, but I cain't answer for what the men'd think." He stood and helped her up. He pulled her briefly into his arms. "I don't expect nothin', Abbie. Just so you know."

She walked beside him as the dusk settled. She felt weak and empty. Without the anger to sustain her there was nothing. She was incapable of feeling. Even the thought of reaching Elliot in a few days brought no emotion. What if she'd been rendered unable to love, unable to feel? *I'm nothing but a shell, God. Put what you want inside.*

Twenty-Six

Abbie jostled in the wagon beside James. She could hardly believe they were back in the yard of the Lucky Star. It felt like forever since she'd seen the pale November sunshine on the white walls and pillars of the house. It almost seemed to shine of its own volition. Her home.

Pearl came out and stood on the porch, clutching her hands at her breast and smiling so broadly her cheeks plumped like popovers. Abbie climbed down the moment the wagon lurched to a stop. "Have Pearl help you unload, James. Will, see to the horses and saddle Zephyr for me. Matt, find Breck and . . ."

She saw Pearl's smile die as she shook her head and came down the steps. "Mizz Abbie . . . Mistuh Breck, he die of the typhoid. Mistuh Skeeter, too."

Abbie's breath left her chest. "What?" Not Breck and Skeeter both . . .

"And Mistuh Curtis, he alive but weak like a baby. I been nursin' him myse'f dese last weeks."

Breck dead, and Skeeter and John Mason. It stabbed at the numbness inside. No, she didn't want to feel again, not like this, not more death. She glanced at Cole, whose mouth had set in a firm line. These men had been his friends, his companions.

"It been real bad here," Pearl continued. "De fever took fifty-eight folks."

"Fifty—oh, dear God. Elliot?" The rush of fear was all too familiar.

"The chillen, dey's fine. Dey with yo mama still."

Abbie turned. Will had Zephyr bridled, and she swung up bareback and pressed with her knees. The horse surged across the yard and onto the rough. Cole cantered up beside her.

"You don't have to come, Cole."

"How you plannin' to carry two young'uns home?"

She hadn't thought of that. She hadn't thought beyond seeing for herself that they were safe and well. But she couldn't likely go there and leave them behind again. She sent Cole a smile and kicked with her heels. Zephyr shot forward with a burst of speed, and she clung with her thighs, one hand in the gray mane.

Cole kept pace beside her, and they held an easy lope until Pa's homestead came into view. Her heart beating in her chest, she urged Zephyr again. She slid off before the mare came to a full stop in the yard.

"Mama?" Elliot came around the porch and flew into her arms.

Abbie could hardly breathe, so full was her chest with emotion unleashed. She was not incapable of love or feeling. On the contrary, she thought she would burst with it. His soft, dark hair needed cutting, and one cheek was smudged, but he was the most beautiful thing she'd seen in too long.

Jenny pranced over, and Abbie reached an arm to her. They shared a three-way hug, then she noticed Jenny's glance behind her. Abbie stood as Cole dismounted.

"Howdy, Jenny."

She stared up at him frankly. "Do I know you?"

"You likely don't remember. But I remember you. I never forget a purty face."

Abbie felt a guilty pang. "Jenny, this is Cole Jasper, the man who carved your animals."

Elliot's eyes widened as though he'd just seen Father Christmas.

Jenny smiled. "I think I remember."

Cole smiled gently. "It's okay if you don't. You were a real small mite the last time I seen you."

Abbie watched Jenny walk over and take his hand. "Did you bring Aunt Abbie home?"

"Yup."

Elliot wiggled from her arms and reached for Cole's other hand. "Will you make me some animals?"

Cole squatted down. "Well, I ain't sure yet how long I'll be here. But we'll see what I got time to do." He ruffled Elliot's head. "You're a fine boy. You got the look of yer pa."

Abbie stiffened. Of course Cole couldn't know they'd never spoken to Elliot of Monte. Looking at the light in Elliot's eyes from Cole's remark, she wondered if she'd done the right thing.

Having taken care of business, Elliot came back to her. "You were gone too long, Mama."

"Elliot cried, but I didn't." Jenny still held fast to Cole's hand.

Abbie took Elliot up into her arms, and he wrapped her neck tightly. Nothing had ever felt so good. She wished she could savor it alone until her cup was full, but Mama was in the doorway rubbing her hands on her apron.

"Welcome home, Abbie. Cole, how nice to see you again." Mama's voice was warm as new milk and just as wholesome.

Cole took off his hat. "And you, Mrs. Martin."

Abbie knew Mama must be pleased. She had not approved of her sending Cole away. And the warmth in her welcome told him so.

"Won't you come in for coffee?"

Cole rubbed his hand through his hair. "We're trail worn and dusty."

"All the more reason."

Abbie carried Elliot onto the porch and inside.

Jenny proudly dragged Cole to a chair in the kitchen. "I have my own tea set, but it's at home."

"I'd like to see it sometime." Cole said the words without a trace of scorn.

"I'll invite you for tea. Pearl makes scrumptious apple tarts."

"Pearl's a fine cook." He took the cup of coffee. "Thank you, Mrs. Martin."

"Goodness, Cole. You're like family. Please call me Selena."

"Yes, ma'am." He drank. "Now, that hits the spot."

Abbie felt uneasy. With so much unsettled, Mama was being too familiar. And she didn't want Jenny growing attached to Cole again if . . . She caught his glance and smoothed the concern from her face too late. He read her thoughts with ease.

She dropped her gaze to the coffee in her cup. "I'm sorry, Mama. Would you mind if I made some tea? I'm sick to death of coffee."

Mama smiled. "I'd imagine you are after months on the trail. How did you fare?" Mama took the cup and poured the coffee back into the pot, then put tea leaves in the kettle to steep.

"As well as we could, though we didn't fetch the price I wanted." *Or needed*, Abbie added silently. "We went too late."

"Well, the Lord provides."

"I know." She felt Cole's gaze. "Sometimes it would just be nice to know how." She watched Mama strain the tea and took the cup offered. Elliot rested his hands on her leg as she sat. He'd not left her side except to ask Cole for animals. She hoped he'd have time to make something for the child.

What was she thinking? He wouldn't leave again, would he? But if he didn't, what then? They could hardly go back to the way things were, not after the day on the prairie, not after . . . She closed her eyes and sipped. Maybe the steam would hide the flush her thoughts had caused.

Except for not barking orders at her, Cole had maintained his previous demeanor. He had not once referred to their discussion, nor touched her, nor made any move to further his advances. She had caught a gentle look now and then, but beyond that he'd made no show of his feelings.

Perhaps it had been nothing more than a confused response to her grief. Part of her fervently hoped so. She'd come treacherously close to feelings she feared more than typhoid fever. But what if he left? She smiled down at Elliot, still pressed as closely to her side as possible. She had her son and Jenny and Mama and

Pa. She had Nora and Clara and her other friends. Surely that was enough.

◆◆◆◆◆◆◆

As Cole rode back to the Lucky Star with Jenny in the saddle with him, he recalled carrying her when her head had scarcely reached to his chest. He'd had to hold tight or she'd slide off the side. She was a slip of a girl now, but there was the same haunted look behind her smile. A look no child her age ought to have.

He wondered if Abbie realized what Jenny felt when she petted Elliot. Not that he wasn't a fine boy. He was so like his pa, though with Abbie's eyes. The ladies would be lining up some years hence. And he could hardly blame Abbie. That baby had likely brought her through as nothing else could.

But Jenny was a queer little thing. Tough on the outside, but not so tough within. She needed someone who preferred a saucy little sprite with big brown eyes and a fetching smile. He wouldn't mind filling the bill if he knew he'd be staying awhile. 'Course, that was up to Abbie, and there was no telling how it would go.

He'd made sure not to pressure her, and though she'd not had a sharp tongue for him recently, neither had she shown any romantic inclination. He knew better than to hope. Maybe he could stay awhile if she asked, but it wouldn't be easy. Here he was again, waiting on a word from Abbie to decide his road. How many years had it been now?

Jenny's head bobbed against his collarbone. "I have my own mare, Snowdrop. Elliot has a pony, but it's small."

"Well, he's a small boy right now. What color's yer horse?"

"White, silly. That's why she's Snowdrop."

Cole chuckled. "Yeah. I shoulda known."

When they reached the yard, he handed Jenny down to Will, who had already taken Elliot from Abbie. He swung down and stood uneasily. These were uncharted waters all right. Will led the horses away as the children ran to greet Zena on the steps.

Abbie approached. "What are your plans, Cole?"

He couldn't read her eyes. Maybe her thoughts were as muddled as his. "Cain't say as I have any."

She looked as skittish as a new foal, not at all the Abbie he knew. That woman had given as good as she got and come back for more. This one looked storm tossed and weary.

He shrugged. "I reckon I can find a place in town to stay. Or if yer needin' help . . . with Breck gone an' all . . ."

"Oh, Cole, I don't know what to do." Her eyes came up to his, and he realized again just how young she was. "I've hardly made enough on this sale to cover debts until a new beef herd is ready. I've only two men left, and they surely can't handle the ranch themselves . . . if they'll even work for my wages without . . . extra . . ."

She let her breath out sharply and spread her hands. "Maybe I ought to sell after all."

"Then what?"

She dropped her face in her hands. "I don't know."

"From what I hear you got gents lined up wantin' to marry you."

"That's the last thing I want." She spoke into her hands.

So there it was. He looked up at the house, around the yard, the outbuildings, the land. She could get a fair piece for the place, enough to set her well enough. If that's what she wanted. "You got Will."

She looked up. "What?"

"He's a fair cowboy. That'd give you three hands if you don't mind lookin' after yer own stables. You might get a boy to come out twice a week and muck 'em for you."

Her eyes lit. "I know Tucker would. I could spare him a little something."

"I reckon he'd take to it right well. Sounds like all you need now's a good foreman." He quirked the side of his mouth. "I got some experience in the job."

She shook her head. "I couldn't pay you anywhere near what Monte paid. I'm sure you could do better elsewhere."

"I'm sure I could, too. But it's a right pain in the neck tryin' to keep tabs on you from Santa Fe to Cheyenne to El Paso."

She got that coltish look again, and he felt sure she'd tell him to go on anyway. "I . . . don't know, Cole."

"What happened out there on the prairie ain't likely to happen again. You got yer grievin' out, and . . . I'd bunk in the bunkhouse." Her obvious relief sent a pang through his chest, but he ignored it.

"The men take their meals in the house now, since Charlie passed."

"You cover my expenses and feed me on Pearl's cookin', and we'll call it even."

"I wish I could do more."

"When you can, I'll let you."

Abbie smiled, and it took all he had not to pull her into his arms. *A dern fool indeed.*

♦♦♦♦♦♦♦

Abbie almost felt hopeful as she drove the buggy the next morning toward the mission with Jenny on one side and Elliot on the other. Elliot pushed the dark strands from his eyes. ". . . and Tucker fell in with the pig, and Grandpa . . ." Abbie smiled. He hadn't stopped talking from the minute she slapped the reins.

She glanced at Jenny sitting primly beside her. "What's the matter, Jenny?"

"Nothing."

She could feel the child's tension, and reached over to stroke her neck. "You're awfully quiet."

"Elliot's a chatterbox."

"That's not kind, Jenny." And she knew that wasn't what bothered her. "What is it?"

"Katie's getting a new baby."

"I know. Not for a month yet, though."

Jenny turned her serious brown eyes to her. "Are you going to get a baby, too?"

Abbie was amazed how the words hurt. It wasn't as though the thought never occurred to her that she would not have another child, but hearing it spoken so directly . . . She steadied her voice. "No, Jenny. I haven't a husband."

Jenny turned her chin up. "But I thought Cole . . ."

Abbie's heart lurched. She raised her eyebrows in surprise.

Jenny rushed on. "I thought you brought him home to be our pa."

Her pa. How could Cole be her pa? It jolted Abbie somewhere deep. Even if they married, which thankfully Cole had no intention of pursuing, he would not be Jenny's pa unless . . . Was there something deeper Jenny was saying? Did she feel . . . separate?

"Cole is a friend, Jenny."

"Oh. Like me."

Abbie reined in. She turned Jenny toward her. "No, Jenny. You are not a friend. You are family. You're my niece, but you're like my own little girl, and I love you as though you were my own."

Jenny fingered the ruffle on her dress.

"Don't you believe that?"

Jenny shrugged. "I guess. But it's not the same." She looked up. "Could I pretend Cole is my pa?"

Abbie felt her chest quake. "I don't . . . think so, Jenny. One shouldn't pretend things that make people what they're not."

"But we pretend I'm a princess, and I'm not. And Elliot pretends he's a pony. And—"

"Yes, I know. But you see, you're pretending for yourself, not for someone else. Cole might not understand."

"Doesn't he know how to pretend?"

Abbie had a very hard time picturing Cole pretending anything. "I don't think so, Jenny. But Katie does." She took up the reins and slapped them.

"Aunt Abbie?"

"Yes."

"If you got a baby girl . . . would I still be like your own?"

The pain again. "Yes, Jenny. Always."

She had a cup of tea with Glenna, then left the children to play while she drove to see Nora. As she approached the mission house, she saw a rider leaving at a canter. She reined in outside the chapel and led the horse to the trough, then knocked on Nora's door.

"I already told ya no, ya fool lad. Give a girl a minute to think, will ya." Nora flung the door open.

Abbie smiled. "Was that . . ."

"Aye. Davy McConnel's makin' me daft."

"Is he courting you?"

"Aye. He thinks I like the looks of him."

Abbie laughed. "And do you?"

"I'd never tell him if I did." Nora took her arm. "Come an' have a cup. It's a long time ye've been away."

"Seems like forever. I don't think I'll ever sit quite the way I used to."

"I canna believe you drove the cattle yourself, Abbie."

"Not exactly myself. Cole—that is—the men drove the cattle. I mainly saw to the horses and cooked. Poor James nursed his back all night."

Nora handed her the tea. "It's glad I am you're home. And in one piece, as well. But I'm sorry about your workers. What'll you do?"

"I'll manage. The man who used to be foreman for Monte is back. He helped me drive the cattle and said he'd stay on a bit." She tried not to reveal anything but the bare facts of Cole's business with her. The rest was too muddled, too precarious.

Nora nodded. "I don't know how you do it. It's hard enough takin' care of Father O'Brien comin' in at all hours from visitin' the sick and what not."

Abbie tried not to imagine taking care of Cole, but the memory of his cut and bleeding side, his stoic face, his wry smile . . .

Nora waved her hand. "I'd not like to be responsible for too many men at once."

"I imagine you could handle Davy." Abbie gave her an impish smile. "He's the mild McConnel."

"Mild is he? More like mule headed if ye ask me." But she flushed.

"Oh, Nora, I am glad. Four years is a long time for him to still be paying attention. He's a good man."

"Don't be thinkin' ye hear weddin' bells. You're a fine one to talk. What's it up to now? Nine proposals, last I heard."

Abbie stared into her cup. "That's different."

"Not to my thinkin'."

"How was your harvest?"

"Oh fine, an' the weather's been nice an' Father O'Brien's rheumatism isn't near as bad here in the dry, but that's not what we were discussin'."

Abbie smiled. "I knew when you came that we were alike. Four years has turned us into peas in a pod."

Nora laughed. "And a pair of hard, dry ones we are. What if I up an' marry Davy? Where'll that leave you?"

"Has he asked?"

"Aye. Fourteen times a day lately. He's found so many ways to say it, he could put them in a book."

"I never considered Davy McConnel a man of words."

"I suppose any man pushed far enough can find a thing or two to say."

Abbie smiled and sighed. "I suppose so." Monte had been a man of words. He was so well read, knowledgeable about so much. He enjoyed discoursing. How she missed their discussions, their arguments even, the way he'd raise his eyebrow to concede a point. She would never have that again.

Nora sipped her tea. "It's never the same, is it? If I keep waitin' for Davy to be Jaime, I'll die on the vine. I know that here." She tapped her head. "But I'm afraid."

"Of what?"

Nora shrugged. "Maybe comparin' 'em. Maybe . . . forgettin'."

Abbie's throat tightened. "I have a picture of Monte. We had it made in Charleston. I look at it every day to keep him in my mind."

Nora's finger dragged over her cup. "Maybe . . . it's time ya put it away."

♦♦♦♦♦♦♦

Abbie lay awake. Time to put it away . . . to forget? No. To go on? How? *Lord, I can't see my way. I don't know your will. Help me.* She looked at the picture in the shadows. It had taken months after Monte's death for her to look at it, and only the fear of forgetting had brought it out.

But once she had, she kept it where she could see it. High enough to be out of Elliot's reach, but never out of her own. *Oh, Monte.* There was a shadow in his eyes from the loss of Frances, but his smile was there. The photographer had wanted a serious pose, but she insisted he smile.

Her arguing had amused him enough to manage it. Her own picture in the hinged frame beside his was prim, but Monte had sworn he saw a naughty streak in her expression. She clasped her hands at her throat and looked to the ceiling. Too many thoughts, too many memories. She could never tuck them all away. She closed her eyes.

But maybe there was room to live, as well. She had much to live for. The children, the ranch, the men who worked it loyally, and the servants who were more family than not. She might never again love a man as she had loved Monte, but her heart was full nonetheless.

Elliot's kisses were soft on her cheek. Jenny had shown an affection deepened by the sharing of her fears and Abbie's assurance of her love. And there was no arguing Cole's place in her heart, though she couldn't yet probe its depth. He was willing to stay, and that was enough.

She felt grateful beyond words for her blessings. Whatever tomorrow held, whatever fears, whatever grief, God's grace would see her through. Whatever His purpose for her life, He was mighty enough to accomplish the work He had begun. Warm drowsiness stole over and lured her deeper.

"Mama."

She opened her eyes to the white-gowned, tousle-haired boy beside her bed.

His small hand snaked into hers. "I thought you might be afraid."

Abbie translated and raised the covers to admit her little son. As he snuggled into her warmth, wiggling and burrowing, she wrapped him in her arms. "I'm so blessed to have a fine, strong man to care for me." She kissed his soft head and smiled.

But the words conjured another face, rugged and mustached; green eyes that could ignite with sulfurous flames or hold such aching tenderness they melted her knees; arms strong and capable; hands as adept with rope and gun as they were gentle on her cheek. She felt a quickening inside, a tentative searching. Maybe . . . in God's time . . . maybe . . .

Acknowledgments

All thanks and praise to my Lord and Savior,
for whom and through whom all things are accomplished.

And thanks to the people on earth He has provided
to love and support me through this work.

To Him be the glory and honor forever.

Honor's Disguise

KRISTEN HEITZMANN

Honor's Disguise

BETHANY HOUSE PUBLISHERS
MINNEAPOLIS, MINNESOTA 55438

Honor's Disguise

Cover illustration by Joe Nordstrom

Unless otherwise identified, Scripture quotations are from the King James Version of the Bible.

Published by Bethany House Publishers
A Ministry of Bethany Fellowship International
11400 Hampshire Avenue South
Minneapolis, Minnesota 55438
www.bethanyhouse.com

Printed in the United States of America
2 in 1 ISBN 0-7394-0594-2

To Jessica,
my daughter, my joy, my inspiration

She opens her mouth in wisdom,
And the teaching of kindness is on her tongue.

PROVERBS 31:26 NASB

Rocky Mountain Legacy

Honor's Pledge

Honor's Price

Honor's Quest

Honor's Disguise

KRISTEN HEITZMANN was raised on five acres of ponderosa pine at the base of the Rocky Mountains in Colorado, where she still lives with her husband and four children. A music minister and artist, Kristen delights in sharing the traditions of our heritage, both through one-on-one interaction and now through her bestselling series, ROCKY MOUNTAIN LEGACY.

One

The slanting light of the bright November morning glinted off the polished silver fork in Cole Jasper's work-worn hand. With its flowered handle and tapered tines, it looked too fine and dainty for the job of taking food from the plate to his mouth. As out of place in his hand as he felt in the room.

Cole glanced around the long cherrywood table at Matt and Will and Curtis. They shoveled in the stringed beef and hot cakes as though they were eating Charlie's grub in the bunkhouse. Weren't they even aware of the fine china, the lace cloth . . . Abbie at the end of the table? It nearly took his appetite.

Abbie glanced up, her quick, eager eyes taking in his hesitation. Her thick brown curls were pulled back with combs, but they framed her face and slender neck and hung long down her back. Too clearly he recalled the feel of that hair, his fingers threaded through.

"Aren't you hungry, Cole?"

"Yeah, I'm hungry, a'right."

"Do you want something different?"

"Nope. This is fine." Too fine. He'd never get used to eating in here, in the fine dining room of the big house. He'd take a chaw of jerked beef on horseback over all this fancy—

"You wants eggs, Mistuh Jazzper?"

He picked up his fork again and eyed Pearl in all her

mahogany girth. "No, ma'am. This here's just fine."

Cole caught Abbie's smile before she masked it. So she was amused, was she? He took a bite of the stringed beef. It was fork-tender and seasoned just right. He dug in, careful to keep the gravy from his mustache. It wouldn't hurt for the others to learn some manners, too.

Now that he was running this ranch again, he'd slap them in line so fast. . . . Take Will's rubbing his mouth on his sleeve, and Matt eating a bite from his knife. No one might care when they ate around the fire, but there were young'uns at the table.

Cole glanced at four-year-old Elliot working his knife awkwardly through his hot cakes. The boy set down the knife, switched the fork to the other hand, and took his bite. There now. Even the little one knew how to do it right.

Beside Elliot, Jenny had hardly taken her dark eyes from him. Her little pointy face was too grave for her seven years, and he felt as though she were sucking him in. Why or how he didn't know, just that her clutch on his heart nearly staggered him. But he saw a wariness, too, as though she thought he might up and disappear any moment. Maybe now he'd have a chance to convince her otherwise.

Cole swigged his coffee. It was strong and black as he liked it, without being bitter. That was an accomplishment only female hands seemed to master. Good coffee or not, he might feel more at ease if Pearl and James joined them at the table. But having them hover about, filling his plate and cup and dern near wiping his mouth, was powerful uncomfortable.

He caught Abbie smiling again and realized he must be wearing a scowl the size of Texas. He tossed his napkin in his plate, stood, and eyed the men. "Y'all know your jobs for the day. Hit the range as soon as you're through." Which might be a week from Sunday the way they were slopping down. He started for the door.

"May I be excused?" Elliot chimed behind him, and Cole kicked himself.

"You may." There was a laugh in Abbie's voice that he did not appreciate.

"Mister Cole?"

Cole stopped at the doorway. "Just Cole."

"Have you made my animals yet, Cole?"

"Nope." He squatted down. "What animal would you like me to start with?"

"Can you make my pony?"

Cole rubbed his mustache. "I reckon I can." The boy's blue eyes fairly shone. Who'd have thought his little carvings would cause such a look?

"Can you make it today?"

"I'll see about that. I got a heap of work to do for your ma."

"She won't mind." He shook his head confidently.

Cole glanced back at Abbie's indulgent face. He reckoned Elliot was right at that. She'd no doubt grant the boy's every wish, within her means. He ruffled Elliot's small, dark head and went out.

The air was brisk and the breeze rattled the drying leaves. He stood on the porch beneath the soaring portico supported by tall white pillars. He breathed the air and felt the faint sunshine on his face. He looked south across the yard of the Lucky Star ranch to the buff-colored range and beyond to where the mountains wound around from the west in a hazy blue.

A man could get used to the sight. Especially if he'd spent years sweating and worrying over the place. No matter that the ranch was Abbie's, not his. He'd been branding the cattle, mending the fences, irrigating the land, and riding herd with its cowhands long enough to put down roots he never expected.

Even during the four years after Abbie ran him off, the Lucky Star was his first concern. With the promise he'd made to her late husband to look after her and the children, it couldn't have been any other way. And he'd done it in the only way he could, by secretly sending money to her headman.

How Abbie had bucked when she found out! Maybe it still stung her, but they'd reached a tentative peace. At least he hoped so. He heard her skirts swish as she joined him on the porch. Her blue eyes held more than a little mischief, and he knew she'd seen his discomfort.

He frowned. "That bad, eh?"

"You'll get used to it." Abbie smiled, showing even, white teeth between the soft lips he avoided thinking on.

"No, I won't. I nearly coldcocked Matt when he blew his nose in the napkin."

She laughed, and it sounded so good he grinned back. How long had it been since she'd laughed like that? Something about her seemed different this morning, as though . . . a storm cloud had been lifted.

She almost looked like a girl again, as she had when he first saw her the day she came looking for Montgomery Farrel . . . the man she loved and married. She wasn't a girl now but young yet, younger than her grieving made her seem. At twenty-six—even more than before—she made a man stand up and take notice. The hard part was keeping it to himself.

"You mind if I take an hour an' carve Elliot a critter or two?"

"I'd consider it a supreme favor. Those animals have been a point of contention between the children since Elliot was old enough to notice."

"That right?" Cole felt the need of a grin but fought it off.

Abbie put a hand on his arm, and he felt it clear through to his soul. "I appreciate your staying." Her lashes drooped over her eyes, and they seemed to deepen and draw him in till he felt like a mouse in the gaze of a bull snake. If she opened up he'd hop right in, death or no.

He cleared his throat. "That's a'right, Abbie. No thanks required."

Abbie looked up into Cole Jasper's sage green eyes, high cheekbones, and rugged jaw. His peaked brows drew down to the crease above the bridge of his nose as he tried to shrug off her gratitude. She couldn't express how thankful she was that he was there, not just to run the ranch, but . . . but what?

She wasn't ready to admit there might be more, wasn't willing to recall what she'd felt in his arms, feelings that went beyond comfort. She'd bared her grief, the desperate pain of losing Monte. She'd opened the pit of fear and sorrow that had kept her bound these last four years.

Cole had been shaken by her tears. She'd sensed his helpless distress. But he'd reacted as a man, and his lips had wakened emotions she thought never to feel again. More than that, her heart had reached out and met his waiting. He'd made her want and hope and need. He'd almost made her believe.

But since that kiss, he'd kept back, careful not to offend—so careful she wondered if that moment of passion had been as foreign to him as to her since losing her husband, her love. Yet here he was, solid and capable and willing to work for next to nothing. Was it only his promise to Monte that kept him?

Cole had loved her once; Abbie knew that. But out on the prairie when she'd shamelessly clung to him, he'd been the one to step back. She was thankful for that—and so many other things. More grateful than words could say. But she felt the need to try.

"I wonder if you know how much it—" She halted as a rider came up the drive at a gallop.

Cole looked up and frowned, then slipped Abbie's hand from his arm and walked down the stairs, stopping squarely in the yard. His slightly bowlegged stance was wary, but he made no other move.

Abbie looked from Cole to the rider, whose broad leather chaps flapped as he swung down from the horse. In two strides, he reached Cole and swung a fist to his face. Cole sprawled in the dirt. Abbie gasped, but she knew Cole could take him. She'd seen him fight two men his size and send them running. She waited for him to spring up and show the man what for.

Cole gained his knees before the man kicked his ribs and punched his jaw. Cole's head snapped back, but he didn't raise a hand. Why didn't he defend himself? The man kicked him again, hard in the ribs, pulled him up by the shirt and—

"Stop!" Abbie rushed down the stairs, ready to scream for help if needed, though the men had reached the range by now and only James would hear.

Cole staggered up. "Stay out of it, Abbie." He thrust her aside.

The stranger punched him squarely in the mouth.

She pressed in between them. "Who are you? What is this?"

The man shoved her away and hurled himself at Cole. Cole sprawled with the man on top and took a punch to the cheekbone.

Abbie tugged at the man's collar as he dragged Cole up, arm raised to strike again. She reached into her pocket, took out the pistol, and cocked it next to his head. "Don't think I won't use it."

The man froze, but she felt his rage still and hoped he wouldn't call her bluff. His breath came thickly as he knelt, undecided. Her own pulse throbbed in her ears while her finger hugged the trigger. Slowly he released Cole's shirtfront. Cole collapsed, rubbing the blood from his lip with the back of his hand.

The man kept his eyes on Cole, and she saw his large hands shaking with each labored breath. His voice came low and gravelly. "This ain't the end of it. You'll pay for Auralee if it's the last thing I do." He picked up his hat and lurched to his feet.

Abbie held her breath, half expecting him to charge again. But he mounted, then dug his spurs and galloped from the yard.

Abbie dropped to her knees beside Cole. She was shaking worse than he. "Come into the house and I'll take care of—"

"I'll take care of myself." He held his ribs as he stood and spat blood.

Her anger kindled. "Oh yes, I saw that. Why didn't you fight back? You could have taken him."

"It ain't your business." He picked up his hat from the dust and limped to the pump. It squealed as he filled his hands and doused his face. The icy water dripped from his sun-streaked hair and dark blond mustache. He turned away.

"Cole!"

He kept walking for the bunkhouse.

An ache started in Abbie's chest. Something was wrong. Very wrong. She followed him to the bunkhouse and watched as he rolled his belongings tightly into a blanket from the bunk.

Surely he wasn't leaving. He'd as much as promised to stay on. She could see the swelling beneath one eye and across his jaw. He winced and grunted when he bent, and his breath came in shallow gasps as he tied the roll.

"Cole, who was that man?"

He buckled his gun belt on his hip and checked the loads in the Colt .44 revolver. "My brother."

"Your . . ." Now Abbie realized the resemblance. The hair had been darker but the eyes just as green, the same rough-hewn features, the lean, lanky build. "What's going on? Why would your brother . . ."

Cole holstered the gun and reached for his sheepskin coat. She saw the pain in his eyes from the motion. "Where are you going? You can't ride like this."

He laid the coat beside the bedroll. "I gotta work this out with Sam."

"Not if you can't even—"

He caught her into his arms and kissed her hard enough to split open his lip.

Abbie's heart beat her ribs. She tasted his blood and clung to him. "Please, Cole . . ."

"Don't." His arms tightened, and he searched again for her mouth, softly, then desperately.

Abbie felt a matching need, but he pushed her back at the sound of horses in the yard. He limped to the door and pulled it open. Over his shoulder she saw two men with rifles. Cole stepped out as they dismounted, and Abbie tried to see past him through the narrow doorway.

The older of the two men took a paper from his vest. "Cole Jasper, you're wanted for the murder of Auralee Dubois."

Abbie's breath caught in her throat, but before she could move, the man swung his rifle butt into Cole's belly. The heavy-set one smacked the back of Cole's head with a length of iron pipe. She cried out as Cole crumpled.

The gray-haired man thrust up his hand to her with a look that froze her blood. "It says here dead'r alive. Dead's easier, but if you don't interfere, we might give 'im a chance."

Anger surged through Abbie. "Who are you? You're not lawmen."

"No, ma'am."

"Bounty hunters?" She watched as the second man roughly bound Cole's wrists.

Cole groaned. Abbie's heart wrenched. She was shaking all over as they pulled off his boots to find a knife, then unbuckled his gun belt and hauled him to his feet. He staggered, and the second man crammed his hat onto his head.

"You're making a mistake. Cole's been here with me. He can't possibly be involved. . . ."

They hoisted him to the back of a third horse they had in tow and tied his wrists to the pommel. "How long's he been with you?"

"The last two months, straight through."

"It's taken us near four to track 'im down. He's wanted down in El Paso for the murder of a harlot."

Abbie's breath left her chest. "That's not possible." Her voice came thin and pale.

"That's fer the law to decide. We're haulin' him back to Texas to stand trial . . . if he makes it there." The man swung astride his piebald mare.

She tried to catch Cole's eye, but he was dazed. He winced when the horse jolted to a trot, pulled by the reins in the other man's hand. They headed south, but not toward town. She stared after them. *Dear God* . . . She looked down at Cole's black leather boots lying in the dirt. She picked them up and held them to her chest. *Oh, dear God* . . .

Two

G*rant.* The thought came to Abbie with sudden clarity. Her brother would know the law. He would help her, help Cole. Her chest squeezed as she ran to the stable, still clutching Cole's boots.

The men were out on the range and hadn't heard a thing. What if they had? What if they'd come running? Would the bounty men have shot Cole then and there? Abbie shuddered. She could get Will and Matt now, but she hesitated to do so. She had to think this through.

She saddled Zephyr, every step taking longer for the shaking of her hands. *Why now, Lord? Why must trouble come just as I started to trust, just as I started to hope?* But for once the trouble wasn't hers. It was Cole's.

Cole Jasper. Cowboy, trail boss, foreman. He'd been a friend to her and Monte both. He'd been a hard and loyal worker, and more than that, he'd been honest and outspoken enough to set her straight when she'd needed it most.

He'd been with Monte when he died, and though he hadn't been responsible for his death, she'd blamed Cole in her heart. She knew the truth of it now, and every accusation she'd flung at him stuck in her throat. He'd done his best to save her husband from the crazed bull that gored him, but that wasn't God's will. Abbie felt a cold shiver.

Though she believed in God's sovereignty, she still feared

His will. Sometimes it just hurt too much. But now was not the time to brood. Cole was in trouble, and his trouble was hers. Abbie mounted and rode for town.

Every mile seemed to take twice as long as usual. Her thoughts rushed and surged and circled back on themselves. *Grant will know. Grant will tell me what to do.* Her brother was not in his office, so Abbie rode to his yellow frame house and banged the door.

He pulled it open. "For heaven's sake, Abbie, Marcy's upstairs with a headache." He caught her as she staggered against him, and his brow furrowed. "What is it?"

"They've taken Cole."

"Who? What are you talking about?"

"Bounty hunters."

"What?" Grant took her by the shoulders and his brown eyes searched over her. "Come in here and sit down. You'd better start at the beginning."

She let him take her into the parlor. She hoped Marcy would stay where she was. It was bad enough with four-year-old Emily Elizabeth staring out from behind the curtains. Abbie sat down where he placed her.

"All right, tell me." His voice was gentle, but insistent.

She tried to gather her thoughts, but words came faster. "A man rode in this morning, Cole's brother, and they fought. No . . . Cole didn't fight, he just let his brother beat him. Sam, that's Cole's brother, said something about making him pay for Auralee. I broke them up, and Sam rode off."

Abbie pushed the hair from her eyes. "Cole meant to go after him, to work it out, he said. But before he could leave, they came."

"The bounty hunters?"

She nodded. "They knocked him unconscious, and—" Her voice broke. "Can they just take him like that? Without proof, without . . ." She spread her hands and saw they trembled.

"They said he's wanted for murder in El Paso. They said dead or alive and dead's easier."

Grant's face was grave. "Did they have a warrant or . . ."

"A poster. I think it was a poster."

"Did you get a look at it?"

She shook her head. "Not clearly."

Grant sat back. His jet buttons glimmered on his vest, and his sleeves were linked crisply at his wrists. "I'm sorry, Abbie. Assuming the poster is valid for Cole's arrest, he's fair game."

"Arrest for what?" Marcy stood at the landing to the stairs, wrapped in a blue silk gown tied high on her bulging waist.

Abbie dropped her face into her hands. The last one she wanted in on this was Marcy. "Is there nothing we can do?"

Grant released a slow breath. "Technically, until he's in the hands of the law, anyone has rights to him."

Abbie shuddered.

"If these men have been sent by Texas authorities to track him down and bring him back, then their claim has weight. But if they're working off a poster, they may just be out for the reward money, in which case . . ."

"Is anyone going to tell me what's going on?" Marcy flounced into the room.

Abbie shook her head. "But you know as well as I do that Cole can't be guilty of murder."

"Murder!" Marcy sank to a chair.

Abbie was too distraught to heed her. "There's obviously some mistake, but those men were . . . brutal. I'm afraid for Cole. I don't trust them. Why didn't they turn him in to Sheriff Davis? Why haul him to Texas when they could collect the money here and be done with it?"

"There's some validity to your question, but . . ."

"It's because they'll get the money for him dead, even if he had nothing to do with this . . . Auralee."

Grant's frown deepened.

"What is it?" Abbie's voice was scarcely above a whisper.

"I don't think that's very likely—not if his brother also mentioned her name. Cole must be involved somehow."

Abbie closed her eyes.

Marcy huffed. "I always said . . ."

Abbie flew from her chair and stopped with a finger just short of Marcy's smug face. "Marcy, if you say one thing against Cole, I'll slap you silly."

Marcy shrank back, ashen, but two spots of color rose up on her cheeks. "Grant, are you going to let her speak to me like that?" Her whine set Abbie's teeth on edge.

Grant turned. "Perhaps it would be best if you went back to bed, dear. You don't want to tax yourself in your condition."

"*Well.*" Marcy pressed her hand to her belly. "It's clear where your loyalties lie." She tossed her blond curls and stalked upstairs.

"I'll pay for that one." Grant smiled grimly. "Now, then. Abbie, I'm afraid your hands are tied."

Abbie winced, remembering Cole's wrists roped to the saddle.

"Unless you think you can take him physically from the men who found him, he's their booty, so to speak. If Cole goes along peaceably and doesn't try to escape, he should make it safely enough to trial. Did he give you any indication that he was on the run?"

"Of course not. He was as stunned as I was. He knows nothing about this, you can be sure."

"Can I?"

"What do you mean?"

"First off, he gave no argument to his brother's accusations . . . or did I miss something?"

"No. He didn't."

"He let his brother beat him. That's the behavior of a guilty man. Second, Cole's first thought was to pack up and leave.

That sounds like a man on the run."

"But—"

"I'm only saying how it looks. Maybe when he learned his brother was on to him, he guessed others would follow. Cole may have suspected his brother would lead them to him."

A low wail started in Abbie's throat. *No. It isn't possible.* But she thought of the way he'd held her when she'd begged him to stay. There was desperation in his grasp. "I can't believe it."

"I'm not saying it's so."

She looked up at Grant with tears stinging her eyes. "I'm afraid for him."

Grant reached over and held her hand. "I know. But you're going to have to let the law handle it."

The law. But Cole wasn't in the hands of the law. He was in the grip of two merciless men driven by greed. Abbie stood. "Thank you, Grant. I'm sorry about Marcy."

"I'll make up to her. She always comes around." He smiled, then squeezed her arm. "Are you all right?"

Abbie nodded, but she wasn't all right. She owed Cole more than she wanted to think. It weighed on her like lead. Honor? Did she at last know how Monte felt, bowed down by a debt of honor? Cole had risked his life for her more than once. He had met her needs again and again. She could not abandon him now.

Abbie went outside and unfastened Zephyr's reins. But what could she possibly do? The helplessness overwhelmed her. She was one woman. Where could she turn? The sky was clouding over with cold, gray clouds and the air smelled of snow. Cole had no coat, no boots, and he was in no condition to ride.

She felt desolate. For the first time this morning she'd been able to breathe as though something hard around her heart had cracked open. Watching Cole's discomfort at the breakfast table had amused her, but she appreciated his concern even more. For all his rough edges, Cole cared about things. He wanted them right.

It was not possible that he was involved in some lurid murder of . . . Grant's arguments were powerful, but he didn't know Cole as she did. Did she? Did she know anything about him, really?

What had he done before he signed on with Monte? Where had he been for the last four years? Abbie thought when she had told him to leave he'd take a position with one of the nearby ranches, but he'd gone away. To Texas?

What had he said? *It was too hard keeping track of her from . . . El Paso.* Was he in El Paso four months ago? Abbie's heart pounded. Could he have taken the cattle drive to Kansas with her, knowing he was hunted? Was it just another way to keep moving, to hide himself?

She felt his arms around her as he'd held her on the plain. *We got to sort things out.* Did he know then he was in trouble? Zephyr stamped, and Abbie clutched the reins. What she really ached to know would not be stilled. Who was Auralee Dubois?

The emotion attached to that thought frightened her. She hadn't felt such . . . jealous anger since Monte married Sharlyn. What was wrong with her? What was it to her if Cole . . . Abbie dropped her forehead to Zephyr's neck. Even if he knew this . . . woman, Cole could not have hurt her. It wasn't in his nature. Abbie knew that to her core.

She swung astride and heeled the mare. Zephyr bolted away, and Abbie scarcely cared where she ran. Confusion swirled inside—anger that he was in this trouble along with a burning need to help him. Somehow she must help. Somehow. She passed through stands of scrub oak and headed up the rocky slopes. Yes, the mountains. She had always gone to the mountains to think, to pray, to find answers.

Oh, Lord, what can I do? Did you bring Cole back only for this? How can I leave him in the hands of men who think nothing of his life? She shuddered, hearing again the thud of the pipe on Cole's skull. "*Dead is easier.*" She had no doubt the men would kill him if it suited them.

Zephyr lunged upward through the pines, and Abbie governed her thoughts. Where could she turn? Whom could she trust? Pa? He would agree with Grant, and Grant thought Cole was guilty.

Sheriff Davis? He would consider justice was already being served. Her men? Matt and Will could not be spared from the ranch again so soon after the last drive, and Curtis was too weak from the ravages of typhoid.

Oh, Lord, Cole showed me what a mockery I made of your grace. Help me now to follow where you lead. Show me what to do.

Zephyr had slowed to a walk, her breath expelled in white huffs. The craggy mountainside was steep and cold. They had left the sun behind, and fog swirled through the pines. Higher up there would be snow, but here in the foothills it was no more than gray breath that masked what lay ahead. Zephyr's ears perked and stood up. Abbie straightened in the saddle. What was it? What did the mist hold?

Suddenly Abbie sensed that she was not alone. She listened intently. No sound of movement, but a chill ran up her spine like so many spiders' icy feet. Then from the mist came a man. Buckskin pants and woolen coat, quiver and bow, black hair twined with feathers and fur. She breathed with deep expectancy.

He looked like he had the first time she'd seen him, only now there were fine strands of silver in the black of his hair. Then he'd ridden a paint mustang instead of leading the horse Monte had given him some years before. That was the day he'd been hunted for a crime he didn't commit, hunted as Cole was now. He had found her in his need, and now he came in hers.

Had God conjured him from the mist? Abbie waited until

he stopped beside Zephyr's head, then swung down and stood before him. "Gray Wolf."

"Wise One rides with fear."

Had God put an urging on Gray Wolf's heart to find her here? Was he connected in a way that God understood, but she could not? She felt a stillness inside and realized her fear and confusion had fled. Here was one who could help. Gray Wolf must certainly be God's answer to her plea.

"I must find a man who's been taken captive. Will you ride with me?" Until that moment Abbie hadn't considered actually going after Cole herself. Somehow it had been impressed on her heart, and she spoke it without knowing. But the stillness remained.

He looked at her steadily. His broad face, angular cheekbones, hawklike nose, and straight down-sloped mouth revealed nothing. Then he inclined his head slightly. "Gray Wolf will ride."

Her relief was immediate, followed closely by a stabbing ache at the thought of leaving the children again.

♦♦♦♦♦♦♦

Samuel Jasper held his hand in the icy flow of the mountain stream. Nowhere in Texas did water run so clear and cold. The edges were ice, but the center of the creek ran swiftly, and it was there he soaked his damaged hand. Cole had always possessed a hard head and bony jaw.

He grimaced as he clenched the hand and drew it from the water. He'd ridden a long way to give Cole that beating. He wasn't nearly satisfied when that woman pulled the gun and made her threats. Would she have shot him? Maybe. Cole seemed to have a mesmerizing way with the ladies these days. He certainly had with Auralee.

Sam's blood boiled. Dern him! He splashed the water angrily, then rubbed his wet hands over his face. He hadn't gotten the answers he'd come for. Did Cole do it? Was it possible his little brother was guilty of what they said? He groaned with dark memories, memories that had tainted him. How badly did they still burn Cole?

He stared at the rocky bottom of the creek. His breath formed a cloudy mist above the running water. He knew Cole could kill. Did he kill Auralee? Sam's heart withered inside him. *Oh, Auralee. Why? Why did you choose him to throw your heart away on?* He staggered back to the bank and sank to the dry, frozen earth.

Tears froze on his cheeks as he fought the grief and fury. "Why!" He gripped his head between his hands. His anger wasn't half spent. He wanted to bloody Cole until . . . Images filled his mind, visions of Cole's young back slashed with bleeding welts, his face and arms blue and swollen.

Sam groaned and looked at his hands. He'd taken after his pa in size. Cole hadn't grown so tall, holding up at six foot one, while he had the extra four inches his pa bragged on. Sam felt the throbbing in his hand.

He looked at the fingers, splayed, then fisted them. He'd raised his hand to Cole before, when it was due him, when he'd stepped too far over the line. He'd taken him down when Cole was strong enough to clean his whistle, though he never had.

But Sam had never before taken after him with such murderous rage—one he wasn't sure he could stop. He sagged against the pine trunk, its sappy roughness supporting his limp weight. He closed his eyes and felt the furrow deepen between his brows.

Cole would come to him. He knew it. Whatever that woman might try to say or do, Cole would come to settle it. They had blood between them.

Three

Cole's head swam, and he realized he was cold. Where in the blazes was his blanket, and what was he doing on the ground? He raised his head and pain shot through like fire. He stifled a groan. Why couldn't he think? His head felt like tar, thick and heavy.

He tried to raise a hand to feel the lump at the base of his skull, only to realize his arms were tied at the wrist. Memories rushed in, and with them every ache and bruise in his body. He was so cold his joints were stiff, and he noticed the ground was covered with a thick white hoarfrost that stood up like needles before his face.

Cole looked up without moving his head. Every blade of grass, every branch of sage and juniper was outlined in white. The sun was pale through the milky sky, but well up. He risked raising his head and saw the men lying near the embers of their fire. He was near enough the fire himself that it kept him alive, but little more.

He must be lying where they had dumped him from the horse. Cole had a vague recollection of the pain that had shot through his ribs when he hit the ground. He tried to move his legs, but they were tied at the ankles, his heavy stockings crusted with frost. He dropped his head back to the ground. At least the cussed wags could have given him a blanket.

Cole looked up at the sky again, tried to get his bearings.

His eyes went in and out of focus. His head throbbed. He was in no condition to think, much less move. He closed his eyes. If the bounty hunters meant to waste good daylight, he'd take advantage of their sloth.

A kick in the ribs brought him around, and he clenched his teeth against the pain. Rough hands yanked him up to sit. With his frozen fingers, he could hardly hold the tin cup shoved his way, but the coffee thawed his innards. His lips were cracked and bruised and it hurt to breathe, but he wasn't dead yet. Not that he held much hope of that continuing for long.

He needed a smoke. He felt his pocket for papers and tobacco. They were there, but with his hands tied and stiff with cold, he'd never get it rolled. He looked across the fire at the two men. Something stirred in the back of his mind, but it was like a blue-tailed fly flitting in and out of his muddled thoughts.

One man squatted beside the fire. His duster was more black than tan, but his boots were snakeskin. Where would a man like that get snakeskin boots? He pulled out a thin cigar, and Cole watched him smoke it. He reckoned the fella knew he wanted a smoke, but no offer was made. Cole felt every draw somewhere deep in his chest, but he kept the need from his face.

"You thinkin' on that night?" The man's voice was thin and grating, too small for his bulk.

"What night?"

"Ninth of August. The night you killed Auralee Dubois."

The man put the emphasis on *Du*. Where had he heard that before? *August ninth*. Cole's head swam. Why couldn't he think? He turned and examined the other man.

He was older, maybe sixty. Again that fleeting unease of something trying to get through. The man opened a can of peaches and held it out. Cole had to stick his hands nearly into the fire to get it. If he held them there long enough he could burn off the rope. Only by then his hands would be crisped like Mr. Farrel's.

The thought brought Cole up short, and he realized he'd been trying real hard not to think of the Farrels, one in particular. Sheez, what must Abbie think? And what on earth happened to Auralee? He couldn't drag up a memory of her in trouble, leastwise none beyond her own making.

He brought the can up and poured the peaches into his mouth the best he could. He needed to remember, but his mind was confused. There was something about Sam. Did he dream Samuel came after him? The bruises on his face and body told him that was real enough.

Paying him back for Auralee. Well, he'd expected as much. The rift had been spreading between them long enough. Only . . . Cole squinched his eyes and tried to force the memory. He'd thought his leaving town would put an end to it.

Cole winced when the younger, dark-haired man sliced the rope that held his legs and yanked him to his feet with a cheap six-shooter to his head. "Git on your horse."

"You suppose I might take care of nature first?"

The man gave a curt nod. "Right there in clear sight."

When he was done, Cole gripped the pommel and pulled himself painfully up. "Don't suppose you gentlemen have a blanket I could make use of."

The older man untied the woolen blanket from behind Cole's saddle and threw it over his shoulders. By maneuvering his legs, Cole tucked it around to cover his feet and stuck them in the stirrups. There. At least he might go to the noose with all his toes.

The horse's hooves crunched on the frost until the sun broke out and turned it soft. Everything was so dazzling white it made his eyes water. The frost dropped with soft plops from the twisted branches of the piñon pines and the yuccas stood like upended icicles. Abbie would like this scenery. He frowned.

With all the long miles ahead in the saddle, the last thing he wanted was to start thinking on her, the look of her eyes with them lashes, the feel of her hand on his arm. . . . Funny how clear that was, when so much else was like mud. He could have sworn she'd taken down her wall. If Sam hadn't come when he did . . .

Samuel Jasper. Where in tarnation was his older brother? Did he lead these fellas onto him like Judas to the Lord? Though he hadn't thought on it for years, he pictured that scene his ma had described to him. It had both terrified and fascinated him to think a trusted friend could turn on a good man like that. But it was no kiss that marked Sam's betrayal.

Cole moved his jaw side to side. He was lucky to have his teeth. A couple felt loose in the sockets, but he figured he'd keep them. For all his lanky arms, Sam's wallop wasn't so bad. Still, this wasn't the first time his brother had thrashed him, nor the first time he'd deserved it.

What happened to Auralee? He'd thought Sam's fury was jealous rage. He understood that. By the time he had realized what she meant to Sam, she'd sunk her hooks, and no amount of wiggling could shake her free. But that didn't account for this other business. Not murder. Not by a long shot.

He tried to unravel his thoughts. He could conjure up a clear enough picture of the vixen. She was alive and fuming when he'd seen her last . . . wasn't she? The dull ache at the bottom of his skull spread upward, and he stopped trying to remember. It would come in its own time. Meanwhile he had only to stay alive.

◆◆◆◆◆◆

Abbie ducked her face to the cold, biting wind. The morning's frost lingered, the sun swallowed by sullen clouds that hung heavy through the fourth day of riding. Gray Wolf was like a shadow ahead in the dimming light.

Beside her, Will led the two packhorses and Whitesock. Abbie felt a surge of comfort that Will had insisted on coming. Matt and Curtis could handle the ranch, but he'd go after Cole.

Will's claim was as good as her own. Cole had looked after him better than she suspected, and Will was adamant. He wasn't wild about a Comanche guide, but he kept his head and bolstered her. He was the one who thought to bring a spare horse for Cole if they found him—when they found him.

Abbie insisted it be Whitesock, as Cole had developed a fondness for the gelding after losing Scotch. The chestnut was fresh, its one white sock stepping out eagerly, Monte's Winchester .44 rifle resting easily in its scabbard against the horse's side.

She stared at the empty saddle and tried to imagine Cole filling it. *He will*, she told herself again and again. They would get to him in time, and somehow they would get him away.

Gray Wolf kept to himself. Sometimes he galloped out of sight. The first time he did, she feared that he'd left them. But he appeared again without a word, and they angled to the east. At times she could pick up the tracks he followed, though on the frozen stubble it was harder than any tracking she'd done. The horses' hooves chipped the dirt like marble, leaving only the slightest mark to be seen.

They had come across rope discarded at a campsite. The fire was cold, but she had lifted the rope and held it to her chest. It had likely bound Cole, and that meant he lived still. If he were dead, the men might have him tied, but they would have no need to cut the restraints.

Abbie watched Gray Wolf riding straight-backed on the roan gelding Monte had parted with. The horse was lean, she noted, but not ill treated, though Gray Wolf had slit its ears in the Comanche manner. He bent and studied the ground, then leaped forward on the horse and rode in a wide loop to the right.

When he came back, they went on as before, as they'd been for days. She looked up at the first swirling pellets of corn snow. The wind was cruel and her spirits sank. She had hoped to overtake them before now, but they must be pushing hard, as well. Her urgency was now shot with dread. Would they be too late?

Will rode in close. "Thought for a minute he'd lost the trail. I can't see for the life of me what he's finding to follow."

She nodded. "We can't do better than an Indian guide. Gray Wolf knows what he's about."

"Let's hope we don't find he's led us off to some Comanche war chief."

Abbie smiled. "Is that why you came? To protect me from Comanche war chiefs?"

Will flushed. "Partly. Mostly cuz Cole needs help."

"Well, Gray Wolf rides alone. Too many of his people have been killed or taken off to reservation lands assigned them by the government. He chooses his solitary path over either alternative."

"I still don't get how you found him and—"

"I didn't find him. He found me. It's always that way."

"I don't like the sound of that."

Abbie pushed the hair from her forehead. "Don't worry, Will. Gray Wolf is a godsend. How would we do this without him?"

Will shook his head. "I don't know. But I never thought I'd be trusting my way to a redskin."

Will's attitude didn't surprise her. Gray Wolf *was* something of an enigma. Comanches were not native to Colorado, though they hunted there at times—especially if fires or war sent them north. But in other areas, their reputation for brutality was well deserved.

She knew Gray Wolf could be as violent and bloodthirsty as any man. She'd seen him kill, seen him glory in it. With the outlaw Buck Hollister's scalp on his belt, he'd gloated and crowed, his face smeared with other men's blood.

But she'd accepted his hand fresh from the kill, and he'd brought her home to safety. What was it Cole had said? She must have some powerful medicine over the brave. Maybe, but she didn't know what.

She didn't fear him. That had earned her the title "Wise One." She recalled his first words to her, "*Wise One, not afraid.*" And she'd been stunned that he spoke her tongue, though in a way, they'd communicated better without words.

They understood each other, shared a love for freedom and for the land. No, she didn't fear Gray Wolf, though she couldn't come close to understanding him, not in his complexity. Nor did she tell Will her belief that God had sent him. Not even Will's simple faith could be stretched that far.

Like many, Will likely doubted Indians had a soul. But how else to explain Gray Wolf's appearance, his answer to her need, just like the first time she'd prayed and Gray Wolf came to her rescue. He was open to the moving of God's spirit, and she firmly believed God used whomever He chose.

Sam slouched in the threadbare chair in a room at the Rocky Bluffs Hotel, the plain hotel whose purpose was to room travelers, not the folks who meant to gamble and wench. He had no intention of either. As far as he was concerned, if he never saw the inside of a bawdy house or gaming room again, that would suit him fine.

He ran his hand over his beard-roughened cheeks. The road to sin was paved with good intentions . . . and a whole hell full of heartache. Knowing Cole might agree didn't assuage the situation. Knowing he hadn't yet sought him out both irked and confused Sam. That woman must have a greater hold on Cole than he imagined.

He'd give him three more days, one solid week, and if he hadn't come by then, he'd drag Cole out from behind her skirts and thrash him before the woman's eyes. Then he'd get his answers. Then he'd know. His heart told him it couldn't be Cole. An eyewitness said it was. Cole would tell him which was true. Sam prayed he could let his brother live if Cole confessed.

Four

The warmth of the crackling fire sank into her back as Nora Flynn sat beside the hearth in the spacious kitchen of the adobe mission house. Across from her, Davy McConnel crouched on the three-legged stool, his hulking shoulders bent forward. He'd only just settled there but already looked uncomfortable enough to pick up his hat and take his leave.

"What is it on your mind, then?" Nora sounded more snappish than she meant, but she had a good idea what filled his mind, and the day was too cold and stormy to tussle inside where the warmth ought to bring laughter and merriment. At least that was how it used to be. "Spit it out, will ye?"

"I'm workin' up to it." His eyes were like two robin's eggs sunk into nests of lashes in his blunt, freckled face.

Nora liked his freckles. They matched her own in number, though hers were more tawny to match her copper hair. She liked him all right, though it irked her to think so. Hadn't she tried every way imaginable to shake him loose? Worse than the potato blight, the way he hung on.

"Well, work it up, then, for I haven't all day to sit waitin'."

"That's sort of what I mean to say, too." He drew a long breath. "Nora, it's like this. I've talked myself out, askin' you this way and that way to be my wife. I've come today with an ultimatum. Either you agree to a Christmas wedding, or I'll consider that your final no."

Nora suddenly felt as heavy as the iron kettle hanging over the fire. Here he was offering to leave her be, and she had no doubt he meant it. Four years was a long time to expect a man to keep calling, not that she'd expected it. Davy called by his own wanting, not by any needing of hers.

So why was her heart a lump of lead in her chest? She pressed her hands together, desperate for a fitting remark, one to let him know it was nothing to her if he finally took her at her word. Abbie would have one ready to her lips. Abbie would know what to say. Hadn't she turned down all of nine suitors in the last four years?

"Davy . . ." It stuck in her throat. Could it be that she didn't want to turn him down?

He kept his big hands on his knees, his blacksmith's hands. He wasn't a farmer as her Jaime had been. He hadn't the quick wit or fiery temper. He hadn't the fine dark Irish looks or the lilting Irish in his voice. Davy had his American ways, his frontier speech, his muleheaded, plodding stubbornness.

But she'd worn him out. She'd used up his patience, and now he waited for her answer. "Davy, I . . ." She stared down at his brogans. How many times had he muddied her floor with the heavy work shoes, coming through any weather to do a chore, bring a gift, or sit here at the fire?

How many backbreaking hours had he spent seeing to her needs, to all their needs: her sister Glenna and Glenna's husband, Alan; Mary and Nolan Donnelly; her smaller sister, Maggie, who lived with her and Father Padriac O'Brien. He'd helped them all, her brother Doyle and Kyle Donnelly included. They all liked and accepted him. Did she?

Like, yes, but *love*? How could she? How not? How many times had he teased and cajoled and asked her to consider him? But never had he worn the frank, serious face with which he now brought his ultimatum. This was the last he'd say on the matter, and it was up to her.

Nora brought her eyes to meet his. He waited with the same fortitude that had kept him courting her four years with little reward but a sharp tongue. She tried to respond and felt herself gasping. His eyes softened. She'd never told him about Jaime. But somehow she suspected he knew. Maybe one of the others . . .

She pictured Jaime burning with the fires of freedom, throwing his life energy into the fight, the cause, the land and country that gave so little in return. She saw him raise a stick to the red-coated soldier who gave the order for their cottage to be pulled down on the heads of her mother and grandmother within. She saw his back stripped of flesh by the lash until no part remained. She saw the life leave his body, clutched in her arms though he never knew she held him.

Nora trembled. Her voice came thinly. "It's a fearsome thing to love again."

"Aye." He said it with the soft inflection of the Isle-born.

Her heart swelled inside. Tears stung her eyes, and she suddenly sat straight up. "What'll I tell Abbie?"

Davy's brows raised, and he spread his hands. "It's what you'll tell me, I'm waitin' for."

"Yes, you fool man, of course yes. I already said it."

He furrowed his brow, but she pushed his shoulder roughly. "I said I'd do it, now, didn't I? If it's a Christmas wedding you're wantin', then let's be about it."

His smile broke broadly across his face. "Are you sure?"

"No, let me think awhile yet."

Davy jumped up from his stool and caught her up with him. "Not a moment more, Nora, or you'll talk yourself out of it. I know you will."

"Then perhaps you'll be wantin' to kiss me."

He stood dumbfounded, and she felt a pang. Jaime had never been so reluctant or shy. But Davy took her in his arms and brought his mouth to hers warmly. "I love you, Nora."

"I know it."

"And maybe there's a bit of love in you for me, too."

"Aye, maybe."

"You won't be sorry."

"I'm sorry already the way you keep runnin' on." But she said it with a smile and planted a kiss square on his mouth. He pressed his hands into her back and returned it.

"And in me own kitchen, no less."

They both spun at Father Paddy's words. But he was wearing a grin nearly as broad as Davy's.

"I'm marrying the girl, Father."

"And that you will, laddie." Father Paddy laughed. "If it's my blessing you're after, you have it and more. The very saints are smilin' on you both."

Nora felt her cheeks burning. Was Jaime one of those saints? Now she clearly understood what Abbie had said, feeling her late husband so close sometimes that she gauged what she did by what he would think. Nora raised her eyes to the ceiling.

Will you forgive me, Jaime? It's a terrible lonesome life without home and family.

But what would Abbie say? They'd shared their lot and their hearts a long while, now. Would she feel betrayed? Nora looked back at Davy and sighed. It had to be. He'd given her an ultimatum, and she'd answered as she knew she would. Abbie would have to understand.

♦♦♦♦♦♦

Cole coughed, sending fire to his chest above and between the racking pain in his ribs. He shifted in the saddle and tried to control the shakes that seized him. The single blanket did little to cut the cold as he rode in the failing light. But he guessed some of this chill was his own.

They'd been riding six days as near as he could figure it, if his first waking had been the morning following his capture. He suspected so by their location now, high up Raton Pass. They were heading due south, and once they left the mountains behind, the cold of the upper altitudes would give way.

He coughed again. Even if he could roll his tobacco, the cough would keep him from smoking it. And the cravings were growing less frequent. Likely due to the burning in his chest. His tongue was thick with thirst, though the little food they fed him was more than he wanted.

A wave of heat rushed over Cole, but he kept the blanket in place. It would be chills again soon enough. If he could just clear his head, he might figure a way out of this. He studied the man riding ahead of him. That niggling familiarity would not go away.

And the one riding behind with the packhorses. Something in his voice and the tilt of his head . . .

The man caught up from behind. "Crete, you see that?"

Crete. Cole grasped the detail and tangled with it. Why did that name resonate . . .

"See what?"

"I seen somethin' in the rocks behind us."

Crete looked back over his shoulder, drew his gun from the holster, then swung around.

"You expectin' company, Jasper?"

Not likely in this life. Cole held his peace, though a cough was fighting its way up his throat.

"Maybe that brother o' yourn?"

He doubted Sam would raise a finger in his defense. Not anymore. Cole pressed his elbows to his ribs and coughed. It felt as though his lungs were tearing out. Maybe it was time to give up the tobacco for good.

"Whatcha think, Crete?"

Crete. It was there, but he couldn't dredge it out. What was it . . .

"A'right, Finn. You stick on Jasper like a burr. I'll have a look."

Crete Marlowe and Jackson Finn. Cole's breath made a slow escape from his lips. And here he was, weak as a cub.

Cole hung his head and fought the exhaustion. Whatever it was in the rocks gave him his first chance at them separately. Not that he'd call it a chance with his hands tied and the fever making him sick as a dog. But he'd worked the rope loose on the pommel, though it still bit his wrists. He just . . . might . . . work it . . . off. . . .

He stopped trying when Finn looked his way, then pulled again when the man looked back at Crete heading into the rocks and pines behind. Cole reckoned four or five minutes for Crete to reach the top and have a look at the back side. And if Finn called out, he'd tear back down like a hellcat or shoot from where he was. But Cole had to try.

He guarded his strength until he had the rope free of the pommel, then looked up beneath his lowered hat and gauged the distance between his horse and Finn's. He'd have one try at Finn in the saddle. If he made the leap and caught him clean with his fists at the temple . . .

Crete was nearly up. Cole gathered himself, drew a breath, but the cough broke loose from his throat, burning, hacking. When Finn's eyes fixed on him, he slumped.

"Here." Finn unscrewed the cap of his canteen and brought his mount one step nearer.

Cole lunged, smashed his fists into Finn's face, and fell hard with him to the ground. Finn rolled and hollered, but Cole brought his fists up under Finn's jaw and heard the teeth smack together. He scrambled for the gun at Finn's hip, but Finn kicked with his knee, and Cole took it in the chin.

His head snapped back, but his fingers reached the pistol butt. Finn smashed his cheekbone with a fist, and Cole lost his hold of the gun. As he raised his hands to strike Finn's head, he heard the whiz of a bullet, felt it hit, then heard the report just as pain exploded in his left shoulder.

He staggered up, but Crete was on him, diving from the horse. Cole went down under his weight. A burst of light filled his head, and he spat blood, then lay gasping and wheezing. Crete held a gun to his chest. The way Cole felt at that moment, he'd welcome a bullet to end it.

Crete gripped the shirt at his throat and dragged his head up. "If I didn't want so bad to see you swing, I'd blast your heart an' leave you lie."

Cole drew a slow, wheezing breath. He didn't doubt it for a minute.

Abbie's heart pounded in her chest as the echo died away. Gray Wolf had ordered them not to move as he crept alone through the dusky light into the pile of boulders and piñon pines. But with the gunshot, her fear rose up like a living thing. *Please, God. Please.*

She wanted to bolt up into the rocks where the echo died, but she was held back by the force of Gray Wolf's command. Had they seen him? Had they shot at him? One shot only? They would have kept shooting at an Indian in the rocks.

Cole? She couldn't bear to think that Cole was shot. It could have been anything, a squirrel, a rabbit, a misfire. She stared up into the mounds of moss-covered rocks on the sharp incline, where the pass narrowed before dropping steeply down. She could see nothing of Gray Wolf, hear nothing of his movements.

Her heart beat painfully. God had sent Gray Wolf, and she must trust him. Abbie stared at the spot where he had disappeared into the rocks, knife in hand. She felt Will beside her, as tense as she. "Pray, Will."

He nodded.

She bit her lip. The silence seemed ominous, heavy. Where

was Gray Wolf? Why didn't he . . . She caught her breath when his head appeared over the boulder to the left of the cut. He crept back with more speed and stealth than she thought possible. She left her crouch and ran to him.

He held up a hand. "Your friend is shot."

Her chest lurched, and Will caught her arm as images flooded her mind, blood-crusted, gunshot bodies, cold, pale flesh. *Cole shot.* The gun's echo sounded again in her head. They were too late. Too late. *Why, God, why?*

Abbie forced her voice to come. "How badly is he shot? Did he move?" She steeled herself for the answer.

"He lives."

Her legs felt weak. "Tonight . . ." She cleared her throat. "We must take him tonight." This was the best country for it. The land before the pass had been too open and desolate. "Are they moving on now?"

Gray Wolf shook his head.

"I want to see."

He looked back at the towering rocks, then started walking. In the near darkness, she followed, crouching where he crouched, stepping where he stepped, making scarcely more noise than he. Below them, the camp lay in the open some small distance from the ridge. The men were not fools. They had a fire lit, and she could make out the silhouettes of one . . . two . . . Her heart leaped to her throat. Where was Cole?

One of the men leaned over the fire, and she caught the glint of a knife. He stepped back and kicked a bundle on the ground. It moved. *Dear God. Cole.* She felt a tremor inside at the sight of him helpless. Cole, who had always managed everything, who had faced down a stampeding herd, who had seemed strong and indestructible. She didn't want to think of him as vulnerable. It struck terror in her soul.

The shorter man blocked her view a moment, then hunched down and gripped Cole where he lay. She saw a flash from the knife in the other's hand, then Cole screamed. Her chest constricted as he bit off the scream and thrashed against the man's hold. They were digging out the bullet.

He hollered again, a string of words that raised the hair on her head, then fell silent, and she guessed he'd lost consciousness. She wet her lips, realizing her mouth had gone dry. How long they sat there in the darkness, she couldn't tell. Gray Wolf was silent.

They watched the men eat, heard snatches of voices but no words. One rolled out his blankets and lay down. The other sat huddled with a rifle across his knees. If Cole wakened at all, he made no move. Her heart sank.

She couldn't tell from what part of him they'd dug the bullet. They wouldn't have bothered if he was gutshot. But any gunshot wound, not to mention his other injuries, would take its toll. What if he were too weak to ride?

Oh, Lord, help me. This looks impossible, but I know all things are possible with you.

Gray Wolf motioned, and they crept back down as quietly as they'd gone up. Abbie answered Will's questioning look with a nod. "He's alive. They dug the bullet out." She kept her voice steady. "We have to get him away, but we can't kill the men. Whatever we do will be held over Cole."

She heard Will's shallow breath. He was afraid, but then, which of them wasn't? Except maybe Gray Wolf. Had she thought to this point? Yes, but had she considered the difficulty and danger of taking an injured prisoner from two armed bounty hunters?

She wouldn't let fear stop her. "We can do it. We have the will and the courage. All we need is a plan." *And a miracle.*

Five

Through his stupor, Cole heard the coyote howl. It struck him strange somehow, like he should know something he couldn't grasp. He wanted to slip back into the daze that covered the pain. But the sound kept niggling, and with a rush he knew. It was no coyote call, it was a Comanche, a sound he'd heard all too often and one that haunted his dreams.

Maybe he was dreaming now. Maybe he was slipping into a place where the mind wandered. He cracked his eyes only enough to see Finn sitting with the Henry rifle across his knees. Blood encrusted the place where his fists had connected with Finn's nose, and he looked sore and cross and ornery.

The horses stirred, and Finn looked up. He stared into the darkness, then stood and walked slowly toward the rope that tethered them, rifle poised in his hands. He must suspect coyotes were troubling the camp. He wouldn't know the difference. Cole saw the shadow move before Finn did. It looked like a Comanche crouched and leaping. . . .

Strange. Comanches kill silently, but he saw no glint of a knife. . . . He saw Finn crash down, heard the rifle shot and watched them roll. From where he slept, Crete scrambled up, then froze with the click of a gun hammer.

"Hold it right there."

He must be dreaming. It sounded like Will using a voice two times his size.

"All right, drop it."

Cole opened his eyes fully and rose to one elbow. The pain almost blacked him out, but not before he caught a solid side view of Will's young face. What on earth . . . He felt hands and shook his head clear. Abbie. Now he knew he was crazy as a loon. Well, if this were dying, it sure beat the living he'd done these last days.

Abbie tried to rouse Cole, but he seemed to slip back into a stupor. "Cole. Cole, wake up."

She heard Will order the man by the fire to drop his guns and kick them over. He stooped and stuffed both pistols into his belt. "Now strip. Down to your long johns and be quick. Toss me your boots."

The man's voice was gruff and snarling. "You'll regret this. You won't get away with it."

Will waved the gun, and the man obliged.

Abbie looked to where Gray Wolf was disarming the heavyset one near the string of horses. She prayed Gray Wolf had understood and the limp man still breathed. She returned her attention to Will.

He stood firm, his anger giving him strength. "Kick the knife over." Without taking his eyes or his gun off the bounty hunter, Will tossed the knife into the dirt beside Abbie.

She took it and cut the ropes at Cole's wrists and ankles. He moaned when his arm fell free and reached for his shoulder. Blood soaked the dressing carelessly tied there.

"Cole." She shook him gently.

He opened his eyes.

"Can you walk?"

He appeared lucid. Clenching his teeth, he half rose, barked an ugly cough, then sank to his side. Sweat shone on his forehead in the flickering light. Cole was not a small man, standing at least six feet tall, lean but muscular, and Abbie fought her mounting alarm.

Gray Wolf came to her, and between them they got Cole to his feet. They half dragged him to the horses and shoved him astride the nearest. The men had kept the horses saddled and bridled, no doubt in case of trouble. That made her job easier.

Abbie kept an eye on the man by the fire, who now kneeled in his red flannel long johns on the frozen ground, hands behind his head, face ruddy with rage. He narrowed his eyes and glowered darkly, taking Will's measure but making no move. She suspected he was the sort to bully when the odds were in his favor, but had a streak of cowardice when the cards turned.

Gray Wolf had trussed the other man and removed his boots. The man was coming to, thank the Lord, but Gray Wolf stood inches from his head, knife in hand, should he make a move. Abbie swung onto the bay gelding beside Cole and gathered the reins of the bounty hunters' other two horses, one of them the piebald mare. Gray Wolf leaped astride the black.

Abbie pointed the rifle from the scabbard on her saddle squarely at the man on his knees. "All right, Will." She watched him back slowly toward them. She held the rifle on the gray-haired man who had smacked the rifle into Cole's belly.

Abbie held it steady while Will hung all the gun belts over his saddle and mounted, then she addressed the kneeling man. "You'll find your horses some miles north. Don't you set foot on my ranch again if you value your skin."

Will took the rifle back and waited until the others had started off with a rush, then he swung around and followed. Abbie heard the bounty hunter's hollered curse but kept riding hard and praying Cole would not fall from the horse's back. They would indeed leave the animals ten miles north, but she was uncertain what to do from there.

She slowed as they reached their own horses. She looked at Cole hunched over his horse's neck. He had kept himself astride by grit alone, but his shoulder was bleeding badly, and he seemed more than half dazed. *Give me wisdom, Lord. Gray Wolf calls me wise, but I feel lost.*

She swung down. With Will's help she got Cole onto Whitesock, whom she knew would carry him better than an unknown horse. He tried not to show the pain, but when Will clasped his hand, Abbie caught the look that passed between them. Gratitude and understanding.

Will spoke low in her ear. "We can't go back the way we've come." He glanced up at Cole. "He'll want to clear his name. I think we gotta head for El Paso."

She released a slow breath and nodded. *Thank you, Lord.* She nodded. "We'll circle round and go as far as he can stand tonight." She took Cole's coat and boots from the pack. As she eased the coat over his shoulders, he brushed her hand with his.

The soft touch nearly undid her, and she pulled away. She could not think of his pain or his gratitude or . . . any of the other emotions that rushed in with that one touch. She looked around. Where was Gray Wolf? There, in the night, circling, sniffing the air and listening.

Will helped pull on Cole's boots, and the difference was immediate. She hadn't realized how vulnerable he had looked without them. Now, even though he still hunched weakly, he looked like a man. Will strapped on Cole's gun, then Abbie took the horse's reins and handed them up to him.

One side of his mouth quivered with a smile. She knew what it felt like to be bound and led like an animal. Buck Hollister had shown her. She mounted Zephyr, and with Will leading the packhorses and Gray Wolf leading all of them, they started out into the night.

♦♦♦♦♦♦♦

Cole's coughing jarred Abbie. They had only settled in perhaps an hour before, having made better progress than she'd believed he could stand. But now huddled in the blankets on the bedroll, he breathed in wet, rattling breaths and coughed out the fever that had settled in his lungs. Her own breath suspended each time his caught before staggering into a cough.

They had dared a fire, agreeing to extinguish it at first light, but still Cole shivered uncontrollably. Abbie crawled out of her bedding and put more of the twisted cedar branches on the fire, then moved the water pot over the flames. Gray Wolf watched from where he sat wrapped in a blanket against the side of the hollow.

The water was still hot and boiled quickly. She dipped a cup and added Pearl's remedy for congested lungs to the boiling water. She was thankful Pearl had foisted on her the whole pack of "medicines and cures."

There was scarcely anything in the pack Cole didn't need. One for cuts and swelling, one for infection, another for fever, and this one for coughs. Coughs. It sounded as though his lungs would disengage with each bout.

She stirred the powder in the boiling water until it dissolved and cooled enough for Cole to drink, then dropped to her knees at his side. His eyes flew open. They held a tinge of yellow, but she couldn't tell if that was the fire's reflection or the fever burning there.

With an arm behind his head, she helped him rise up to drink. In the morning she'd doctor his other wounds, but his lungs wouldn't wait. When he'd finished drinking, she put her hand to his forehead and felt the heat emanating before her hand touched his skin.

He startled her when he reached up and took her hand from his head and pressed it to his chest. "I ain't dyin', Abbie. Git some rest."

Whether it was bravado or prophecy, she crawled back into her blankets. The last thing she saw was the glint of Gray

Wolf's eyes shining in the firelight.

♦♦♦♦♦♦♦

When Abbie woke, the sky was dim. The air was keen on her nose and cheeks, and she knew the fire was dead. Will snored softly, no doubt exhausted. But he had proved both formidable and cool-headed. She rolled over and sat up at the sight of Gray Wolf standing over Cole. Something in his stance chilled her as he rose to the balls of his feet, chanting low under his breath.

Her breath came sharply. *Cole?* He lay unmoving, but with irrational relief she heard his tortured breaths. She sat up. "Gray Wolf?"

He didn't turn but stopped chanting.

Abbie climbed out of her bedroll and reached for her coat, then walked to his side. She pulled the coat close in the fresh wind and glanced down at Cole. He slept soundly, a patina to his skin showing the breaking of fever. "What is it? What's wrong?"

"This man. He is Death Rider."

Death Rider? She stared at Gray Wolf, his face set and hard, something . . . savage in his eyes. *Does he mean Cole rides the edge of life and death?* She felt a prickling of fear. "I don't . . ."

"He has passed years, but Gray Wolf knows him."

This was crazy. How could Gray Wolf know Cole? He must be mistaken. Her mind reeled. She knew the Comanche lands were in Texas, and Cole had spent years there, but . . . Abbie recognized then the look on Gray Wolf's face—neither fear nor concern but pure hatred.

This was something she couldn't grasp, something ominous. *Death Rider.* The very sound of it made her quake. "Gray Wolf . . ."

"The Great Spirit demands his life."

Abbie's throat constricted. She stepped between the men,

acutely aware of Gray Wolf's physical power. Did he have a conscience to which she could appeal? She wouldn't believe otherwise. "The Great Spirit sent you to save his life. He made you strong last night and silent as the dark."

He gripped the hilt of his knife. "Death Rider will die."

She saw the tension in his face and neck, the bloodlust in his eyes. *Dear God, please help us. . . .*

Will stepped up behind Gray Wolf with the Winchester rifle balanced in his hands. His face was stern, absent of his boyish uncertainty. He would risk anything for Cole. But she would not risk Gray Wolf. They were bound together by an honor that transcended their races. She must make him understand.

Abbie drew herself up. "Gray Wolf, I know the wrongs done your people. But there were wrongs on both sides. If Cole fought against you, it was to protect his own."

"He is Death Rider."

"Not anymore."

Gray Wolf's eyes turned to flint. Abbie felt them cutting her with all the suffering of the Comanche tribe. But she was right. The Comanches were brutal themselves, shockingly cruel. If Cole had fought them, he was justified. *Please, God. Speak to Gray Wolf's heart, make him see.*

The muscles rippled in Gray Wolf's forearm. His knuckles whitened on the knife, and Abbie saw Will tense. If Cole woke . . . She reached up and opened the neck of her shirtwaist to reveal the string of claws that hung there, given to her by Gray Wolf when she had secreted him to safety.

It was the seal of their unspoken pact. She untied the leather thong and held it out to him, hoping to bargain for Cole's life. She would hold Gray Wolf to his debt and demand his honor.

Gray Wolf's jaw set rigidly; his eyes flamed. Suddenly he thrust his hands out, flat palmed, and knocked the claws to the dirt. "I ride no more with this man's shadow." He turned, strode past Will, and swung astride his horse.

Her heart ached as they shared one last glance, then he kicked his heels and galloped off. Cole jumped awake at the sound, reaching for the gun belted on his hip. The motion made him cough, and he doubled over in its violence. Abbie dropped to his side.

Will stepped close, legs spread and rifle ready, taking no chances with Gray Wolf. He eyed the retreating figure, then crouched beside her. "Now we'll watch our backs for both the bounty hunters and that Comanche."

"Comanche?" Cole wheezed.

Abbie supported his shoulders. "Gray Wolf carried you free last night."

"Thought I was dreamin'. Must be still." He sagged against her arm.

Looking at him, a crushing fear came on her. She didn't want to feel the wrenching compassion the sight of him conjured. The daylight showed everything she'd missed in the dark. His head was battered and cut, his shoulder bleeding, his wrists rope-burned. By the way he moved she suspected internal bruising, and she could only guess at what else.

Cole sat up and coughed again, a wretched, thick barking. Her own chest burned just listening. She kept her voice steady. "You're in no condition to travel, but we've no choice. I'll doctor you first, though." She walked to the fire. The iron pot of water was still warm beside the quenched flames. "Will, please see to the horses. We'll start as soon as I've finished."

She carried the pot to Cole's side, dipped a cloth, and pressed it to his cheekbone. He winced, and she felt an angry satisfaction. *If he had defended himself against Sam, against the bounty hunters . . . if he had not been involved with that . . . Auralee, he'd be safely at the ranch instead of coughing out his lungs on this death trail to Texas.*

He sat silently as Abbie washed the cuts and bruises. Every

few minutes he turned away to cough and held his ribs as he did. There was a dreadful lump at the base of his skull, and through his hair she saw the purple and yellow flesh. No wonder he was dazed. She wouldn't be surprised if there was a crack in the bone beneath.

The water ran red when she dropped in the cloth. Blood. Cole's blood. She unbuttoned his shirt and long johns and peeled them off his shoulder. She bit her lip, forcing herself to focus on the blackened, ugly gash where the bullet had entered and been cut from the flesh.

The ball must have lodged in the sinew and bone near the center of the joint, for they had dug deep. The skin around the wound was angry red and even hotter to the touch than the rest of him, though the fever indeed seemed to be subsiding.

Her fingers shook as she rubbed the wound clean and fresh blood flowed. "We've been here before. I'll need to sew it."

In spite of his efforts, Cole jerked and sucked in his breath as Abbie washed his wound with carbolic acid. It hurt like blazes, but he bit back the cry. The pain cleared his senses and helped to convince him she was real. He watched her take the needle from the box. Her fingers were nimble as she threaded and snipped.

"I don't expect this will hurt anything like what they did last night."

"Go ahead." Nothing could hurt worse than the agony that lodged somewhere near his solar plexus every time she touched him.

Abbie's face was set as she poked the needle through and tied off the stitch, then stabbed it through again and again. He kept the pain from his eyes and fought the cough clawing his throat. She packed the wound with alum and tied on a clean dressing.

He balked when she wrapped his arm tightly to his chest

to immobilize the shoulder, but the look she gave him silenced his argument. The minute she sat back, he let go the cough and fire filled his chest. Whatever she'd given him last night had helped, but obviously the cure was not set.

"I don't suppose you thought to ask for a coat or boots or a blanket."

He was surprised by the anger in her eyes. "Some o' the time I had a blanket."

She turned away. Her breath came sharply, and he saw she was fighting tears. He touched her hand, but she pulled away like he'd burned her. "I can't do this" came her whisper.

"Cain't do what?"

"Love you."

The pain spread from his solar plexus to his throat and put gravel in his voice. "I ain't askin' you to."

She looked at him, her eyes pools so deep a man would never touch bottom. "I don't want to care what happens to you. I don't want to live afraid that one day I'll see you in the back of a wagon. I . . . don't want to feel . . . anything for you." Her voice broke.

Cole's throat was so tight the air hardly passed through. "Fair enough." He pulled the shirt back over his shoulder and fumbled one-handed with the buttons.

She stood and walked away. He kept his eyes from following. If that was how she wanted it, that's how it would be. Wasn't like he hadn't been doing it for the last eight years of his life. He coughed again and pressed a hand to his chest. Then he gathered his strength and stood.

His legs were weak as a new calf's, but he reckoned if he stood a minute they'd come to speaking terms with his head. He checked the gun at his hip, broke it open to see the loads, then slid it home. From the looks of the countryside, they'd continued south last night. Quite a surprise, considering his escort. He'd have thought Abbie would try to take him home, but then, he reckoned that was the last place she wanted him.

At any rate, it probably threw off Crete and Finn. They'd expect him to head any way but Texas. Yet that was exactly what he intended to do. He'd wanted to shake loose of them, but not because he wasn't going to El Paso. He just didn't trust them to get him there.

He took one feeble step. At this rate, he might not get himself there. But he meant to try. If his suspicions were right, if his reckoning wasn't awry, if Sam had . . . could Sam have killed Auralee? It pained him to think it, but he knew only too well what a driven man could do. Even a man like Sam.

Cole shook his head. If he was right, he had no choice but to get to El Paso and stand trial for murder. In a way, he figured, he was as guilty as his brother. He glanced at Abbie packing up with Will. What was she doing coming after him with a boy and a Comanche brave? *Guess she feels beholden somehow.*

Well, he'd take care of that. Better to get quits of them now. He joined them resolutely. "I appreciate what you done, but I'll be goin' on myself. You git on home." *Dern.* He bent and coughed. It staggered him, but he steadied himself with the saddle horn and met Abbie's eyes. He would've sooner faced Crete's gun barrel.

"First of all, you won't make it one day by yourself. And second, don't you ever tell me to *git.*" She spun, stalked to Zephyr, and mounted.

He stood like stone until he saw Will's half smile. Why did he suppose the kid knew exactly how it was?

Will drew his horse up alongside. "How're you feelin', Cole?"

"At the moment, catawampously chawed up."

Six

Jenny wrapped her knees with her arms and pulled them to her chest. The valley between her bony knees made a resting place for her chin as she made herself as small and compact as she could. She didn't like the hollow feeling in her stomach. It didn't go away like a bellyache. It just got hollower and hollower.

Even when she woke herself up at night, it was there waiting to gobble her up from inside. She should have known better. She should have never liked Cole so much. Everyone she liked went away.

Jenny pinched her arms above the elbows where they held fast to her knees. *Say it, stupid. He hasn't gone away, he's . . .* But she couldn't say it. She wouldn't. Her folks were dead; there was no denying that. She wasn't sure she remembered her pa. Not much more than his waxy mustache and the smell of his hair pomade.

She remembered Mama. Jenny couldn't squeeze her like Aunt Abbie. Mama wrinkled. *That's silly. People don't wrinkle; their clothes do.* But somehow in her mind she couldn't separate Mama from her clothes. She remembered the feel of hoops and skirts, but had she ever felt her mama?

Stupid, stupid. Of course I did. I was just too little to remember. Jenny knew how Aunt Abbie felt, all warm and smelling of honeysuckle. Even when Elliot was in the secret place and Aunt

Abbie's belly was hard and round, she had pulled Jenny close and held her. Aunt Abbie's hugs made Jenny want to laugh and cry together, so she never let it last too long.

What if, just once, Aunt Abbie pushed away first and smoothed the wrinkles? No, better to be the one pushing away. Except for Cole. Jenny trembled. It was scary how much she wanted him to hold her, just like a daddy would. She thought she remembered it. She was almost sure she recalled his arms hard around her, and not just when he had her in the saddle.

She remembered the smell of his neck against her cheek, the roughness of his jaw. How else would she know that if he hadn't held her? Jenny was sure he had. Maybe when he gave her the carved wooden critters. She hadn't called them that for a long time. *Critter* was Cole's word.

The hollow grew harder.

She looked out from the lacework of gray scrub oak twigs to the side of the bunkhouse where the bad men had taken Cole. She hadn't seen them. She had heard Aunt Abbie telling the cowhands what had happened. If she had seen them . . .

A rustling in the crisp, frozen leaves brought her head up. She peered over her shoulder at Elliot crawling through to her. She frowned. He was allowed in her special place, but right now she wanted to be alone.

"What are you doing, Jenny?"

"I'm thinking."

He pressed himself between the trunks in the frozen ground until he was close against her. "Thinking what?"

"What I'd have done to the bad men who took Cole."

Elliot's eyes widened as she'd known they would. "What would you do?"

"I'd have snuck up behind, quiet as a rabbit in the snow, and I'd have lassoed them with the lariat, the way Cole showed me. Then I'd . . ." She hesitated at the sound of a wagon in the drive. "It's Nora."

Jenny released her knees and crept back through the tunnel of branches. She could hear Elliot behind but didn't wait for him. She gained her feet and ran for the yard. Nora had just secured the ox as she rounded the pink stone wall and walked staunchly forward.

"Afternoon, Jenny. Is your aunt about?"

Elliot skidded to a stop behind her, but Jenny didn't turn. "Aunt Abbie is on a dangerous mission."

"Is she, now?" Nora smiled.

Jenny drew herself up. "This is not a laughing matter. She's getting Cole from the bad men."

Nora sobered, but Jenny could tell it was the forced seriousness grown-ups used when they were trying not to laugh and thought they could fool her.

"Are you short of coal, then?"

"I'm speaking of Cole Jasper." Jenny took a step forward and considered her words. She took a tight breath. "My pa."

Nora's eyes widened more than Elliot's. He tugged her arm and stood on tiptoe to whisper noisily in her ear. "He's not your real pa."

Jenny shrugged Elliot off and kept her eyes on Nora.

"I'm afraid I don't understand you, Jenny."

"That's all right. When Aunt Abbie brings him back, you'll see."

Nora looked toward the house. "Maybe I'll just say hello to Pearl and Zena."

Jenny felt the hurt of being doubted. She tossed her head. "You can ask them. They'll tell you the same thing. Aunt Abbie isn't here." She gathered her woolen skirts and ran back around the house. Why did the tears burn now? She wouldn't let them come when anyone could see. She wouldn't.

Jenny heard Elliot's pumping feet on the ground behind like her own shadow. She turned fiercely. "Go away."

He stopped and stood with his look of pained obedience.

Jenny felt the power she had over him, and with it the pang of guilt. She didn't care. She couldn't think about his feelings when her own heart was near to splitting. He had a mama. She had no one to call her own—no one but the man who looked as lonely as she felt.

Her legs flew beneath her skirts, and this time she ran alone.

Nora climbed the steps between the massive pillars. Even after four years she still felt strange approaching Abbie's fine house with its towering portico. In Ireland, wealth like that meant English landlords or turncoat Irish deep in the pockets of the English. She would sooner have spit on the stairs than climbed them to find a friend.

But Abbie was that. They'd grown close as sisters these last years. Aye, she loved her as dearly. And she was grateful beyond expressing to know Abbie returned it. Nora looked up at the looming twin doors. Was Abbie within?

Jenny was such a queer one, people were never certain how to take her. Back home they'd have said the child was fey. Nora didn't believe that. Jenny hadn't the look of one with the second sight. She was normal enough in most ways, just had an overactive imagination and a precocious manner.

She applied the knocker, and James opened the door to her, his grizzled head and shoulders more stooped than ever. "Good afternoon to you, James. Is Mrs. Farrel in?"

"No'm. She gone after Mistuh Jazzper."

Nora stared. She couldn't help it. Hearing Jenny's own declaration from the lips of the old Negro . . . "But . . . who is Mr. Jasper?"

"You come on in now."

Nora followed him in. Here she'd come to brave her news to Abbie, and it was she getting the surprise. Who was this man

Abbie had gone after? Surely she'd not held out on a secret love . . .

She followed James into the parlor, and Zena turned from dusting the mantel. Nora must have looked dazed because Zena put down the duster and came to her. "Don' you worry none. Mizz Abbie, she gonna be fine."

Pearl arrived with tea, and Nora accepted the cup with relief. She sipped the steaming brew and calmed herself. "I feel as though I've stepped into a fairy circle, my head's that spinnin'. What's happened? Where's Abbie?"

The two Negro women exchanged a glance, then Pearl swung her head side to side as she spoke. "She gone after dem bounty hunters. Dey took Mistuh Jazzper off, and him hardly back with Mizz Abbie three days."

"But I don't understand. Who is this Mr. Jasper?"

Zena clenched her hands to her chest. "Mizz Abbie's sweetheart."

"Hush yo mouth." Pearl puffed her cheeks. "He Mizz Abbie's foreman. He come back to work for her."

Nora took another swallow of tea. Why hadn't Abbie told her? Or had she? She had mentioned the man who'd worked for Monte and helped her drive the cattle. But her sweetheart, was he? She tried to remember anything in Abbie's tone or expression that would have betrayed such feelings.

Pearl wiped her hands on her apron. "You set now."

"I'll just be finishing my cup."

Pearl nodded, then left the room with a final dark look toward Zena. The young woman picked up the duster and ran it lackadaisically over the china shepherdess on the mantel.

Nora seized the chance. "Is it true about this Mr. Jasper? Is that why Abbie turned away all the others? Was she waitin' for this'un?"

"I wouldn't know about that." Zena looked sheepishly over her shoulder. "I only know what I seen with my own eyes."

"What have ye seen, then?" Nora raised her brows and fought a smile. She wasn't the least surprised Abbie's help knew her secrets.

"Oh, Mizz Nora." Zena dropped the duster and swept across the room to drop beside her on the settee. "Mistuh Jazzper, he plain crazy 'bout Mizz Abbie. He been that way for years. When she run him off, it like to break his heart, the way she done blamed him for Mistuh Monte dyin' an' all."

"Blamed him . . ."

"It was Mistuh Jazzper brought poor Mistuh Monte's body back home. And him what made her fight back to life." Zena wrung her hands. "After the baby was born, Mizz Abbie fired him straight off. But he come back, an' I knows how he feels."

"But what about Abbie?"

"Well, I don' say for sure." Zena swung her head. "But she went after him her own self with Will an' the Indian."

"The Indian?" Nora was more certain each moment she was in the grip of the little people. She gulped the tea. It tasted real.

"Yessum. A real Comanche buck as a guide."

Nora sat back against the seat. Och, that was Abbie all right. She was always one to up and handle matters herself. But if she had fired the man and gone four years without mentioning him to her closest friend . . . Wasn't that even more a sign than the rest?

Nora's heart leaped. But then she shuddered. Bounty hunters. Comanche guides. What had this Cole Jasper done? Was Abbie's man a scrapper as Jaime had been? Did he burn with the fires of travail? Her chest seized. What would be the end of it this time?

♦♦♦♦♦♦♦

Abbie rode beside Will, each of them leading a packhorse. Cole rode ahead since he knew the way, but he still hadn't the strength to more than keep himself in the saddle. Abbie's fury kindled as she heard him cough, hunched over and weak, and fear for him gnawed at her. Fear tinged with anger.

Three days they'd traveled so, creeping along slowly and arduously, scarcely making eight to ten miles a day before he had to stop and sleep, all the while watching their backs. If the bounty hunters found their trail, they'd run them down with ease, but she guessed now her ploy had worked. The men didn't suspect they'd go on the same way.

Not that she felt particularly gratified for pulling it off. Though Cole had not once looked at her with hurt and condemnation, she knew he felt it. What more did he expect from her? How many loved ones had *he* put into the grave? How many times had *he* risked his heart to have it crushed and sacrificed on the altar of honor?

Honor. Why had that thought come to her? What did Cole know of honor? Was he not mixed up somehow in the murder of a . . . strumpet? Grant's words suddenly rang truer than she had thought. Had Cole spoken one word of explanation? Had he once said, "Abbie, I have no idea what this is all about"?

She studied him as he tried to keep straight in the saddle and bear the pain and chills and fever. *Death Rider*. How much more did she not know about Cole Jasper?

"I think he's better." Will sent her a furtive glance as though he read her angry thoughts.

"Better than what?"

"Than he was."

Abbie tightened her grip on the reins. "What makes you think that?"

"He's not swaying in the saddle so much."

Hallelujah. So her heart should leap for joy now that Cole Jasper was not swaying in the saddle so much. She frowned. The hard shell tightened around her heart. She was sore and weary and missed Elliot and Jenny almost more than she could bear. Why had she come on this . . . rash, harebrained ride?

To keep him alive. To get Cole away from those men who meant him harm. And she'd been right. He might not have made it to El Paso alive. Their digging the bullet out seemed the most they'd done for his injuries. If he was better now, it was due to her doctoring and Pearl's remedies.

She'd made him drink the powder when they stopped to rest the horses and eat cold rations, then watched him stalk from the camp and cough his lungs clear. She'd changed the dressing on his wound and felt the burning of his flesh. She'd watched him sleep fitfully, obviously in pain.

She glanced at him now. Cole did seem a little stronger. At least he wasn't shaking with chills. The air was warming as they left the high mountains behind, and the wind had calmed in the night.

Abbie sighed. He'd never admit it, but he needed her. He couldn't do this alone, and . . . she couldn't let him. Somehow, someway they were bound together until this was over. And then? She shook her head and looked away. There was no *then*, only today.

Seven

Cole coughed, but it didn't rack him as it had a couple days ago. Whatever Abbie put in those cups these past three days took the burn away, and he'd slept like a baby last night. He pressed his ribs. Better. He hardly felt the jolting of the horse.

The shoulder was the worst. It burned and ached and throbbed. He tried to keep it still and let the healing happen. The sling helped, but it was hard to be one-handed on horseback, especially over rough terrain. One thing was certain, his left arm would be no good in a fight for a long while.

His head was clearing, and it was time to decide what to do. Hands down, Abbie was the most determined woman he knew, and she'd set her teeth and dug her heels. But she was in danger as long as she traveled with him. And beyond that, he'd be derned if he'd take her down to El Paso to watch him hang.

The problem was, he couldn't turn back to get her home. Did he dare send her off with Will? What of Crete and Finn? Those two must be carrying a chip the size of Texas, getting bested by a lady like that. They'd be mad enough to whip their weight in wildcats.

And there was the Comanche. Abbie might think she knew this one, but Cole knew his kind better. If this Gray Wolf was half what he expected . . . Doggone it, why couldn't Abbie have stayed where she belonged?

He glanced over his shoulder, then up at the sky. She'd been yapping with Will all day, though she hadn't said a word to him. But it was coming on to night, and maybe she'd be reasonable once they had made camp. Cole turned in the saddle. "We'll stop the night at that stand of pines."

Will nodded. Abbie refused to look his way. Sure as shootin', when Abbie Farrel got something stuck in her craw, she sulked but good. He patted his shirt pocket, dug inside for his tobacco, then shoved it back in. He'd gotten this far without it, he'd gut it out. He coughed. The dern thing wouldn't let loose of him as it was.

Cole swung down from Whitesock's back, slid the bridle off with his good hand, and let him graze. Abbie and Will dismounted. Abbie took a tin plate from the packs and filled it with water from the canteen for the horses.

They'd crossed, then followed the Canadian River nearly two days, but now they were veering west toward Santa Fe, and they wouldn't hit the Pecos for another three or four days of steady riding. It wasn't desert yet, but water was chancy this time of year. Cole cleared his throat. "Go easy with that. We got a ways to go before we find more."

She nodded curtly. Acknowledgment but nothing more. Fine. It would make sending her home that much easier. Will gathered sticks for a fire, and Abbie took out the Dutch oven and the blue enamel coffeepot. Cole almost felt hungry tonight. Guess that was a good sign.

He looked back the way they'd come. The miles stretched long and hilly to the hazy mountain pass. There'd been no sign of Crete Marlowe, and that bothered him. He loosened the cinch of the saddle. Crete was not one to be defeated by losing his boots and walking for his horses.

He motioned to Will, and the boy came. "Tell me what happened the night y'all got me away. It's a mite fuzzy to me yet."

Will shook the hair from his eyes and shrugged. "Gray Wolf jumped the one on watch, and I took the other. Abbie got you roused, then she and the Comanche got you on a horse and we rode out."

Cole smiled sardonically. "That's about what I recall. Now gimme the rest. What was said?"

Will scrunched his brow and chewed his lip. "Well . . . I told the one to strip down, so I could look for weapons. That's how I found his boot knife, same as he found yours." He looked up. "Maybe it is yours. It's in the pack, there . . . an Arkansas toothpick if I ever saw one."

"Go on."

"I told him to toss over his guns and his boots, but mostly my revolver did the talking. I got him on his knees and held him there till the others had you ready."

"What else? Was anything more said?"

"He claimed we'd be sorry, but he was just spouting. Gray Wolf never so much as breathed heavy. Oh . . . Mrs. Farrel, she told them where to find the horses, and never to come on the ranch again."

Cole frowned. "Can you recall how she said it?"

Will kicked the dirt with his boot. "She talked real tough. She said, 'You'll find your horses some miles north.' Then she told 'em to never set foot on her ranch again if they valued their skin."

The sinking in his gut told him as much as anything. Abbie had put them off their trail all right. Not knowing her as he did, Crete and Finn would easily believe she was stupid and sentimental enough to take him back to the ranch, especially when she'd headed that way and left the horses before circling around in the dark. Cole narrowed his eyes out over the desolate land. He wished she'd sent them anywhere but there.

He rubbed a hand over his face. Well, there was no help for

it now. Crete Marlowe would likely add this vexation to the injuries he already carried. But then, Cole had injuries of his own. Memories of his ma flooded in, and the old anger settled at the base of his chest.

So Crete was now hunting bounty. It figured he'd stoop so low. Or was it just him they came after? He could well understand Crete taking a personal interest in seeing him hang. They had bad history between them. Bad history.

"A'right, git these saddles off. I want the horses well rested tonight." Cole patted Whitesock's flank, then joined Abbie at the fire, more sore and tired than he could remember being. He wasn't snapping back as quick as he'd like. Two more days, three maybe, before he'd feel quite himself again, discounting the shoulder.

He watched Abbie pour beans and tomatoes into the pot. Her hair was tied back with a strip of rope. Even trail worn and dirty she was beautiful. But it was no good thinking like that. He might drink in the looks of her so he wouldn't forget, but he couldn't let it get inside where it made him hurt.

Cole crossed the camp and stared out across the land. He smelled the air. It would get dryer still as they pressed south and west. He took out his tobacco and felt the pouch between his thumb and fingers. He breathed the aroma, then clamped his fingers around the pouch and dropped it back into his pocket. His lungs needed all the help they could get.

He felt Abbie at his side and turned. Holding that cup of medicine out to him, she looked like an angel. His heart jumped. *Dern sentimental fool.* He drank it down, handed back the cup, and expected her to leave, but she stood there, working herself up to talk to him. Shouldn't be so hard. "What?" he questioned.

She put up her chin. "I want to know what this is all about."

"Don't we all."

Her eyes flashed. "Don't try to put me off. You must know . . ."

Cole took her arm and turned her. "Ever seen the sun set over the New Mexico Territory?" He looked out as the bright edge of the winter sun crept away over the brown nubby hills. There was always something in that final moment that made him ponder. He watched the streaks fade from orange to yellow to gray. It created a sadness inside. Or maybe the sadness was there already and moments like this just reminded him of it.

"What are you going to do in El Paso?"

Her quiet query brought him back, but he couldn't think how to answer.

"Who was Auralee?"

He swallowed, but still the words clogged.

"Why do they think you killed her?"

Cole dropped his chin and hooked his thumbs into his jeans. "I don't know. She was alive when I left her." He felt her stiffen next to him. What did she think, that he'd lived thirty-six years without meeting another woman?

"The men who took you said she was a . . ."

"She was a saloon girl, Abbie."

She made no move, but it suddenly felt like she'd put miles between them. "Did you love her?"

He could answer that simply, but the narrowing of her eyes and the jut of her chin betrayed her double meaning. She'd already judged him, and heck if he'd try to change her mind. He turned and met her gaze squarely without reply.

Abbie looked away. "What was she like?"

"Purty. Red hair, green eyes. Had a spark to her . . . it reminded me of you." For two short weeks he'd thought Auralee could make him forget. Two weeks was all it took to see he'd never forget. "But she had a bad streak, somethin' inside that made her mean. She'd take your heart an' twist it if you were fool enough to turn it over."

"Which you weren't, though you availed yourself of her charms."

He looked into the scrubby branches of the cedars. "I ain't the one that killed her."

"But you know who did."

He jolted. "What makes you say that?"

She eyed him with feminine insight.

"Sheez." Cole jammed his fingers through his hair. "If I knew that, would I be ridin' to a rope?"

Her lip trembled. "I don't know."

He took hold of her arm. "Abbie, I want you to go home. I don't know how this'll turn out. I gotta go on and do what I must. But if it comes to it, I don't want you out there when I swing."

He saw her breath come in short gasps.

"Go home to your young'uns."

Angry tears sparkled in her eyes. "Jenny is torn apart over losing you. Did you read her note?"

"What note?"

"I put it in your coat pocket."

Cole reached in and pulled out the paper. He frowned. "You know I cain't read."

She took the paper from his hand and unfolded it. " 'Dear Cole, Aunt Abbie says not to tell you, but I pretend you're my pa. Please come home.' "

The pain flared up in his heart. And he'd thought Abbie was the only one who could put it there. *I pretend you're my pa.* He couldn't meet Abbie's eyes. What had he done to make Jenny think a thing like that? No more than offer a kind word and understand her need.

Abbie's eyes were honed blades. "How do you think it'll be if I go home without you?"

The tightness in his throat kept him from speaking. He cleared it dryly. "I reckon it'll be hard on her. I never meant to . . ."

"You don't understand a single thing about love, do you? It's not something you make happen. It just does."

He understood more than she thought.

A flicker of hurt showed through her anger. "Jenny needs you. And here you are throwing your life away."

"I don't know what you—"

"Oh yes, you do."

He swallowed down the argument. There wasn't any use. "I thought you meant for me to go on down there."

"I do. But to defend yourself."

"What makes you think I ain't?"

"The way you're talking about a rope. The way you're muttering and gazing around like you might never see things again. The way you wouldn't fight Sam."

She was hitting too close. "So?"

"I know you, Cole. Is it Sam you're protecting?"

He kicked his boot in the dirt. "You're thinkin' crazy."

Her eyes glittered dangerously. "Am I?"

He nodded toward the fire. "Them beans are gonna burn."

Abbie's chest rose and fell. Her hands balled at her sides, and he thought for a moment she'd hit him. Then she turned and walked away.

Cole stared after her straight back. Was his mind a window to her? She'd voiced what he hardly dared to think. Was it Sam who killed Auralee? They looked enough alike that someone could mistake them, especially in the dark as it had been when he'd left her.

Had Sam known? Had he seen her carry on? Had she baited him, tormented him with it? Back at the Lucky Star there'd been a familiar look in Sam's eyes when he pounded Cole's face, a purely murderous look. One he'd seen in their pa's face.

If Auralee had pushed Sam over the edge . . .

Cole's throat went dry. Abbie was right. He'd do whatever it took for Sam. Cole jammed his hand into his pocket and felt Jenny's note. His groan made him cough. He looked up at the darkening sky. What in heaven's name was he supposed to do?

◆◆◆◆◆◆

Abbie wrestled with her bedroll, then drew its blanket around her. She knew that inside, too, she was sealing herself off. This journey was something she had to see through, but she would not let it cost her. She was beholden to Cole Jasper for all the times he'd helped her in need, but she would not risk her heart. This was duty. Monte would say honor. Either way, she owed a debt.

Hadn't he ridden down Templeton Gap to ransom his life for hers, expecting the rustler's bullet at any moment? She had known that day that he loved her, more so than when he asked for her hand in marriage two years before. The love in his face that day when he had taken the rope from her wrists had been raw, sacrificial love.

Abbie frowned. There was no indication that a trace of that remained. And she was thankful. When he'd kissed her on the plain it had been for his own pleasure. She knew that now. She'd seen him with the saloon girl, Lil Brandon, and could imagine him with Auralee Dubois. *All the time I'd thought he cared, he was . . .*

No, that wasn't fair. Hadn't she sent him away? Hadn't she despised him, hated him even? Didn't she still? Abbie looked at him sleeping by the fire. Cole Jasper was the only man she knew who could sleep the minute he lay down and wake faster than lightning.

She rolled over. But then, how many men had she seen sleep? *Monte.* She remembered his voice growing drowsy, and how she'd rest her head on his chest and he'd curl his arm around. She remembered the gentle rise and fall of his breath, the low drum of his heart. It seemed too far away and long ago. Now she just felt empty.

She watched Will toss about in his blankets. He reminded her of Elliot when he would pad into her room and climb between the covers, then wiggle and squirm until he had every possible part of him against her before he promptly fell asleep.

Oh, Elliot. Every day away was one she'd never have again. Her only baby growing week after week without her there . . . Monte's son. The ache of separation was no longer debilitating—the panic and nightmares had only come once since she'd set out with Will—but she yearned for her little boy.

She missed the way he slipped his soft hand into hers, the sound of his laugh, the quirk of his eyebrow, so like Monte's . . . Was it possible she had thought of Monte just now without the dreadful ache? Had healing begun? Maybe, just maybe, she would soon be at peace.

Cole coughed, and her heart wrenched. What was she thinking? She was lying out in the New Mexico Territory with bounty hunters searching for them, and only God knew what waited at the end of the trail. How was it in one breath, Cole could steal her chance at peace and replace it with such wretched . . .

Abbie heard a low raspy rumbling, and in the same instant Cole's eyes opened. She saw him move under the blanket and knew his hand went to his gun, but he hadn't lifted his head. She felt her own pistol in the pocket against her thigh, but could they risk a gunshot? Anyone within miles would know their location. Will slept on soundly.

She caught Cole's glance and confirmed with her own that she had heard the sound, as well. Slowly he raised his head and folded the covers off, then sat up. She listened. Nothing except her breathing and Will's. She raised her head and saw movement beyond the clump of piñon pines.

Zephyr snorted, and the other horses stamped and tugged at their ropes as they whiffed too late the downwind scent. She caught the glow of eyes reflecting the firelight like flat fiery disks. Cole stood and took up a stout stick with his one good arm.

A flash of tawny hide confirmed her guess, and her heart rate quickened. The cat kept its distance. That it braved their camp at all amazed her, but the fire was no more than coals, and the animal's gaunt condition bespoke its hunger. It limped past the cluster of pine trunks. It was old and mangy, but that didn't make it any less dangerous.

What could Cole do against a mountain lion that size? He'd have to shoot. He couldn't . . . Slowly Cole lowered his boot onto a twig and snapped it. The cat's head swung around. He raised the stick.

For a long moment they bound each other with their eyes. The cat's muzzle peeled back from its fangs. With ears flat against its head, the animal wore the scars of too many battles on its face. Abbie's fingers were on her gun, but she dared not move to bring it out of her pocket.

Cole stood, legs spread, slightly crouched and ready. If the lion jumped him he would have no chance, one-handed with a stick. But the cat was wary now, as though only realizing its predicament. A cornered animal was twice as fierce, and this one looked nearly starved. Would it be so brazen?

Abbie lay mesmerized as the two of them held their stance, neither backing down, neither showing fear. What was Cole thinking? What did he feel? He looked hard and . . . deadly. Slowly, so slowly she hardly saw at first, he raised the stick and inclined his shoulders. She held her breath. He was challenging the animal.

The rumble in the lion's throat took on a raspy yowl as it took one pace back, then opened its mouth in a low hiss. The horses strained against their tethers, and Will stirred. In a flash the cat spun and bounded into the night. Cole stood unmoving, and Abbie felt frozen by the sheer force of his will.

A moment later Cole lowered the stick, and her breath returned. She sat up as he hunkered down beside the fire pit. He held a hand over the remainder of the coals, then gave the coffeepot a testing touch. Satisfied, he poured a cup of coffee and breathed the steam.

Trembling, she pulled on her coat and joined him. The rock she sat on was hard and cold through her skirts, but sleep was as far away as the dawn. She glanced at him curiously. "How did you hear that first sound in your sleep?"

"How did you?"

"I wasn't asleep."

He drew a slow sip. "How come?"

There he was, turning things back on her. Well, she could give a little to get a little. "I was thinking. Of Elliot."

He drank. "You must miss him somethin' fierce."

She nodded. "It's not as bad as last time. When we first started out on the cattle drive, I thought I'd never survive, it hurt so much."

"You didn't let on."

Abbie shrugged. "You just thought all my pain was from the horse."

His mouth quirked. "You ride a mite better now than you did three months ago."

Cole's teasing smile tugged her heart, but she clamped it down. She pulled a bur from her stocking. It clung to her finger, and she flicked it away, leaving a tiny prick of blood. She felt her throat work around the words that wanted to come. She drew a shaky breath. "Why do the Comanches call you Death Rider?"

Cole stared into his cup until she thought he wouldn't answer. Then he slowly raised his head. "Gray Wolf told you that?"

She nodded.

He looked out into the night. "I ain't proud o' some things. That's one of 'em."

She waited, and at last he spoke. "Livin' in Texas, you expected run-ins. Apaches, Comanches. Most times they settled fer stealin' food and livestock. If you stood your ground they tended not to bother you much, though some were wicked mean. Others seemed peaceable enough, but folks bein' what they are . . ." He swirled the coffee in his cup, then drained it and set the cup on a stone.

"Samuel and I had a healthy respect for our scalps, but we weren't afraid to do a bit of tradin' now an' then, mainly with the Comanches. Got to know some of the camps pretty well, got to understand their ways some, too. Beyond that, the Comanches left us mostly alone. Guess they figured we weren't much of a threat."

Cole rested his forearms on his knees. "We'd gone prob'ly a year without a single raid on our ranch. Samuel was twenty-one, and I'd just turned nineteen. Then a man by the name of Crete Marlowe sold a wagonload of whiskey to the Comanche camp. Samuel an' I were workin' at a neighboring spread when they come."

Abbie heard his voice thicken.

"They hung our ma from the tree by her arms an' set her dress afire." The muscles rippled on the side of his jaw. "While she burned, they shot her full of arrows and ran on to the next place and the next. Thirty-one dead, mostly women and children, tortured, raped, and disfigured. Babies with their heads crushed in."

Abbie felt the horror rise inside.

"When I saw her hangin' there, somethin' snapped. I wanted to kill."

"What did you do?" Her voice was scarcely a whisper.

His answer was low and cold. "I joined the rangers."

"You were a Texas Ranger?"

"One year. Went on a campaign of revenge, ridin' with others who'd seen the butchery. The Comanches come to know when I was ridin'." He bowed his head. "I didn't care how many I killed. I kept seein' my ma hangin' there . . . prayin', Abbie, that they'd burned her before they'd done worse."

She felt his pain like a knife to her heart. What had she said out on the plains of Kansas? That he'd never suffered anything to compare to her loss? She felt paralyzed. She wanted to drop to her knees beside him, take his hands in hers, and cry. But she couldn't move.

"I burned Crete Marlowe's cabin to the ground. There was enough liquor in there to shoot the blaze halfway to the stars. Then I beat him a hair's breadth short of hell and hoped he'd die when I left."

She hated what she saw in his face. This was a Cole Jasper she had never guessed existed. This was Death Rider, and his bared anguish awakened her own. Too much death, too much pain. She couldn't bear it. She turned away.

He stood up from his crouch. "Better get some sleep."

She heard his steps on the frozen ground, heard him pull his blanket aside and lie down. She crept to her bedroll and curled up with a dry, hollow ache inside.

Cole could be brash and insolent, cross and infuriating. But underneath he was loyal and kind and steadfast. Was he also capable of a rage that spurred him to such destruction? *Vengeance is mine, saith the Lord.*

Abbie closed her eyes, remembering the horror she'd felt when she killed the young rustler. She recalled Cole's penetrating gaze that horrible night, his words, "*You done what you had to.*" He had understood only too well what she felt. Though he tried to hide it, there was agony behind his telling tonight. He was indeed not proud of his name, Death Rider.

Eight

Aunt Pearl! They's two men in the yard a hollerin' for Mistuh Jazzper. They knocked Mistuh Matt senseless, and they's comin' for the house."

Pearl spun to face Zena. "Lawd ha' mercy." Hadn't she had a premonition all morning? She swooped down on Jenny and Elliot at the table with their fingers in the bowl of sponge cake batter. "Take the chillen down Mastuh Monte's wine cella'." For once she felt thankful it was there. She shoved them toward the door at the end of the kitchen.

James rushed in. "They gonna break the door down."

"He'p me here." With James, Pearl pushed the walnut cupboard in front of the cellar door. Then she sat him at the table and stuck a napkin in his collar as the pounding on the front door ended with a mighty crash.

James pushed back from the table with his gnarled hands. "What's all this? I can' eat, not with . . ."

"Hush yo' mouth." Pearl ladled a bowl of chicken dumplings and set it before him. She stuck the spoon in his hand.

The kitchen door burst open and two men filled its space. Pearl plastered her fists to her hips and scowled her fiercest. "Who are you? Why you bargin' in my kitchen?" She took up a broom and started toward them. "Get out. Get out where's you belong."

The younger man backed out, but the second grabbed the

broom from her and threw it. "Where's Cole Jasper hidin' out?"

"Mistuh Jazzper ain' here. He been took off."

The men looked around the room. The older one jutted his chin. "What's that in the pot?"

"Chicken dumplin's."

"Sure a big potful for one old man."

Pearl held her tongue. If ever there was a time for falsehood this was it, but that was how the devil worked, and these two were the devil's own.

"Don't stand there gawkin', woman. Dish us some. And be quick." He pulled a gun. "'Fore I shoot off this old man's head."

Pearl ladled the bowls, muttering. It was a crying shame to waste her dumplings on trash. For once she wished she made them heavy as old Esther's. They'd hang in their bellies like stones. She smacked the bowls on the table, but the men didn't sit. They gobbled like hogs, spooning the food into their mouths with the bowls held to their chins.

The younger one finished and wiped his mouth on his sleeve. "You got whiskey to wash it down?"

Pearl jutted her lower lip. "I got no use for the devil's tool."

The other man took James by the shirt. "How 'bout you, old man? You got whiskey?"

"The massuh got some."

Pearl held her piece. James always spoke as though poor Master Monte was still master.

"Git it now."

Pearl watched as James stood and walked stoically to the parlor. The men followed, and she stayed close on their heels. Now that they were out of the kitchen she meant to keep them out.

They shoved past James to the cabinet. The younger one eyed the elegant room. "Whooee. Looks like Jasper got hisself a fancy position."

Pearl scowled when the older man pulled the stopper and drank from the decanter. Master Monte's whiskey had no right in that man's belly. It had sat in that cabinet four years now, except on the rare times Miss Abbie offered it to a gentleman caller.

He passed the bottle and the other man drank, then he took it back and slammed it on the cabinet shelf. "Finn, you take upstairs, I'll take down. Tear it apart till we find his hidey-hole."

"Mistuh Jazzper ain' here. I tol' you."

The men separated. Pearl heard the crashing and smashing. She backed toward the kitchen as the gray-haired man started that way. She rushed in ahead of him and took up the marble rolling pin Master Monte had brought her all the way from Italy. "You break somethin' in my kitchen, I'll crack yo' skull."

"What's that door?"

Pearl's heart pounded. She turned, then almost gasped with relief. "Tha's the washroom." She huffed over and opened the door to reveal the pantry shelves and the washtub with the small stove beside it. "They's nothin' there. Mistuh Jazzper, he gone."

"What about the missus?"

"What missus?"

"The girl what sprung him loose with that Injun."

So they'd gotten Mister Jasper free. Pearl felt elated but didn't let it show. "Mizz Abbie ain' here neither."

"Where is she?"

"I don' know." And that was God's truth. She worried sick when each new day failed to bring Miss Abbie home.

The look in his eyes near froze her marrow. This man was the devil's own for sure. He turned and bellowed, "Finn!"

Finn bounded down and followed the first man back to the parlor. They shoved the whiskey and the brandy into their shirts. Pearl held her tongue. Good riddance and she hoped it rotted their bellies. The older man took up the lamp.

"Whatcha doin', Crete?"

"Repayin' a favor." He smashed it against the wall. The oil splattered down the lace curtain and over the carpet.

"No!" James hollered as Crete tossed the match, then knocked James to the floor.

Crete and Finn ran from the house as the fire rushed up the wall. Pearl took up a rug and beat it against the flames. The fire jumped from one curtain to the next. James staggered up and ran. "Mistuh Matt! Mistuh Curtis, come quick!"

Pearl's arms ached, and tears streamed as she beat the flames. In the spreading flames she choked and swung the rug with all her strength. What would Miss Abbie do now? Lawd A'mighty! That woman had troubles in this world.

Down in the cellar Elliot pressed into Zena's arms, but Jenny made a small ball of herself. With each smash and thump she tightened until she imagined herself growing smaller and harder like one of Cole's animals. Where was he? Had Aunt Abbie found him? Did she give him her note? Did he know how to pretend?

She pressed her eyes shut and saw him. He could be her pa. Of all the people she knew, she liked him best. She couldn't say why. It was something in the way he smelled, the way he smiled at her, the way his voice got growly when he said something nice.

It wasn't easy to be nice. Not for Cole, and not for her. He didn't have to be. He could grumble and holler, and she'd even heard him swear once when he didn't know she was there. She wouldn't tell, though, because sometimes she wished she could be just as ornery.

But she had to be nice. If she wasn't nice, bad things happened. Hadn't she teased Elliot this morning? She'd made him cry, not that it was hard to. She'd told him maybe his mama wouldn't come back at all. She'd wanted to hurt him. Now the wickedness of it made a hard ball in her tummy.

She'd made this bad thing happen, made the evil men come. Would her mean words ruin everything? What if Aunt Abbie never did come back? What if she couldn't get Cole? What if there was no one, no one but Elliot left? What if she was alone . . . again. . . . Jenny stared into the reddish candlelit darkness.

The shelves of dusty bottles loomed over her. Was this what it was like to be buried? They'd buried her mama. She knew that. That grave was far away, but her pa's grave was right here on the ranch.

She didn't remember him, except . . . his mustache. It had hard ends that curled up, not soft like Cole's. At least she thought Cole's was soft. She could almost remember him holding her, remember it brushing her cheek when she wrapped her arms around his neck. Yes, she was almost certain that wasn't pretend.

Jenny drew a long soulful breath. At least that's what Zena called it when she breathed like that. Soulful. It helped the knot in her tummy, and she took another one, then smelled smoke. She shot to her feet and stared at the door at the top of the stairs.

Nothing showed in the darkness, but she smelled it stronger and started to shake. Every part of her felt tight and wobbly at once. If she burned now, she'd go to hell and burn forever. She saw her grandmother's face, heard the words. *"That child will scream herself straight to hell."*

Jenny clamped a hand to her mouth. She mustn't make a sound. Not a sound.

Sam had given him ten days. Time enough for any man to own up to his obligations. He'd never known Cole to shirk before. He'd trained his brother better than that. But he had waited in that hotel too long, and today was Judgment Day for Cole Jasper.

Sam reined in and squinted. Smoke was pouring from the front of the fancy house. He made out two men beating the flames that climbed the tall white pillars. Neither one was Cole.

It wasn't his business, but . . . Sam spurred the horse into the yard. He leaped down, grabbed a gunnysack from the pile thrown in the dirt, and beat at the pillars. "Anyone in the house?" he hollered over the ruckus, but he saw for himself a moment later.

Inside, a Negro woman rushed past the window just as the glass exploded. She fell clear, grabbed up her rug, then beat out the flames licking the window frame. Another figure, a Negro man, staggered behind her.

Where in tarnation was Cole? Where was the lady . . . Sam straightened. He took one step and hurled himself through the shattered window. He gained his feet, but the Negro woman raised her rug and swung.

Sam tumbled over and rolled. "Wait! Stop! I'm here to help." He clutched the gunnysack as proof.

She took his measure with a hard eye, then went back to beating the flames. He worked beside her. "Is anyone else inside?"

"Dis fire ain' leavin' dis room. You want to he'p, he'p here!"

Sam quickly eyed the doorway. The paint was blistering, but no flames showed past it. He ran over and scanned the hall. Smoke, but no flame. He shut the paneled wood door, then stomped and ground the fire at the edge of the thick rug, swinging the sack into the worst of it.

The old man was wheezing, his gnarled fingers scarcely gripping the broom he swung at the flame running along the ceiling molding. Any moment he'd ignite the broom and spread the fire worse.

Sam rushed over. "Here, get clear." He grabbed the broom and swung at the ceiling, pounding out the flames even as they sprang up anew. Sweat poured from his skin, and he felt his lips burning. He plunged the broom up again and again.

The old man hunched against the wall—a good sign. If it was cool enough to support him, it wasn't likely to ignite. This house was well built. Plenty of lathe and plaster. Sam beat the broom against the wall, then into the thicker flames at the window, his arms aching with each whack.

He turned. The big rug was smoldering, and he lunged to it and rolled the end until the would-be flames suffocated inside. He covered his face with his arm and choked. A wrenching groan brought him around, and he watched the elegant portico come crashing down outside. One of the men leaped free, and Sam suspected he'd purposely brought it down to keep the fire from jumping over the stone face to the wood siding above.

The dark-haired man cast a bucket on the pillar flaming in the yard. The other followed suit, running from pump to pillars, but they were salvaging only. The danger was past, unless . . .

Sam yanked open the parlor door and staggered down the hall through the smoke. If sparks or embers had blown through . . . He cleared the haze with his arms, keeping one wall at his elbow. The place was massive. He felt a warm body behind him and made way for the woman.

She pushed past like a nursing cow on her calf. He followed. They barreled into the kitchen, and she flung open the door to a washroom and then an outside door. Cold air rushed in, and the smoke swirled. The woman came back and put her weight to a cupboard. Sam caught her intention.

He shoved with her until the door behind was free, then yanked it open. A waif stood at the foot of the stairs, still and solemn in the column of daylight. Sam stared through the smoke at the child, and she stared back.

Then she opened her pinched little mouth. "Cole?"

The voice was plaintive, and he eyed the young Negro behind the child, holding a tiny white boy on her chest. He saw their hopeful eyes. They were looking for Cole, and mistaking him in the smoke. He swallowed hard. "Come on up now. The fire's out."

The little slip of a girl came by herself. She stepped onto the slate floor and swiped at the smoke. She blinked, then tightened her lips and brought up her chin. "You're not Cole."

"I'm Sam. Cole's brother, Sam." He heard the heavy woman mutter and turned. "Is that everyone?"

"Tha's all."

The other two came up from the cellar and the small boy stared at him with incredible eyes. Sam had seen eyes like that, only angry . . . that lady must be his ma, the one who had held a pistol to his head as cool as you like. The child's eyes teared in the smoke, or maybe he was scared.

Sam faced the woman who had felled him with the rug. "Where's Cole? And the lady?"

The Negro woman puffed her lips and scowled but kept her peace.

"Look, I don't mean to make trouble. . . ."

"Mistuh, you brung trouble."

Sam looked from one face to another. They could've hardly been more hostile if they were Comanche squaws. He slouched against the cupboard. "My brother and I had some personal business, but this is different. I got word there are bounty hunters . . ."

"They done took him off. An' Mizz Abbie, she gone after him."

Sam frowned.

"Now they come back lookin' for him again. Who you think lit that fire?"

Sam ran a hand through his hair. Was he getting this straight? "The same ones that took him came lookin'?"

"They was hoppin' mad Mizz Abbie got Mistuh Jazzper loose."

Sam stared at her, not certain if this was some tale meant to throw him or . . .

"If you're Cole's brother, how come you hurt him?"

Sam turned to the little girl and met her angry stare. "That's his business an' mine, little miss."

Her fists clenched at her sides. With one swift stroke, she swung her shoe into his shin, clearing the boot by an inch. "Aah!" The pain shot up his bone.

She turned and fled out the back door. The little boy ran after, and the young woman after him. The large woman folded her arms across her chest. One look into her face and Sam felt decidedly unwelcome.

He reached up and realized his hat was gone. He nodded, turned on his heel, and went back to the damaged front room, hoping it hadn't been trampled or burned in the ruckus. He'd been two years training that hat, and it was just now the best fit he'd yet accomplished.

He saw it lying against the wall where he'd rolled from the woman's first blow. He scooped it up and put it where it belonged. He wasn't about to make the long, fast ride with a hat that didn't fit.

Nine

The terrain they'd covered that day had been thickly treed and hilly. They had forded the Pecos River and camped on its far bank. Abbie stirred the thin beans in the pot, wishing for corn bread or biscuits, anything to properly fill their stomachs. They were at the end of their provender, and they'd soon be scrapping for roots and rabbits.

She glanced to where Will sat with his knees poking up like grasshopper legs. He'd sleep with a rumbling stomach tonight. But he seemed cheerful enough as he watched Cole with something close to worship.

"You been through this way before, Cole?"

Cole nodded. "More or less. I've taken herds along both the Santa Fe and the Chisholm trails, among others, from the time I was seventeen. Some herds up to three thousand head."

"Was it difficult driving the big herds?"

"Every drive's difficult, Will. Every drive's different. You never know from one trip to the next what you'll encounter by way of weather and trouble."

"What sort of trouble?"

"All sorts." Cole's eyes took on a faraway look. "The first time I drove a herd as boss foreman, I thought I knew all there was to know on the trail. I was twenty-three years old, and half the men in my outfit were twice that. But I was a cocky son of a gun and had wheedled the job from old man Black."

Cole rubbed the dust from his boot. "We'd gotten word that some herds ahead of us had turned back for lack of water. Well, I knew the land and figured those herds must have been driven by less experienced men. I didn't reckon on the last summer's drought. But that's what it was."

He ran his fingers over the tracery on the leather. "Once we'd crossed the Colorado River, things looked pretty scaly. Where there should have been water, there was mud. We dug wells, but they scarcely filled up enough to satisfy our saddle stock. There was none for the cattle."

He shook his head. "The heat was fierce and sapped our strength. Dusters twisted 'round and stung us fierce. But I knew the way clear and figured we best push on. The herd could go some days, though their tongues were hangin' out and they were bawlin' like babes. They wouldn't lay down, and they wouldn't graze. It took every man ridin' twenty-four hours straight to keep 'em from turnin'."

Will whistled low.

"By the fourth day, the cattle were millin' so bad we spent more time breakin' up the circles than movin' forward. Then they turned. We snapped our whips and shot our six-shooters, but they kept comin'. One bull trampled clean over a calf like he'd never seen it. And I realized they were blind. There was nothin' for it but to let 'em get back to water."

"They were really blind, Cole?"

"It wasn't permanent if their other senses could get them to water in time. We couldn't drive 'em. All's we could do was try to contain them as they trailed on back."

"Did they make it to the water?"

"Well, nature smiled on us. The next night it rained, comin' down so fierce it sounded like nails on the hard ground. Kept on all through that day and the next. The cattle, they stood and licked at the water round their hooves like they'd never tasted it before."

Cole shook his head. "It was a sight to see. Come mornin' of the third day, we felt right hopeful that the streams were runnin' good enough to see us through."

"Had you lost any cattle?"

"We lost two that gave up and keeled over less than one hour before the rain begun. But in roundin' up the strays, we gained a number of range mavericks, as well. Times bein' what they were, we let the extras stay, no charge."

Abbie caught Cole's slanted grin as she handed Will his meager plate.

Will nodded his thanks. "You mean you rustled them?"

"No, sir. I never rustled a steer in my life. 'Cept down in Mexico, where they're free for the takin' if you've guts enough to face down the vaqueros."

"What's a vaquero?"

"Mexican rancher. It's kind of a give-and-take across the border. They raid ours, we raid theirs. Most times you hardly know what rightly belongs to one or the other anymore, and it's like a game—only a hazardous one if you ain't quick and quiet."

"But isn't that rustlin'?"

"Not if you're takin' back your own with a few unfortunates mixed in."

Will whooped. "Tell us another one, Cole."

Abbie slopped the beans into the tin saucer and handed it to Cole.

"Thank you, Abbie." He turned back to Will. "Talkin' of rustlin' puts me in mind of the time we met a band of true cow thieves at the crossing of the Brazos. I reckon I'd been trail boss two years or so, and I hadn't had much trouble of that sort to speak of."

Cole took a bite of beans and chewed slowly. Abbie sat down and watched him. This was the most talkative he'd been the entire trip. Of course the cough was nearly gone, and his strength was returning.

"We'd got word from a previous herd that rustlers had set up at the crossing, and sure enough, as we neared the river some fellas came along claimin' to be cutters. Well, I gave the orders to start the herd across before I asked what brand they were searchin'."

"How come?" Will wiped his mouth with his sleeve.

"That way if these men caused us trouble, we'd have the river behind us to catch our herd. Well, they sparked good at that, but I told them I had a job to do and didn't want to risk the river risin'."

Cole chuckled, obviously enjoying his tale. "Once across, they started claimin' cattle that they recognized as this outfit's or that's, and always the brand was close to another or maybe blurred some. Anytime we contested, they demanded we throw it. Bein' of a tractable sort, I obliged, throwin' the steers in spite of my suspicions."

"And?"

Cole swilled his bite down with his coffee. "Once we cut the hair away, our road brand was as clear as day. The fellas acted embarrassed, but I could see they was riled. I told them to take what they had and shove off."

Will's eyes shown. Abbie saw the signs of true adulation as he hung on Cole's words.

"Well, they'd only cut six head of the brand they were scouting, and they were mighty peeved. Their lead man scowled somethin' fierce and acted like he'd been wronged."

Cole fixed Will with a steely gaze. "We figured they'd try to stampede the herd come nightfall, or come back with gunmen and put up a fight. So we night-herded the cattle and kept a scout on through all the watches."

Will's eyes were aglow. "What happened?"

"Nothin'. Next mornin' I sent a man out, and he come back

with the answer. And a mighty grizzly one at that."

"What?"

"Apaches. A war band met up with them on their way to us. Passed within six miles of our herd and never knew we were there."

Abbie released her breath, caught up in the story in spite of herself. "That was lucky."

Cole shrugged. "We felt kinda gypped. Seemed hardly fair the Apaches got all the fun of the fight we picked." He winked at Will.

Will laughed heartily, but Abbie frowned. There again was a peek into Cole's character. As though shooting it out with ruffians was a pleasure to be sought.

Will wiped the brown drizzle of bean juice from his chin with his thumb. "Cole, you got family in Texas?"

Cole swirled the coffee in his cup, then took a swallow. "I got my brother, Sam, but I ain't sure where he is just now."

"Are your parents dead?"

Abbie tensed, but Cole stirred the fork around in his beans. "My ma is. Ain't seen my pa since I was ten years old. But I reckon he's somewhere in hell."

Will nodded slowly. "My pa was killed in a fight when I was a kid."

"You're still a kid. Barely more than a colt with wobbly legs."

Abbie bit her lower lip. Cole was certainly a master at diverting the subject.

"I had my twenty-first birthday the day we crossed the Canadian River."

Abbie glanced up. "You never said. I'd have managed something special for supper."

Cole frowned. "Such as?"

"Well . . . beans." She met his eyes and suddenly laughed. "With a whole side of beans." She liked his answering grin and felt the tightness between them ease.

"We'll be comin' on to Santa Fe by sundown tomorrow. We'll get stocked there."

Abbie nodded. Cole talked as though this were no more than another trail. Try as she would, she could not get one word from him as to his plans once he got to El Paso. Would he turn himself in? Would he clear himself of the charges?

Surely he had some explanation that would clear things up, but she had an ominous weight on her spirit. It was fear. Fear that he had no intention of clearing things up. Fear that he would not defend himself. Fear . . . of losing him?

"What if someone recognizes you in Santa Fe?"

"You an' Will can go into town. I'll keep shy of it."

Abbie swallowed her bland bite of beans. "So we load up there and go on to El Paso?"

"Should find most anything you need there, if you don't need nothin' fancy."

She sighed. "I can't say I wouldn't mind a fine Lucky Star beefsteak just about now."

"That's your own doin'. I've sent you home twice now."

"And I've already told you, we're going all the way with you."

Cole glowered at his plate.

Abbie felt a stab of anger. Why did that disturb him unless he expected the worst? If he thought he'd be turning around and coming home free, wouldn't he be glad for the company? "Have you given thought to your defense?" There, she'd said it. "We could wire Grant and . . ."

He set down his plate, stood, and walked away. So that was his answer. Well, she wasn't about to accept it. She slapped her own plate down on the ground and followed him. The night sky was like jet set with diamonds. She saw only his dark form against the black hills.

If Cole heard her approach, he ignored it. His stance was

firm, stubborn. Abbie felt her irritation rise. Why did he get under her skin so? She stepped around and faced him. "I think we should have a plan."

"I think you should quit meddlin'."

"You're just stubborn."

"Like you ain't?"

She felt the tendons tighten in her neck. "I want to know what you intend to do in El Paso."

"How can I tell you that when I don't know m'self?"

She put a hand on his arm. "You must have ... an alibi. Grant says if a person has an alibi ..."

"I was with Auralee the night she died."

Abbie felt as though a rock hit her stomach. *With Auralee?* She pulled her hand from his arm. "But you didn't kill her."

He set his jaw. "I a'ready told you that."

"Then someone else must have been there ... when you left." After completing the business he had with a saloon girl. ...

It could almost be a smirk on his face. "Leave it alone, Abbie. The subject's distasteful to you."

She hadn't meant to show her displeasure. But she couldn't help recalling his hand under Lil's fingers. Why would that burn itself on her memory? It wasn't as though twenty men a day didn't do as much and more. But she'd expected better from Cole. Even if Auralee was a red-haired beauty.

Fury and a feeling of ... jealous dismay burned up inside. She turned and stalked back to camp. What had she been thinking? How could she have thought she cared for him? He was a rake and a scoundrel, as far from the man she thought him as ... as from the man Monte had been.

Will looked up from his perch by the fire. His eyes were worried. "He didn't answer?"

"He's a bullheaded ..." Abbie closed her fists at her sides. "If I ever come to you again on Cole's behalf, tell me I'm plumb crazy!" She flounced to her bedroll and climbed in.

Cole stood in the dark. The moon was a sliver amid the stars swarming the sky. He'd have liked to lie on his back and let his gaze search out the farthest pricks of light. He'd have liked to have Abbie beside him, searching out the same stars with that look of wonder she got sometimes over the littlest things.

But she was angry as a polecat, and he'd done it on purpose. Sure he didn't want her prying, sure he hadn't a decent answer, but more than that, he needed to shake her loose. It was eating away his resolve to have her with him. Every day that passed made it harder to keep his focus on what he meant to do.

What did he mean to do? Could he save his neck and Sam's both? If Sam killed Auralee in a fury, was it right to stand in for him? It was, if Cole was the cause of that fury. He'd seen it building, but he hadn't known how to stop it.

Those first two weeks in El Paso he'd been like the blind cattle, feeling nothing but the water on his belly, tasting a lick or two as though he'd never drunk before. He'd spent three and a half years secretly looking after Abbie from wherever he could make the most money, hoping she'd call him back, hoping she'd need him. But she hadn't called.

So he'd gone home. He'd thought to look up Sam, maybe find some of the boys. He'd thought to go down Mexico way and drive a herd for old times' sake. He'd thought to put his feelings for Abbie behind him once and for all. But he hadn't reckoned on Sam loving the one woman who caught his eye.

Auralee Dubois was poison in a silk gown. How Pablo Montoya got hold of her, he'd never know. She was as out of place in La Paloma Blanca as a fish in the desert. With her fair skin and red hair, she stood out, but it was her fire that caught him cold.

He had wanted a woman who'd fight him, a woman who'd exorcise the memory of blue eyes and creamy skin and a tangle of brown hair. For two weeks he had eyed and baited her, until the blindness passed and he saw Sam's face. By then it was too late. Auralee was up to the challenge and not to be put off. That he refused only fueled her fire.

Cole drew a long breath. Sometimes a body just couldn't get it right.

Ten

Nora looked at the wooden walls rising up from the piece of property Davy had acquired. It was no mansion he built. Not like Abbie's fine house, and she was glad. She would never be at home in so much glass and polish. This one would suit her better.

It was near enough to town for Davy to travel to and from the smithy each day, yet far enough out to support a small farm. A half-day's ride from the mission made it impossible for her to look in daily on Maggie and Father Paddy, but Mary Donnelly's mother was to live there when she left.

That was a good arrangement, though Nora felt a twinge at leaving her sister to Father Paddy and old mother Donnelly. Father Paddy was too busy to keep an eye on Maggie now that she was eighteen and as bonny a lass as ever turned a lad's head. Her young sister had enough fire to keep them at bay, but nary the will to do it.

Nora carried the steaming pot of coffee to where the men worked. Though the weather had warmed after the brief snow, there was still enough chill to be chased by the hot brew. And Davy preferred coffee to tea.

He looked up from the architectural pattern he held and smiled. Her heart warmed, though she wouldn't show it. She gave her head a coquettish tilt and met him with the coffee.

"I've something to keep you goin'."

"That you have." Davy's smile broadened, and he reached a hand to her hair and tugged. The coppery coil sprang back from his fingers.

"I mean the coffee, ye daft man."

"Who are you calling daft? Don't you see the walls rising to your house?"

"Aye. But will they hold the roof, I'm wonderin'?"

"They will that and more. They'll hold the family we'll be growing inside them."

Nora flushed. "And if you propagate as well as you boast, where will we put them all?"

"We'll add on as we need to." He took the coffeepot. "Cups?"

"Aye." Nora pulled them from her shawl, one cup for each of the men—Davy, Alan, her brother, Doyle, and big Connor.

The others smelled the coffee Davy poured and left their places on the walls. Alan pulled off his hat, though Davy had no more than tipped his, western fashion. "Mornin', Nora. A bonny day made bonnier."

Nora smiled, his soft speech warming her further. Like his cousin, Jaime, Alan had the way of words that turned a woman's head, though it was only banter built of habit and growing up together. She held up her own side with the retort, "I'm knowin' why Glenna put up nary a fight when you came callin', Alan O'Rourke."

She noticed Davy's frown and regretted the words as soon as they were out. She hadn't meant to spark his jealousy, nor remind him how long it had taken him to win her. It was only that Alan and Jaime had been so close. Part of her linked them together always, and she knew no other way to be with Alan.

"Glenna had never your stubborn temper." Alan said it gently, but she felt the barb. "Davy's the man for the job."

"Aye." Nora tucked her arm into the crook of Davy's to assuage his hurt.

Alan clamped his shoulder. "It's a walk you're needin', Davy lad. A stroll in the winter sunshine with your betrothed."

Davy rolled the plans and slid them into the tube. He slurped his coffee with gusto, then set down the cup. "A walk it is, then."

They headed out across the land. Davy tossed the hair from his forehead as he walked. "Here's your vegetable garden and the plot for potatoes. Over yonder's where we'll pasture the sheep."

"And who'll watch them, I wonder, while you're beating iron into nails and I'm seeing to our home and garden?"

"They don't need to be watched all the time. In case you haven't noticed, there are no rocky cliffs in the vicinity, no roaring falls or flooding torrents. But I have been thinkin'."

"Och, Lord save us."

Davy took the gibe with grace. "I wondered how you'd feel about Mariah staying with us. Ma and Pa haven't had a year to themselves, what with Mack coming so soon and the rest of us following after. Ma's aged so since Blake and Mack . . ."

Nora held her breath. Davy never spoke of the brothers he'd lost. She'd learned more about them from Abbie than him.

He shrugged. "I was just thinkin' Mariah could help you in the house and watch the sheep some. She's good with animals, and it's not likely she'll marry. Not the way she is. Not . . ."

"I'll have your sister, Davy. It'd be an honor."

He stopped in his tracks, and she was shamed by his surprise.

"Did you think you'd have to fight me for it?"

"I . . ." He shoved his hands into his pockets. "Guess I didn't know."

"Alan's right. I've always had a temper and more stubbornness than suits me. It takes the likes of you, Davy McConnel, to have your way with me."

He stood a long moment, then took his hands from his coat and pulled her close. He kissed the crown of her head. "I love you, Nora."

"Aye." She pushed back. "And soon enough you'll be sorry for it."

"I won't be sorry."

She sighed and allowed him to take her hand as they walked again. "I hope Abbie will be back for the weddin'."

"Truth be told, I hope she's not."

Now it was her feet that halted. "Why?"

"Abbie's bad luck to us McConnels."

"Sure an' that's the Irish in you to say that."

"It's just the way it is. Mack would never have gone if Blake hadn't put him up to it. And Blake was tryin' to win Abbie's heart with gold."

"Then it was his foolishness."

"You've seen what she hankered for. You've been in her fine house, crossed the miles of her land. How could Blake compete with that?"

"It wasn't the things Abbie wanted. T'was the man. She loved Blake, but not enough to stop her from lovin' Monte."

"Is that how it is with women? Is there always one who keeps you from loving any other?"

Nora felt the heaviness weigh her down. Her throat was as dry as the ground she tread. "Not always, Davy."

"Just my luck, huh?"

She dropped her gaze to the brown dormant grass. "I wasn't speakin' of me."

"But it's the same, isn't it? You love me, but not enough to stop you wanting Jaime."

Hearing his name spoken aloud jarred her. So Davy did know, and he felt justified throwing it at her. Nora's voice trembled. "What's the use of wanting someone from the grave?"

"No use. But you do, don't you?"

"Aye." The whisper escaped before she could stop it. Nora raised her eyes to his face. "Is it off, then?"

Davy clenched his hands at his sides. "No. I just wanted to know where we stood." He wet his lips as though he'd say more. But he only shrugged and started to walk back. "If Mariah will come, we can start a flock in the spring. Just a few ewes and a ram."

Nora nodded, allowing the change of subject to cover her shame. "You'll stay on at the smithy?"

"What else? Pa needs me. He'd planned on Mack, or maybe even Blake. They had the shoulders for it."

"Seems to me your shoulders are plenty broad themselves."

Davy walked silently. She wished she could take back her words. Did she want Jaime back from the grave? What would she do if he crossed her doorstep, all afire for the cause? Could she sit and listen to him speak his death again and again as she had once?

Nora glanced at Davy plodding beside her, his heavy brogans placed solidly step after step. His big hands were gentle, his dreams close to home. He would be a good father, a fine husband. If only she could let Jaime go.

◆◆◆◆◆◆◆

Santa Fe was a quaint cluster of pole and adobe buildings and dusty streets filled with burros, wagons, and a saddle horse or two. Dried red peppers hung from the whitewashed houses, and Abbie drank in the unhurried bustle and the flavor of things foreign. After the miles of travel, Santa Fe looked as welcoming as any place she'd been.

Abbie searched the street for a bathhouse, but the only hope was the low hacienda with a sign on the front that said, *hotel y cantina*. "Will, I can't do anything else until I've washed."

"I wouldn't mind a bath myself."

"I know Cole's waiting, but I won't get supplies until I've scraped the grime and dust and—"

"I know exactly how you feel." Will smiled boyishly, and Abbie almost hugged him. How good it was not to knock heads with someone. Cole was worse than ever since she'd questioned him. He almost bit her head off when she suggested shaving his mustache and disguising him so he could come to town and have a decent meal.

"We'll wash and have a hot meal without a single bean on the plate."

"Sounds too good to be true."

She curled her hand into Will's arm and saw him blush. It made her feel young, and she realized she was. Twenty-six was not near old enough to feel as dry and bitter as she'd been.

Minutes later, Abbie sighed blissfully as she slipped into the tub. She wished she could have seen Nora before she left. Her friend would have told her straight and clear she was crazy to even think of doing this. And what if she hadn't come? Would Cole still be trailing along with the bounty hunters, more dead than alive? Though he was not yet at the top of his strength and the shoulder troubled him, he was mostly hale, thanks to her.

She splashed the soap down into the water of her bath and rubbed it furiously between her palms. Would she have told Nora all the reasons she came after Cole? Would she have admitted what passed between them only a month ago?

Abbie lathered her arms. No, she would have spoken of her duty, her debt. But she would not have admitted the traitorous feelings that almost led her into more heartache. Thankfully Cole's own behavior had put that to an end.

When she had thoroughly scrubbed in the small galvanized tub, she brushed the dusty skirt and shirtwaist and donned them. She would never take her back-room bathhouse for granted again. When she got home she'd bathe every day without fail, maybe twice a day if she felt like it.

Abbie met Will in the hall. He had used the twin tub on the other side of the canvas wall and looked as though he'd squeak when he walked. Even his nose had a shine. She laughed. She couldn't help it. Then she thought of Cole, dusty and worn back at the camp, and felt a pang of remorse.

Well, he could have come with them. There were few enough people in town to worry about, but he'd been stubborn . . . again. She raised her chin. She would not feel guilty. Will deserved a good meal, and so did she. She stalked to the large room that housed the cantina, determined to dine at leisure.

The meal was hardly worth sitting for, and not without beans. They were mashed and fried in grease with hot peppers, served with beef so tough Abbie suspected they'd been served a leggy longhorn cow. It stuck in her gullet, seasoned with remorse. They should have gotten their supplies and headed back. Cole would be hungry and cross, and they'd wasted plenty of time.

She would make it up with special purchases—canned smoked oysters if they were to be had. She knew Cole had a fondness for them. And perhaps a sweet or two. With her conscience eased by good intentions, she and Will hoofed it to the general store. She stopped with dismay at the closed sign in the window.

"Closed. How can they be closed?"

Will rubbed his cheek where he'd been nicked by the barber. "I thought the town looked a little sparse. Let's try somewhere else."

Nearly every door and window they passed was barred and locked, shades drawn. Will drew his brows together. "Maybe they're havin' a siesta."

"According to Cole, that's over the noon hour, not in the evening."

Will caught her arm and held up a finger. "Hear that?"

Abbie listened. She did hear a commotion and turned toward the sound. It seemed to be coming from a corral behind the livery. "What is it?"

"I don't know." Will started walking, and she followed.

An immense crowd around and inside the corral seemed frenzied. They hollered and gesticulated, made coarse jokes and spat. Will self-consciously shielded Abbie as they drew near, but she climbed the low roof of a lean-to and peered over their heads. A terrible shrieking filled the air, and she caught a glimpse of feathers amid the dust.

A cockfight. Abbie's anger and disgust grew as she caught snatches of the activity through the men's backs. Each time the cocks flew apart, their owners snatched them up and threw them back at each other. She turned her head away from the crazed, bleeding birds. Such cruelty for sport was inhuman.

"Maybe we better wait back at the store." Will lifted her down, and she went mutely, though many choice words perched on her tongue. He shook his head. "It won't be a long wait. They're almost at an end."

Abbie hung her head. She'd wrung enough fowl necks to have little sensitivity toward the creatures themselves. What bothered her was the delight the men took in violence for its own sake. They were more like animals than the creatures they pitted in the ring.

She sat on the bench outside the general store window and closed her eyes. When the proprietor arrived, keys in hand, he tugged his vest and smoothed wisps of hair across his pate. "Sorry to keep you waiting, Señora."

Abbie stood with all the hauteur Monte's late sister, Frances, might have managed and walked inside. By the time they purchased their supplies and had them packed onto the horses, the sun had set. It was dark before they made it back to camp. Cole did not greet them. Was he hiding, fearing foes?

The fire was banked, and Abbie felt a vague disquiet.

"Cole?" Even as she spoke, she knew he wasn't there to hear it. She released a slow breath and closed her eyes.

"You reckon he went on without us?"

Abbie slipped down from Zephyr's back and walked to the fire. He had buried the coals to keep them warm without leaving them free to blow. And at the side of the fire ring, he'd lined stones in an arrow toward the direction of home. For a man who couldn't write, his message was clear. Why did she feel so betrayed?

Eleven

Cole pressed on through the darkness. Whitesock was pretty near stumbling, but he wanted as many miles behind him as possible. These last days he had intentionally misled Abbie as to his condition. He'd kept on at a diminished pace, making more of his weariness than need be in order to slow them down and see to it they finished off their provender before Santa Fe.

It was the logical point to split up. She and Will could gather supplies and head home before the going got really rough. And Abbie wouldn't suspect the distance he could put between them.

Cole felt a twinge of guilt and even more concern, but he didn't figure they'd meet with trouble if he wasn't with them. Will had a good head on him, and Abbie . . . well, even Crete Marlowe was no match for Abbie with her back up. Besides, she'd likely thrown Marlowe so far off the trail, he'd lost interest.

She'd get home safe. He had to think so. He'd tried and tried to send them off before this. Now Abbie just had more miles to cover than before. He had few qualms about leaving her to Will. The kid was solid stock. He'd look out for her.

As for himself, Cole shrugged, he'd eat what he found and make his way. He'd done it before. He headed southwest toward Albuquerque and long past sundown he reached the banks of the Rio Grande. He was as stiff and weary as the horse when he swung down.

He pulled the bedroll off and unsaddled the gelding, wincing at the painful strain it put on his shoulder. He'd unslung his left arm as soon as Abbie was out of sight. He had to. There was no way he'd cross this territory with one arm hobbled to his side. Cole tossed his bedroll to the ground and lay down. By morning, Abbie and Will would start home, and he'd work his way down to El Paso.

It was chilly this high up, but he'd do without a fire. He wanted nothing to give away his position. He'd left coals for Abbie and Will. They'd be all right. They'd be . . .

The muffled sound of hooves on turf brought his hand instantly to his gun. No one rode this time of night without ill intentions. Cole sprang up and faced the gun barrel at the rider in black. Every muscle, every nerve was alert, ready.

The rider stopped short. "Easy with your gun, cowboy. I didn't see you there with no fire. I've come a long way this night."

Cole sized up the man and eased only slightly. "What're you doin' ridin' past dark?"

"I could ask the same of you, brother."

"I'm doin' the askin'."

The man took his broad-brimmed hat from his head. "I'm Brother Lewis, bearer of good news and preacher of the truth. I've just quit a camp of evildoers who cared little for the light. I am unashamed to admit they drove me from their midst. As the Good Book says, I shook their dust from my feet, and it shall not fare well for such as they on Judgment Day, for they received not the Lord's messenger."

The rider's pointed features eased into a handsome, charismatic smile as he swung out of the saddle. His face was cleanly shaven; his dark hair cut neatly. Cole couldn't tell in the dark whether it contained streaks of gray or whether the starlight tricked his eyes.

The preacher inclined his head to the side. "Mind if I water my horse?"

Cole appraised the man, sizing him up at about five foot ten and none too brawny, then nodded toward the bank of the Rio Grande, just visible in the moonlight.

"Thank you kindly." Again the stranger's smile flashed.

Cole wasn't sure why he'd agreed. It wasn't from any fear of Judgment Day, nor any hankering after the truth. He wasn't looking for company, and he wasn't eager for talk. This fella seemed right likely to want both.

After watering the animal, Brother Lewis staked his horse and joined him in the grassy hollow. "I appreciate your hospitality. It's always a pleasure to find companionship along my road."

"What's your road, mister?"

"Circuit rider, preacher of the Gospel."

"I meant your direction."

"Wherever I'm called."

"Where'd you leave the evildoers?"

"About seven miles east. A camp of men bound for trouble by the quickest route—greed."

"How many?"

"Eight, plus a deaf mute."

Cole breathed easier. It wasn't Crete, and they weren't anywhere near Abbie and Will.

"Which way were they headin'?"

"West for California."

Cole nodded. "And you're headin'?"

"Wherever the Lord points me."

Cole eyed the man. Underneath his well-defined brows, the preacher had a wide-eyed exuberance, but Brother Lewis was no fool. Cole could feel himself being sized up, as well.

"Are you versed in the Scriptures, Mister . . ."

"The name's Cole."

"Very well, Cole. This place beside the river puts me in mind of the prophet Amos. 'But let judgment run down as waters, and righteousness as a mighty stream.' "

Cole narrowed his eyes and kept silent. What was this talk of judgment? Did the man guess he was wanted by the law?

"Doesn't it awe you to cross the wilderness and suddenly come upon a flowing river? The water seems to have a life of its own, rushing onward like the river Jordan, or the very river of life. To drink your fill when your throat has first known thirst is to find riches and joy."

"I reckon so." He was a spellbinder, all right. Cole wondered if he was as sincere as he looked, or if he was one of them that made his living fleecing the unwary.

"Our God is mightier than our need. 'I will bless the Lord, who hath given me counsel: my reins also instruct me in the night seasons. I have set the Lord always before me: because he is at my right hand, I shall not be moved.' "

Cole felt his pocket for the cigarette papers and pouch. The urge lodged at the joining of his ribs. He needed a smoke and the cough was nearly gone, but he rubbed his hand down over his chest and resisted. "That ain't one I'm familiar with. More like, 'Wherefore I abhor myself, and repent in dust and ashes.' "

The preacher betrayed mild surprise, but Cole simply shrugged. "My ma had the book of Job by memory. It was closest to what she lived."

Brother Lewis nodded. "The world can be harsh to our sisters."

Cole wasn't about to tell him how harsh.

"But have you read—"

"I cain't read, nor write more than my own name."

The preacher pursed his lips. "Yet you live by your wits. I knew that at once. In my travels I've seen many an intelligent man with scant learning and many a learned man with scant intelligence."

Cole half grinned.

"The Lord endows what he sees fit. It's up to us to use the gift or bury it."

Cole stared at the darkness around them. He reckoned he'd buried a portion of his, but maybe he'd done the best that circumstances allowed. He drew a long breath and relaxed. He was tired and had a long ride ahead. He couldn't sit jawing with a preacher all night.

"You're welcome to share this spot. I'm turnin' in now."

Maybe he ought to warn the man that he was a fugitive and others might be coming on them with less honorable intentions, but he didn't want to provoke a sermon. So he lay down and went to sleep.

♦♦♦♦♦♦♦

In the cold morning light, Abbie tightened Zephyr's breastband and rear saddle girth before turning to Will. "Do you know what way Cole meant to take?"

"Not exactly. But it's purty obvious what way he meant us to take."

She brushed the hair back from her cheek. "We've come this far. I've no intention of turning back now."

Will nodded. "Till now we've roughly followed the Santa Fe Trail. I expect he'll keep on that way."

"Then so will we. He has a start on us, likely a good one. But he has no supplies beyond his canteen, some jerky, and hard biscuits. He'll have to provision himself somehow, and that'll take time."

"If Cole wants to keep shy of us, he'll do it."

"Maybe so, but even if he gets to El Paso ahead of us, I'm going down there."

"What can we do?"

"I don't know. But I mean to find out." Why? Why not go home to her children? Cole wasn't her responsibility. Hadn't he made that clear by leaving them behind? He wanted to be free of her. He wanted to handle this in his lone wolf way. But something inside drove her on.

She searched the ground and found Whitesock's tracks. From the hoofprints she saw that Whitesock stepped more heavily on his right foreleg and kicked out slightly with the left hind. That would help distinguish these tracks from others she might encounter along the trail.

"It seems he's headed more west than south here. Think back to your geography. Doesn't the Rio Grande lie that way?"

"It's along there somewhere."

"Then we'll know if we wander from the trail."

Will looked less certain, but he manfully shouldered the task. In his own way, he was as determined as she to see this through. Was he also disappointed by Cole's departure? If so, he didn't show it. Well, the sooner they started the better.

Their provisions would go far since she'd bought for three, but she wouldn't waste time cooking more than she had to. With each of them leading a packhorse, she and Will set off. The day was cold and clear, with a sharp wind. Abbie wrapped a scarf around her face against the blowing dust and followed the tracks.

Angling southwest, they rode doggedly throughout the day. As the sun lowered to the western rim of land gouged by a great white stone canyon, Abbie saw the river valley. It lay like a long strip of life through a barren, buff-colored land.

The Rio Grande was edged with low yellow sand hills that gave way to flat, bare mesas. Those to the south were arid, cracked mounds of earth bleached and bled by the sun. Those to the north were covered with sage, rolling up to foothills with scattered mounds of juniper and nut pines. In the far distance, almost like a dream, stood mountains, a jagged, misty blue silhouette.

Abbie reined in Zephyr and sat transfixed. Such extremes of landscape and climate left her breathless. Here was God's handprint, unmarred by man. "Have you ever seen such a sight, Will?"

He glanced the way she was looking. "A sight such as what?"

"All of it. This wide incredible stretch of creation."

He shrugged. "No, I guess not."

Abbie wanted to shake him awake. How could anyone lay eyes on something so new, so wild, and not be moved past words? She shook her head. "We'll camp at the river."

"Yes, ma'am."

As they neared the water, they left the sandy hills and crossed a narrow strip of coarse grassy marshland. At the river's edge grew cottonwoods, some twenty feet high, others small, taking root upon the sandbars. Leafless box elder and wild grapevines choked the bank where there were signs of regular flooding. She guessed without the growth, the river would take the valley again and again.

Abbie looked up at the gray trunks and branches of the cottonwoods, draped with mistletoe. It made her think of Frances's husband, Kendal, and his story of Frigga, the goddess of love and her son, Balder, the sun god. She wondered what gods were worshipped in this untamed land and shivered.

None could contend with the true God, but the followers could be hard to convince. Once again she questioned whether she was doing the right thing. Was it only her pride that kept her going? Her unwillingness to give up? She sighed. What would tomorrow bring?

◆◆◆◆◆◆◆

It was obvious the preacher meant to travel with him indefinitely. Cole had allowed the man to ride along the previous day, expecting he'd take a turn soon enough. But Brother Lewis had shown no signs of parting ways.

Cole scowled. He'd wakened as sour as he could remember, and a dose of the preacher's gab was not the cure. "Look, I gotta cut a good pace today."

"Where are you heading?"

"El Paso."

"I'll do my utmost to keep up."

Cole sucked his cheek. "No offense, preacher . . ."

" 'Where two or three are gathered together in my name, there am I in the midst.' "

Cole rested his arm across Whitesock's saddle and eyed the man. "You sayin' if I allow you to tag after, God himself will ride with us?"

"It's a matter for thought."

Cole wasn't expecting a godly escort, and he'd not have chosen Brother Lewis for company at the best of times, but he shook his head and mounted. "Suit yourself."

They rode in quiet long enough to settle some of his annoyance. But then the preacher started talking, and Cole steeled himself to bear it.

"You're a man who travels alone."

He would be, if the preacher had taken a hint.

"I don't just mean out here on your horse. I mean the journey of life, of the heart and soul. I, too, am a solitary rider, but I'm never truly alone."

Cole reached for the cigarette papers in his pocket. He took one out. He could almost taste the tobacco, feel the smoke filling his lungs. Why not? What difference did it make if he spent his last days enjoying a smoke? But he'd be giving in. He crumpled the paper and let it fall.

"If you once take Jesus into your heart, you never walk

alone from that moment on. For as the Good Book says, 'Whosoever shall call upon the name of the Lord shall be saved.' "

Saved. Cole wasn't asking to be saved. He was sticking out his neck to keep another from the noose. Where was Samuel? How many times had Cole looked to him as a kid, scarcely able to keep from bawling when he hurt so bad there wasn't a position he could find that didn't make it worse?

He remembered the day Sam put his own shoulder between him and the board their pa was wielding. He remembered the smack of it and the welt it had raised on Sam's arm. He remembered Sam telling him to run, and to his shame he recalled running.

His ma had brought in the doctor for Sam that time, and his pa had disappeared for six months. He remembered the fury he'd felt when his pa returned. And he knew he'd never run again. No matter that his ma had told him never to raise a hand in anger. The next time his pa came after him with a stick, Cole wrenched it free and wielded it like a club.

"Come on, come on and take me like a man if you got the guts." His pa was too stinking drunk to hold his own against a ten-year-old with the devil in his blood. Old man Jasper had stumbled away, then drunk himself near to death and left them for good. Samuel had taken on his rearing, Sam and Ma, but it seemed like his ma quit caring, and only Sam was left. Cole realized the preacher was waiting for an answer.

"What's that?"

"I said, have you surrendered your soul to the Savior?"

"Mister, I ain't sure I got a soul to surrender."

Twelve

Cole crouched beside the river and looked up where the ridge of land met the strip of turquoise sky in the growing darkness. He'd expected, and now saw clearly in the failing light, the silhouette of the Comanche. Cole knew better than Abbie the limits of her pact with the Indian.

Maybe Gray Wolf wouldn't attack while she was present, but Cole wasn't at all surprised to see him now that Abbie was heading home. He heard Brother Lewis come up from the water beside him. He turned briefly to warn him, but Brother Lewis eyed the line of sky and smiled. "Ah, the close of day. God is good."

Cole drew his brows together. Was the man blind or just stupid? He looked back. The turquoise had shrunk to a thin band above the black line of earth. Pale stars dotted the darkness above. The Comanche was gone.

Not far, or for long, Cole was certain. Glancing up at Brother Lewis's rapturous face, he held his tongue. He wouldn't disillusion the man.

♦♦♦♦♦♦♦

Six full days of Brother Lewis was wearing him thin. Cole had quit responding, quit giving him any encouragement, but the man was like a bad toothache. He wouldn't go away. Cole swung down from the saddle.

"No man who puts his hand to the plow and turns back is worthy of the kingdom."

Cole loosened the cinch and heaved the saddle to the ground, wincing with the strain to his shoulder. If it kept breaking open and bleeding as it was, he'd expect some degree of permanent damage. He led Whitesock to the riverbank.

They'd followed the Rio Grande through the better part of New Mexico without seeing more than the native Indians, who were peaceful enough, and a few fellow travelers. Most of them were drawn to Brother Lewis's friendly greetings, then cleared off soon enough. No doubt his own expression urged them on. A pair of turkey buzzards circled overhead in the dusky light as he watered the horse.

"And there will come a reckoning. Every man will stand before the throne of God and make an account of himself before the Almighty. Don't think you'll escape that, Cole."

The horse drank, and the preacher's mount lowered its head, as well. At this rate Brother Lewis would be screaming fire and brimstone as they rode into El Paso. Cole felt the tendons knot at the back of his neck, and his gut twisted.

The rabbit he'd shot yesterday hadn't gone far between them, but it wasn't hunger that gnawed. It was fear. He might as well face it. Two days' rides would bring them into town. What kind of crazy man walked into a hangman's noose for a crime he didn't commit?

But what if Sam did? Could Cole stand back and let them realize their mistake, when he'd driven Sam to it? No, he hadn't. It was Auralee herself. She knew Sam loved her. She stoked the flames until they roared inside him, then she turned to his little brother instead . . . and rubbed Sam's face in it.

Cole shook his head. If he'd seen sooner . . . if he'd realized his holding back would so infuriate her, he'd have plunked down his money and done it. How was he to know she'd take it personal that he wouldn't use her? In a million years he'd never understand the mind of a woman.

Not Auralee; not Abbie. The ache that coursed through him now had nothing at all to do with impending death. Why had he allowed her to come so far? Why had he ridden so many days with a woman he'd loved too long? Why had he allowed himself to imagine she cared, to think . . .

"For all have sinned. Not one is without sin. Repent and . . ."

Cole spun, caught the preacher by the collar, and pressed his Colt revolver to the man's well-shaped chin. "Preacher, you make your livin' by movin' this jaw, but if it don't stop now, I'll blow it right up to kingdom come."

Brother Lewis's throat worked, but no sound emerged.

"You just blink if you got my message."

The preacher closed his eyes and opened them.

"Good." Cole released him. He picketed Whitesock and stalked off to gather wood, such as there was. They'd have a fire tonight. The air was cold. He felt it in his bones. He felt it in his innards. He felt it in his soul. Was he doomed to hell?

Was there truly a place of fiery wrath that forever burned those who failed to account before the throne? He lifted a stick and gripped it in his hand. He'd held the stick his pa had used on him just so. He'd wanted to crack it against his pa's head to see him bleed the way he'd made his sons bleed.

It was easier to think there was nothing past this life, that a man died and went back to the earth, that it just ended. If there was a hell, he sure as heck didn't care to meet his pa there. What worse torment could there be than spending eternity with him?

Cole tossed the stick. All those years away, all those years working for Mr. Farrel, he'd scarce thought of his past once. 'Course, there'd been Abbie to hold his thoughts. He didn't like to recall how many nights he'd spent thinking on another man's wife.

He'd tried not to covet, took pride in the trust Mr. Farrel put in him. But he reckoned that wasn't good enough to state before any throne. Fact was, if she'd ever given him the least invitation, he might have fallen as low as the next man. He sensed Brother Lewis behind him.

"Why don't you unburden your soul? Take the free gift of salvation the Savior has won for you."

The man was a slow learner.

"Pray with me the sinner's prayer that will open the gates of heaven."

Cole turned. The preacher didn't flinch, he'd give him that. "The name's Cole Jasper, preacher. You might'a seen my face on a poster, wanted dead or alive for the murder of Auralee Dubois. I'm ridin' to a hangman's noose in El Paso."

Brother Lewis folded his hands over the black book he held to his chest. "I know who you are. I saw your poster in Santa Fe."

Cole fought his surprise. Brother Lewis had knowingly ridden alone and unarmed, day after day, with a man wanted for murder?

"I told you, I ride where the Lord points me. But Cole Jasper was a name known in these parts long before the charge of murder."

Yeah. They didn't consider Indian slaughter murder, did they.

"And I don't just mean your days as a ranger. It's a name many consider a hero's handle. A name many have counted on, looked to, and blessed. In my opinion, you'll have a hard time convincing folks you're guilty."

"Well, I ain't askin' your opinion."

"What sort of man rides alone to face his crime? How many others would flee the consequences? Either your character is rare or you're innocent of the charges."

Cole's jaw tightened. If folks were thinking that, they'd

look elsewhere for the culprit. His anger rose. "I said I ain't askin'."

"You like to depend on yourself, don't you, Cole? But there will come a time when there's nothing left, when it's too late. Don't wait until the rope is on your neck or a bullet finds you in the dark. Throw yourself now on the mercy of our heavenly Father."

Mercy? Since when did life offer mercy? To his ma? To a little boy with welts on his back thick as a washboard from his own earthly father? Cole felt the anger burning. Was it anger ... or fear? He'd refused to recognize fear the day he swore never to run again. And he'd refused any heavenly balm that rang as false as his pa's apologies.

He saw the preacher's eyes burning with the intensity Cole had seen long ago in his ma's. She'd wanted him to believe. Even after she slipped into that place where she hardly knew him, there were times when her eyes burned with that same hope.

His chest seized. She'd died not knowing if she'd done her job, maybe most of her not even caring. But somewhere inside, the hope burned. Why would this preacher mirror that now? What was it to him if Cole Jasper burned in hell?

Cole reached for his tobacco. He didn't care that the urges had almost passed. He was going to smoke one now.

Brother Lewis put a hand to his shoulder.

Cole's throat went dry. "God help me."

"Oh, He will, I assure you."

♦♦♦♦♦♦♦

Abbie woke to the cacophony of birdsong. Waterfowl of many sorts dotted the river valley: ducks and geese and cranes. Turtledoves flitted from the branches of box elders and welcomed the day with song. The sun rose sharp in the clear air.

It lightened her heart after the dark and tiresome dreams that had filled her sleep.

She stood and walked to the water's edge. The tracks they'd followed were evident in the sand along the river. But now she saw new tracks beside Whitesock's. Her chest seized, and she searched the ground in sudden concern. There was no sign of struggle. Maybe the second traveler had come later, merely watered at the same spot. But the tracks seemed to match in age.

"What you got?" Will's voice was sleepy, but concerned.

Her troubled thoughts must have shown. "New prints with Cole's."

Will fit his foot inside the boot mark beside the hoofprints. "Do you suppose it's a bounty hunter?"

"I don't know." She stood, refusing to let worry take hold in her heart. She followed the tracks up from the water to a spot near where she and Will had slept, then crossed to the broken ground where the horses had grazed. She picked up Whitesock's marks easily enough and saw the second horse's hoofprints alongside.

She let out a slow breath. "They're traveling together, whoever he is. I guess it doesn't matter now. They'll be in El Paso long before we are."

"We could make better time if we started now. I don't mind chewing hardtack and jerky."

Abbie felt the overwhelming futility. The wonder she'd felt coming upon the river was swallowed today by the endless miles, the continuous strain to keep hopeful. "Yes, you're right. We won't waste time cooking." She packed up their tents and bedding while he watered and saddled the horses, and they struck camp in nearly no time.

Will looked thoughtful as he mounted.

"What is it, Will?"

He shrugged. "Do you suppose he did it?"

The question came from nowhere, but she knew what he

asked. Abbie swung up into Zephyr's saddle. "No, Will. Cole did not murder Auralee Dubois."

"One time when I was in town a couple toughs jumped me, tried to steal the wad I'd been savin' up. Cole was on them like a hawk on a mouse. He thrashed 'em so bad they staggered away, thankful for their lives."

Yes, she'd seen that, too, the night he defended her from the assailants in Dodge. Cole was a powerful man, but that didn't mean he was guilty now. She headed Zephyr away from the wetlands to the flat, level plain of the valley that paralleled the river's course.

Will spoke low. "If he was really mad, I mean like outta control mad . . . he could . . ."

"He didn't kill Auralee. Cole would never raise his hand to a woman."

Will shook his head. "You don't know, Mrs. Farrel. Some women aren't . . . ladies."

Lil Brandon flashed before her, the clear disdain—something near hatred—that had been in her eyes with her rude remark, "*You lost, lady?*" "Even so, Will. You know Cole well enough to know he'd never—" She gripped the saddle horn as Zephyr stumbled and nearly went down.

Will wheeled. "You caught a varmint hole." He jumped down and settled Zephyr, then eased her leg up and examined the fetlock.

Abbie slid down. "Is she hurt?"

"Nothing's broke. Let's see how she does."

Abbie led her gently, but the mare resisted, holding her leg gingerly with her hide twitching and eyes wide. Abbie stopped pulling. There was no point forcing the animal. Even if she rode one of the others, Zephyr would have to carry a load. "I guess we'll have to stay here awhile after all."

Will nodded. "Looks that way."

Abbie prepared biscuits in the Dutch oven and roasted the

duck Will shot from the water. She boiled rice with red peppers she'd purchased in Santa Fe and opened the can of smoked oysters. It reminded her that the extra time in town had allowed Cole to get so far ahead. Would it have mattered? She was too vexed now to wonder.

Abbie kept her thoughts to herself, and Will did the same. He seemed to read her mood as easily as the sky before a storm. Maybe it didn't take much to see that she was in high dudgeon.

She set to exploring the land on foot, noting that there were plant and cactus varieties she'd not seen before. She tried to mentally match them with the illustrations in her botanical manual, but her mind was too restless.

What were the children doing? Were they being cared for with the loving attention she longed to give? Where was Cole? With whom did he ride now? Was he in pain, in danger? There was no way to know, and no way to help. She sighed, shook her head, and returned to camp.

Will was whittling a stick of cottonwood into the shape of a duck. It gave her a pang to recall the knife in Cole's hand, forming the wood into fine creatures. His hands seemed to caress the wood as he worked down to the core, bringing it to life.

The sculpture he'd done of Sirocco had been so lifelike it looked as though the horse would leap from the desk, mane and tail flying. Even Monte had been impressed. She'd often caught him studying it as he mused.

Abbie sighed again as she sat on a stump of driftwood beside Will. "Did Cole show you how to do that?"

Will nodded. "He worked with me some. Cottonwood's not good for carving. Not much good for anything, really. Burns like paper, can't be sawn into lumber, can't hardly make timbers from it at all. It's junk wood, worthless."

Abbie looked along the line of cottonwoods. Leafless, they looked worthless indeed, yet . . . here they clung where little else could. How often did the river rip them out and churn them along its bed, though they tenaciously reseeded and grew again? It was easy to miss the importance of things, easy to judge by sight alone.

"Well, it looks as though you'll get a duck out of it."

"Yeah." Will grinned. "I might that."

Thirteen

Abbie woke discouraged. The morning light revealed swelling on the base of Zephyr's fetlock. The mare's hide still quivered at any touch near the injury, and she was skittish. Abbie's spirits sank deeper, discouragement weighing like wet plaster on her soul.

She stood and gentled the horse, then dropped her head to Zephyr's neck. "What are we doing, Will?"

"Seeing it through for Cole."

Seeing it through for Cole. What craziness was that? He'd sent them home. He didn't want them. He had his plan, and she had no place in it. Abbie looked at Will's earnest young face. He didn't want her to give up, even if he wouldn't say it. But she was as close to quitting as she'd ever been.

She fought the weight of her thoughts, the drag on her spirit. "I think we'll have to stay put until the swelling goes down."

"I'm afraid so."

Abbie had hoped keeping the mare quiet one day would be enough. Now it seemed something as innocuous as a gopher hole would set them back and cool the trail even further. She felt Cole pulling away, putting distance between them. It brought an unexpected ache.

She raised her chin defiantly. "I'll make a plaster for Zephyr's leg. Let the others loose to graze on whatever they can find in this desert country." The grasses were probably as hearty as those in Colorado. And they had the river. Cole seemed to be staying relatively close to its course.

"Yes, ma'am." Will nodded. She saw the relief pass over his face. What was Cole to him that he should care so?

After a leisurely breakfast, she washed their clothes in the river and hung them to dry from the cottonwoods. Then she sat across from Will and set about mending the tear in his shirt sleeve. He wore his spare while she worked on his favorite. He had worn the elbows thin, but she had no scraps for patching, so she merely sewed up the tear as best she could.

If Will chafed the delay, he handled it better than she. A wave of annoyance passed through her. She turned her thoughts. "So tell me, Will, did you know Cole was sending money to the ranch?"

He flushed. "Yes, ma'am. That is, I never saw it come, but . . ."

"But everyone knew."

"I guess so."

"Everyone but me."

"I suppose Cole should have asked."

Abbie half smiled. "But I would have refused."

"I reckon he saw it that way. We all thought it would be sort of hard for you to accept. Though I don't know that the men could have stayed otherwise. Especially when Sutler and Fredericks set up headquarters. They were paying top dollar."

Will's confession should have incensed her, but now it just added to the weight. Abbie imagined them all with this unspoken pact. In an odd way it pleased her that Will had been included. He was left to himself too much.

Monte had cared enough to give Will the position in his stables when he was just a ragamuffin boy. But in true aristocratic fashion, Monte hadn't thought much past his physical needs. She'd seen to Will's schooling, but she could do little more for a mostly grown boy. Cole had been the one to fill in the gaps.

Though gruff and sharp with the men under his control, he saw things others missed. He was a man of contrasts. He could rile her to the boiling point one minute, then wash it away with unexpected kindness the next.

Abbie shook her head. She was thankful she'd set herself straight on Cole Jasper. A man like that was more dangerous than any sweet-spoken suitor come calling.

♦♦♦♦♦♦♦

Cole awoke to the cold stillness before the dawn. In the dusky light, the grass beside his face was stiffly outlined, and he smelled the remains of the fire, the dry earth, and something else. His ears sharpened, his breath arrested, and his fingers found the cold metal of his gun.

He sensed more than heard the stealthy step. In one motion he threw back the blanket and drew the gun, rolling to his feet. Brother Lewis startled awake as Cole stepped over him and scoured the half-circular ring of scrub.

"What is it, Cole?"

"Hush." His eyes could scarcely penetrate the lingering darkness. A flicker of movement brought him around, but he could see nothing clearly. A bird flitted to a box-elder branch, then mounted to the sky. A moment later Cole released a slow breath and holstered his gun.

That Comanche had intentionally shown himself the other night. He'd known how it would work on a man's mind. But Cole didn't think he'd imagined this. He'd have to wait for daylight to be sure. If he was right, the sun would show the moccasin prints.

Cole rubbed his hands down the sides of his jeans. That derned Indian was toying with him, wearing him down. He glanced at Brother Lewis. The man looked concerned, but not afraid. Maybe it was time to change that.

Cole squatted beside him. "Why don't you get up now, preacher. I've a mind to tell you my Indian name."

Brother Lewis listened to the story without interrupting. Though the preacher blanched when Cole described his ma's death and the reckless hatred that had followed, Brother Lewis sat without comment until he'd finished. Cole spread his hands. "I reckon that lone Comanche thinks it's his solemn duty to send me on to the Great Spirit. And I reckon he won't mind sendin' you, too."

Brother Lewis nodded slowly. "Yes, that would seem to follow."

"It'd be in your best interest if we part paths now. He's only one and cain't rightly track us both."

"That's true. However, as I told you, I go where the Lord leads, and I've not been given marching orders in any other direction."

Cole cocked his head. "Maybe you ain't heard me. I'm Death Rider to that Indian. He won't pause to shake hands before he slits your throat and takes your hair."

"Yes, I'm familiar with their methods. But have you read . . . heard the story of Jonah?"

Cole stared at him. The man was dense as unshorn wool.

"You see, Jonah heard the Lord's call but went the other way. He thought he knew better than God how to spend his time. But God got his attention, had him thrown into the sea and swallowed by a great fish. After three days in the fish's belly, Jonah thought better of ignoring God's call. I can't do any less."

"I reckon you'd be a sight more useful to God alive than dead. Maybe you ain't heard Him right, either."

"That's possible. I am only human. But He'll honor my intention as long as I mean to hold fast to His will."

Cole scrubbed his bearded jaw with the back of his hand.

"What's to keep you, preacher? You've saved my soul a'ready."

Brother Lewis smiled. "Not I. Jesus Christ."

"So your job is done."

Brother Lewis only smiled broader.

"Look, not to be rude, but what good will you be in a fight? You're not even armed."

"Oh, but I am." Brother Lewis reached for the black Bible. "No enemy in the world can stand against God's Word."

Cole felt a stirring inside. As ridiculous as the man's words appeared, they drew a response deep within him. It showed him just how shallow was his own fledgling belief. Maybe his inability to read made it hard to put his trust in a book. Maybe he was too ignorant of God's ways to fully reckon the change Brother Lewis assured him he'd undergone.

He stood. "Suit yerself, preacher. You've been warned."

"Thank you, Cole."

Cole shook his head. There was no figuring a man like Brother Lewis. Maybe the man had spent time in the belly of something worse than a fish. Or maybe he'd never seen anything to scare him enough to run. Either way, Cole felt shamefully glad for the company.

He pulled a hard biscuit from the saddlebag and tossed it to the preacher. "We'll look for game as we ride. I feel the need of a meal."

"Amen, Brother Cole. Amen."

◆◆◆◆◆◆◆

Abbie swung into the saddle at last. Two days of rest had given Zephyr the chance to heal, and it was time to move on. Ever since rescuing Cole, they'd made dismal progress. His wounds and illness had made traveling more than ten miles a day impossible, though he seemed to have taken off like the wind after leaving them in Santa Fe.

Abbie and Will hadn't done so well. The animals were

weary, no doubt contributing to Zephyr's injury. Now she wasn't certain what the mare could do. But even if they couldn't travel as long as before, it was better than sitting and stewing.

She glanced at her companion, tying up his bedroll. Will was more than eager to strike camp and head out. Thank goodness for that, because she felt cross enough for them both.

They'd hardly left the camp behind when she turned at the sound of hooves. A single rider with a remuda of two chestnut mares and one pack mule cantered over the hill and started down. Abbie felt for the pistol in her pocket and saw Will unstrap his.

There was something familiar about the rider, and she realized he rode like Cole—the same motion, the same easy control, the same set expression. *Sam.* Her heart thumped. It was Samuel Jasper.

Her sudden fury surprised her. Sam Jasper, the one who had led bounty hunters to his own brother. The one who pummeled Cole without once asking for an explanation. The man who got them all into this.

He looked fresh, as well he might with spare horses to trade off riding. He'd likely made fifty miles a day that way. Why hadn't she thought to bring a remuda of her own?

He reined in and stared at her. Was it recognition, or just surprise to see a woman? He tipped his hat. "Ma'am."

She raised her chin. "Good afternoon, Mr. Jasper."

His eyes narrowed, and the skin pulled taut around a small triangular scar on his right cheekbone. "You're the lady from the ranch."

She neither admitted nor denied it.

His look darkened. "Where's Cole?"

"Do you honestly think I would tell you that?" She held steady under his gaze.

He turned and searched the land around.

"He's not with us. He was taken by the bounty hunters you led to him."

"I led . . ." Sam shifted in the saddle. "You mean Crete Marlowe?"

Crete Marlowe. Wasn't that the name . . . the man who sold whiskey to the Comanches, the man Cole had beaten and left to die? Surely . . . Could he have been one of the bounty hunters? Was it another personal vendetta? Did it never end?

Abbie tightened her jaw. "I didn't ask their names when we got Cole away."

"You broke him loose of Crete Marlowe and Jackson Finn?" He tipped his hat back and eyed her.

"If that's who they were."

"Oh, that's who they were, lady. So where is he?"

"I don't know. He went on alone. We've been tracking him since, but he's riding with another now. Maybe the law, maybe someone else looking to make a profit on an innocent man."

The furrow between Sam's brows deepened as he scowled. "What makes you think he's innocent?"

"He's your brother and you ask that?"

Sam rubbed the back of his hand across his jaw, a motion so like Cole's it gave her a pang. He looked out along the broad Rio Grande valley. "Looks like he's headin' to El Paso."

She nodded.

"And you're followin'."

She didn't deign to answer.

He almost smiled. "How far ahead is he?"

"Far enough."

Sam raked his eyes over her, but with curiosity more than insolence. "I ain't caught your name."

"I haven't given it."

He nodded. "I reckon we started out wrong. I'm Samuel Jasper, but you already know that. Are you Cole's woman?"

Abbie felt Will stiffen beside her. "I beg your pardon?"

"I didn't mean that how it sounded. Are you the one who's kept him busy these last years? The widow?"

Her blood pounded in her ears. "I'm Mrs. Farrel, and yes, my husband is deceased."

Sam nodded. "I addressed an envelope he sent off to your foreman. The money he sent."

Abbie felt her ire rise. Did everyone in the country know? "I never asked for Cole's money."

"Don't I know. He said you'd be mad as a peeled rattler if you ever got wind of it."

Abbie turned away. The air carried a dusty film that settled on her cheeks like talcum powder. She was amazed how little the money mattered now. She just wanted to be done with this. "If you'll excuse me, we have a lot of ground to cover yet."

"You sure you want to go on?"

"Why wouldn't I?"

He fixed her with his green eyes, too like Cole's for comfort. "I figure you ought to know Crete Marlowe don't take kindly to meddlin'."

"I don't care a fig about that."

"You might care to know he set your house afire."

Abbie spun in the saddle, her heart caught in her throat.

Sam raised a hand. "Don't fret. Your folks're safe. We got the fire put out."

"We?" Her breath was tight and thin.

"I got word Marlowe was huntin' Cole and went to the ranch to settle things. Got there in time to beat out the flames."

"I don't understand. You led them to him . . . the day you came. Why would . . ."

"I had fire in my blood to take Cole down myself and pound him square, but I never brought Crete alongside."

"But they came right behind you. They . . ." Abbie shook

her head. She didn't know what to think. It was all too complicated, this life of Cole's. How could she help him? How could she possibly make sense of it? Where was Crete Marlowe now? What about the children? A cold fear snaked down her back.

She had to go home. She had to turn back. *What if Crete returns, what if he* . . . She gripped the reins with white knuckles. She felt Will's concern and turned to meet his eyes. He wouldn't tell her one way or the other, but his need was to see it through for Cole.

Oh, Lord, help me. I don't know what to do. My heart's divided, torn in two. My children . . . She looked back over her shoulder. Everything cried out to flee for home, to see for herself they were safe and to keep them that way. But a still, small voice said *Trust me.*

Trust God? Fear closed around her heart. She couldn't. How could she? She had lost too much, suffered too much. "*It's honor, Abbie. Doing what you must, even when your heart is against it.*" She heard the echo of Monte's ardent drawl.

Her breath made a slow escape from her throat. *Oh, Monte. How can I?* But she had to. She owed Cole a debt of honor. She owed Cole her life. The edges of her teeth met as she turned her head back toward El Paso.

Sam brought his horse alongside. There was something in his expression, some measure of . . . esteem in his eyes. He slowly tipped his hat. "Seems we're travelin' the same way."

Abbie glanced weakly at Will. By his expression, he was no more eager to have Sam join them than she, but maybe this way they could keep an eye on him. If he still meant trouble to Cole, they'd know it soon enough.

Fourteen

Jenny stared up at the blackened front of the house. Without the tall portico it looked naked, like a face without a nose. The wide stone steps still led to the door, but the pillars lay on the ground beside the house.

She didn't know why the sight frightened her. She had never liked the pillars. They reminded her of Grandmother's house, and she hated Grandmother's house. But somehow, lying on the ground, blackened and peeled, they looked worse, far worse.

Jenny turned away from the house and studied the long field beyond the yard. Her breath made a cloud when she sighed. It was cold and gray, but the snow wouldn't come. It hung in the sky, but wouldn't fall. The dry air had cracked her lip, and she chewed on it. She felt lonelier than she could ever remember.

Pearl would not drive her over to play with Katie. Pearl was afraid to leave the house unguarded, but Jenny knew if the bad men came back they couldn't stop them doing more bad things. Elliot cried in his sleep. The last two nights he'd woken up hollering.

Jenny clutched her hands together. She wished Aunt Abbie would come back, though she didn't tell Elliot so. He cried if she talked about it. She searched the empty range. If Aunt Abbie had found Cole, why didn't she bring him home?

She frowned. She felt little and helpless, like the rabbit dragging its leg she'd seen in the scrub oak. She was sad and scared and angry, and she couldn't do anything about it.

Jenny kicked the dirt. "Why?" Her voice was hoarse, but she didn't know whom she asked.

Pearl came out of the house with her great-uncle Josh. They carried bundles of hers and Elliot's things. Her heart jumped unsteadily. Something was happening. She turned sharply. "Where are we going, Uncle Josh?"

His smile crinkled his eyes, and with his graying beard he looked the perfect grandpa. Elliot's grandpa, not hers. "You're to stay in town awhile."

"In town?" Jenny's stomach tightened. "Where in town?"

"With your Aunt Marcy and Uncle Grant."

The tightness became a knot. She opened her mouth to argue, but Aunt Selena appeared in the doorway, with Elliot grasping her hand.

"Hold on, Selena. That stair's uneven." Uncle Josh deposited the bundles into the buggy and assisted her great-aunt and Elliot.

Jenny fought the angry feelings the knot was making inside her. Had she been bad . . . had she said something wrong? Why were they sending her to Aunt Marcy? Were they punishing her? She turned to Pearl and saw the old woman soften.

"You be fine in town, chile."

She didn't want to be with Aunt Marcy. Especially if it meant being away when Cole came home. Jenny searched the land again as though he would suddenly ride up in time to save her. She felt Uncle Josh's hand on her shoulder.

She mustn't complain. She mustn't . . . He lifted her into the buggy and she waited while he helped Aunt Selena and Elliot up to the seat. Then he squeezed in beside her and took up the reins.

She watched the first tiny snowflakes swirl in the air

around them. The horses bobbed their heads as they pulled, and she watched the flakes catch in their manes. Uncle Josh clicked his tongue and the pair quickened their pace eagerly. Maybe they wanted to hurry out of the coming snow.

Jenny blinked against the thickening flakes, but she was in no hurry. She glanced at Elliot. He seemed quiet, too. He wasn't chattering as he usually did. Aunt Selena looked worried. She probably knew things, things they wouldn't tell her and Elliot. Grown-ups didn't know it was scarier having to guess.

The snow kept on but didn't worsen as they neared the end of town where Uncle Grant and Aunt Marcy lived. She saw the glow in the windows of the house. It had grown dim outside and the windows would have looked welcoming, only she knew better. She was amazed the snow dared to land on the walk without Aunt Marcy's permission.

Jenny drew a shaky breath. "Why can't we stay with you, Uncle Josh?"

"You'd be welcome, but this way you're close to the school." He climbed down and reached for her.

She rested her hands on his shoulders as he lifted her down. "You could bring me in with Tucker."

"It's more practical to have you here."

He meant safer. He thought the bad men wouldn't come to Uncle Grant's house. This was all Pearl's fault. Jenny had heard enough through the door to know Pearl had been worked up to a tizzy after fretting for two days over what to do.

Jenny'd been plenty worked up herself when Zena had hidden her and Elliot in the cellar. After kicking Cole's brother, she had run and run, but it hadn't helped. She still smelled the smoke, still feared the flames. The flames that burned the house . . . and the ones that burned her heart. Those she couldn't outrun.

She looked up at the door where her great-aunt Selena waited with Elliot. Aunt Marcy had yet to open the door. Then Jenny would have to face her cousin, Emily Elizabeth, as well.

She liked Emily Elizabeth far less than her adopted cousin Tucker. Tucker could spit through the knothole in the barn wall. Emily Elizabeth tattled when he did. Without realizing, Jenny had pressed close to Uncle Josh on the porch while they waited. He smelled good. Not the same as Cole, but clean and comforting.

Cole didn't wear pomade or wash with the smelly green soap Curtis and Matt used. When she grew up she'd have nothing to do with dandies or men who washed with smelly soap. She'd marry a man like Cole who smelled of horses and the range. Her belly suddenly hurt again.

The door swung open, but it was Uncle Grant who smiled down at her, then tussled Elliot's hair. "Hello there. This is a surprise."

Aunt Selena stepped forward. "Sorry to get you from supper."

"You haven't. We've just finished." Grant motioned them in.

It was warm inside, and the clock chimed prettily on the mantel. Jenny watched it, ignoring the low voice with which her great-uncle asked his favor. She held her breath, hoping Uncle Grant would say they couldn't stay. She snuck a glance.

He looked concerned, but she guessed it was more the news of the burning as they discussed the matter. He was not the one who would refuse them. Maybe Aunt Marcy. Oh yes, if her aunt had her way . . .

Marcy came into the room, all pinched and pouty. She would be pretty if she didn't always look like she'd sucked a chokecherry. But she put on a smile and swept her skirts behind her. "Well, well. Nothing's the matter, is it?"

Jenny scowled when Aunt Marcy fixed her in her gaze as

though any trouble must naturally be her doing. She stood silent as Uncle Grant explained the request. Jenny felt like a young foal at auction, only she wasn't sure anyone truly wanted to bid.

She looked at Elliot. He seemed happy enough. But then, Aunt Marcy liked him. He put up with Emily Elizabeth's airs. Jenny eyed the plump and dimpled four-year-old who pushed in behind her mama. Jenny bristled automatically. She couldn't help it. Emily Elizabeth was prissy and altogether spoiled.

Jenny turned her thoughts back to Aunt Selena, whose next words sealed her fate. "Are you certain you can manage?"

Jenny held her breath, hoping.

But Aunt Marcy smiled her molasses smile. "They'll be fine, I'm sure. Emily Elizabeth sees so little of her cousins, with Abbie always running off somewhere."

"Now, Marcy . . ." Uncle Grant patted her shoulder. "She hasn't exactly run off."

"Traipsing after some outlaw cowboy isn't what I'd call responsible. Trouble will come of it. Mark my words."

Uncle Josh cleared his throat. "It may not be what we'd have advised, but Abbie did what she thought right."

Aunt Marcy looked like a crow swallowing a worm when she jerked her nose up in the air. "I would never leave Emily Elizabeth in this kind of danger."

"Not even to save me?" Uncle Grant gave her a playful pinch.

Jenny appreciated his joke more than her aunt.

"Hah. As though you'd be mixed up in something so vulgar. Why, I—"

"Well, now." Uncle Josh replaced his hat. "I think we'd best try to beat this storm home."

Aunt Marcy followed his gaze to her and Elliot as though suddenly remembering they were there. Jenny wasn't fooled.

Aunt Marcy meant for them to hear. She wanted them to think badly of Aunt Abbie . . . and of Cole.

Jenny jutted her chin and met her aunt's gaze. "Aunt Abbie isn't afraid to leave us. She knows we can take care of ourselves." She wrapped Elliot's shoulders in her arm.

"There's no need for that." Uncle Grant stroked the top of her head. His eyes were like brown sugar drops. They soothed her temper when she didn't want to be soothed. "We're glad to have you stay with us."

Jenny's heart sank when Aunt Marcy stiffly agreed. It seemed that was the final word. Her aunt turned and fussed with Emily Elizabeth's hair bow. "Now run along and play, sweetheart."

Emily pranced over and took Jenny's hand. "I want to play castle, and I'm the princess."

Jenny resisted making a face. "All right." She used her sweetest tone. When they were alone, she'd announce her role—the wicked, fire-breathing dragon.

Selena climbed into the buggy with the aid of Joshua's strong arm. The snow had mostly stopped, but she agreed with his timely interruption. What was Marcy thinking speaking so carelessly in front of the children? Did her animosity never cease? Nonetheless, Abbie truly was trying the limits this time.

Joshua patted her knee as he joined her on the seat. "What do you think?"

"I wish I could feel settled about all this."

"So do I."

"I've sought the Lord time and again. Perhaps if I understood . . ."

He slapped the reins. "She's following her conscience."

"But to abandon the children . . ."

"Not abandon, Selena. Abbie left them in the care of those she trusts. Pearl and James and Zena . . . and us."

"And now Marcy and Grant."

"They'll do right by them."

Selena knew that. It was only . . . the little ones suffered so. Didn't Abbie realize how they needed her? Jenny's brave front and defense of her aunt had not dispelled the haunted look in her eyes. She was too young to be deserted so regularly, whether or not Josh considered it desertion.

And Elliot . . . Selena sighed. Perhaps it was too much to expect Abbie to settle down like other women. Grant had tried to warn her, but she was always one to throw caution to the wind. The town still buzzed with it all—thanks to Marcy, no doubt—particularly the incredulous news that Abbie had gone with an Indian guide.

Selena half smiled. *Oh, Lord. You do work in mysterious ways.*

"I know that look."

She smiled up at Joshua and saw the answering mirth in his eyes. "I can't help smiling each time I recall poor Ruth Bailey fainting clean away, right in the middle of Marcy's parlor, when she heard Abbie'd gone off with a Comanche."

"Bet that was a sight."

"And Judge Wilson. Do you suppose he'll ever forgive Grant his wayward sister? I suppose it's God's mercy Darla passed on before hearing the news."

"A man's got to choose his in-laws with care. It's a package deal when you set your eye on a pretty face."

Her smile faded, and she sighed again. "I never wished any of this on Abbie. I thought with Monte . . . God's ways are higher than ours, but I wish He hadn't seen fit to take Monte so young."

"God has a plan for our girl. You can rest assured of that."

"But will Abbie stand still long enough to see it?"

"Maybe it's not a standing still sort of plan. I think God's equal to catching her on the run."

Selena laughed softly. "How you do comfort a mother's heart."

Joshua chuckled back. "Would you really want her any different?"

Would I? She'd seen Abbie lose her spark. She'd seen the light go out of her eyes, the spring from her step. She'd watched the bitterness set in and the hollowness follow. Cole's return had seemed such a boon. Then this.

Selena shook her head. "I don't know, Joshua. It seems all these years I've been trying to mold her in ways she just can't go."

"Maybe it's time to see her as she is."

Selena linked her gloved fingers together. "Maybe it is."

"After all, we're none of us perfect."

"No, indeed." *For none is perfect but the Father.* Whose better hands in which to entrust her daughter . . . and the children, and the rest of them—especially Cole.

Fifteen

Not for the first time, Cole wished for a good Sharps rifle. Heck, he'd settle for any rifle. Bringing down an antelope with nothing but a handgun was next to impossible, and once again he had to set his sights on a long-legged jackrabbit. Cole returned to the camp.

Brother Lewis had the fire ready and a spit rigged. He must have expected small game. "I'll skin that. It's the least I can do toward your providing."

Cole held out the rabbit by the feet. He'd spent two bullets catching it, and he'd replace them shortly, once he'd cleaned and oiled the weapon. The shots would have given their location to anyone handy, and he wouldn't be caught with less than a fully serviced gun.

He pulled the chamois from his pack and laid the gun upon it. Beside him, Brother Lewis worked the meat free of the hide. Cole noticed his ability with frank interest. Maybe the preacher hadn't spent all his days with books. "You handle that knife right smartly."

"I've had cause to procure victuals along my trail."

"How? Without a gun, I mean."

Brother Lewis paused in his work and glanced up. "A snare."

"What sort?"

"Whatever I can come up with. Rope and sticks and bait."

Cole raised a skeptical brow. "Sounds chancy at best."

"Can be." Brother Lewis sliced the skin free of the hind leg. "But if the good Lord means me to go hungry, I accept that. More often than not He sends a creature my way for sustenance."

Cole eyed him curiously.

"You see, Cole, God isn't interested in our souls only. He oversees every part of our lives, spiritual and physical. He knows we need to eat, and He provides."

"Well, I'd've preferred an antelope to this here rabbit."

"It's not always what we want that's best. In fact, I've stopped setting expectations whenever possible. What God chooses to send my way is fine by me."

Cole eyed the rabbit as the last of the hide fell free of the knife. The preacher made it sound simple. It was hard to get disappointed if a man had no expectations. He ought to be thankful for the rabbit. Food had been meager enough these last miles, and a man could only go so long.

His stomach rumbled confirmation, and he tried not to think of Abbie's corn bread or biscuits or apple dumplings. Right now, anything she made would be welcome. He refused to envy Will. That only opened up a whole passel of thoughts best not dwelt upon.

Brother Lewis looked up from the spit on which he'd skewered the rabbit. "If you fill my small pot with water, I'll brew some coffee to go with this hare."

Cole nodded, took the blue speckled pot from the preacher's saddlebag, and headed upstream. The water beside their camp was slow, and he walked to where the river narrowed and plunged a scant foot or two. He stooped and dipped the pot into the flow, then flipped the lid down.

The scent came on him like a storm. His senses reeled, and he dropped the pot and spun. His hip felt empty even before he reached, and he pictured the Colt .44 lying on the leather cloth beside Brother Lewis at the fire ring. Cole faced the Comanche bare-handed.

Gray Wolf wore ceremonial paint on his face and chest. His legs were spread and bent, his arms parted, his knife gripped in one hand. Cole eyed its razor edge. That the knife wasn't already lodged in his back was some tribute to the brave. Likely he meant this to be a contest, giving his deed greater honor.

Gray Wolf wove to one side and stepped to the other. Cole followed the motion, imitating the crouch, but kept his eyes on the knife. The Indian thrust, and Cole dove, rolled, and slipped his own knife from his boot. That evened the odds a bit. Gray Wolf's eyes narrowed but showed no surprise.

They circled. Cole feinted left and swung right with the knife. Gray Wolf dodged, then returned the swipe. They were fairly matched. Cole had an edge on the Indian in reach, but his shoulder wound would cost him if they went hand to hand.

Cole dodged a thrust, but Gray Wolf swung out with his leg, and it caught the back of Cole's knee. At the same time, the tip of the Indian's blade cut his side. Cole hissed sharply at the pain, then forced a swipe at Gray Wolf's chest. The brave avoided him easily, but Cole had backed him off and regained his footing.

From the corner of his eye, Cole saw the foliage move. Brother Lewis crouched in the reeds, his Bible clutched to his chest. Cole frowned. If the man had to grab something, why couldn't it have been the gun?

Gray Wolf's knife sliced his shirt sleeve and drew blood. Cole made a poor jump and lost his balance. He went down and rolled as the brave dove and gouged for his eyes with clawed fingers. Cole kicked Gray Wolf in the side with his boot, but the Indian gained his feet and spat.

"The white dung fights like a woman."

"I have no quarrel with you, Gray Wolf. What's past is past."

"My people are dead."

"So are mine."

Gray Wolf lunged, slamming his head into Cole's belly and knocking him backward. Cole fell with the Indian on top. The brave's teeth bit into his collarbone while he gripped Cole's wrist and smashed his arm to the ground. His knife flew free and lay in the dirt.

Cole grasped Gray Wolf's arm as the Indian blade swung toward his throat. His left arm was perilously weak, but he caught hold with his right hand as well and forced the blade back. He brought his knee up with all the force he could muster and shoved the Indian aside.

Gray Wolf sprang to his feet and kicked dirt in Cole's eyes, then jabbed with the blade. Cole rolled. His breath came hard and angry. He was bleeding and his shoulder burned like fire. He saw Gray Wolf's guard drop and shot a right hook to his jaw.

The brave staggered back, and Cole dove for his knife. Gray Wolf sprang like a cat, but his thrust went wide and his knife plunged into the ground. Cole pressed his knee to Gray Wolf's wrist as he fought to free the blade. He felt the bones shift and delivered a punch to the brave's face.

Blood spurted from Gray Wolf's nose, and he seized Cole's arm and yanked him over. Again he tugged his knife, and it came free. Cole kicked it from his hand and it flew, glistening, end over end toward the water. Gray Wolf lunged after it, and Cole threw himself onto the brave's back.

They splashed down together and rolled, sputtering to their feet. Gray Wolf's knife sank beneath the muddied current. Cole tossed his to the shore near Brother Lewis. "Hand to hand, Gray Wolf. Your strength to mine."

"You have no strength. You are wounded."

"That's my misfortune." Cole's blood was up, and no words

from this Comanche were going to cheat him of this scrap. "Come on!"

Gray Wolf's chest heaved with his heavy breaths. He narrowed his eyes like a stoat. "This day you will die."

Cole answered in Comanche. "Then it is a good day to die." The Indian saying registered in Gray Wolf's expression. It seemed to feed him, and he leaped without warning.

Cole caught the full force of the man's weight on his left shoulder and went down. Gray Wolf pressed his head beneath the water. Straining for breath, Cole thrashed free and used the brave's own power to plunge him into the water. His shoulder throbbed and the arm felt numb as he yanked Gray Wolf up. He concentrated his strength and smashed his fist into the brave's right temple.

Gray Wolf went limp, stunned, and his open eyes rolled back. Cole gripped him by the hair and held the back of his head to the surface of the water. When Gray Wolf's senses returned, Cole held him there firmly. "If I were Death Rider, I'd have drowned you like a dog. Because I'm not, and because of your service to Abbie, I let you live. Our score is settled." Cole let him go.

Gray Wolf caught himself from sinking into the water. His black hair was carried by the current as he held himself up by his elbows and returned Cole's stare. Cole saw the vein pulse in his neck and waited. He knew the Comanche temperament well enough not to turn his back.

Gray Wolf shook his head as though just now coming to. He pressed his hand to his temple. "Death Rider has fist like a bear."

Cole lurched to his feet. The current tugged at his calves. He waited while Gray Wolf scrambled up. "Maybe that's a more fittin' name to wear now." He roughly translated "fist like a bear" to Comanche.

Gray Wolf eyed him. "You speak the tongue of my people.

Yet you return to the land of death."

Cole bent and pulled his hat from the shallows. "Is that your concern? You worried that I've come to bring harm to your people?"

"My people are no more."

"Oh, there are Comanches yet. Plenty of 'em. Just none you want to run with."

Gray Wolf scowled.

"I reckon you were a renegade before your clan was broken up. You're a man who rides alone. I recognize it." Just as Brother Lewis had recognized it in him. Cole glanced toward the bushes. Brother Lewis was on his feet now.

Gray Wolf drew himself up. "My people were strong, their ways good, until the white man came to their land."

"I won't argue that, though I know the Comanche ways. I've set aside my fight." He waited. This was the man who had saved Abbie's life, who had helped to save his, unknowingly. Perhaps Gray Wolf's need to avenge was understandable. But Cole wanted no more of it.

Gray Wolf nodded slowly. "I will contend no more with Fist Like a Bear."

Cole felt his tension ease. Gray Wolf's use of his new name signified more than it would to a white man. In the Comanche's eyes, he was still a fighter, but perhaps no longer a killer. Cole clasped his hands in front of his body with the back of his left hand down. After a moment, Gray Wolf returned the hand sign for peace. At least for a time, the brave would honor it.

Gray Wolf turned and strode to the gelding with the Lucky Star brand. Cole noted the slitted ears and the overall gaunt and shaggy condition of the animal. One day he'd ask Abbie how Gray Wolf came by the horse. If he ever had the chance.

The brave mounted and held his head erect. He drew a breath and spoke in Comanche. "Perhaps tomorrow will be a good day to die." He wheeled the horse and pressed with his knees.

When the dust settled, Cole turned to Brother Lewis. "I'm not certain I'd choose you for my corner, preacher. That was a little touch and go. Did it ever occur to you I might need help?"

"From the very start."

"You just didn't mean to give it?"

"Indeed I did."

Cole felt his side where the shirt clung to congealed blood. "My mistake. I must've missed it."

"You may not have heard, but God did. I beseeched Him on your behalf the entire time you fought. I'm certain He gave you strength."

Cole swallowed his laugh, then pictured Gray Wolf, dazed, in his hands. In truth, the power of that punch hadn't seemed to be his own. He eyed Brother Lewis sharply, then bent, dug the coffeepot from the shallows, and refilled it. That rabbit must be just about cooked.

◆◆◆◆◆◆◆

Abbie drew the canteen from the water and twisted the lid tightly. She raised her face and let the slight breeze cool her brow. They had dropped down out of the high country, and the approach of the southern climate was evident.

All along the river valley they'd seen Indian pueblos rising like queer formations of the earth itself. Dwarf corn had grown in patches of land trenched with ditches to bring the river to the roots. Though the fields were harvested of their bounty, she could see they'd been productive. The Pueblo Indians had watched but not harassed them as they passed. They seemed a garrulous, uncomplicated people.

At Sam's direction, they had stopped briefly in Albuquerque, but skirted Socorro. Its reputation was such that he wouldn't risk it. The place attracted the worst sort of Texas cattleman and too many others looking to live by the end of a gun.

He'd said bringing her there would be like holding a beefsteak before a pack of wolves, and to Abbie's dismay, she'd blushed furiously. He was as incorrigible as Cole in his understated sort of way. She glanced up as he joined her now at the river's edge.

In physical characteristics, he was more like Cole than she'd noticed when he first descended on the ranch. As they'd ridden, she'd noted features and expressions, intonations and motions that all betrayed their kinship. Were they close?

Cole talked as though they had been, but now . . . was Sam still bent on revenge? And was he as dogged in that as Cole could be? Did revenge run in their blood? Was it bred in this rough, desolate country where mile spread upon mile without end?

She shook away the gloomy thoughts. Whatever Sam had in mind, she'd have something to say about it. Just as she would concerning Cole's intentions, which he had left unspoken when he deserted them. She frowned and dipped the last canteen into the river.

Sam nodded her way. "Fill everything we have. In a few miles our route will leave the river."

She was instantly suspicious. "Why?"

"Well, you see, this road we've been on is the *Camino Real.* Been here since the Spaniards came lookin' for gold. Runs all the way from El Paso to Santa Fe. But along here the river changes course and runs through some wicked arroyos, so most travelers keep to the old bed."

"For how long?"

"Some ninety miles."

"Ninety miles! That's days without fresh water."

"There are a couple of springs, though one is frequently

run dry. The other's full of arsenic, but so many have drunk from it in desperation that the stretch of road's known as *Jornado del Muerto*. The journey of death."

Journey of death. Abbie glanced uncomfortably at Will. And they were following Sam into it. How Sam had assumed leadership of their small band, she wasn't sure. Like Cole, he had simply fit the role.

"Will we have enough water for us and the horses?"

Sam shrugged. "We'll have to go lightly. We don't have the blistering heat this time of year, but it's still desert. Whether there's water at the spring depends on how many have used it before us. There's enough traffic on this road to deplete it, and plenty who've counted on it are bleaching their bones now."

Will shouldered past to face Sam. "Did Cole go this way?"

"I reckon so."

"You don't know?" Will's tone was almost belligerent.

"The trail we're trackin' has been chancy ever since we hit the road. But it don't matter. Either way gets you where he's goin'. This way's just shorter and easier."

"It doesn't sound easy with all this talk about bones and arsenic."

Abbie touched Will's arm to quiet him. "I think we need to trust Mr. Jasper here, Will. It's his risk, too."

"Not if he means to get himself through and leave us to die of thirst."

Abbie saw surprise and offense color Sam's expression.

If Will saw, it didn't keep him from continuing. "How do we know you haven't joined up to keep us from reaching Cole?"

Sam held his ground and wisely kept his cool under Will's insult. Abbie did not intervene. Sam could answer for himself. "You can travel on yourselves if you think you can get through better without me."

"And have you at our backs?"

Now Sam did bristle. "I'm neither a sneak nor a backstabber. You best learn to govern your tongue, son, or a better man might govern it for you."

"If you think . . ."

"Will." Abbie caught his arm. "We're all on this road together. We may as well see it through to the end."

Sam turned his attention to her. "It's plain foolishness your comin' this way at all. The road only gets worse. There's bandits and ruffians and all manner of things a lady don't want to meet in the night."

"Well, unless you know yet another way, I'm afraid we'll have to chance it. I intend to reach El Paso and see Cole freed."

"You'll reach El Paso, maybe. As for the rest, who can say."

"God will stand by a just man."

Sam frowned. "Depends how you define justice, lady."

Abbie raised her chin but refused to argue. "Now, then, Mr. Jasper, are we equipped to proceed?"

"Oh yes, ma'am. I'm certain the very sands will part for your righteous journey. I just hope you don't find your trust misplaced and call down the wrath of God on us all."

Abbie, Sam, and Will alternated riding the remuda horses with their own. Sam was wise to have brought them, as it eased the burden of the beasts through this desolate stretch. In places, the river had flooded, then receded, leaving stagnant alkaline water that bred hosts of mosquitoes. Abbie slapped at their stinging bites but kept her complaints to herself.

She watched a striped water snake slither into the quagmire to her right. On either side of the stranded pool the land was white with poison and cracked. There was nothing to recommend the place at all, nothing but the fact that it led toward the goal.

Her righteous fury had burned to ashes inside her. Her

trust in Cole was nearly as sapped. She glanced at Will. Funny how he'd taken up the cause as she'd felt her own wane. Now she kept on because it was all she could do. They were wrapped up in this to the end, but somewhere along the way she'd lost heart.

Sam rode in surly silence. What strange twist of fate had brought him to them? Or had he merely followed a path known to both him and Cole and found them upon it? Abbie's throat was thick with thirst, and she forced her thoughts away from cold, clear mountain streams.

Two days of travel had nearly emptied their canteens. Every swallow now was precious, not to be taken without need. Desire had no place in survival. Her voice rasped even when she cleared the dust from her throat.

Sam glanced her way. There was concern in his eyes, but he didn't voice it. If they spoke of their thirst it would be worse. He shifted in the saddle. "Not long on past that bend is the spring. With any luck it'll be more than mud."

"I don't depend on luck, Mr. Jasper."

He gave his smile a quirk. "Then I hope you brought your staff."

Abbie turned away. His mockery would not divert her, though her prayers had dried up like the land around them. The horses plodded on. They rode and rode but the land never changed. Distance made sport of progress.

She was scarcely aware of the motion any longer. Her legs and backside were numb, her mind torpid. The landscape became a blur of bland desolation. The sky seemed to merge with it. Part of her was aware of falling, the rest just didn't care.

Abbie tasted the dust in her mouth as she settled into a heap. Then even that was gone until she felt the metal pressed to her lips, the grip of a hand behind her head. She shook away the clouds and drank. The water coursed down her throat, not a single meager swallow, but a flow, gulp after gulp of paradise.

She opened her eyes. For an instant Sam's green-eyed stare was Cole's. Then her mind corrected. He drew the canteen from her lips, but gently. She looked from him to Will, standing just behind, then back to Sam.

"It's all right, Mrs. Farrel. There's water in the spring."

She pushed herself up to her elbows, then sat.

Sam steadied her, then removed his hand. "We'll rest here, though we'll have to be on guard. Anyone on this road will head for this spot. And out here the six-shooter is god."

Abbie half smiled. "Even here, Mr. Jasper, there's only one God."

Sam nodded toward the water filling a shallow pool. "You may be right, ma'am. But I'll keep watch nonetheless."

Abbie curled into the shade of a ragged cut in the land. The water had revived her, but still her thoughts were dull. How much longer could she go? Surely they must be close to the end. "How much farther, Mr. Jasper?"

He settled cross-legged on the ground a short distance from her. His rifle lay across his thighs. "Should reach the river again by noon tomorrow. We'll be nearer the Organ and Franklin Mountains. Two days' journey between them and the river brings us into El Paso."

His voice gruffed as though the thought of reaching the town pained or angered him. Abbie felt a flutter inside, as well. Her thoughts had been so focused on completing the journey, she'd not yet figured her plans once she got there. Much would depend on how she found Cole.

A flicker of fear stirred inside her. What if they came too late? She straightened. "I'm quite recovered now. We should continue."

Sam gave her a slow look down. "I'm glad to hear that. But we'll let the horses drink their fill and rest a bit. There's a dry stretch yet to cover."

She felt like a schoolgirl who'd just received a dressing

down. Who was Samuel Jasper to speak to her so? It must run in the Jasper blood. Cole, Sam—they both thought a good deal too much of themselves. Abbie turned away without a word, though her heart seethed at the low chuckle she was certain she heard.

Sixteen

El Paso-Juarez looked much the same to Cole in the slanting evening rays—low, flat-roofed, plastered adobes with arched doorways and square columned galleries across the fronts. The smell of dust and refuse and even the tang of the river filled the air.

He heard the Ysleta Mission bell some ten miles away and imagined the padres making their silent way through the arched adobe passage. Now theirs was a life free from trouble. But no—hadn't two of them been killed several years ago, when Mexican bandits came after a wounded man they'd sheltered?

The town had been outraged, but that was no help to the two who were buried. Maybe there was no escaping the evil of the world. Maybe it just swept a man up, whether he liked it or not.

Though he looked straight ahead, Cole sensed Brother Lewis's calm presence beside him. He didn't feel much different since praying with the preacher or taking the river dunk that the man set such store by, but it had stopped the sermons some. Strange, but with his innards twisting the way they were, he wouldn't have minded a word or two now.

Brother Lewis straightened in the saddle as though reading his thoughts. "Remember, Cole, in this world you will have tribulation. But be of good cheer, for the One who holds your soul has overcome the world."

Cole didn't answer, but the words had a settling effect. He'd just ride it out. Soon as he walked into the jail, it was out of his hands anyway. They passed the first buildings.

From the corners of his eyes, he saw faces turned his way, folks pausing in their business to watch him pass. One short fella held his hat to his chest, funeral-like. Ignacio Perez, the mule skinner who treated his animals like children and trusted everyone. He'd been the butt of too many jokes, and Cole had taken him under his wing a number of times.

At the end of the block, a woman stared with grief in her face. Cole recognized Sonja Bjork, the Swede's widow. Cole had pulled her young'un from a well. His jaw tightened. He didn't want to put names to the faces, though he likely knew most everyone on the street.

Cole kept his focus at the end of the street. Already a small crowd gathered at the jail's door. Texas Ranger Captain Henry Gates stood at the front. Cole swung down from the saddle and handed Brother Lewis the reins. "Would you find some way to return this horse to the Lucky Star in Rocky Bluffs, Colorado?"

The preacher nodded.

Cole turned and faced Captain Gates. "I hear you got paper on me that says I'm wanted for murder."

The ranger cocked his jaw to the side and nodded. "Got an eyewitness, Cole."

Cole drew a slow breath. So he was right. It must've been Sam if someone thought they saw him do it. The crowd parted as Cole stepped forward and held out his hands.

Gates cuffed him. "I'll question you inside." He kept his face expressionless, but Cole saw something soft in his eyes. Cole couldn't let regret and old times keep Captain Gates from carrying out his duty. Not when that duty kept Sam safe.

They went inside the square, stone building. Two Mexican *caballeros* argued in the center cell. Cole understood most of the words, though they spoke fast in their anger. They broke off to watch darkly as Gates motioned him to a chair. Cole sat.

Gates fixed him in his sights with one brow lowered. "I had no choice but to follow through on the testimony of the witness. You know the law, Cole. But it does me no pleasure to bring in one I served with."

Cole was silent.

" 'Course, it's her word against yours. If you have an alibi that can stand up, prove her wrong—you're a free man. Where were you the night of August ninth?"

Cole wet his throat with a swallow. "I was with Auralee Dubois."

The ranger stood and leaned a hand on Cole's chair. "And what happened?"

Cole stared down at the cold metal cuffs on the skin of his wrists. The truth, and they'd be removed. The truth, and he could go back to Abbie. He drew a slow breath and answered. "We fought. You figure out the rest."

Gates swore and circled his desk. "Give me something, Cole. The last thing I want to do is hang you for the death of a—"

"Lady?"

"That's not the word I would choose to describe Auralee Dubois."

"Don't matter."

Gates lowered his face near Cole's. "Are you tellin' me you did it?"

Cole pictured Sam's eyes aflame with rage and ... gut wrenching grief. "You got your witness." It came out a dry croak, all the more convincing. His thoughts went back to the night he left El Paso, to Auralee's whisper in his ear, begging—or as close as she'd come to it—for him to come up.

He'd thought she was in trouble, needing something, but she'd tried every wile in her bag once she had him alone. She'd wrapped him in her arms and pressed her body close, offering more than what she did for a living. Offering her heart—something she never included in the price.

Cole was probably the only man in town who hadn't paid to prove his love or his lust. Was it her need to conquer him, too, that made her eyes so bright, made her lips like coals against his? He still felt her slap when he'd pulled away.

He should have walked out then, should never have tried to explain, should have left his love for Abbie buried deep in his heart where it belonged. But no, he'd dragged it out, confessed it to a woman who would never understand unreturned devotion. She'd gone cold like the edge of a knife, dug her nails into the back of his neck and tried to force a response he couldn't withstand.

But he'd come to his senses and got clear. Had Sam known? Had she taken delight in tormenting Sam with her version of their moments alone? Had she pushed Sam too far? Pushed him to murder? If any woman could bring a man to murder, it was Auralee Dubois.

Gates turned from the window where he'd been waiting for a response. He was a good man, straight and mostly square. He wasn't above a little rowdy blowing of steam, but he kept control. They'd had some good times.

Cole cleared his throat. "I reckon you'd better choose me a cell."

Gates expelled his breath in an exasperated whistle. "This is no different than the Comanches, Cole. That woman had men tearing each other's throats out. I figure you did the town a favor."

"But that ain't the law." Cole felt his pocket. No bulge of tobacco pouch, no crinkle of paper. He'd tossed them away after praying with the preacher. Kind of a private acknowledgment of his leaving the old self. *Sheez.*

"Listen to me, Cole. Most of the folks out there owe you a debt of gratitude for one thing or another. They want you to walk out of here. They'll buy you a drink, slap your back, and welcome you home." He leaned his head to Cole's ear. "Give me something that will satisfy the law, and you can walk away."

Cole sat silent. *Walk away*. He'd ride to the Lucky Star and explain it all to Abbie. He'd tell her how he felt, how much he cared, how he loved and needed her. He looked into the ranger's face, his friend, a man he respected. Gates wanted that word, his testimony against that of the witness.

Cole again dropped his gaze to his shackled hands. Gates was itching to unlock them. This was sure different than the treatment he'd had from Crete Marlowe and Jackson Finn. And a whole lot harder to take.

Where were Marlowe and Finn now? He felt a grim satisfaction at having cheated them out of the bounty reward. But he reckoned they'd be along to see him hang. At least Abbie would not.

♦♦♦♦♦♦♦

Abbie saw El Paso with the afternoon light beating on the white-plastered adobe walls. Most of the town lay on the far bank of the Rio Grande, or the Rio Bravo, as it was called from the part of town across the river. El Paso del Norte, or Juarez Chihuahua on the Mexican side, was connected by a ferry at the crossroads.

Nearer at hand, a U.S. mail coach drawn by six mules clogged Santa Fe Street while men and women in colorful woven shawls and ponchos pressed through beside it. They had an air of dogged independence and camaraderie that stung her heart. These were the people who would condemn Cole.

Abbie studied the flat, rounded features, the gaunt faces, the smiling, the bronze, the proud aquiline countenances. This conglomeration of peoples were those who had called for justice against Cole. Yet they seemed oblivious, busy with the details of their daily lives.

Abbie shivered. A few cottonwoods stood bare in the cold, dry air, casting small inkblot shadows at the base of their trunks. In two weeks it would be Christmas. The children would spend it without her. She was too weary to hurt.

Under Sam's direction, they'd made it in the time he'd said. She glanced his way. He'd grown silent and introspective as they neared the town. Even Will's enthusiasm failed to provoke a response.

Abbie looked back over the town. There were the usual taverns, blacksmith, livery, and corrals. Her gaze rested briefly on a sign marked *El Paso Sentinel*, leaning against a wall, but its use as a newspaper office like Pa's must be past. She sighed. They had reached their destination. But what could she do now? She felt staggered by the helplessness, lost in the miles, and so, so tired.

"I reckon you'll go straight to the jail?" Sam's voice startled her.

"The jail?"

"You said Cole meant to turn himself in."

"Well, I . . . I'd hoped he'd clear himself." She still clung to it, however foolishly.

"Maybe he did. If you'd rather go to the hotel, I can ask around."

"No." Abbie was suddenly certain she'd find Cole behind bars. She searched the street and found the jail at the end. Raising her chin, she determined to let Cole Jasper know exactly what she thought of his predicament.

She tapped her heels to Zephyr's sides and pulled ahead of Will and Sam. She would do this alone, and she'd do it before any renegade emotions kept her from speaking her mind. She swung down, dust billowing from her skirts. She must look a sight, but she didn't care.

She stepped onto the creaky boardwalk and reached for the latch, but the door swung open, and the stocky man who opened it stopped short. He wore a cropped beard and mustache, mostly gray, but the hair that hung to his shoulders was brown beneath the gray Stetson he hastily removed.

"Afternoon, ma'am. I'm Captain Henry Gates. Can I help you?"

"I'm looking for Cole Jasper." She dared to hope he'd tell her Cole was gone.

Instead he eyed her with fresh interest. "Well, ma'am, he's inside, but I hesitate to let you in there."

"I assure you it's nothing I can't handle."

Captain Gates scratched the side of his beard. "I dunno . . ."

"May I ask on what evidence you're holding Cole?"

"On the testimony of an eyewitness, and his own failure to discount her."

Abbie raised her brows. "The witness is a lady?"

"Well . . . uh . . ."

"I see." Abbie frowned. Good heavens. With how many saloon girls was Cole involved? "If you'll permit me, Captain Gates, I've come a long way. I want a wash and a good meal. But first I want to see Cole."

"Yes, ma'am." He pushed open the door.

Abbie stepped into the stale air of the jail. She saw the three cells along the back. Cole sat in the one on the left with his head on his palms. He had several days growth of beard and looked as though he hadn't slept in as many nights. She stepped past the captain, and Cole looked up.

She watched surprise, then dismay, then fury pass over his features. It was fury that settled in his eyes. She felt a surge of her own and stepped up to the bars. A catcall and a string of

Spanish vulgarities came from the next cell, but she didn't look. She kept her eyes on Cole.

He stood slowly and jammed his thumbs into his belt. "Abbie, what in the blazes are you doin' here?"

She drew herself up. "I might ask you the same."

He growled something that might have been a word she didn't care to hear.

"Why won't you tell the ranger what you told me? You didn't kill Auralee."

"This ain't your business. I told you to go home." His words were as sharp as the report of a gun.

Oh, he'd sent her home all right. But now he'd see she had a mind of her own. "You didn't really expect me to go, did you?"

"Call me a fool, but yes, I did."

Why did it hurt that he believed she would leave him to face this alone? He would never have left her in trouble. Didn't he realize she owed him the same? "As you can see, I chose to ignore your stone arrow, though I assure you its meaning was clear."

He scowled. "You and Will crossed all that territory alone?"

"And Sam."

His jaw went slack. "Sam's here? In town?"

She turned to the captain. "Cole Jasper did not kill Auralee Dubois." She heard Cole's sharp breath.

"Is that right, Cole?" Gates seemed eager to believe her. Abbie hadn't expected his support.

Cole didn't answer, and she glanced his way. His expression was close to what she'd seen the moment after she'd slapped him on the prairie. He narrowed his eyes and looked past her to the captain. "I reckon you'd better stick with your witness. Mrs. Farrel has a vested interest. She needs me to run her ranch, and she'll say anything to get what she wants."

Abbie felt as though he'd slapped her right back. He made

her sound petty and self-serving, after all she'd been through to . . . Her spine stiffened. "May I see you outside, Captain Gates?"

"Yes, ma'am." He sent Cole a penetrating look, then escorted her out.

Abbie settled her thoughts, determined to speak her mind without letting Cole's insult fester. "It is true that Cole is in charge of my ranch in Colorado. It was from there the bounty hunters took him, quite viciously, I might add."

"Bounty hunters?"

"Crete Marlowe was one of them. We . . ."

"But Cole came in alone, ma'am. Leastwise he came with a preacher, not a bounty man."

Abbie filed that, but it was unimportant at the moment. "We relieved Crete and his partner of their quarry."

His eyes widened, then narrowed. "Who's we?" he asked like a lawman.

"My friend, myself, and a Comanche brave named Gray Wolf."

He shook his head. "You'll forgive me, ma'am, if I don't believe you. No Comanche would come in sight of Cole Jasper without slitting his throat."

"When Gray Wolf realized it was Death Rider he'd rescued, he was more than ready with his knife."

That registered truth to the ranger. Cole's name must be known to him. "But?"

She knew this next would sound incredible, but she prayed he would believe her. "Gray Wolf and I . . . have an understanding. We've both had occasion to save the other's life. He refused to ride farther with us, but, on the strength of our pact, he let Cole live."

The captain looked as though she'd just told him the biggest fish story of his life. No doubt he heard plenty in his line of work. He pulled a handkerchief from his pocket, turned and blew briefly, then turned back. "Well, ma'am, I don't rightly know what to say."

"Cole is not guilty."

"Maybe he is, maybe he's not. I know Cole Jasper well enough to say he's actin' mighty queer. Another man in his boots would be sayin' anything to get out of there. Cole, well, he's settlin' in for the trial, and by law there's got to be one."

"When?"

"Whenever Judge McFee comes through."

"Is there nothing you can do?"

"It's my job to uphold the law. Until he's cleared . . ."

Abbie clenched her hands at her sides. "This witness . . . where can I find her?"

"You can't. She's one of Pablo's gals. He won't let a lady near. Thinks you'll missionize him out of business. His place is off limits to womenfolk."

"What place is that, Captain Gates?"

"The Paloma Blanca." He pointed down the dusty street.

"And her name?"

"Goes by Birdie."

"Thank you." Abbie looked at the two-story, flat-roofed adobe. So Auralee had worked at the Paloma Blanca. The white dove. What a misnomer. How many times had Cole taken her in his arms inside those walls? Had he whispered words of love? No, Cole wouldn't say it unless he meant it. But he'd no doubt shown it.

A dull ache started in her temples. She wanted to go home to Elliot, to Jenny, to her memories of Monte, a man who would never have entered a brothel. A man of honor so solid and deep it was unshakable. *Oh, Monte.* How could she have thought what she felt in Cole's arms might be love?

It was nothing more than the devil's trap, the same that

had ensnared men and women since the start of time. Her heart ached with loneliness, her body with longing, and she'd allowed herself to imagine Cole a hero. She closed her eyes. No more.

Seventeen

Abbie started for the white, two-story building with the square, columned porch. The sign read *Central Hotel.* Zephyr and the other horses were tethered outside, along with Sam's pack mule, as yet still burdened. She crossed over and went inside. Will and Sam were not about, but they had registered a room for her and left a key at the desk. She went up.

She ached with weariness and frustration as she stripped and stepped into the steaming tub. Soaking in the bath, she pondered her options. She could go home and leave Cole to handle this as he so clearly wanted, or she could stay and help, though how, she wasn't sure. Either way, when this was over, she and Cole Jasper would part paths. Her heart had nearly betrayed her. Almost . . . she had almost forgotten Monte . . . and her grief.

She looked up at the tap on her door. "Yes?"

"Mrs. Farrel?" It was Sam. "I was wondering if you'd join me for a meal."

She sloshed as she straightened in surprise. "Where's Will?"

Sam cleared his throat. "He took the horses to the livery, and I reckon he's lookin' around town."

Suddenly she had an idea. Maybe Will could get to Birdie. She felt a twinge at sending someone as young and impressionable as Will into a saloon of that sort. But he was as committed as she to getting Cole free. If they could just keep Sam from interfering . . .

"Thank you, Mr. Jasper. I'd like that, but first I need to speak with Will. Can you find him while I finish here?"

"A'right. We'll meet you downstairs."

She had already hung her dress to straighten the wrinkles. It hadn't had time to do much good, but she pulled it on anyway and brushed her hair until the curls shone. She studied herself in the mirror. She should be distracting enough to keep Sam's thoughts from Will.

Abbie felt a pang of conscience. Surely he was still grieving Auralee. Who was she to think . . . Good Lord, this was all so confusing. Why did Cole have to fraternize with trouble until he had everyone, including his own brother, out to get him?

She shook her head and went out. Sam and Will waited at the foot of the stairs. She didn't miss Sam's look of appreciation, though it quickly passed.

"May I speak with you a moment, Will?"

Sam tipped his hat. "I'll find us a table." He hesitated. "For two or three?"

"Two." Abbie gave him a smile she hoped was innocent enough, then tugged Will's arm. "I need you to find someone. She's the witness who claims she saw Cole. Her name is Birdie, and she's at the Paloma Blanca."

He nodded solemnly, and she was sure he knew the place. After all, he was no longer the boy she tended to think him.

"I wouldn't ask this, but . . ."

"I want to help Cole."

"See if you can arrange for me to meet her . . . somewhere." She prayed it wouldn't be at the saloon where Cole . . .

Will nodded again, and Abbie squeezed his arm, then joined Sam. He stood and held her chair. Again she saw a flicker in his eyes, but it was mixed with pain. Being back in El Paso had surely opened his wounds. He looked as though he regretted asking her to share his meal.

She sat quietly, uncertain how to handle herself. The waitress brought the food he'd ordered for both of them, and she looked down at the fried steak and mashed potatoes covered with slightly congealed gravy. Sam cleared his throat and said the last thing she expected. "Would you like to pray?"

She barely kept herself from gaping.

He motioned to the table. "Bless the food?"

Abbie understood now, but still his words burned in her spirit. How long had it been since she'd really prayed and turned this whole situation over to God? And how was it this rough brother of Cole's, bent on revenge, was the one to remind her?

She bowed her head. "Father, we thank you for this food. Bless it to our use and guide our steps." *And help me know what to do.*

Sam mumbled his amen and took up his fork. Abbie looked at the crispy fried steak, remembering the meal she and Cole had shared in Dodge the night he told her of his promise to Monte. The night she feared he had let Monte die, maybe even caused it. The night he saved her from her assailants.

"They were closin' the kitchen down till supper. I took a chance you wouldn't mind this choice."

Abbie glanced up and forced a smile, though the hard knot of tears in her throat made it difficult. Would she ever understand Cole Jasper? "I like it fine." And she took a tasteless bite to prove it.

"Mind my askin' something personal?"

"I can't say until I've heard it." Her voice came a little more naturally.

"Are you in love with my brother?"

It stabbed to her quick. *No. Yes.* She couldn't be. "Why is that your concern?"

"It ain't, only . . . if you are, I want to apologize."

"For?"

"Messin' things up."

"I would think you'd consider that fair turnabout." Abbie watched the scar beneath Sam's eye stretch and compress as he spoke.

"Maybe for Cole. But it ain't right you should be hurt."

She sighed. "I've grown accustomed to hurt."

"That ain't somethin' a lady should ever say. Not if things are right with the world."

Abbie wondered how Sam had handled his mother's death. Cole hadn't mentioned any but his own need for vengeance. "But things are not right with the world, are they, Sam?"

He startled at the use of his given name but didn't gainsay her. "I reckon not."

"Why do you think Cole killed Auralee?"

"Birdie says so, and I . . . I saw him go up."

"And after? Did you see him come out?"

"No. I left as soon as he went with her. I figured I knew how it would end. But I never suspected . . ." He spread his hands, and the raw pain on his face reminded her of Cole. For two strong men to bare their hearts so . . .

"He didn't do it." Abbie played her trump. "He thinks you're the one who killed her."

Sam's face darkened as his eyes ignited. "What?"

"That's why he's taking responsibility. To keep them from suspecting you."

He slammed his fists on the table. "I would never have hurt her."

"Not even if she loved Cole? If she—"

"You think I'm blind? I saw how she took to him. I saw how crazy he made her." His eyes held their own bit of crazy. "Auralee changed after he rode in. She wasn't . . . even willing to listen anymore. I tried to get her to marry me, to come out of that place."

Sam gripped his temples between his thumb and fingers, then let his hand drop and slowly raised his head. "I loved her same as any virtuous woman. I didn't hold it against her that she done what she had to. Most times that life's forced on them by hardship or spurious people. Auralee didn't choose what she was."

Abbie did not agree. There was always room for choice, no matter how bleak the circumstances. But she held her tongue and let Sam pour out his heart.

"Sure, it tore me up thinkin' of her with others. But . . ."

"But she didn't love them." Abbie met his eyes with hers. "Until Cole."

Sam scowled. "I raised him up, cleaned him out of more scrapes, stood beside him when things were bad. Then he came in, and suddenly Auralee has eyes for no one else. Even Pablo saw it. He threatened her with the whip if she didn't stop moonin' over Cole and show the others some attention."

Abbie regrettably understood. Cole Jasper had confidence and charisma—not to mention cocky good looks—that were hard to ignore. Sam was all right in his own, but he lacked Cole's energy.

"I'm sorry," she said softly.

He gripped his cup and watched the contents. "I reckon even if he didn't . . . knife her himself, he brought it on. She turned mean as a grizzly whenever he'd been around. I reckon she pushed someone too far. But it's still Cole's fault."

Again she saw the pain that fueled his anger. What could she say? If Cole cared nothing for the woman, then he had no business . . . seeing her. Especially if he knew how she felt. And she doubted very much he hadn't known. *Oh, how muddy everything gets outside of God's plan.*

Again she felt a pang for what she and Monte had known. Even if she freed Cole, she could never love him knowing he'd held other women so cheaply. She suddenly felt empty. "I am sorry, Sam. I'm sorry for your loss. But I must do what I can to see that Cole is freed of a crime he didn't commit."

"You'd stand by him, knowin' . . ."

"Cole is his own man with his own free will. What he does is his business. But . . . I owe him my efforts after all he's done for me."

"There's nothin' more to it?"

No. Her aching heart suddenly throbbed. "There's nothing more to it." She heard the bell on the door and turned.

Will's slight shake of the head told her he'd been unsuccessful.

She wiped her mouth and laid her napkin beside her plate. Except for the first bite, her meal was untouched. "Will you excuse me, Sam?"

He nodded, but seemed lost in his own thoughts. She took Will's arm and stepped out to the street. "What happened?"

"I can't get in to see her. Leastwise, I can't talk to her without . . . money."

"I should have thought of that."

"You couldn't know. And . . ." He reddened furiously. "This Birdie's one of the high priced ones. You can buy her a drink or even a dance, but you can't talk privately without shelling out hard cash."

Abbie closed her eyes. She didn't want to know, didn't want to imagine . . . "How much?"

He mumbled a figure and she stared. If Cole could afford that . . . but maybe Auralee hadn't been . . . but Abbie knew she had. Cole would set his hat for the best.

Will stuffed his hands in his pockets. "Birdie was tight with Auralee. I found out that much."

Abbie frowned. It would cost nearly as much to see Birdie as to supply their trip home. She took the purse from her pocket. "Can you get in tonight?"

"If her dance card isn't full. I'll try."

"And Will . . ."

He held up his hand. "You don't have to say it. I know what I'm there for."

Abbie squeezed his arm. "How did you grow up so fine?"

"Had a good teacher." He grinned, then sobered. "And I had Mr. Farrel's example. I thought I had . . . Cole's, too."

Anger burned her cheeks. "Everybody fails, Will. But look where it's landed him and consider it a lesson learned." She watched him walk back to get his name on the list and prayed he'd withstand what he saw. After all, he'd had Monte's example. Who had been Cole's?

♦♦♦♦♦♦♦

Cole felt the anger spread across his chest and lodge in his throat. For the first time he understood what it was to choke on his rage. Maybe because, caged up, he could do nothing else with it. Hollering, cussing, or throwing things would only provide a show for the Mexicans, and that wasn't his way anyhow.

Why did she come? Why insist on meddling when he'd told her to leave it alone! But that was Abbie, always sticking her nose where it didn't belong. Hadn't she gotten herself in enough trouble for one lifetime? Now she had to mess with his and Sam's?

What could he do about it? She was out there with no one but Will to look after her, and she'd be more likely to mother him. Worse still, Will would be clay in her hands. Whatever she put him up to, he'd do. And with Sam here in town . . .

Cole swore, then felt remorseful. He guessed Brother Lewis's prayer hadn't took so good after all. The preacher shouldn't have wasted his time.

The door opened and sunlight shot into his eyes. Cole looked up, surprised. *Speak of the* . . . He felt a strange elation watching the black-clothed figure close the door and approach, but he hid his grin. "Howdy, preacher."

"Hello, brother. You're in good company, you know."

Cole glanced at the Mexican bandits and raised a questioning eyebrow.

"The apostles Paul and Barnabas spent much of their time in prison." Brother Lewis pulled up a stool.

"That's real comforting."

"The key is to rejoice in your circumstances." Brother Lewis repeated it in Spanish. He must figure on making his sermon count twice. The Mexicans sneered and gave him a string of foul language in return.

"The Lord will turn all things to good for those who love Him."

Cole waited through the translation and the soiled response. Brother Lewis was undaunted. "Cast your cares upon the water and the One who sees and knows all things will bring you peace." He leaned close to the bars. "And the truth will set you free." Brother Lewis's eyes burned with inner intensity. He saw. He knew.

Cole frowned. *The truth will set you free.* Sure it would. But what about Sam? "Brother Lewis, I want you to do something for me."

"Name it."

"There's a woman in town, name of Abbie Farrel. If this turns out as I expect, I want you to get her clear. I don't want to look in her blue eyes when I feel the rope closin' down. And you can return the horse to her. It's hers anyway. And another thing . . ." He got up and leaned close. "I got some money put away in the bank in San Antonio. I want it to go to Abbie and her kids."

Brother Lewis studied him silently. Cole hoped he wouldn't argue. Cole had looked at this every which way and couldn't see clear to do anything different. Wherever Sam went, he'd pay in his own way for the rest of his life. But Cole wouldn't let his brother swing. All those years ago, Sam had taken the punishment meant for him, and he couldn't do less now. It had to be this way. It had to.

◆◆◆◆◆◆◆

When Abbie viewed the handsome minister making his way purposefully along the boardwalk, she recalled Sheriff Gates mentioning one who rode in with Cole. Glimpsing Whitesock tied to the post behind him, she guessed this was he, though as a companion for Cole Jasper, the minister was as unlikely as she was apt to find.

The circuit rider, as she guessed him by the layers of dust on his boots, appeared to be as ardent and sincere a man as she'd laid eyes on in some time. It only raised her hackles to think of his riding in with Cole. Maybe taking an outlaw to jail was his good deed for the day. She frowned as he removed his hat and held it to his chest.

"Good afternoon, ma'am. Would you by chance be Mrs. Farrel?"

She drew herself up respectfully. "On what do you base your assumption?"

"A fair description from my friend and traveling companion, Cole Jasper." The reverend kept his hat to his chest, his intense brown eyes searching hers.

His friend and companion? "Do you always ride with outlaws, Reverend . . ."

"Brother Lewis." He bowed slightly. "And yes, I would say the majority of my time is spent among the godless, the hapless, and the scorned."

Abbie smiled in spite of herself. "Then I presume Cole found himself in good company."

"He may have doubted that, ma'am, until he came to see the light."

"The light?"

"The saving grace of our Lord and Savior, Jesus Christ."

Abbie glanced down the dusty street to the jail. Was he saying Cole had turned to God? Cole, who had told her himself he knew little of God's ways, who had counted himself sufficient and had stubbornly refused her help? If Cole had turned to God, why did he now live a lie inside the walls of that jail?

"Did you have business with me . . . Brother Lewis?"

"Cole requested I return the horse to you." He waved toward the gelding tethered on the street.

"Thank you." Her ire rose. It should be Cole riding the horse home, Cole keeping his word to help her run the ranch, Cole standing tall and sure before her. Not this . . . this . . . "What kind of preacher are you, not to see that Cole is innocent of these charges? What kind of friend would ride here beside him without convincing him of his error? What—"

Brother Lewis raised his hand. "Please. I understand your concern." The sable fabric of his coat sleeve furrowed at the elbow with a threadbare sheen. "But Cole is walking a destiny laid out for him. Through trial and suffering—"

"He'll end up hung."

The minister bowed his head. "I have given him council to speak the truth. But he finds a greater good in laying down his life. . . ."

Abbie spun and stalked to the post that held the roof over the entrance to the hotel. She raised her chin and closed her eyes, drawing in a sharp, hostile breath. The air smelled of dust, the scent of her dreams.

"Mrs. Farrel, Cole has surrendered his heart to the One who knows. If God calls him out of there, Cole will honor that."

And if not? Once again, Abbie felt the pain of hurting for a man who honored something with which she was at odds. Would honor forever be her enemy? What if it was honor to God? Could she dare stand against it? "You've returned the horse, sir. Was there anything more you needed?"

The reverend held his ground. "At his request, I would, regretfully, ask you to leave town. It pains Cole to face his trial with you here."

Abbie turned with fire in her veins. "It pains Cole? It pains him? What of the rest of us? What of Will and Sam and me? This isn't about him alone. It's about . . ." She faltered. Jenny, the ranch . . . her own half-hopeful dreams. They lay now in the dust, trampled by Cole's stubborn self-destruction. It wasn't God's will he followed; it was his own.

Well, she wouldn't stand for it. She hadn't come this far to turn back because her presence pained Cole. She hoped it pained him fiercely. "You may let Cole know that I'll not leave until I've seen him freed. And as for his supposed surrender to God . . ."

"I baptized him myself in the waters of the Rio Grande. I heard his confession of faith, and I assure you the Lord Jesus Christ heard it, as well."

Abbie matched Brother Lewis's stalwart stare, but she had no words to rebut his assertion. *Will Cole now die in peace?* That was the last thought she wanted to allow.

Eighteen

Jenny darted to the back corner of the house and peered around the side. Drawing a sharp breath, she ran for the stable and ducked inside. Uncle Grant's horse was gone, of course, but the gelding, Topper, was there. Aunt Marcy would be furious, but she didn't mean to take him all the way, only to the ranch to fetch Snowdrop.

Jenny couldn't saddle the gelding or hitch the buggy, and she'd only ridden bareback a score of times when she'd escaped Aunt Abbie's watchful eye. But there was no help for it. Jenny took the bridle from the wall and slid the bit into the horse's teeth. Topper was old enough to accept it without much trouble.

She had to stand on a bucket to get the straps up over his ears. That done, she swung her leg up and tugged and wiggled herself astride. The gelding sidled to the wall, but she collected the reins where they hung and took him in hand.

Topper would get her home, and from there she'd set out on her own horse. She adjusted the pack of food she'd strapped to her back. She wished it held jerky and biscuits like Cole's, but Uncle Grant didn't ride the range, so Aunt Marcy's cupboard held neither. What Jenny had taken would have to do.

She clicked her tongue and the horse left the stall and stable. She kicked her heels, and he picked up his stride. She'd have to reach the stable at home without Pearl or James or any of the men hearing her. Maybe she'd leave the horse and creep in on foot. She could sneak quiet as an Indian if she had to.

Mr. Bender looked up as she passed, and she waved shortly. He returned it and went back to loading bags of grain into the waiting wagon. She kicked in her heels again and the gelding broke into a trot. It was painful with no stirrups, and she urged him to a canter. Once away from town, he could slow down, but she didn't want anyone asking questions.

Just outside the Lucky Star yard, Jenny slid from the horse's back and ran for the bunkhouse. This time of day it would be empty, and it afforded a view of both the house and stable. All was quiet, and she crept from her hiding spot to dart across the yard.

If Will were there, he'd catch her, but Will had gone with Aunt Abbie. Jenny found Snowdrop contentedly munching her oats. Curtis and Matt were doing well looking after her. Jenny stroked the soft pink muzzle and white speckled cheek. The horse blew hay-scented breath through her wide quivering nostrils.

Jenny reached for her own small saddle. She could manage that one herself. She stood on the mounting block and fastened the cinch. Normally Will helped her tighten it, but she pulled as hard as she could, then hung her whole weight and dangled beneath the mare's belly. Snowdrop obliged by not bloating her stomach.

Jenny fastened her food bag and a bag of oats to the saddle, then mounted. The yard was still empty, so she walked the horse slowly and quietly. The men must be out with the herd. James was growing deaf and if Pearl was in the kitchen she wouldn't hear. But Zena might see from a window . . . Jenny looked quickly to the house, but all was still.

She walked the mare out the gate and hurried her along. She wasn't sure exactly what way El Paso lay, but she'd ask the travelers she passed. Someone must have seen a man like Cole. They'd notice him for sure, and they'd be willing to help when she told them he was her pa.

Jenny only felt a little twinge now when she said it to herself. He could have been her pa. He should have been. Cole understood her, and he cared. She was now convinced of that. If the bad men hadn't taken him, he might even have told her so. Now he'd have the chance.

She imagined how happy he'd be when she found him. He'd know how hard it was, and how far she'd gone just for him. She pictured his face full of wonder and joy. Aunt Abbie couldn't find him, but Jenny would. She wouldn't give up until she did.

Jenny laughed, and it made a cloud as white as Snowdrop's breath. The cold air stung her cheeks, and she was glad for her heavy woolen coat. Snowdrop would keep her warm at night. She'd snuggle up beside the mare like the picture of Prince Rabadash and his steed, Goldthorn, in her *Tales From Far Lands* book.

When she looked back the first time, the house was small. She looked back again and could scarcely make it out in the vast stretch of land before the foothills and mountains. She'd never been out this far unattended, though she knew the road to the mission as well as anyone.

When she came near the mission itself she'd leave the road and cut over the land, avoiding the homesteads of Miss Nora's friends and family. Jenny wouldn't ask them if they'd seen Cole. But anyone she met after that . . .

Her heart beat quicker. Maybe El Paso wasn't far. Aunt Marcy and Uncle Grant hadn't said how far when she overheard them last night. Aunt Marcy had been whining, of course. She'd said bad things about Aunt Abbie, and Uncle Grant had tried to explain.

Jenny was glad he had because now she knew Cole was in

real trouble . . . hanging trouble. And she knew he was in El Paso. Someone would know where that was. She closed her eyes and imagined him again. That helped her not to be scared.

She pictured the way he rode his horse, so easy in the saddle—like an Indian, Aunt Abbie said. She pictured his walk, his strong stride, his long legs, a little bowed at the knees. She liked that. She pictured his eyes, the color of sagebrush in the spring, with crinkles at their sides.

She pictured the smile he had just for her. It warmed her better than her coat. She raised her face and pretended he tweaked her nose. It didn't bother her when Cole did it. It was affectionate, not teasing.

"Jenny?"

Her eyes flew open. Where had Miss Nora come from? And Mr. McConnel? Her first urge was to kick the mare and run, but that would be no good. Even if they couldn't catch her on foot, they'd send others. No. She had to fool them.

Jenny smiled. "Hello, Miss Nora. Hello, Mr. McConnel."

He tipped his hat and raised a hand to Snowdrop's reins. Jenny felt her heart flip as he took hold.

Nora came close, her hand resting on her hip. "Where be you off to, little Jenny, all by your lonesome?"

"Just riding." Jenny sweetened her smile.

Mr. McConnel glanced around her. "Well provisioned for a ride, aren't you?"

Jenny looked at the food sacks tied to the saddle. "Oh, I just brought a snack for me and Snowdrop."

"And you've ridden all the way from town?"

Jenny looked back to Nora. "From the Lucky Star."

"But I thought you were stayin' with your aunt in town."

Jenny's thoughts spun. "Oh, I was. But now I'm not . . . anymore. Well, I guess I'll just be on my way."

Mr. McConnel tightened his hold of the reins. Jenny's heart fluttered. She felt Nora's hand on her knee. "Suppose you tell us what ye're really about," Miss Nora said quietly.

Jenny felt the blood rush to her face. She'd been caught in a lie. Aunt Abbie would be so shamed.

"Well, I am on a ride."

"That ye are, darlin'. But *why* is what we want to know. And where ye're goin'."

"I'm . . . I'm looking for Cole." Jenny blurted it almost defiantly.

Nora's eyebrows raised, and she glanced at Mr. McConnel.

Jenny felt their joined forces. "You can't stop me, because I mean to find him. Aunt Abbie tried, but she couldn't, and I won't stop until I do!" She felt the fear and fury rising up. Worse, she felt the tears.

Miss Nora stroked her knee. "There, there, *aroon*. We're not meanin' ye harm. Has your aunt come back then?"

"No. But she would have if she'd found Cole. She'd have brought him home by now."

Mr. McConnel steadied the mare with a hand to her muzzle. "El Paso, Texas, is a ways away."

Nora patted Jenny's knee. "Suppose we go to the mission and talk about it over a hot cup of tea with cream."

Jenny felt her indignation fading, and with it her hopes of success. "I think I'll just ride on."

"Come and have a cup, Jenny, and we'll talk it out."

Short of bolting, there was no help for it. Jenny allowed Mr. McConnel to lead the mare. Of all the terrible luck, to meet them on a stroll. She should have been paying attention. She'd never have come this close to the mission with her eyes open. Now everything was ruined.

Mr. McConnel lifted her from the saddle, and Jenny walked despondently behind Miss Nora into the warmth of her kitchen. None of the children were there but Maggie. And Maggie was all grown up now. Jenny gave her a weak smile.

Nora bustled past and hung her coat on the hook. "Now,

then, Maggie dear. Pour us a cup, will ye? And one for Davy. He'll be inside in a minute."

As Maggie poured the tea, Jenny noticed her questioning glance.

All Nora said was, "We've a wee visitor, this day."

"Aye. How are ye, Jenny?" Maggie smiled warmly.

"Fine, thank you." But she didn't feel fine. She tried to keep the sorry look from her face, but she knew it was there. Now she'd never find Cole. She'd never get away again. Aunt Marcy would see to that. She imagined all the dark places Aunt Marcy could lock her up.

Maggie slipped a plate of oatmeal cookies under her nose. They smelled of cinnamon and molasses, but Jenny shook her head.

"Och, that's a gloomy face if ever I saw one." Miss Nora caught her chin and raised it. "Suppose you tell me about this Cole Jasper. I think ye said he was your da."

Jenny flushed. "Well, he's not exactly my pa, not in the real pa way. But I pretend he's my pa. I wish he were."

"And why is that?"

"He's . . . well he likes me, for one."

"Of course he does, darlin'." Nora glanced at Mr. McConnel coming into the room. "So does Mr. McConnel and lots of others. Ye're a fine lass."

"But Cole . . . he's different. He needs me." She hadn't meant to say that part. That was her own secret thought.

"Does he, now? And why is that?"

"Because no one loves him as I do."

Miss Nora sat back. "Now, then, I've not seen for myself, but I think yer aunt might have a thought or two for him. After all, she's gone a'lookin'."

Jenny shook her head sadly. "I thought so, too. But I asked her if she'd brought Cole home to be our pa, and she said no." Jenny saw the smile Miss Nora hid.

Mr. McConnel slid to the bench beside her. "That's not always a good indication." He took the cup before him and slurped the tea. "Sometimes grown women don't admit the things they feel. Not to children, not to the ones they feel it for, and not even to themselves."

Jenny watched his eyes. He had kind eyes, but she felt as though he wasn't speaking just to her. "Why wouldn't they admit it?"

"That's something I can't figure, but I can tell you unequivocally that it's so."

"Then you think Aunt Abbie loves Cole?"

"I think it takes a lot for a woman to go after a man in trouble. Most would say he made his own bed, now let him sleep in it."

Jenny frowned. "Cole didn't do anything wrong. Especially not what they say he did."

Miss Nora nudged her cup toward her. "And how would you be knowin' what they say?"

"I heard Aunt Marcy. I don't care if it was eavesdropping. I never get told things, and I had to know. He's in bad trouble. Hanging trouble, Uncle Grant said. And I mean to find him and get him out of it."

"How?" Mr. McConnel's question was softly asked, but it hit her hard nonetheless.

Jenny clutched her stomach, hoping the knot would go away. "I don't know." She fought the tears. Miss Nora held the tin cup to her and Jenny drank. It was warm and sweet. She took another gulp, and a tear started down her cheek.

"It's all right, aroon. It's in God's hands, ye know."

Jenny shook her head. "No. God takes people away and they never come back. My pa and mama . . . I won't let Him have Cole, I won't!" She threw the cup down and tea splashed all over the table and her dress. She tried to stand, but Mr. McConnel caught her into his arms and held her to his chest.

"Let me go! Let me go!" Tears flooded her eyes.

"Now hold on a minute. We're not gonna stop you doing what you must. But you need to listen here."

Jenny didn't want to listen, but there was something in his tone she couldn't ignore. She sniffed. She'd hear him out if it meant they would let her go on.

"Now, you have to think this thing through. El Paso's hundreds of miles away, close on a thousand maybe. You think you can go a thousand miles on that little mare with what you have in the bag?"

A thousand miles? Could it be so far? Jenny shook her head slowly.

"Even sayin' you could, it's a mighty big world out there. How will you know the way? How will you keep shy of people who wouldn't be nice to a sprig like you? What about bobcats and coyotes . . ."

And wolves.

"And supposing you did find Cole Jasper. What then, Jenny?" Mr. McConnel looked as though he really wondered.

If she could give him an answer . . . But what answer did she have? Jenny felt the lump growing in her throat again.

He cocked his head to the side. "It's an awful big task you're takin' on. It'll be gettin' dark soon and mighty cold. Where are you gonna sleep?"

Jenny looked out the window. Already the sky was the color of her velvet dress at home. Soon it would be black. She felt a shiver creep up her back. All her imaginings had dissolved. What could she do for Cole? How could she even find him?

Miss Nora squeezed her hand. "Ye'll need more than ye have in the bag. I've a fresh loaf and apple jelly if ye want it."

Jenny's stomach rumbled. She'd hardly touched the lunch Aunt Marcy put out, so nervous was she about breaking away. But it was silly to think a loaf of bread would go much farther than the things she'd stuffed into her bag. Not for hundreds of miles.

Jenny shook her head again, the sadness settling deep. "I can't go, can I?"

Miss Nora stroked her cheek. "Ye can if ye've a mind to. But ye won't be gettin' far."

She sniffed. "Aunt Marcy will be hotter than a gunfighter's pistol."

Miss Nora gave her a sympathetic smile. "She'll be that and more. But Davy and I will speak a word on yer behalf."

Jenny realized Mr. McConnel still had a heavy hand on her shoulder. She glanced up at him.

He smiled. "That we will."

"I stole her horse, only I didn't keep it. I just rode it to the ranch to get Snowdrop and left it there."

Mr. McConnel frowned. "I reckon you'll catch it on that one. Some things can't be talked past."

Jenny nodded. "I reckon so." She drew herself up. She'd suffer it for Cole. She'd done it all for him anyway. "I better go now. Before it's all the way dark."

"I'm needin' to go that way myself, sprig," Mr. McConnel said softly. "How about we ride together?"

Jenny's heart skipped with relief. Visions of sleeping under the stars beside Snowdrop had vanished with the sun, replaced by ghostly wolves. She nodded solemnly. "I don't mind."

"Wait for me at the front door. I'll just say good-night to Miss Nora."

Jenny nodded again. Part of her hurt, and she figured that would get worse, but just now she felt a little glad Miss Nora and Mr. McConnel had found her out.

Nora's heart was pounding as Davy sent Jenny off, then turned to her. He'd been wonderful with the child, his arms about her, his gentle concern, his honest discourse. He had neither lectured nor scolded, but had taken her need seriously, though Davy saw well its futility. That was one thing Jaime had lacked. He couldn't see the importance of anyone's fight but his own. And he hadn't had time for the lads and lasses.

As Davy eyed her, Nora's heart kept up its dance. She could hardly keep it from showing through the layers of her bodice. He must have sensed it, for his eyes took on a depth she'd seldom seen. She cleared the awkwardness from her throat. "What is it ye're wantin'?"

He stepped close. "Just a proper sending."

"Well, have it then."

He took her in his arms. "Thank you for the walk, Nora." He bent and kissed her.

Of their own volition, her arms wrapped tightly about him. Was she daft to give her mind and heart away so? "You were fine, Davy. With the lass."

He drew back only inches. "And with you? Just now?"

"Aye. That was fine, too."

He kissed her again, and Nora didn't hold back. What was the use against a heart as big as Davy's?

He smiled broadly. "Now, that's a proper sending."

"Be off with ye, then. Ye've taken more than yer share."

"Oh no, Nora. It's all mine. Soon."

"Go on, or the child'll be off to the wolves without ye."

Davy sent her one more smile. "Soon."

Nineteen

Will didn't get in to see Birdie. Her card was full the first night, and Abbie fretted all the next day. Sam had disappeared, though she suspected she'd find him at the town's graveyard if she looked. But she stayed in the hotel, though the walls were starting to close in on her. She wanted to draw as little attention to herself as possible while Will tried to learn what he could.

Now night was drawing on, and still she sat, fully clothed, drowsing in the chair in her room, waiting. The letters she'd penned to the children lay on the table beside her, sealed and ready for the next day's mail coach. There were a thousand things she could have said to them, but she'd kept the notes short and cheerful.

The letter to Pearl told more, but even it held only a fraction of all there was to say. In neither letter did Abbie explain her current plans, nor express a time for her return. She didn't know either of those herself. When the knock came, it jarred her from her dozing. She rushed to the door and opened it.

Will stood sheepishly in the hall. "I hated to wake you, but you said . . ."

"Yes, Will." She stepped out into the hall. "Tell me."

"I saw Birdie. She's a real small thing, but kinda . . . hard, like she's scarcely a girl at all. I think she's scared. She said she wanted money to see you. I told her I already paid, but she said that was for another thing altogether, and she wouldn't see a penny of it herself."

"How much does she want?"

"Twenty-five dollars."

"Twenty-five! How will I come up with that?"

"I don't know. Maybe you could wire for it."

"But . . . isn't there any other way?"

He shook his head slowly. "She said when you had it, I was to have a drink at the Paloma Blanca. She said not to come in until you had the money. She'll meet you outside the back at four." Will swept the hair off his forehead. "That's in the mornin' as she usually . . . works till then." He slouched. "She acted real tough, but . . . I kinda felt sorry for her."

Abbie frowned. He sounded like Cole. Sorry for a brazen minx who demands that kind of money to see her? "Did you ask about Auralee?"

He shook his head. "I didn't want to scare her off. She already thought I was crazy for not . . . you know."

Abbie suddenly felt exhausted. "Would you go with me to meet her?"

He nodded.

"Thank you, Will. Get some sleep. I'll work on finding the money tomorrow." Abbie sighed. Twenty-five dollars. Even if she could find it . . . No, she refused to think about all the things she needed it for.

* * *

Samuel stood before the rough chalky stone marker on the edge of the graveyard. AURALEE DUBOIS. That was all. At least they'd marked the grave, though he couldn't read it any longer in the darkness. His legs were like stone themselves from standing so long, his hands loose and weary at his sides.

He couldn't picture her dead. He'd not seen her. He had been nursing a drunk headache the day she was buried. He hadn't even heard she was killed. He'd thought . . . thought she was with Cole. Thought maybe they'd ride off together. Thought no man, not even Cole, could withstand her once she got him alone.

The anger was cooling, but he couldn't let it. Mrs. Farrel had planted doubts in his head, but he wouldn't listen. Why would Cole go after Auralee if he had someone like her to love? But he recalled the night they'd sat together, brothers not yet divided.

Hadn't Cole told him then that Mrs. Farrel would have no part of him? She blamed him for her husband's death. She'd given him the kidskin boot. *Cole tried to forget her with Auralee.* Sam stiffened. Cole would get what he deserved. Auralee was dead because of him. His Auralee . . .

The pain choked his thoughts. Sam dropped his face to his palms. She was never his. He'd never laid claim to her because he wouldn't dishonor her. But she'd only laughed at him and made crude jokes he flushed to recall. She'd questioned his manhood, but she'd never questioned Cole's.

Had Cole used his woman? Sam dropped his hands into fists. Knowing wouldn't help. It wouldn't change things. But not knowing was making him crazy. If Cole had used Auralee, he'd . . . what? His brother was already waiting to hang.

Because Cole thinks I did it. Sam looked down at his hands. How? How could Cole think . . . He recalled the knuckles crushing against Cole's jaw. He recalled the fury, the desire to see him bleed. Sam swallowed the tight lump that filled his throat.

He could have killed. If he had found them together he could have. All these years he'd thought he could control it, the rage that burned inside. He felt again the board ripping his flesh, felt the point of it dig into his cheekbone, saw Cole running for his life. A kid too scared to feel shame. Sam felt again the blood spurt from his ear, the dazed numbness he thought was death.

He recalled the smell of the doctor's fingers, the burn of carbolic acid searing his wounds. For the first time he had taken on himself what Cole had endured for years. For the first time he knew what it was to hate his pa. But he'd never let on. He never told Cole he understood. And they never spoke of the man who walked out of their lives a miserable wreck.

Sam and Cole had each other and their unspoken pact to care for their ma. They'd failed there, too. Cole took that bad. He'd gone a little crazy. Sam drew a long, slow breath. Maybe the rage was there in all of them. Maybe the ability, the desire to maim, to kill, was embedded in a man's soul.

Maybe Cole did believe his brother could kill Auralee. So why was Cole taking it on himself? Sam recalled the look in Cole's eyes when he'd stood at his bedside, staring at the bandages. He'd stopped being a boy that day. He'd been shamed into a man. Was it that shame that drove him now?

Sam felt a wicked satisfaction. Hadn't Cole started it all with Auralee? Hadn't he played her fiddle until she sang for him alone? Hadn't he made her crazy when he changed his tune? Hadn't he seen the damage was done?

Sam shook his head. The damage was done. She was gone. Auralee. His Auralee. Never his. Never again. Never at all. He felt the sob rise up from his chest, and this time he didn't fight it.

****

Every time the door opened, Cole expected to see Abbie. Every time it wasn't, he felt relieved and hurt at once. He didn't reckon she'd left town, though she hadn't been in but the once. His last sight of her had been her angry response to his cruel words.

What was it that made them spar so? He should have

thanked her, should have told her how much it meant that she would care enough to come. He should have told her if there was any other way, any way at all . . . But doggone it, he'd told her to go home!

Cole stretched and felt the sharp pain in his left shoulder. The wound hadn't poisoned, thanks to Abbie and, grudgingly, Crete's burning knife. Still, it pained him plenty, especially after the tussle with Gray Wolf.

It was closing into a dark, puckered scar that matched the one on his opposite thigh, just above the knee, the one he'd gotten on Abbie's wedding night. That night he'd been hurting worse inside than any bullet hole. They'd had a right purty wedding, and Mr. Farrel had won her fair and square, but that didn't stop the pain.

Cole leaned against the wall. The Mexicans in the next cell smelled, and he figured he'd be the same if he hadn't asked Gates for a basin of water and a shaving bowl. Even in a hole like this it felt good to be clean. He ran his hand over his mustache.

And if Abbie should come in . . . The hours dragged. He watched the Mexicans play cards for stones. He ignored their sneers. Gates had told him they were in for robbery and murder. They would hang. There were witnesses . . . just like there was for him.

Captain Gates returned from his rounds and stopped outside his cell, holding a pack of Genuine Blackwell Bull Durham smoking tobacco, maybe not the best on the market to Cole's mind, but mighty tempting nonetheless. "Smoke?"

Cole reached automatically, then heard Brother Lewis in his head. "'*If any man be in Christ, he is a new creature.*'" But there was nothing in the Book about smoking tobacco. That was Cole's own idea, first to help his cough, then to prove he could do without it. Now . . .

Cole withdrew his hand. "Naw. I'll pass." He could almost

taste it, but what he wanted even more was a stiff shot of whiskey, the kind Mr. Farrel kept in the house. 'Course, the whiskey might not be there anymore. Abbie had little use for it.

He pictured the big white house with the pink stone and tall pillars. It was fitting she should have a place so nice. She deserved it and any other comforts that came her way. But it was unsettling sitting around that big fancy table, though Cole felt a pang at the thought of never doing it again. Little Elliot with manners like his pa's, Jenny and her saucy ways, Abbie . . . He felt the darkness descending on him. He might be ready to meet his maker, as Brother Lewis claimed, but it sure didn't feel that way.

The daylight faded from the single small window high on the side of his cell. One of the Mexicans snored; the other tossed pebbles at his boot, gathered them up, and tossed them again. Cole felt the wall grow cold against his back.

Gates brought them their supper. It was decent food—beef brisket and roasted potatoes Gates's missus had sent over. This whole time Cole had been showered with gifts of food, some given anonymously through Gates, others by the hands of those who thought they owed Cole something.

Gates snuffed the lamp and left them as night settled. Cole ate, then set the empty tin plate on the floor by the bunk. He cleaned his teeth and washed his mustache, then sat again on the edge of the bunk. His companion's eyes glittered in the dark. The man was staring his way, and Cole just made out a hint of teeth that could be smile or snarl.

"Hey, *gringo*. You are ready to die?"

Cole said nothing.

"Your preacher, he thinks you are ready. I think you are scared."

Cole shifted his legs up on the bunk and lay back. No, it wasn't fear. Not anymore. More like wondering. He'd sure done a whole lot wrong in his life. He would have liked a chance to do some good. For little Jenny maybe, or others.

He'd helped where he could, but it didn't seem complete somehow. He hated to think of Abbie on that long ride home. Would she grieve for him as she had Mr. Farrel?

No, not like that. Not likely. But she might some. It pained Cole to think of it. But she'd go on. Abbie was a survivor. She was made of stiffer stuff than some men he'd known.

Maybe she'd marry again. She was plenty young yet. She ought to have more children. She was real good with kids. Cole tried not to think they could have been his. It'd be enough for her to be happy. He felt a drowsy acceptance of the way things were. *Thy will be done.*

Strange, it wasn't Brother Lewis he heard in his head. It was his ma saying the prayer that contained those words. *Thy kingdom come; Thy will be done.* Cole understood it now, but as a boy he'd wondered what "thy" was.

What exactly would be done? Something that should be, but never was, at least to his ma's way of thinking. Maybe things were better for her now. They must be. They must be real . . . nice. . . .

◆◆◆◆◆◆◆

Abbie stood outside in the dark, afraid that even after all her efforts, Birdie wouldn't show. It had taken four days to transfer Grant's loan from Mr. Driscoll's bank to the bank in El Paso. Had Birdie forgotten her promise? Will had taken a drink at the bar in the main room, just as they'd agreed, but Birdie had paid him no mind.

Now he stood beside Abbie at the back of the saloon, waiting. The watch that hung on her neck said half past four. Abbie searched her heart. Had she misunderstood? Was she outside of God's will? Had she followed the wrong path? She jumped when the door clicked open and Birdie stepped out.

It had to be Birdie. She was small . . . and hard. More like an old woman than the delicate child she appeared. Abbie guessed her true age between fifteen and twenty, but her eyes said fifty at least. The light from the lantern above the back door of the saloon showed that much clearly.

Abbie breathed her relief. "Thank you for seeing me, Birdie. I was afraid you wouldn't come."

Birdie raised one slight shoulder. "I was busy." She flashed her eyes toward Will and back. "You have the money?" She spoke English with a Spanish accent.

Abbie wondered which was her native tongue. Probably both. She handed Birdie the money wired from Grant, the money Abbie could ill afford to lose.

The girl shoved it down her low-cut bodice with a lewd glance at Will. "So talk. He said you wanted to talk." She thumbed Will rudely.

Abbie looked at the narrow oval face, large dark eyes, and straight black hair hanging loose to her waist. The girl's skin was a flawless olive tone, and she recalled Cole's description of Auralee's beauty. Obviously Pablo Montoya carefully chose his wares.

Abbie's throat tightened. "I want to know about Auralee." She hadn't meant to be so blunt, but thoughts of Cole had brought it out.

Birdie's eyes narrowed. "Who are you?"

"Mrs. Abbie Farrel. I'm a friend of Cole Jasper's."

Birdie looked over her shoulder, then searched the woodpile and trash heap. "Who sent you? The captain? Does he not believe me? I saw it all." She clenched her hands at her sides. "Did Cole send you?" A brief concern showed, then passed.

"No one sent me. Do you know Cole?"

Birdie raised her chin with a slight smirk. "Of course. Why wouldn't I?"

Why indeed? Abbie wanted to walk away. Pinch that smug smirk from Birdie's face and walk away. . . . She didn't want to know what Birdie had to say. With sheer will, she drew her next breath. "Please tell me what happened."

"I told the captain. Ask him." She turned for the door.

"Birdie."

The girl stopped, and with the light full on her face, Abbie saw she was no more than sixteen, if that.

"Cole didn't kill Auralee. Who did?"

"You are wasting your time. I have told what I know." Birdie reached for the knob.

"Please . . ." Abbie's spirit sank. "I paid you . . ."

Birdie turned with a shrewd eye. "Perhaps if you come tomorrow, I might remember something I forgot. But remember, my time is valuable."

Abbie clenched her teeth against the furious words that flooded her mind. She closed her eyes and felt her breath come sharply.

Birdie's voice was smooth and clear. "Same time. Same price. Tomorrow."

Abbie felt Will's hand on her shoulder and opened her eyes. Birdie was gone, and they were alone in the alley. She felt close to tears but held them back for Will's sake. She glanced up, but he was staring at the door through which Birdie had disappeared. "Will?"

He startled as though coming to himself and turned to her. "She's afraid to talk."

Abbie's jaw dropped. He could hardly have said anything more naïve. Her anger flared. "Afraid? She's no more afraid than a . . . a rattler or a rabbit. She's using me. Blackmail, plain and simple."

"What are you going to do?"

"I don't know. But I certainly won't put another cent down her sultry little bodice."

Will flushed, but Abbie ignored him. "Come on. We've no more business here."

♦♦♦♦♦♦♦

Abbie tossed in the bed, more restless than she'd been all the nights sleeping on the ground. She flounced to her side and punched the pillow under her cheek. What could she do? Even if she convinced Sam to tell Cole he didn't do it, even if Cole gave up the charade, there was still Birdie's testimony.

It would go before the judge whether Captain Gates wanted it to or not. It was the law, and it would be Cole's word against hers. What man wouldn't deny a crime that would have him hung? If Birdie was convincing . . . and Abbie had no doubt she could be convincing. The little vixen had more tricks than a riverboat gambler.

What grudge did Birdie nurse against Cole? Why would she claim to see him, unless . . . maybe she had seen him. Hadn't Cole said he was with Auralee? Maybe Birdie had seen him there, but not seen what happened. Maybe she just guessed or thought to gain something by lying.

Abbie shook her head. She had to get the truth from that woman. She dropped to her knees on the floor beside the bed. *Dear God, help me to find the truth. For Cole's sake and all those involved. Help me to know your will. . . .* What if it was His will that Cole die?

No. It couldn't be. Not the will of a just God. She had to trust. She had to believe. As Cole did? Had he truly surrendered his heart? Was he following God's will? Was she storming the gates of heaven in vain? Abbie shook her head against the despair inside.

Lord, help my poor faith. I trust you with Cole's life. Guide and direct me to accomplish your will. What else was there but God's will? She could either fight it or accept it. Either way, His will would be done.

Father, make me an instrument of your purpose. Use me as you will. Forgive my doubt, my fear, my weakness. Make me strong. Make me wise. Make me obedient.

Abbie dropped her face to her hands. What if that meant she must fail? Could she watch Cole die? Her chest constricted. *No. Please God. I beg you for his life. Even if I never see him again, please don't ask me to face another death.*

She felt ashamed of her faithless plea. Tears stung her eyes. Here she was thinking of herself when Cole . . . *Dear God, he's in your hands.*

Faith.

There it was, the still small voice she had learned to trust from her youth. Peace washed her, and she closed her eyes, then bit her lip with renewed determination. Now that she knew there was no hope of loving Cole, she could help him unselfishly, for his sake and for the will of God.

Twenty

Nora stirred in her sleep, the dream fresh upon her. *Abbie, walking in a shadowland, huddled in a shawl and staggering, uncertain where to turn. Nora saw the path clearly and tried to call out, but Abbie seemed blinded, dazed, and either she had grown deaf or Nora's cries were mute.*

She shook herself awake. What an odd dream, to picture Abbie uncertain of her path—Abbie who always knew what she intended and went forward to it. But that was the way of dreams. It was Nora's own fears coming out. For on the morrow she'd marry Davy.

She'd held out for Abbie to stand with her, but Davy wouldn't hear it. He had overnight become the stubborn Irishman she'd suspected him to be. She had given him a fingerhold the night Jenny came, and he'd gripped it with both hands. And his hands were the size to wield the tongs and bellows at his da's smithy.

The thought of letting Davy McConnel into her life was fearfully wonderful. But the deed was done. She pressed her face into the pillow's softness. Och, it was her own nerves bringing the dream. Surely Abbie knew exactly what she was about. But just in case, Nora lifted a prayer for her friend.

♦♦♦♦♦♦♦

Abbie walked through the field behind the scatter of buildings that made up El Paso. She listened to the burros bray and the group of black-haired children holler and laugh as they scrapped behind the smithy. The confidence of her prayer the night before was greatly diminished this morning. The doubts had crowded in, and she'd sought the solitude of the fields until Will found her there.

He turned to her and took the grass blade from his teeth. "Maybe I could talk to some of the others, see if anyone else knows something about the night Auralee died."

"That won't change Birdie's testimony." Abbie bent and picked up a white stone, round as a marble. "It all rests with her, but I don't know how to get through."

Will hung his head. "What I don't see is why Cole won't tell the truth. I thought he was honest. He lectured me often enough."

"It's not as though he's lied, Will. He just won't say he didn't do it."

"Isn't that the same thing?"

Abbie fingered the stone and closed it in her hand. "I suppose it is. If only Sam would tell Cole he didn't do it. If only Cole knew he didn't have to protect his brother."

"Have you seen Sam?"

Abbie shook her head. "I don't think he's in town."

"Where would he go?"

She shrugged. "I don't know, Will. I just don't know."

At Will's frown, Abbie sensed his concern. "What is it?"

"Just . . . I heard that judge fella—McFee or something—is expected by the end of the week."

Abbie stopped. "So soon?"

"I only heard it. Down at the general store."

She bit her lip. "Then I have to see Birdie again. There's no help for it."

"But . . . the money . . ."

Abbie spread her hands. "What else can I do?"

"I wish I had it."

She smiled up at him. His hair needed cutting again. He always looked in need of a haircut. Abbie reached out and squeezed his hand. "Thank you, Will."

Half an hour later she stood at the window while the teller counted out the money. Grant had left his last loan open-ended, should she need more, and as the integrity of his standing with the bank in Rocky Bluffs was already established, the bank in El Paso would draw the loan against his account, for a slight amount of interest. Abbie had only to sign the note.

Doing this rankled, but at the moment Birdie held all the cards. She trembled to think what would happen if the demands continued. At what price would she value Cole's life? At what point would she stop paying and let him hang?

With a sigh Abbie slipped the cash from the teller into her pocket. She turned from the counter and met Sam's gaze. He must have come in behind her. By the look of his eyes she wasn't sure he'd slept in days, but there was no smell of whiskey, and he seemed sober and lucid.

"Good morning, Sam." Her voice came softly.

He tipped his hat automatically. "Mrs. Farrel."

"Will you join us for breakfast? Will is at the hotel."

"No, I . . . think I'll be movin' on."

Abbie stared at him. "You can't mean that. You won't leave town with Cole in jail, waiting to . . . to hang for a crime he thinks you committed."

Sam dropped his chin. "Cole can stand on his own two feet. It's time he did."

"But he won't if he thinks they'll come after you."

"That's his problem. No one's said anything about me bein' with Auralee. If he hadn't gone up there, he wouldn't be in this fix."

Abbie saw something flicker behind his eyes. Was it a twinge of conscience or a lust for blood? "At least talk to him,

Sam. Tell him you had nothing to do with it."

"If he had half your sense, he'd see that for himself. He knows me."

"Does he?" She felt her anger besting her. "Would he die for a brother who hasn't the guts to stand up for him? Will you let him die because Auralee saw something in Cole that you lacked?" Abbie saw Sam's jaw stiffen, but he held his peace. "Can you live the rest of your days knowing the real killer is living free?"

He spread his hands, then closed them into fists. "It don't matter. It won't bring her back."

"And hanging Cole will?"

"He don't have to hang. That's up to him. He ain't in there to protect me. He's in there to ease his guilty conscience."

"That's not true."

"Ain't it?" Sam's cheek twitched. "Suppose you ask him. Suppose you find out why he took to Auralee."

Abbie's chest constricted. "I know why. Does that mean I should hang, too?"

Sam cocked his jaw to the side and held her angry gaze. "I reckon only you know that." He slowly tipped his hat and walked away.

"Sam!"

He stopped at the door and turned.

"I will free Cole."

He shook his head. "Not likely. Not with the tale Birdie has to tell. Not even you can change that."

Abbie wet her lips. "I've spoken with her once. I'll see her again tonight."

Sam drew his brows together and scrutinized her. "You're messin' with things you don't understand. If Pablo gets wind of your meddlin'—"

"I'll just see that he doesn't. No one knows but you and Will."

"And Birdie."

Abbie thought of the money in her pocket. Would Birdie double-cross her? Did this Pablo put her up to it? Or was Birdie playing a game of her own? "I'll just have to take that chance."

Sam spoke slowly, as though the words came from a recess in his mind that had grown dusty with lack of use. "I wish you luck, Mrs. Farrel." Again he tipped his hat, then walked out.

Sam stepped into the street, and for a moment he envied his brother. Abbie Farrel might be a hard nut, but at least Cole had hope. Maybe that's what hurt the most. There was no hope now, not once a person was gone.

He'd looked that truth in the eye these last days. He'd cried like a baby, holed up in the shack where he'd grown up. He'd been tempted to lose himself in booze. Instead, he'd let the raw pain sear him like a smelting fire. He wasn't sure what was left. Maybe nothing. Nothing at all.

◆◆◆◆◆◆◆

This time Birdie seemed edgy. Abbie watched her eyes dart back and forth across the yard, saw her flinch at any sound. Birdie caught the hair back from her face with her fingers and let it cascade over her shoulder like silken thread. The motion was practiced, but her fingers trembled.

"What do you want? Why are you doing this?"

Abbie tried to look determined and not as desperate as she felt. "Because an innocent man will hang unless you tell the truth."

"Innocent? What is innocent? I have men at my door all night long. But they are not there to protect me." Her voice held a bitter edge.

"Protect you from whom? If Cole is guilty, who do you fear?"

Birdie's eyes shot to the door behind her, and Abbie thought she might run. What had happened between now and their last meeting? Had Abbie's questions made the girl consider what she was doing? Or was it something else?

Birdie rubbed her wrists and hesitated, then drew a sharp, sudden breath. "If I talk, I'm dead, too. This life, it's better than lying in the graveyard."

Abbie searched for words of assurance. Could she appeal to Birdie's conscience? Could she—

"We'll take you out of here."

Abbie spun with Birdie at Will's words. What was he doing? What was he saying?

He straightened. "Tell us the truth, and we'll get you out of here safe."

Abbie watched the doors close in Birdie's mind. Her eyes grew dull and hard, absolutely dead. Abbie had never seen eyes so cold, so void of feeling.

"Sure you will, caballero." Birdie's voice was mocking and cruel. "You and a hundred others." She swept the hair in a shimmering stream from her face. "What do you want in return? A little sugar?" She stretched her delicate fingers to Will's shirt, and Abbie watched the shock of it register in his face.

"We want to help Cole." Abbie said it plainly. "And we'll help you, too." She hadn't planned on that, but Will's intent was clear. And it might be the only way. "I give you my word."

"Your word?" Birdie's eyes stabbed her with the same derision she'd seen in Lil's. "Oh, *sí*, the word of a lady. You know the best part of all this? The judge will take my word." She smacked her hand to her breastbone defiantly, but Abbie saw a confused mixture of pain and hatred in her face.

Birdie narrowed her eyes. "What is Cole to you?"

"A friend."

"You lie."

The words sank deeply into Abbie's soul. How dare this . . . this . . . woman call her a liar? Was it a lie? Was Cole only a friend? Was he even that? Was he more? How could this person think to know her heart, when she didn't know it herself?

"You think I do not know a lie when I hear one? 'Oh, Birdie, you are the only one. I love you. I will come back and marry you. Just you wait.' "

Abbie swallowed her indignation. One angry word now could ruin everything. At least Birdie was listening. She'd almost admitted her story was untrue. . . .

Abbie drew a long breath. "We will take you out of here."

"Why should I believe that when you lie about Cole?"

Abbie forced her heart to steady. "The truth is I don't know what Cole is to me. I . . . care for him, and I don't want him to hang for something he didn't do."

Birdie dropped her eyes. For a moment Abbie saw a young girl, uncertain and . . . afraid. Will was right. He'd seen something Abbie's eyes had missed. Birdie's head jerked up, and she whispered, "I cannot tell you. He'll kill me."

"He?"

Birdie shook her head, trembling. "He will knife me as he did Auralee."

"He won't." Abbie held her gaze, willing her courage.

"My room and hers, they join up. I wasn't working. I was sick. I heard . . . I tried not to listen, but then he came into my room. He had blood all over him, all over the knife. He asked who'd been with Auralee. I only knew Cole. I had heard them talking just before, arguing."

Birdie shuddered. "He was pleased when I said Cole. He told me to name Cole. Then he . . . rubbed her blood on my throat. He said I would be next if I crossed him. I know better than to cross Cre . . ." Her mouth froze in a grimace.

"Crete? Crete Marlowe?"

Birdie moaned. "You must get me away. If Pablo knows I told . . ."

"Pablo Montoya knows it was Crete?"

Birdie's voice rose a pitch. "He knows Crete was last with Auralee, but he said Crete was with me."

"Why? Why would he protect Crete Marlowe?"

"Money. He can make Crete pay for his silence." Birdie gripped the doorframe. "You take me out of here as you promised, or I will swear it was Cole and watch him hang." She heard a step inside and paled. She pointed to Will. "Send him after me in one hour." Birdie pulled open the door.

"*¿Que pasa alli?*"

Abbie heard the male voice, but Will pulled her out of the light and away before she caught Birdie's reply. She held tightly to Will's large-boned hand as they rushed through the alley to the back of the hotel. Then she leaned against the wall and caught her breath.

Crete Marlowe. The one who came hunting for Cole was the one who'd killed Auralee? He had hunted Cole for his own crime?

"You're shaking."

She gripped Will's hands. "What are we going to do about Birdie?"

"I'm goin' for her tonight. I'll take her straight to that Captain Gates, then light out of town. Can I . . . take her to the ranch? I mean, if she has nowhere else to go?"

Abbie felt the pulse in his hands, and they warmed. What had she gotten him into? "I guess so, Will, but . . ."

"Be ready to go in an hour."

"I can't leave until they let Cole out."

Will shook his head. "I don't know . . . that Pablo . . . You didn't see him, Mrs. Farrel. He has eyes like . . . He's a man who will kill."

She rubbed her temples. "I can't leave, not without seeing Cole freed."

"Then follow as soon as you can. And don't let anyone connect you with Birdie. No doubt Pablo will be lookin'."

Abbie was amazed by Will's manly tone. But then, she reminded herself again, Will was no longer a boy. She went up to her room and lay without sleeping. The few hours of sleep she'd gotten before meeting Birdie left her weary but unable to sleep again.

What was Will doing? She pictured him pacing his room, waiting for the hour to pass. But no. He would be packing up, making preparation to travel. They still had supplies from Santa Fe. They'd used little of it since reaching El Paso.

What of a horse? A horse for Birdie? Abbie's thoughts spun. She forced them to still. Will would figure it out. This was his cause, not hers. She must see Cole freed. Abbie sank her head back into the pillow.

With Birdie's testimony removed, they would have no cause to hold him. Cole might even be out that day. Her heart quickened, but not with the elation she might have expected. She pressed her fist to her forehead and closed her eyes. It would mean another good-bye.

Her task was accomplished. Her honor satisfied. Cole would be exonerated and now . . . What? Abbie's breath came in a half sob. *Oh, Lord. Give me strength to do the right thing.* She would be alone, but alone was better than compromising what she knew love could be.

A tear crested and made a slow channel down her cheek to catch in the hair at her temple. If only it hadn't been so right with Monte. Maybe then she could have loved again. Her heart was willing, but her mind, her memories . . . God had given her one perfect love. She could never expect that again.

More tears burned and fell. The short years she'd had with her husband would have to sustain her. And she had Elliot, the fruit of their love, Monte's legacy. She had her memories. What more did she need?

Twenty-One

Cole was jarred awake by the door banging open and a streak of pale daylight. He rose to one elbow as Captain Gates passed in, much too early for any normal matter of business. The captain looked as though he'd been roused in a hurry. Had the judge arrived?

Gates strode forward, jammed the key into the lock on Cole's cell, and turned it. "Cole Jasper, I'm tired of havin' you in my jail." Both of Cole's neighbors stared wide-eyed as the cell door swung open. "Well, go on. Get out."

Cole came fully upright on the bunk. "What the heck are you doin', Gates?"

"Charges against you are dropped. The witness gave us the real story. It wasn't you she saw at all."

Sam. Cole felt his chest lurch. His throat went dry. "Who, then?" The rasp was pathetic.

"Marlowe. Crete Marlowe."

Cole stared at the captain as if he'd spoken some language Cole didn't know. "But you sent Marlowe after me."

"I didn't send him. If he came after you, it was his own doing. Anyway, the warrant's out for him now, and you are a free man."

Cole stood, but he wasn't sure he was awake. "Why'd your witness change the story?" He hadn't bothered to ask who the witness was, but now he had his suspicions.

"Your lady got through to her."

"My . . ." *Abbie.*

"Seems Marlowe threatened Birdie with the same as he did to Auralee if she named anyone but you."

Cole frowned, picturing the little raven-haired wisp. He could hardly blame her. She must've been plenty scared. It suddenly hit him. "You mean I've been rottin' here in place of Crete Marlowe?"

"Looks that way, you stubborn son of a gun. What the heck did you think you were doin'?"

Cole buckled on the gun belt Gates handed him and reached for his hat. "I figured someone mistook me for Sam. You know how he was about Auralee."

"So you were gonna hang in his place?"

"I was hopin' it wouldn't come to that."

Gates quirked an eyebrow. "Ever consider bein' a lawman again? Anyone with your kind of death wish ought to do just fine." He clamped Cole's shoulder. "I could use a deputy."

"I'll think on it." Cole quirked his mouth. "But not too hard."

"I guess not—not with that purty lady waitin' for you."

Cole felt none too sure about that. "Where is she?"

"Guess she headed back to the hotel after the young fella skipped town with Birdie."

"Will?"

"He's takin' her out of harm's way, back to your lady's ranch."

His lady. Cole's heart jumped in his chest, but things were far from settled in that area.

"I got Birdie's *X* on her statement, should we catch up to Marlowe anytime soon. But I may be calling for her if it comes to it."

What was Gates running on about? Oh, Birdie. Little Birdie with a smile of promise and a heart of quicksand. God help

Will. It suddenly sank in what the boy was up to. And what would Pablo have to say about it? This was trouble Cole hadn't counted on. Did it never end?

Cole almost wished he could go back to that sleepy place of acceptance. But no, he was a free man again. His grin probably looked as stupid as it felt. He didn't care. *And the truth shall set you free.* The truth. Could he tell Abbie the truth?

"As for the lady, I wouldn't be looking any further if I were you, Cole."

"I ain't plannin' to. But she's got a mind of her own."

"No mistaking that." Gates clapped his back. "But you're up to it, I reckon."

"We'll see." Cole took a step toward the door and inhaled the early morning air. He cleared the doorway and stepped out onto the walk. Every step seemed a true pleasure. He could direct his feet, go whichever way he chose. He was free.

He eyed the street, the hotel, and Abbie's horses outside it. She was shy a packhorse and Will's bay, but the others stood ready, packed up. So she was leaving. Without word. Or had she wanted him to come to her? Cole started along the walk, hesitated, then continued on. He owed her his thanks at the least.

He stopped outside the hotel door. Should he go in? The eastern sky glowed orange under a hazy pink. It was early yet. What if she'd gone back to sleep? He could wait. He could . . .

She came out dressed to travel in a riding skirt and fitted jacket buttoned to her neck. She looked prettier than any woman had a right to be. But her face was set, determined. He knew that look. It had shut him out more years than he could count.

Cole pulled the hat from his head and forced the lump from his throat. Still, the words were slow in coming as they stood and looked, one on the other. "I came to thank you." He was gratified that his voice showed none of his distress.

Abbie's expression softened. "No thanks are needed, Cole. I only did what you'd have done for me, what you have done in the past."

The past. "You're ridin' this mornin'? Alone?"

"If I travel fast, I'll catch up with Will. Birdie won't be used to the saddle." Her words were frank, her tone matter-of-fact.

"I reckon not." Cole ran his hand through his hair and replaced his Stetson. It was now or never. Could he live with himself if he didn't take the one last chance he'd likely have with her? "I got someplace I'd like to show you before you go, if you can spare the time."

Abbie nodded slowly and none too eagerly. "I can spare it." She motioned toward the horses tied at the post. "Brother Lewis returned Whitesock, but I intended to leave him for you."

"Thank you, Abbie." He took the bags and bundles from her and tied them onto the horse beside Zephyr. "What's Birdie ridin'?"

"Will purchased a mare from the livery with the money I . . . money Birdie had."

Birdie? Unless she'd gotten a whole lot better at pinching wallets, Birdie had no such wherewithal. Abbie must have paid to make her talk. That would have set Abbie back badly, if he knew Birdie.

Cole saw Abbie's flush and knew his guess was right. How much had it cost her to get him free? And why had she done it? Why not? She had a good heart, even if it was as closed to him as it seemed.

Abbie had meant to seek out Cole before leaving, to say good-bye in as sensible a manner as possible. She wanted it to be brief and unemotional. She had not expected to come upon him with the morning sun in his hair and its reflection in his eyes.

She didn't want to know what he felt, what he wanted. It was better for both of them to part friends, without saying or doing anything they'd regret. It was better to leave the possibilities in the dust of El Paso. It was time to go home.

But Abbie couldn't refuse him the simple request, and now she felt the silence grow between them as they rode the horses away from the ferry after crossing to the older Juarez. She fought to keep her emotions from rising to the fore. They were too confused, too dangerous. Yet she was painfully aware of him beside her as they rode the river valley to the edge of town and beyond.

Abbie looked ahead and saw a weathered earthen hut. The door was lost or stolen, and the opening gaped darkly. As they drew close, she saw a piece of canvas hanging from a window like a flap of skin on a sightless eye. The stoop was choked with weeds and likely crawled with things better left undisturbed.

Cole reined in and crossed his wrists over the saddle horn. His gaze looked pensive and . . . pained. Surely this wasn't what he meant to show her, this desolate, forsaken place. But he didn't move on.

Abbie turned to him, confused. "What is this place?"

He swung down and led Whitesock a couple paces forward. "This is my home."

Abbie felt her lips part as she looked at it with new eyes. The heap of rotted wood on the side might have been a barn or shed at one time, and her gaze was drawn to the burned-out stump of a tree. Images of a woman hanging by her arms, flames and arrows . . . Pressing her eyes shut, Abbie shuddered and slowly climbed down from the saddle.

Cole didn't look her way. "Belongs to Sam now, though it ain't worth much. Not like those across the river, stateside. The place was goin' down even before my pa left. Sam and I scratched the ground some, raised enough to fill our bellies.

Ma tried to patch up the place as best she could, but with the floodin' and the droughts . . ."

He spread his hands. "After pa left, she hadn't much to go on, so Sam took jobs where he could find 'em. When I was twelve we signed on together at a spread owned by cattlemen up from San Antone."

He looked along the river valley as though imagining the herds grazing there. "When we weren't workin' the herd, we were drivin' mules and haulin' freight, or raidin' the vaqueros' range and drivin' home the wild horses. At night, Sam taught himself to read and write. I learned to bust broncs."

Cole let the reins hang and rubbed the back of his neck. "Good money in that, but it's hard on your innards. You void blood often enough, you get to thinkin' there must be a better way. Only sometimes no other way shows itself. So you do what you gotta do till you're the best there is. But that don't keep you from makin' mistakes."

Abbie listened. Though the picture he painted was painful, it explained his fierce independence, his gruff and caustic ways, his need to control and his commitment to good. From what she'd overheard during her days in El Paso, the town's esteem for him was unparalleled.

"You were born here, in Mexico?"

"I was born in San Antonio. We moved here when I was five. I suspect my pa was runnin'."

"From the law?"

He shook his head slightly. "I doubt it. Most of his crimes were legal."

Abbie waited, but he didn't elaborate.

Cole stood without speaking, then kicked the dirt. "I've never brought anyone here before."

She heard the vulnerability in his voice and resisted its tug on her heart. She couldn't, she wouldn't . . . Abbie drew herself up. "Not Auralee?" Her voice had an edge she hadn't intended.

"Or Birdie or any of the others?"

"The others?"

"You've traveled around. I imagine there are broken hearts in more than just El Paso."

"I ain't sure where you're gettin' your imaginings." Cole turned to face her. "Abbie, I . . . never had relations with Auralee or any other."

She felt the blood rush to her face. "What?" It came out more breath than voice. "But you told me . . ."

"No, I didn't. You were just so ready to believe it, I didn't argue."

Abbie's temples started to throb. What was he trying to do? "I saw you with Lil . . ."

"You saw what you wanted to see. You marched in believin' the worst."

Now her anger gained strength. "You made very little effort to dissuade me. And how did Birdie know you, then? And Auralee? You said you were with her the night she died."

"I hate to be the one to educate you on how those places work, but there are different levels of involvement. The downstairs is public, just like the saloon in Rocky Bluffs. A man can pay for a drink and a dance and pretend for a while that somebody cares. Least until the music stops."

"And that's all you did."

"The one time I paid entrance to an upstairs room was the night Auralee died."

"Why then?" Abbie's throat cleaved, and her voice came out thin and tight.

"I thought she was in trouble."

Abbie felt her defenses crumbling. She didn't want to believe it, but how could she not? Cole could no more resist helping a woman in need than . . . Her anger stirred. "Why were you there at all, in that sort of place?"

Cole slouched. "Well, Abbie, the truth is a man gets lonesome for a purty smile and a soft voice. With another kind of woman you set up expectations, and that ain't fair. But those in the business, they're just doin' their job."

Abbie heard the gentle compassion he felt for the women who offered him a soft word and pretty smile. The fight left her, and she felt . . . ashamed; ashamed for condemning Cole for seeking solace in his loneliness and judging the women who gave it.

It didn't make it right, not by a long shot. Some things were wrong no matter the circumstances. But it wasn't for her to condemn. If Cole had never more than kept company . . . How could she know? How could she be certain?

He must have seen her doubt. "Two things my ma taught me—never underestimate a woman and never take advantage of a lady. Some folks draw a line between the two. Me, I consider them all ladies."

Abbie's conflicting shame and relief were swallowed by the sudden pulsing rush that swept her. She couldn't help thinking how much he'd changed from the cocky trail boss who'd told her dancing was just like roping only gentler. But then, maybe he hadn't changed so much after all. Maybe now she just saw beyond his crusty edge.

What had Cole said with that confident grin all those years ago? "*Dancin's easier than ropin' cuz every girl wants to be caught.*" Abbie fought now to keep from proving him right.

"If you were lonely, Cole, why did you never marry?" It was a feeble attempt.

"I reckon you know the answer to that."

Abbie was sure he must hear her heart pounding from where he stood. She took one step closer, drawn by his green eyes, by his suntanned features, straight nose and jaw, by his firm mouth half-covered with a mustache in need of a trim. She remembered the feel of his mustache. . . .

He didn't move, didn't reach for her.

Her lips trembled. "Aren't you going to kiss me, Cole?"

He parted his mouth slowly. "No, I ain't."

His expression betrayed nothing. Abbie was suddenly young and uncertain. "You don't want to?"

"I want to."

She searched his face, trying to discern what he felt. Anything at all?

"If I kiss you now, it won't stop there. I'll want to kiss you tomorrow and the next day and every day after. I've spent too many years wantin' to kiss you, Abbie. But if you tell me one more time that you cain't love me, I'll walk away now and not come back."

Abbie's heart rushed in her chest. She reached for his hand, firm and strong under her fingers, but he still made no move. His own honor, disguised behind the character of a cowboy, kept him back. He wouldn't settle for less than everything, not this time.

Lord, help me. I don't know which way to turn. Lose him forever or . . . or risk . . . A deep, fearful warmth passed through her, then peace so profound it took her breath. She almost felt the hand of God nudging her onward. Her gaze met Cole's, the waiting evident in his eyes. "I love you, Cole."

Abbie wasn't sure if she'd actually said the words, or if her heart had just thrummed it through her being. But Cole's expression deepened with a look almost painful as he enclosed her hand in his.

"I asked you this a long time ago. Now I'm askin' again. Abbie, will you be my wife?"

His face held the same raw, unconditional love she'd seen the day he meant to die for her. She didn't deserve it, didn't deserve his steadfast devotion. She knew him now. She'd seen into the depths of his soul, his failings and his goodness. He seemed no longer rough but . . . noble.

"Yes."

Cole stood a moment as though she hadn't spoken, then pulled a slow grin. "I'll be. I'd have gone down on my knee if I thought you'd say yes."

Abbie gave him a shaky smile. "You still could if you're inclined."

He drew her close. "I reckon I could. Or I could take care of that need."

"What need?"

"As I recall you were just beggin' a kiss."

"I wasn't begging."

"What then?"

"Offering."

He wrapped her cheek in his callused palm. "I accept." He kissed her long and slow.

Abbie's heart beat a powerful response, drawn in by the call of his own. She caught her breath, then tried to sound frank and sensible. "We can speak with Father O'Brien on the way home."

Cole cupped her face in both hands. "We can speak with the priest if you like, but first we'll have us a ceremony with Brother Lewis. Sheez, Abbie, I've waited eight years."

Twenty-Two

Abbie stood facing Cole under the cottonwoods on the rise above the old cabin. In her blue woolen skirt and jacket bodice, brushed clean of trail dust, she looked presentable enough, but it was hardly what she'd call wedding clothes. Cole had purchased a six-dollar suit that looked as out of place on him as Monte had looked in dungarees.

No, don't think about it. Don't question. Don't doubt. But how could she not? Had her feelings once again held sway over her judgment? Had she only imagined God's blessing? Why else would she now feel so . . . terrified? The December air was cold, but her palms were slick in Cole's hands.

She'd thought to have time to let the decision sink in, to get used to loving Cole, to . . . let go. This immediacy, this . . . finality, the irrevocable words . . . and what would follow . . . *Oh, Lord.* Yes, she loved him, but . . .

Cole cocked his head just slightly, and his eyes narrowed, making fine lines at the edges. The chilly wind ruffled his hair like a cockscomb, and the creases on either side of his mouth deepened. He saw her hesitation; he knew.

No. Yes. Abbie's throat was tight and dry. The wind caught her hair and carried it. She should ask him to wait. *Wait? Until when?* Would she ever be ready? Would it be different two months, six months from now, a year, five years, or ten?

Brother Lewis's question hung in the air, caught away by

the wind, but there ... waiting for her reply. *Do you take Cole Matthias Jasper to be your lawfully wedded husband ... until death do you part?*

Until death. Joined until death. Did death part two hearts that beat as one? Was she severed from Monte by the grave? If Cole took her in his arms and loved her, would they join? Would it be the same? Could it ever be the same?

Please, God. But no voice came. Had God already shown her the way? Was it now hers to accept or reject what He had given? Cole waited, impassive, neither forcing nor pleading. Cole Jasper who had been part of her life so long now. Cole who forgave even her ugliest parts ...

Abbie didn't know what to feel, and for once she was glad of that. She didn't want her emotions to make the choice. She must take this on faith, choose to commit her life to this man whom God had provided, no matter how unlikely.

Had Cole truly surrendered to God? She thought for a moment of Gray Wolf. Hadn't God used him? Was it any less likely that Cole was in His hands? She had a hard time seeing Cole submissive even to God, yet ... there was something, some depth she hadn't seen in him before, a humility ... an acceptance. Trust.

Brother Lewis cleared his throat.

Abbie trembled. "I do." It came from her, but her throat shook, bearing witness to her doubt.

The tension in Cole's jaw released, but his mouth kept the same line as he slipped the ring on her finger. His eyes probed, offering ... what? A chance to turn back? Take back her vow?

Brother Lewis covered their joined hands with his. "Cole and Abbie Jasper, I now pronounce you man and wife, and may God guard your promise all the days of your life together." He smiled. "Cole, you may kiss your bride."

Cole bent and brushed her lips with his. There was nothing of his passion in the kiss. It was the seal of their testament, but no more. Abbie waited in surprise, but he straightened, turned to Brother Lewis, and extended his hand.

"Thank you, Brother. It was a fortunate bend that brought our trails together."

Brother Lewis matched Cole's grip. "Fortune had nothing to do with it, Cole. It was God Almighty and His wondrous ways."

Cole turned, and Captain Gates gripped his hand. "Congratulations, Cole." He tipped his hat to Abbie. "Ma'am." Then he and another man Cole had introduced, but whose name Abbie forgot, signed their names as witnesses and strode away down the hill.

Cole took the license from Brother Lewis and tucked it into his vest. It was done, settled and permanent according to the law. Cole and the preacher spoke briefly, saying their goodbyes, but Abbie felt rooted to the ground.

Brother Lewis gripped her hands warmly. "God bless you, Mrs. Jasper."

Mrs. Jasper. It jolted her as though she'd been suddenly changed. She was no longer the person she'd been, the person she'd dreamed of being and become. She was Mrs. Montgomery Farrel no more. Her mind closed in, and she felt dazed.

Abbie stood alone with Cole on the hill. He was silent, but his questions, his disappointment shown in his eyes. She offered him a thin smile. What was wrong with her? This man had proved again and again his integrity, his fidelity, his love. An hour ago her heart had pulsed with passion for him. Why did it now beat with fear and uncertainty?

Cole reached for her hand and brought it to his lips, then closed her fingers between his palms. "How much of a start did you give Will and Birdie?"

She felt thick-headed and stupid. "What?"

"Will and Birdie. When did they start out?"

"This morning, before dawn."

"Then I reckon we'd better ride." He kept hold of her hand and started down the hill at a saunter.

Abbie stumbled beside him. Did he mean to go, to leave without . . . would he not consummate their marriage? Didn't he expect . . . "Cole—"

"Mr. Farrel told me something I never forgot. He said when you get a new foal, fresh into the world, you go over it with your hands real gentle. You don't rush and you don't force it. That way it comes to know you and remembers your touch."

What was he doing? Why was he speaking of Monte now? Why churn up old memories, emotions, sorrows?

Cole stopped and turned. "He said he wouldn't touch you until he had a touch he wanted you to remember."

Abbie's heart seized. Was Cole intentionally hurting her, paying her back for her indecision?

He cupped her cheek with his palm. "I reckon now I know what he meant. It has to be right, and here and now there are too many things workin' against us. When you're ready, and when we ain't fightin' time and trouble, then I will love you."

Abbie felt the warmth of his palm on her face. She heard the tenderness in his words. He was giving her time. Without her asking. He knew her heart, and it again surged with love for him. Would she ever get it right?

She touched her fingers to his jaw, felt his wind-chapped skin, smooth shaven for the occasion. Her gaze went to his mouth, to the line of his lips, to the overhang of his freshly trimmed mustache. She felt a quickening, and she wanted his kiss, wanted it badly.

His mouth pulled slowly sideways. "Don't make it hard on me, Abbie. We got a lot of miles ahead."

"Don't you even mean to kiss me?"

"Sheez!" Cole pulled her into a rough embrace and kissed the crown of her head.

That wasn't what she meant, but he set her back and

started down at a quicker pace, tugging her along. "I reckon by the time we're packed up and on our way, those two will be restin' the horses and settin' off again. We'll have to cut a good clip to catch them by nightfall."

"Well, if not tonight . . ."

"You don't know what you're sayin'. You set that boy's foot in a bear trap, sendin' him off with Birdie."

"But surely . . ."

Cole gathered Zephyr's reins and held her while Abbie swung up. Then he mounted Whitesock and brought its head around. Once more he was the cowboy, one with his horse and in control. "Trust me, Abbie. We ain't got a spare minute."

She followed him into town at a canter. His words were clear enough, but she couldn't help wondering if it was Will he feared for, alone with Birdie, or himself.

♦♦♦♦♦♦♦

Cole led the packhorses at an easy lope, with Abbie riding beside him. His wife. On paper at least. It shamed him, the disappointment he felt. What did he expect? He'd rushed her. He'd thought her acceptance was more than it was. Maybe she loved him as she said, respected and accepted him, but her heart wasn't his. Maybe it never would be.

Could he live with that? Cole shrugged away the doubt. He would, if it came to it. She'd made the vow, though it took everything in her to get it out. She could have refused, but she didn't. She took him as her husband, the same as he pledged himself to her. They would build on that promise.

The daylight was nearly spent. If they didn't find Will and Birdie soon, they'd have to camp separately—something he'd just as soon avoid, all things considered. But it was getting cold, and they couldn't go on in the dark. Will had probably stopped already and set up camp with whatever he had.

Abbie had sent them minimally supplied so they could ride

fast. And that was good. Birdie's fear of Pablo Montoya was well grounded. He didn't let his doves loose without a fight. Cole had heard the whispers of a search beginning as he and Abbie packed up and resupplied in town.

So far the runaway hadn't been connected to them, but as soon as she was, Pablo would make his move. Cole looked back over his shoulder. With Abbie's conditioning, they had made good time and spread some miles behind them. The same wouldn't hold for Birdie.

If she'd ever been on horseback, it couldn't have been much. Pablo kept a tight rein on his girls. Abbie had no idea what she'd done in freeing that bird. But now that they were in it, they'd see it through.

"There." Abbie pointed. "There's a fire, Cole."

He picked out the prick of light in the darkness ahead. "You're right. I don't suppose too many folks are travelin' this time of year, but we'll take it slow anyway." He reined to a walk, unwilling to mention all the possibilities of who could be sitting around that fire. They'd see soon enough.

But once the blaze was a discernible glow, Abbie hurried the mare toward the camp.

"Abbie . . ."

She kept on, and Cole matched stride, trying not to take her eagerness personally. Two figures huddled near the flames, one large, one small. Cole relaxed. They'd found their party, but that didn't mean they were out of trouble, from without . . . or within.

Abbie swung down and rushed to Will. "You did it!"

He rose awkwardly and caught her outstretched hands. He grinned like the boy he was, regardless of his size and years. Then something caught his attention, and he stared from Abbie's hand to her face, then to Cole's. "You . . . you got hitched?"

The ring. He'd noticed the gold band with rose-colored

tracery. Cole hadn't meant to make a deal of it, but that Will, he was observant. And there was Abbie with her hands still caught in the boy's, though she was none too quick to explain.

"Yeah, we got hitched. Now, why don't you see to these horses while Abbie cooks up some grub." Cole hadn't meant to sound so gruff. He saw Abbie's puzzlement and hurt. Well doggone, he was only human. How many emotions could a man juggle in one day?

Cole looked at last at Birdie. Her dark eyes were sharp on him, like those of a hawk. She was a twisted-up child with enough wiles to outsmart the nation's governing body. Her gaze went to Abbie, and he didn't like what he saw.

He rubbed the back of his neck and crouched beside the fire. "Pablo got any idea what you're up to?"

Birdie shrugged. "It may have occurred to him by now. He has eyes to see."

"I mean, does he know you took off with Will?"

"I did not take off with Will." Her voice dripped scorn.

"Does he know you're travelin' with us?"

She fanned the glimmering veil of black hair over her shoulder with one splayed hand. "He may. He is not *estúpido*, eh?"

"Did you tell anyone else what you were doin'?"

"Oh sí. I mentioned it to all the upright citizens of El Paso."

Cole felt like shaking her.

"Listen, Birdie, we're in this together. If Pablo comes lookin', it'll take all of us to keep you safe."

"What is it to you?" She turned so the fire outlined her fine profile. "You are free now, regardless."

"That ain't the point. Abbie gave you her word . . ."

"Oh sí." Birdie's chin raised. "Her honorable word." She combed the hair back with her fingers. It was a calculated move. She knew what that hair did to men. She knew how to use her beauty to slice through men's defenses. Pablo had trained her well. "But she has kept it already, no?"

Cole wet his throat. "It's not likely we'll abandon you now." *Unless you're more trouble than it's worth*, he wanted to add.

"How gallant, Cole Jasper. And on your wedding night." She shrugged and both the blanket and blouse slid off one shoulder.

Cole restrained the urge to shake her silly. He stood and helped Abbie gather up the pots and supplies to make their supper. Things could get real difficult if Birdie kept up that chatter in Abbie's hearing. He had a sudden need to hold his wife, but he resisted that as well. *Oh, Lord, you do try a man.*

♦♦♦♦♦♦♦

Abbie waited as Cole spread her bedroll. It was near his, but not touching. That's how she felt, near him but not touching. He kept her at a distance. Was he angry? Had her hesitance hurt him more than he let on? Didn't he know it wasn't him; it wasn't anything but her own disabling fears?

Will and Birdie were at opposite angles across the fire. Will at Cole's head, Birdie at hers. How had adding one slight girl to their number so changed the ease with which they'd traveled before? Will was tongue-tied and fumble-fingered, Cole gruff and short-tempered. He'd barked at Will twice.

But Birdie wasn't the only change. She and Cole were changed, man and wife, though somehow things had gone awry. Why had he insisted they marry at once? Had he thought if they waited she would change her mind? Would she have?

Abbie caught his gaze in the flickering light. When she was ready, he'd said. What if she went to him now, asked him to hold her, spoke of her love? Birdie shifted in her covers, and Abbie glanced over her shoulder. When she turned back, Cole wore his insolent grin.

What he found funny in the situation was beyond her. She

raised her chin and showed him her back, but he took one stride and caught her shoulders. "Good night, Abbie." He kissed her forehead. His lips were warm, his mustache soft.

She raised her face. If he just kissed her, she'd know. He couldn't keep his love from his lips, not if he really kissed her.

Cole tapped her lips with his finger. "Get some sleep." He let her go and waited while she climbed into the bedding and pulled the oilskin cloth over the blankets.

The ground was hard, the wind cold with more than a hint of rain, and Abbie felt a surge of temper. *Lord, what were you thinking when you made men so all-fired stubborn and impossible? I might offer an improvement or two, if you've ever a mind to listen!* She breathed an immediate apology and settled into a dismal mood. If she slept at all it would be a wonder.

Twenty-Three

The bed felt so deep and soft it wrapped itself around her. The flannel sheets were thick as fur, and someone's arms held her. *Cole.* She heard his deep breathing, felt his beard-roughened cheek against hers. With her eyes closed in drowsy content, she reached a hand to stroke his jaw.

Her fingers grew confused trailing over features they knew, only . . . he felt so cold. She ran her hand down his neck, over his chest. Her hand went inside him, and she felt the gore through shattered ribs. *Monte!* But the cold, dead face was Cole's.

Abbie jolted awake in teeth-chattering fear. The blankets slid down as she sat up, trembling. The sun had not yet risen, and the sky was a dull gray. She turned to Cole, but his bedding lay empty. Fear crawled up her spine.

She threw off the covers and stood. The camp was still, the embers low. Whitesock was not with the other horses. Cole was gone. A burning pierced the ice inside her. She felt betrayed all over again.

Abbie stalked to the fire and cleared away the rain-soaked ashes. She stoked the coals beneath with a vengeance and added damp cottonwood to make a sullen blaze. She scooped water from the river into the coffeepot and filled the insert with grounds. She shoved on the lid and set it to heat, then mixed up cornmeal batter.

When the lard was melted in the iron skillet, she poured in the batter and set it to cook. After washing out the bowl, Abbie wiped it dry and set it to be packed when they moved on. She moved with controlled determination, every action, every thought sharp and calculated.

Both Will and Birdie slept through her clatter, Birdie completely submerged in the blankets and likely too sore to move. Will snored like a hog in slop. What did they have to worry about? What troubled their dreams? Nothing. She looked up at the sound of hooves and stiffened.

Cole dismounted and joined her at the fire. "Coffee ready?" He reached for the pot.

She gave him a curt nod.

"Somethin' wrong?" He released the pot.

"No." Abbie turned the skillet to brown the other cornbread edge.

"Then why are you in a huff?"

"I am not in a huff." Abbie shoved the skillet and stalked away. She heard Cole's boots on the crisp turf behind her. She picked up speed.

"You cain't outwalk me."

She stopped, keeping her back stiffly toward him. He wrapped her from behind and rested his chin beside her head. "What's the matter?"

"Where were you?" She knew he could feel her trembling start up again.

"I went to see if we were bein' followed."

Abbie dropped her head forward, fighting the tears. She was unfair in her anger, but it gripped her nonetheless.

Cole turned her in his arms. "I'm sorry. I didn't know that would upset you."

"Well, you ought to have." She bit the words tersely. She couldn't tell him she was ashamed a dream could shake her so, ashamed to dream of Monte still, even if it was twisted and distorted. Besides, he should know better than to sneak off and leave her to wonder.

Cole looked at her with a frown between his brows, as though he were trying to piece her together. Oh, what was the use? Abbie shook off his arms and stalked to the fire. The corn bread was blackened at the edges, cracked and crusty on top. With a wadded cloth, she yanked it from the heat.

Cole bent and poured a cup of coffee, then he nudged Will awake and sent him to graze the horses. The grass was coarse and swampy from the icy rains, which looked to be coming again right soon. He would let Birdie wake her own self, or Abbie could rouse her if she'd a mind to.

He slid Mr. Farrel's Winchester rifle from its scabbard on Whitesock's saddle and checked it over. He'd have preferred a Sharps or something with more kick to it, but the Winchester used the same caliber load as his Colt revolver, so that was one benefit. He hoped it wouldn't see use, except maybe to hunt some meat. But he'd make sure it was in working order, just in case.

When Cole had cleaned and oiled and reloaded it, he did the same with his revolver and saw that Will was caring for his, too. Birdie woke, and he saw the pain in her movements. They'd not get far this day. He would pad her saddle with a blanket and shorten the stirrups some. Maybe that would help. He just hoped they'd have no need to ride hard.

They ate in silence around the fire. It was not Abbie's best effort, but then, he reckoned he'd distracted her. She put out a more frigid chill than the wet wind kicking up off the hills. Well, he'd apologized. It was up to her to accept it.

They rode slowly and made poor time. The rain came and beat on them relentlessly. It would wash clean their tracks, but there was really only one path to take through the desert country. Pablo knew that, and he'd know Birdie's condition. If he was of a mind to claim her, he'd do it this day or the next. Cole chafed. Two women, a man, and a boy were no match for the plug-uglies Pablo would bring.

Will rode up beside him, rain running from the brim of his hat. "You worried, Cole?"

"Does it show?"

"Not to the ladies, I don't think. Birdie's in too much pain, and Mrs. Farr . . . Jasper, well, she's . . ."

"Yeah, I know." Cole eyed Will. He'd filled out plenty these last years. He was what they'd call strapping, and he even carried a decent beard from the whiskers on his cheeks today. Twenty-one years old. Maybe it was time he stopped thinking of Will as a boy.

Cole dropped his chin. "I got a bad feeling. It ain't just that the girl's a valuable commodity, it's that Pablo might take it personal we saw fit to remove her."

Will nodded. "I suppose he would. She was pretty shaken up when we snuck out. That Captain Gates didn't promise anything as far as holding Pablo back."

"Nor could he, even if it was his job to. Which it ain't."

"What do you mean?"

"Well, Birdie's like property. Ain't right, but Pablo's invested in her keep and her clothes and the like. The way he sees it, she owes him, and on account of that, we've stolen from him."

Will shook his head. "She's a person, not a thing."

Cole noted the heightened color and vehemence in Will's face. "Look, kid, maybe you best know a thing or two." He lowered his voice and watched Will color as he explained the ins and outs of Birdie's life as he knew it. "So you watch yerself, you hear?"

Will nodded, but there was a manly set to his jaw that told Cole he might have done more harm than good. If Will took it on himself to conform and win over that vixen, he'd be a man right quick. Luckily, Birdie seemed to think Will had fallen off the face of the earth. Just now that was the best news Cole had.

♦♦♦♦♦♦♦

Under the stormy night sky, Abbie finished scrubbing the dishes in the creek. The rain had stopped long enough to permit a fire, but what wood and peat they could scrounge had burned with a sulky flame, and they'd eaten lukewarm beans and hash. So far, Birdie had not lifted a finger, but Abbie supposed that was due to her pained condition. Abbie remembered how it was but could conjure little sympathy for the girl.

Birdie's tongue was sharper than a viper's, though most of her virulence was directed at Will. The remarks she sent his way made Abbie's hair rise, though most of the time Birdie ignored him as completely as she did Abbie. It was to Cole she looked for everything.

Abbie watched him now, standing beyond the fire's smoky glow, looking out . . . for what? Trouble? His stance was solid, his thumbs hooked in his belt, his gun hanging at his hip. She felt a stabbing remorse.

She'd snubbed him all day, responded in monosyllables or not at all. What kind of wife was she proving herself to be? Not that he'd yet taken on his role of husband. Or had he? Wasn't he taking seriously his care and protection of her? But hadn't he done as much before their vows were said?

He'd protected her since the first time he found her dazed in the snow. He'd been checking their safety this morning . . . at his own risk. And there it was. The cold, clawing fear. She'd awakened and seen his blankets empty, just as she'd seen the empty bed beside her, morning after morning when Monte . . .

The dream images filled her mind—irrational, confused, but potent in their terror. She stared at her hand as though it would actually be red with gore, then clenched it into a fist.

With taut arms, she left the firelight and joined him in the darkness of the night.

"You shouldn't have gone out alone." She spoke with the edges of her teeth joined together.

Cole turned, looking uncertain what to make of her sudden attack.

"This morning. You shouldn't have gone alone. It was reckless and . . ."

"Is that what this is all about? You were worried?" He made it sound childish.

"I don't believe in taking unnecessary risks."

"Since when?" Cole raised an insolent brow. "Since it's someone besides you? Seems I recall plenty of times I pulled your tail out of trouble you dug up yourself, takin' risks."

The fury warmed her. "I don't mean doing what you have to do. I mean . . ." Abbie tightened her hands at her sides.

He cocked his head, waiting, seemingly unwilling to join the argument any more than he had to. His self-control threatened her lack and only riled her more.

"What if they'd been out there? What if there were too many for you alone? What if you'd been . . ."

"Killed?"

Her chest heaved, and he took her arms. His grip was solid, hard. "I cain't promise I won't die. Only that I'll live the best I can until then."

Abbie rested her hands on his chest over the buttons of his yoked shirt, inside the flaps of his tawny duster. She felt his heart beating strong and fast beneath her right palm. His breath was warm, with no hint of tobacco. She suddenly realized he'd not smoked a cigarette since they started. It was different to smell him without it. It was nice.

"Tell me what you want, Abbie."

Her fingers trembled. "I want . . . I want to see you without your shirt."

"What?" His voice thickened.

"I need to see you whole. I have dreams . . . bad dreams . . ." Abbie dropped her head to his collarbone. She wasn't making sense and she knew it. He must think her addled.

Cole stroked her hair gently, his breath coming quick and shallow. "Well, back off, then."

She stepped back. He shrugged out of the duster, opened the yoke of the blue flannel shirt and tugged it over his head. In the darkness, she looked at him, his lean musculature, his smooth skin rising with gooseflesh in the stormy cold, the matting hair that spread across his chest. He was whole, undamaged except for the wound in his shoulder, healing now into a dark, puckered scar.

He shifted, and she watched the flex of bone and tendon. He was beautifully made, her husband. The thought caught her short. Abbie reached slowly, ran her fingers down the muscles of his chest and felt his stomach quiver.

Cole caught her hand hard at the wrist. Tears stung her eyes as she dropped her face to him, and he pulled her close and wrapped her in his arms. "Satisfied?" His voice was hoarse.

Her tears fell silently over his skin, and he pressed her head close and kissed its crown. She felt him shiver. He was cold, poor man. She laughed, then sniffed, and looked up at him.

Cole frowned. "I'm glad you find this comical."

"I'm sorry." She bit her lip against another laugh. "You're cold."

"On the outside, yeah. But you've stoked my furnace good."

Her breath caught jaggedly. "Kiss me, Cole."

"No, ma'am. We're in what you'd call a precarious situation. I need my wits about me."

"One kiss."

"Doggone it, Abbie." He pulled her close and kissed her soundly. "Now, let me keep watch in peace and with my clothes on, if you don't mind."

Twenty-Four

Cole dozed as he sat with his forearms to his knees, rifle ready across his boots. His eyes were closed, but his ears stayed wary. He could keep it up this night and maybe the next. After that he'd have to sleep.

He'd expected Pablo before this. But he knew in his gut it wouldn't be long now. With the Jornado Del Muerto less than a day's ride ahead, they couldn't risk the barren stretch where ambush would mean certain death. And if they stayed beside the Rio Grande they'd traverse rough and pitted country, scored by cliffs and arroyos that would make progress slow, if not impossible.

Again he wondered what chance they'd have against Pablo's men. Cole felt his innards twist up with concern. What he needed was a plan, but for once no possibilities seemed to come. Too much rested on this to take a chance he might have otherwise considered. Now he had Abbie to think of. His wife.

He felt wholly inadequate for the job. He'd saved his own skin plenty of times, even on occasion stepped in for Sam or one or another of his men. But he'd never had to risk what he now risked with Abbie—his heart and soul. *His soul.*

What had Brother Lewis said? To put his trust in the One who held his soul? Cole turned it over, but what good was that in a practical sense? Hadn't Brother Lewis had an answer for that? He'd sure filled time with all his sermons. Cole rubbed his brow.

Ah yes. The preacher had said God had charge over all the circumstances of his life. His physical as well as spiritual needs. Well, if Pablo came along armed as Cole expected, they'd sure as shootin' have physical need. Cole pressed his eyes with his right palm.

Lord God, you haven't known me long—leastwise, I haven't known you. But I reckon I need you now even more than when I was sitting in the jail. It ain't just me now. It's the ones in my care, and especially the one you gave me to love. I'd sure consider it a personal favor if you saw fit to get us through this somehow.

He peeled open his eyes and gazed along the line of the river in the dawning light. The storm had passed in the night, dropping rain and hail pellets that left the ground wet and surfeited. The water ran high. Storms had glutted the banks.

Abbie, Will, and Birdie slept beneath their oiled muslin tent covers. The hail had stung but not injured as it might have. They were none the worse for it. They'd move on at first light. He was edgy to get going even now. What kept Pablo?

Cole stood up stiffly. As he worked the kinks from his back, he scanned the distance. Heavy clouds met the earth at the horizon. Another storm would slow them, but it would work against Pablo, as well. The ground was slippery; it had been too dry underneath to receive the rain gracefully. Instead it rushed across the surface, filling the ruts and gullies.

He dropped his head back and stretched his arms, then yawned. He needed coffee. He could make it himself, though he'd gotten spoiled on Abbie's. He turned, but something caught his eye. He squinted out across the land. There it was. Birds.

Several things could raise a flock like that, but Cole knew better than to wonder. He stooped and took up the rifle, gauging the distance as he did. The rain last night had precluded a fire, but even if it hadn't, he wouldn't have allowed one. Now it looked like he wouldn't have coffee this morning, either. Cole gave Will's foot a kick with his boot, then squatted to wake Abbie.

She opened sleep-glazed eyes, then reached for his hand and held it between both of hers. "Pablo?"

Cole nodded. There was no use pretending they weren't up against it. He'd return Birdie before he let any harm come to Abbie or Will. But he'd give Birdie his best shot, as well . . . for what it was worth.

Abbie sat up, and he cupped her cheek in his palm. He had to be careful touching her, so potent were the feelings it kindled. But this morning it was comfort he wanted to give, comfort and courage. She'd need both before the day was out.

"Come 'ere." Cole caught her close to his chest.

After the episode with the shirt, she'd seemed less touchy, but he knew there were fears inside Abbie that he had no way to control. Today might prove her worst ones true. Cole almost wished he'd loved her when he'd had the chance.

He buried his fingers in her hair, and she raised her face to him. Her lips were soft and full from sleep, and he felt drawn beyond his resisting. He leaned close.

"Should I rouse Birdie?" Will's voice was as thick as his head. Hadn't the boy any sense of timing?

Cole drew back. "Yeah. We'll have company before long." He watched Will hesitate before touching Birdie's shoulder, then saw him sag when Birdie shoved his hand away. At least the kid was safe as long as she chose to spurn him.

Safe? They were none of them safe yet. He needed a plan, but his head was as thick as Will's this morning. No tobacco, no coffee, no sleep. And he'd missed his chance at Abbie's kiss. It was working into a sorely trying day.

Birdie sat up, looking scarcely all of her sixteen years and more like she wanted a paddling than saving. She gave him another inviting, almost pouting, smile. Cole turned away without response and stood.

"Listen up now. I reckon we got maybe an hour to decision time." He saw Birdie stiffen. "I don't mean decidin' *whether* to resist Pablo, but how." Cole ran his hand through his hair. "Ain't much use movin' out. Birdie's sore, and there'd be no outrunnin' them. May as well save the horses the trouble."

Abbie stood and pressed her hands to her lower back, shaking out her rumpled skirts. "What do we do, then? There's little cover here."

"That may be, but the country just ahead ain't the sort you can hurry through." The sound of hooves reached him at the same time he felt the vibration faintly in the ground. He stepped around Abbie and stared. He'd miscalculated. Or had he? It sounded like a single rider. As he watched, the rider came into view.

Cole raised the rifle to rest in both hands across his chest. His throat felt dry. Was it Pablo come to make his demands ahead of his men? Would he challenge him personally? A matter of honor? Was there honor among his kind?

Cole spoke over his shoulder. "Get down to the bank and hide yourselves in the bushes."

Abbie raised her chin.

He didn't give her time to argue. "Go on."

She shook her head and waved her arm over their camp. "It's obvious by the bedding that you're not here alone."

"I don't mean to fool anyone. I just don't want you in the path of any stray bullets. Now *git*." He saw her eyes flare and regretted the unfortunate words. Hadn't she already shown how poorly she took to that phrase?

Will stepped up and took her arm. "Come on, Mrs. Jasper. The sooner you and Birdie are out of harm's way, the better we can concentrate on the business at hand."

Abbie seemed surprised, then relieved that Will meant to

stand with him. Cole hadn't intended that at this point, but he wasn't going to argue. Especially as it smoothed Abbie's feathers. But he saw her pull the pistol from her pocket before she moved. He'd forgotten she carried it. And she could shoot. That was one more gun to count on.

Cole squinted at the rider, just visible now. He was coming at a good clip, not as he would expect Pablo to ride with a threat on his lips. Suddenly Cole relaxed and lowered the rifle to his hips. The rider drew swiftly closer, then slowed. Cole held his stance. If Sam meant to whip him again, this time he'd find a rival. He couldn't afford to be taken out now.

Sam swung down from his horse and caught the reins loosely with his left hand. Cole met his gaze evenly but let Sam speak first.

"I reckon you know you have trouble on your heels."

Cole nodded.

"I figured you could use a hand."

"You usin' it as a fist this time?"

Sam kicked the damp earth with the toe of his boot. "I reckon that's out of my system."

Cole drew a deep breath. "How many are they?"

"Baker's dozen." Sam tipped his hat, and Cole realized Abbie had come up from the bank.

He turned and drew her up beside him with a hand to her elbow. "I hear you've met Abbie, but I'll introduce her now as my wife." Cole watched the surprise in his brother's eyes to see if it triggered bitterness that could endanger them. Instead, Sam gave Abbie a questioning look, then extended his hand.

She took it, and Sam brought her fingers to his lips, a hint of mischief in his eyes. "Welcome to the family, little sister."

Abbie seemed taken aback, then annoyed. "Not so little," she stated, though she had to look up considerably to meet his eyes. "And if you've any more thoughts of thrashing my husband, I'll still put a gun to your head."

Sam cocked his jaw and grinned. "I reckon you would at that." He looked past her to Birdie coming back up from the riverbank.

Cole shook his head. So much for his instructions. "Well, if you're all done socializin', maybe you'll recall we're in a bit of a bind here."

Will came forward. "How far are they?"

Sam shrugged. "Twenty minutes, maybe, before they get a look at us."

Birdie tossed the braid she'd made of her hair back over her shoulder. "It is a shame we are on the same side of the river."

"They'd see us anyway." Sam eyed the sparse growth on either bank.

"But they would not reach us."

Cole stood the rifle on end and eyed her. "Why's that?"

"Pablo takes us to the river to bathe. But he does not swim himself."

"Why not?" At least Will didn't stammer when she looked his way.

"He is afraid, no?"

Cole snatched at the thought. "Are you sayin' Pablo won't cross?"

Birdie turned her wide sultry eyes on him. "Pablo believes his death lies on the water. It was spoken at his birthing." One eyebrow raised. "He will not cross."

"His men might." Sam turned as the sound of hooves became faintly discernible.

"Pablo will not lose face. If he cannot cross, his men will not."

"How sure are you?" Cole tried to read beneath her practiced bravado. She seemed smugly certain, but their lives depended on it.

Birdie shrugged one slender shoulder and said no more. It

was for him to decide whether to believe or not, and he didn't know which way to go. Crossing the Rio Grande was not to be taken lightly at any time and certainly not with the water up as it was. He glanced at Sam.

Sam tipped his head to indicate the decision was his. Cole looked across the water. It was a chance he hadn't counted on. But it was a dangerous one. *God, I ain't sure here. If you're listenin'* . . .

Suddenly he thought of Brother Lewis's awe at the sight of the river, his almost boyish delight as he spoke of the water having a life of its own, rushing like the river Jordan or the river of life. This was the same water that had baptized Cole into the kingdom at Brother Lewis's hands. It had ushered him into life once. Maybe it would again.

Cole felt a conviction inside. He'd take the chance. It was all he had. "We'll even out the load on all the horses. Sam, you and I will swim 'em across. Then we'll come back for the others."

He turned to Abbie, expecting support. Instead he saw confusion, uncertainty. "What is it, Abbie?"

Her eyes looked like a young doe's, all pupil and lashes. "I . . . can't swim."

Cole's conviction faded. "Not at all?"

"Where would I learn? The most I've done is wade the mountain creeks."

He looked back at the water, then to Will. "Will?"

"I used to swim some. But it's been years."

"Can you hold your own against the current?"

"I swam the Ashley River as a boy."

Cole turned to Birdie. She smiled confidently and nodded. "I had planned one day to cross the river and leave Pablo cursing on the bank. Today will be that day."

Cole nodded. "Let's go, Sam."

Abbie came up beside him as he reworked the supplies onto

the horses' backs. "Could I ride across on Zephyr?"

"Too dangerous. She's never been tested as a water horse, and any of them could cramp and sink without warning. You'd be dragged under without a chance." Cole yanked off his boots and coat and then stripped down to his long johns, stuffing it all into the packs on the horse.

"Cole . . ."

"Don't worry, Abbie. I'll get you across." He gave her what he hoped was a confident smile.

She looked pale and less than certain. Of all the times for her to lose her nerve . . .

Twenty-Five

Abbie watched Cole lead Whitesock into the water. He and Sam kept the other horses between them, carrying the gear. The animals breasted the water and splashed until the bottom fell away and they swam. Cole caught hold of Whitesock's mane and swam beside him.

As they entered the current it carried them a little, but they angled against it and fought to keep a steady line to the far side. The river was wide and angry, fifty yards at least and far more tumultuous and deep than before the rains. Abbie felt fear grip her. Where was her bold defiance? She felt more akin to Pablo at this moment than her own husband.

Was there nothing Cole feared? She saw him reach out to free a drifting branch from the packs on one of the horses. Whitesock veered and almost dunked him, but Cole brought the animal under control and kept on. His hat hung by its cord, floating behind him like an obedient pup.

Abbie could just make out a cloud of dust from Pablo and his men. It would take a dozen horses moving fast to raise a cloud from the damp and cracking earth. Crossing the river seemed their best chance if what Birdie said was true. Looking at the girl, Abbie wondered. But it was Birdie's own neck at stake as well as theirs. Surely . . .

Birdie turned with a smile too close to a sneer. "You are afraid, no? They say to drown is very peaceful. But perhaps the snakes will get you first. There are nests of them. Their poison is swift."

Abbie's chest seized, but the cruelty of Birdie's words emboldened her. She would not be intimidated by a misdirected snip of a girl. Abbie returned her gaze to the river and watched Cole and Sam reach the bank. They shouted the horses up the side, then paused and caught their breath.

Abbie could see them talking together, but no sound reached her. Cole took off his hat and rubbed his forehead. She thought he looked her way, and she stood tall for his sake. She would face this. She would conquer the fear. She would do it for him.

Then he and Sam were swimming back. She could see them moving through the water like bobbing apples. As they neared she saw the strong strokes of their arms and legs. When they climbed up the bank, both men were breathing hard, their chests heaving and dripping, their skin red with cold.

"The current's strong but steady." Sam spoke between breaths.

Cole looked to Will. "Sam'll swim alongside you and Birdie. Shed anything that might hold you down."

Will pulled off his boots, and Cole tied them together and hung them over Will's neck. Birdie nonchalantly stripped down to her bloomers and chemise. She dipped her narrow foot into the water and splashed it up playfully. "It is cold as death."

Abbie shuddered involuntarily.

Birdie entered the water, walked a small way, then dove in headfirst, gliding like a fish. Will rushed in behind with awkward giant steps, and Sam shook his head. "Guess I'm off." He cut back into the water.

Abbie stood on the bank with Cole. Her reluctance was a weight on her shoulders, dragging her down.

He gave her a halfhearted smile. "I'll turn my back if you want."

She glanced up, confused, then caught his meaning. "It's not that. It's . . ."

"I know you're scared, but it won't get better by waitin'." He looked to the riders coming on. There was movement detectable along the valley, and she could make out figures. In minutes they, too, would be visible. Cole had rested, and it was time.

Abbie unfastened her skirt and let it fall. She stepped out of the petticoats and unbuttoned her shirtwaist. Cole was looking out across the river, watching the progress of the others. They were in the thick of the current now. Abbie shuddered.

He turned back and reached for her hand. He kept his eyes on her face, and she felt grateful for that. This was hard enough without feeling self-conscious, as well. He walked her to the edge and stepped in without hesitation.

The water was cold, but not icy as the mountain runoff waters of Colorado. Abbie let him tug her deeper. It climbed to her knees and kept mounting.

"When we get to where you cain't stand, I'll get a hold of you and swim. You just relax and let me do the work."

Abbie nodded. The water reached her waist and she could feel the power of the river, even though they were not yet into the current. Her ribs were engulfed, and she felt each breath against the slap of the water.

"It drops off here." Cole reached for her waist.

Abbie's foot slipped on the decline, and she went down, swinging her arms and grasping for Cole. She heard him holler, but her head went under and she thrashed wildly. She felt him there and clung with all her strength, but he broke her hold, and she panicked.

Cole trapped her arms and hooked an elbow across her

throat, pressing her head back to his shoulder. Her face came out, and she gasped air.

"Don't fight me!"

She dug her fingers into the forearm around her neck and kicked. His muscles were hard, but she fought to break free.

"Stop it, Abbie!" He covered her face with his free hand and pulled her ear to his mouth. "Stop kicking. You'll drown us both."

They went under, and Abbie understood his words. She fought the fear and released her hold. He twisted her to her back and once again hooked her under the chin with the crook of his arm. She went limp, begging God's mercy. They surfaced, and she felt Cole strike out with a powerful kick and his one free arm.

She let him drag her, sputtering when the water splashed into her face. She held his arm with both hands but didn't fight his efforts. She was helpless, totally dependent on him. The fear filled her chest and formed a scream, but the splashing water kept her mouth shut tight.

After some moments she learned Cole's rhythm and tried to relax into it. Then they hit the current. She felt it thrust them to the side. He'd never hold against it, not with her as dead weight. The panic rose again. She twisted, and he tightened his hold. She was strangling, but it was enough to bring her to her senses. *Don't fight; don't fear.*

Abbie forced herself to slacken, and he loosed her slightly. His chest was heaving against her side, the muscles tight and hard. She felt him straining. How could he go on? What if he let go? The water was grasping, demanding, terrifying. It would take her, drag her under, hurl her along until it owned her, body and soul.

Something whizzed by her head and struck the water. Cole jerked, and the river carried them the moment his stroke paused. Again something splashed the water, and she realized what it was. Bullets.

"Take a breath."

"What?" Terror seized her.

"Take a breath!"

Abbie gasped, and Cole pulled her under. He had hooked his arm over her right shoulder and under the opposite arm. He dragged her down, no longer fighting the current but still angling toward the far side. The water was thick and murky. Her lungs burned. She imagined snake nests and slimy things lurking just past her vision.

She pressed her eyes shut, and fought the reflex to breathe. Her lungs were bursting. They couldn't hold it. Cole would drown her. She kicked and kicked again. She felt the thrust through the water and kept kicking. The air was leaving her lungs. She couldn't hold. Bubbles rushed past her ears.

Abbie broke the surface, gasping once before he pulled her down again. This time she kicked immediately and tried to push with her free arm as Cole did. She scraped her knee on something jagged and tangled. She kicked free and kept on.

Her lungs cried for air. Her throat ached as she clenched her teeth against the need to breathe. Her head was dizzy, and she no longer knew which way was up. Her legs were heavy, her arms like lead. She stopped kicking. The air flew in bubbles from her lips as her lungs emptied.

Cole's arm was hard and unrelenting. Then she felt a quick thrust, and suddenly she thrashed and gasped air and water together. She choked and wheezed, crying and coughing and trying to breathe.

"It's a'right. It's a'right now." His voice was low in her ear, soothing.

But it wasn't all right. She was still up to her neck in water. She sucked a hard breath and clung to Cole. Though she felt earth beneath her feet, the water still tugged. She clawed his arm and sobbed, trying to keep her feet and get free of the river.

He spoke again into her ear. "Keep still. The river's dragged us some, but we're still within gunshot."

Abbie coughed and squeezed tears from her eyes, trying to see the horsemen on the far shore. She felt as though half the river were inside her ears and eyes and throat. She couldn't get a clear breath for the wet rasping of her lungs.

"Go ahead and cough it out. If they see us, we'll go under again."

"I can't." She choked and water spewed from her lips.

Cole pressed her head to his neck. "A'right. Try not to move. We've got that bit of sandbar between us an' them. Maybe they won't notice if we're still."

"I want to get out."

"I know you do. But that's what they're lookin' for. And the minute we start climbin' they'll cut us down."

Abbie closed her eyes and let the dizziness pass. The pull of the water made it hard to keep her feet, but Cole held steady. Slowly he backed through the water, careful not to splash the surface. A shelf rose behind them, and he eased her down to sit.

The water lapped her throat, but he hooked her shoulders with his arm and pressed her close to his side. Her teeth chattered with the cold. They'd freeze if they didn't drown. "Cole, I . . ."

"I know you're cold. Just hold on a minute more." His eyes were fastened on the far bank.

She could see the horsemen clustered there. She didn't know which one was Pablo, but one man held her skirt over his head and danced about. She could just make out the laughs and hoots. "Where are Will and Birdie and Sam?"

"Upriver, just across. Sam's got the rifle as well as his six-shooter."

Abbie gasped. "I left mine in my skirt."

Cole nodded grimly. "I thought of that when we were halfway out. Right about when you tried to drown me."

She flushed. "I'm sorry. I didn't mean to fight like that."

"For once I wished you were more like the late Mrs. Farrel. You nearly had me beat. I was this close to knockin' you silly just so's I could get a hold and keep it."

Abbie gave him an impish smile. "You've got a hold now."

He let out a slow breath and shook his head. "You sure pick your times, Mrs. Jasper."

She felt giddy. "What's the matter, Cole? Don't you feel romantic, up to our necks in freezing river water, fighting for our lives?"

"I've a suspicion that's when it hits you most."

She reached a hand through the water to his chest. "Cole . . ."

"Not now, Abbie."

"I just want to thank you."

"For?"

"Not drowning me."

"We ain't outta this yet."

"*Aiyee!*" The cry came from the far bank and gunshots erupted.

Abbie jumped, but the shots were not toward them. The others must have been spotted. She heard the bang of the Winchester and saw the men scramble from their horses and fall belly down to take cover.

"That's our signal." Cole yanked her up the bank toward dry land. "While they're occupied we'll get loose of this river."

She followed, scarcely able to press her legs through the water. They were farther from the side than she'd thought. The shelf went a good way, and they plodded waist-deep, stooping, expecting any moment to find bullets aimed at them. But Sam and Will were keeping the men busy.

So far Birdie's prediction held true. Pablo kept his men to their side. It would be fatal for them to cross now, with Sam armed and ready to pick them off if they tried. Even outnumbered, the river made a formidable defense. She silently thanked Birdie's good sense.

Abbie climbed onto dry land and fell to her knees in the bushes. The wet underthings clung to her, but she had no time to think of impropriety. A gunshot whistled through the reeds, and she ducked automatically. Cole flattened himself beside her. They'd been seen.

Her breath came in short gasps as Cole rolled to his side against her. He pressed his fingers into her hair and held her face. His eyes were deeply green as a mountain meadow. "I gotta get to my gun. I want you to stay here."

"No."

"Two of us movin' through is a better target than one."

Her fear rose. "Stay here with me. Please."

"I can't. Sam can't do this alone. It ain't even his fight."

"If we just stop shooting, maybe they'll go."

Cole dropped his head. "They won't go, Abbie. They'll wait until dark, and they'll cross."

"But Birdie said . . ."

"Birdie don't know everything, and I don't have time to argue."

Shame rushed to her cheeks, but before she could turn away, he kissed her. His mustache was damp, his chin scratchy, but his lips were ardent as they'd not been before. It caught away her breath, but when she opened her eyes, he was already moving away from her.

She didn't call him back. Cole was doing what he must, what his honor demanded, even though it was not truly his fight, either. Taking Birdie along had been her doing and Will's, though it had bought Cole's freedom.

A bullet thumped the bank beneath his crawling figure,

and he flattened, then crept on. She wished she could go, as well. At least she could help reload. Cole's concern had been for them to move together. If she went separately...

A bullet whizzed past. She wasn't any safer staying where she was. She crawled through the growth. Her wet underthings were already muddy and spoiled. She snagged the lace of her camisole and tore it free, then crept forward. Either they didn't see or didn't bother with her.

Abbie kept on. One shot sprayed dirt in her face, but though she flinched she didn't slow, so intent was she on reaching her destination. She followed the edge of the riverbank, staying as close to the ground as possible. Her knees were raw, her arms shaking and weak, but she pressed through the bushes, grimly determined.

Rounding a bend, she could see Will huddled behind a bush with blood on his sleeve. Sam was out of sight, and Cole, too, had disappeared. Birdie lay flat with her chin on her arms. Only the crease between her brows betrayed her concern. Will startled, then recognized her and relaxed.

Abbie crept to where he crouched. "Are you hurt badly?"

"Just a graze."

"Where's Cole?"

"He and Sam moved down that way for better cover." He motioned with his head.

Abbie looked where he directed. She could see Cole's back bare to the wind. His shirt lay before her on the bank, just beyond the lapping water. "Where are the horses?"

"Sam hobbled them some three hundred yards yonder, down that gully."

She eyed the shirt again. "Cover me."

"What are you..."

She didn't wait to argue but sprang, crouching low toward the shore. Gunshots stung the sand at her feet as she snatched the shirt and ran. Will scarcely got off two answering shots before she was back. She saw Cole turn at the ruckus, his scowl in place. She crawled to his thicket and handed over the shirt.

He frowned. "Do you ever do what you're told?"

"Just put on the shirt and don't bother thanking me. You'll catch your death without it." From the corner of her eye she caught Sam's grin. "I'm going to the horses to retrieve clothing for Birdie and me. Have you cartridges enough?"

Cole shrugged into the shirt and buttoned the yoke. "I've a mind to hobble you with the horses."

Abbie glared. "You're not the only one with wits, Cole. I can handle myself."

"Tell that to the man usin' your six-shooter."

She punched his shoulder, then drew back when he winced painfully. She'd forgotten the old bullet wound. "I'm sorry."

Cole grunted and rubbed the damaged joint. "It's bad enough I have to drag you kickin' and screamin' through a floodin' Rio Grande. Now you . . ." A bullet splintered the thin trunk of the bush beside them, and Cole caught her down. "A'right, go. Fetch what you need an' keep your head down."

Abbie scrambled clear. She took a zigzagging path away from the river and arrived at the horses, winded and with her feet cut and bruised. She had to search through the packs as the things had been redistributed for the swim. She found her one spare pair of slippers, but her boots were either washed away or on the far shore with Pablo and his men.

She pulled on her forest green serge dress, did up the buttons, and began to tremble. She'd been creeping about in bloomers and camisole before God and everyone without a thought to her near naked condition. What would Monte say? The thought stabbed her. It wasn't Monte who mattered now, it was Cole.

Well, he'd hardly noticed. At least he hadn't shown it. He'd had survival on his mind. But she had better get Birdie covered up before Will learned her anatomy by heart. Abbie dove into her pack and found the brown linen dress. It should be just drab enough to dull Birdie's beauty.

Abbie balled it under her arm and started back. It had been awfully quiet while she stood with the horses. Both sides seemed to have ceased firing. She stooped low and made her way back to Will and Birdie.

Birdie sat now with her knees wrapped in her slender arms. She hung her head back and let the sun dry her long shining hair. She seemed not the least unnerved to be sitting half clothed under Will's bashful gaze.

Abbie tossed the dress to her. "Here. Put that on."

Birdie's lips turned up at the corners. It was like a cat gloating over a dead bird. She stood slowly and stretched. Immediately there were shouts across the water.

Abbie yanked her down. "What are you trying to do?"

"I was only obliging you."

"You can dress yourself just as well sitting down. Now see to it."

Birdie held the dress to her chest and looked about to retort when there came a single gunshot. Abbie watched a rider raise a white flag on a pole and walk his horse into the water. She felt Cole creep up behind her.

She turned. "What is it, do you think?"

"Parley."

"They'll ask for Birdie."

"I reckon so."

"What'll we do?" Abbie glanced to see Birdie slipping the dress over her head. She wasn't fond of the girl by any stretch, but she'd given her word. And beyond that, she had to champion the girl's determination to get free.

Cole's focus was on the rider, now advanced to swimming depth and entering the current. He frowned. "His horse is swimmin' deep. It's got a poor breadbasket to handle the water."

"Breadbasket?" Abbie tried to catch his eye.

"Its chest cavity."

"How can you . . ."

Suddenly the horse went down. One moment it was there, the next, horse and rider had sunk beneath the surface. Cole sprang forward to the water's edge. Abbie's breath caught short. Surely he wouldn't go in after the man. He would be an easy target for the dozen remaining guns.

Abbie clenched her hands at her sides as Cole stood and searched the flow. The white flag surfaced on its pole, spun, and shot away down the river's center. Cole stood in plain view of the opposite bank, but no one fired. They all stared at the water. It rushed on, gray and dull, with no sign of the man whose life had been engulfed in its depths.

At that moment the clouds opened and rain fell in thin sheets. Abbie got to her feet and walked to Cole's side. He stood unmoving. She touched his arm, but his eyes remained on the water, his face inscrutable.

His voice sounded dry. "He should've known that was no water horse. It maybe could've swum the river without him, but never with a rider."

"Come back, Cole. They can see you."

He looked out across the river. The dozen men milled uncomfortably. One stood staring into the river even as Cole had. Abbie had never laid eyes on him, but she knew it was Pablo. He was staring death in the face. Slowly he raised his head. She almost felt his gaze meet Cole's.

They stood frozen. Neither moved for his gun, yet neither released the other. A dark man with a broad-brimmed straw hat stepped close to Pablo. He spoke, but still Pablo did not move.

Abbie felt Cole's tension seeping from his pores. His fingers dangled near the gun, immobile like the rest of him. Did he know she was there? Did it matter? She waited, scarcely breathing. What power held them?

Oh, Lord, you are master. Govern Cole now. Give him wisdom and strength. Make him strong enough to let go.

Slowly Cole raised his hand and took the hat from his head. As slowly, he lowered it to his chest and held it there in respect for the man the river had claimed. Across the water she saw Pablo's stance change. Would he go for his gun?

Lightning slashed. Pablo took one step back. He brushed away the man beside him with a gesture. Then, with a last glance across the water, he turned his back and waved his arm at his men.

No sound of argument reached her as she watched, silent in the rain. The men across the bank gathered up their things and mounted. Still Cole waited, and Abbie waited beside him, uncertain what to make of it.

"Are they leaving?" Her voice sounded small.

"I reckon so."

"Why? They were willing to kill and be killed. Why would one man's drowning change that?"

"Superstition, likely. If Pablo thinks that was the river's warning, he won't press his luck. My guess is Pablo figures he beat death once today. Better not risk it again."

"But . . ."

Cole turned. "Do you have to argue God's will? Sheez, woman. Weren't you prayin' alongside me just now?"

"How did you know?"

"You had that pinched up, pensive look you get when you're beggin' the Almighty."

"You never looked at me once."

"Don't think because my focus is elsewhere I cain't see you."

"I don't believe it."

"Oh yeah? Then how about the little blue ribbon you had

woven through the waist and neckline of your . . . whatever it is you swam in."

Abbie felt her jaw drop.

Cole caught her arm and started up the bank. "And whereas under better circumstances I might appreciate it, I'd just as soon Sam and Will not get another eyeful."

Abbie's sudden humiliation left her speechless. Then her temper came to her rescue, but before she could vent it, Will clambered up with Sam on his heels.

Sam sent his gaze across the water. "You reckon that's it?"

"I reckon we owe a word of thanks to Birdie here." Cole tipped his hat to where she sat in the sand in Abbie's brown dress. "Crossin' the river was a wily move, young lady."

"*Gracias, señor.*" Even the drab fabric couldn't dull the flush of pleasure that filled her face. Abbie felt a jealous pang.

Cole took a look at Will. "How's the arm?"

"It's nothin'."

"Better let Abbie doctor it anyhow. No sense it gettin' septic." Cole rubbed his shoulder. "And she has a way with wounds." He gave her a teasing wink.

Abbie raised her chin, scarcely noticing the rain. He'd deserved the sock she gave him. And after his embarrassing comments, she had half a mind to do it again.

Twenty-Six

Cole felt almost giddy riding along the river. They'd challenged death, and the Lord had been with them. He wasn't used to thinking that way, but he'd put his trust where it counted when the chips were down.

Likely none of them would be riding now if they hadn't crossed, and Cole might not have crossed if he hadn't sought wisdom from above. Years ago he'd have called that nonsense. Now it seemed right wise. Still, it had been touch and go for a while.

He and Pablo could have shot it out. The distance across the river was enough to spoil a man's aim, but not enough to keep the bullets from striking. Cole had felt the challenge. Pablo could have taken him in speed, but he was a hothead. The man would have fired wild.

Cole shook his head. He hadn't been of a mind to kill. Surely not in front of Abbie. But he wasn't one to back down. Why it came to him to lay it down, he wasn't sure. Maybe Abbie's prayers. He'd more felt than seen her as he'd claimed to.

He'd struggled, his pride not wanting to give in, to be the one to let go first. Then he'd thought of the man rolling under the river. The one carrying the peace terms. It seemed only right. Doffing his hat to a plug-ugly who'd likely see Brother Lewis's infamous flames was no contradiction. It wasn't for him to judge.

Cole glanced at Sam riding beside him. What had brought his brother around? It had pained Cole to think they'd be at odds for good. Sam meant too much to him for that. But for the life of him he couldn't see how to make it right, except to show he was willing to die for him.

Maybe Sam knew that. Maybe it helped. Likely Cole would never know for sure. That's how it was with them. They didn't talk about the deep things. Those got sealed off, unspoken. But it kept them close, knowing the shared things were there.

Nor had Sam said where he was heading. Maybe he had no plans. Maybe Sam was drifting, just as he himself had when Abbie cut him loose. Maybe Sam would come back to the ranch with them. Cole could sure use him.

But that was up to Sam. Right now Cole was just grateful his brother had seen fit to stand by him. He couldn't have handled the crossing alone. There was a limit to any man's strength, and without Sam he wouldn't have attempted it.

Cole's shoulder was paining him something fierce. Crossing the Rio Grande three times was enough to tax a sound man, much less one with a recent injury. He just hoped he hadn't done any real damage.

He glanced back at Abbie and Birdie riding just behind, and Will bringing up the rear. Will's arm was bandaged, but as he'd said, the wound was little more than a sting. The kid had held his own. He could keep his head up. Cole caught Will's grin and returned it.

It put him in mind of the first time he'd spit in death's eye. Only in his case it hadn't been from a bullet. It was the stallion known as Devil. None of Cliff's men would face the beast, but Cole at fifteen thought he was invincible.

He'd gotten so far as hooking his lariat on the demon's neck when it came straight for him. Another horse would have charged and veered, or reared up to use its hooves. This one came straight on with murder in its eyes. At the last second

Cole had spun, grabbed the mane, and sprung astride.

He'd only kept his seat for a breath before landing so hard the world went dark. He heard later that two of the guys had pulled him free before Diablo's hooves could finish him off. He had three broken ribs, but he was alive.

Cole reached up and rubbed his shoulder. Yes, indeed, he was alive.

Abbie watched Cole's and Sam's backs as they rode. They couldn't travel far after the exertion at the river, but Cole didn't seem to think they'd be followed. She wasn't so sure, but she was too tired to argue. Besides, Abbie had a worse concern—that they would have to cross back.

She pushed the thought from her mind. There were places the river was fordable. Surely they'd take advantage of that. Surely . . . Sam glanced back briefly but looked past her. He'd come along with them, though he hadn't spoken of his plans.

At least he and Cole seemed at peace. Maybe they'd shared words, though she hadn't seen when. Maybe they needed none. She slid from Zephyr's back the moment Cole called a halt. The rain, too, had stopped and the earth gave off a ground mist in the last of the sun's rays. Will led the horses to drink at the river, and Sam collected brush for a fire.

It would be nice to have a hot meal and a fire's warmth. Abbie gave the supper her best effort, though the supplies they carried were plain enough. She managed a cobbler made with a small bag of dried peaches and what flour and sugar hadn't been wet by the river.

The steamed jerky and boiled potatoes filled their bellies while the cobbler perked up their weary spirits. Birdie seemed the least affected by the day's events and sat humming by the fire. As Abbie washed the last of the dishes, her arms ached from her bout with the river.

Her neck was stiff, too, no doubt from Cole yanking her

along. Well, he'd had no choice, especially the way she'd fought him. What was she thinking? She wasn't thinking at all. It was pure reflex, and one that nearly killed them. But they'd made it.

Abbie shook her head and wiped the skillet dry. She set it on the canvas and pressed her hands to her lower back. How she had strained that, she couldn't say. She felt another hand there and turned, startled.

Cole took her arm and led her from the camp. Abbie felt the fire's heat fade as she crossed the stubbly plain beneath the open sky. Cole walked without speaking and stopped at a driftwood tree trunk lying prone and bleached by wind and sun. A prior flood must have wrenched it from the bank and left it stranded there. The moon shone on its silvery length.

"Set there a minute."

She sat down, looking at him curiously. What was he doing? Cole took the harmonica from his pocket and patted it against his thigh. He looked up to the sky, then cupped the metal with his hands and put it to his mouth. The soft wailing notes formed a slow waltz as the harmony chased the melody up and down his hands.

Abbie wrapped her knees in her arms and listened. A smile tugged her lips and filled her heart when he drew out the last note and pocketed the harmonica. She raised her hands to clap, but he caught them in his and pulled her to her feet.

"Now you hold that tune in your head." He hooked his arm around her waist and caught her hand up, palm to palm with his.

"What are you . . ."

"I'm dancin' with my wife."

In the darkness, Abbie heard the smile in his words as he swept her into the slow waltz that lingered in her mind. Cole always was a good dancer. He had both a natural rhythm and personal style, and he danced as though he enjoyed it. She looked up to find his smile, but his expression was deeper, wilder.

"See, on the dance floor, you gotta watch yerself. You hold a girl too close or too long and folks start to talkin'. But out here, there's none but the stars to notice." Cole drew her against him, and Abbie moved where he led as though they were one.

Her heart sped as he increased his steps, sweeping her in widening circles. The cold night air caught her breath as it quickened and shortened. The edges of his mouth deepened beneath the ends of his mustache.

A warmth and tingling shot through her limbs. She felt her pulse throbbing to his rhythm, and the tune he softly hummed. Years of soothing a herd with his voice gave him a confidence and ability she couldn't resist.

Abbie slid her fingers from his shoulder to his collarbone. "I never knew you were so . . . romantic. You weren't like this before."

"As I recall, you didn't want to be courted. You cain't have it both ways, Abbie, but I was kinda hopin' you wouldn't mind now." He brushed her cheek with his beard-roughened jaw.

Cole was right. She hadn't wanted his courting all those years ago. She'd pretended he was merely keeping company, visiting, and he'd kept it that way . . . until he asked to marry her. He had made it easy to say no. But now she'd said yes. Her pulse throbbed almost painfully.

She loved him—his strength, his goodness, this side of him that was tender and deep, even playful. But she was not prepared to be swept off her feet. Could she risk committing all she had to loving him?

Abbie had seen today how closely he walked to death, how carelessly he challenged fate. Even now his eyes had a recklessness, a cocky daring. Was this some victory ritual such as she'd seen Gray Wolf and his braves hold when they'd slaughtered Buck Hollister and lived to tell of it?

She pulled away, shaken. "Thank you for the dance, Cole. But the others must be wondering."

He stood still, his eyes glittering in the dark. Abbie didn't realize she held her breath until he released her by looking away. He made a small laughing sound, bowed jauntily, then hooked her waist in his arm and led her back to the fire.

As they entered its warmth, his hand slipped away, and she had a moment's misgiving, as though she'd been offered a prize and had turned it down. She glanced up, but he wore the noncommittal face she'd seen when they started out. There was only a hint of regret in his eyes, and then it was gone. Abbie wished her own could vanish as easily.

Lord, you ain't making this easy. Maybe I ain't got the right to complain. I ain't served you as long as Brother Lewis. Maybe you only look after the details for them as serve you well, or maybe I'm missing something I should see. But either way, I could use some advice right about now on how to love the woman you've given me.

Cole turned in his blankets to see Abbie lying close by. Her face was soft in sleep, but it had been sharp enough when she dismissed him. Hadn't he shown her yet what she meant to him? She was as skittish as a maiden and twice as wary. He'd never seen her look at Mr. Farrel that way.

Even angry with Farrel, or hurt as she'd been plenty of times, her face had held a yearning, a desire to please. Cole kicked himself for the envy he felt, knowing it was surely not God's intention. If Brother Lewis were near, he'd have a word or two to say on that subject.

Cole shook his head. He'd thought to woo her, to bring her along gently. He'd thought maybe now she'd allow him to do the things he'd always wanted, to court her rightly. Maybe she thought he'd had more on his mind than a dance. Maybe he had.

But what he really wanted was to gentle her. To take away the fear and share the joy of being alive and together and safe. He almost felt charmed. That he walked free was remarkable. That they'd escaped Pablo was amazing. That Abbie had married him was nothing short of a miracle. He shouldn't spoil it with doubts.

But he wished God would show him what to do. Maybe Cole just didn't know how to listen. He'd thought the urging to cross the Rio Grande had been divine, and it seemed to turn out that way. He'd felt the inclination to let go the fight at the opposite bank, and Pablo had gone along. But he sure felt cut adrift when it came to Abbie.

Maybe God didn't cotton to romance. But that was foolish. He'd started it all Himself with them two in the garden. Cole pushed up from the saddle he used as a pillow. He'd counted on a sound sleep this night after the sleepless ones previous. Maybe he was still too worked up with it all.

He climbed out of the covers and started to stand, but instead, he went to his knees. It felt strange, even a little foolish, but he folded his hands as he'd seen Brother Lewis do. The ground was dry and hard, having absorbed all the moisture and secreted it away. Cole bowed his head.

Lord, I reckon Brother Lewis would say surrender this care to you. So here goes. I want to love my wife as I should, and if it ain't too much trouble, I'd like her to love me, too. But as the preacher said, what I want ain't always your plan. So I'll just leave it up to you to make things happen as you will.

Cole opened his eyes and saw Abbie watching. He hadn't prayed aloud, but he felt as though he'd been caught doing something foolish. He kept his thoughts from his face as he unfolded his hands and rocked back on his heels, squatting cowboy fashion. She rose up on one elbow. The question was in her eyes, but she didn't ask.

His own whisper came hoarsely. "Go back to sleep, Abbie.

I'm just gonna have a look around." Cole stood and strode away before she could argue. God sure had a way of humbling a man.

Abbie watched Cole until his silhouette merged with the darkness. He'd been on his knees, hands clasped in prayer. At first she'd thought she was dreaming. She couldn't have imagined a less likely sight. But then she'd realized it was a waking sight. It was real.

Abbie knew Monte had served the Lord, but she'd never seen him pray, not on his knees, not . . . humbly . . . simply . . . seeking God. Yet seeing Cole thus hadn't diminished him. Instead, she felt . . . honored. Had he indeed come to trust God? Could she doubt it any longer?

She recalled the warmth with which he and Brother Lewis had parted. She recalled Brother Lewis's testament to Cole's conversion. Had that been God's purpose in all of this? Had she been only secondary to what God had in store for Cole Jasper?

Abbie felt a trembling inside and recognized it as shame. She'd given Cole so little credit. She'd dared to think he had no trust in the Lord. She'd felt smugly secure in her own faith and inwardly disparaged his lack.

She sat up and brushed the hair from her face. She couldn't see him out in the night, but she slipped from the covers and pulled on her coat. Will and Birdie and Sam slept soundly, no doubt exhausted from the day. Abbie was certain any sound she made would waken Sam, but she crept silently as Blake had taught her.

She made out Cole's frame, hands hooked at the waist, legs apart and slightly bowed. He didn't seem arrogant now, or insolent or even teasing. His back was straight, but his head hung forward. She approached, and he raised his face and spoke low.

"I've lived all my life by my own compass. I think now God wants to give me a new map, but I ain't sure how to read it."

Abbie reached out and clasped his hands but didn't speak.

"I ain't sure why, but . . ." Cole swallowed and looked aside, then fixed her again in his gaze. "I'd like to ask His blessin' on us. Just seems the thing to do."

Her chin trembled as she nodded.

"Lord, you created us, and you got a plan for us. All we want is to serve you as you see fit. Please bless our efforts, as it ain't likely we'll get it right on our own, first off anyhow."

A tear crested her eyelid and slipped down her cheek.

Cole caught it with his thumb. "Doggone, Abbie."

She pressed his hand against her cheek. "I've wronged you, Cole. Can you forgive me?"

"Ain't nothin to . . ."

"Please."

He drew her slowly into his arms. "I forgive you, Abbie. And . . ." He dropped his forehead to her hair. "I love you somethin' awful."

She closed her arms around his waist and rested her cheek on his chest. "I love you, too, Cole. I believe there's a chance we'll be happy."

"One heck of a chance if I have any say in it." He gave her his crooked grin.

She smiled back. It was a start. And maybe the best start they could hope for.

Twenty-Seven

Standing beside her in the yard of the Lucky Star, Cole wrapped his arm around Abbie's slender waist. He felt an awesome rightness in the gesture. She was his to protect, to love and cherish, and right now, his to comfort. Though Sam had told them about the fire Crete Marlowe set, it was still hard to look at the marred face of the house.

He was glad he'd asked Will and Sam to hold back a bit with Birdie while he and Abbie rode ahead to have a look. Cole could only imagine what Abbie was feeling. That house held a lot of memories, both good and painful. It could have been worse. The structure was sound, though the portico and the front rooms were blackened and the windows boarded.

He stroked his thumb down and up her back. "We'll fix it back up, Abbie. I got some money put by."

She pulled her gaze from the house to him. "How?"

"Bustin' broncs paid good. I squirreled away whatever Ma didn't need. And then Mr. Farrel was generous. He paid a good sight more than I could spend." Abbie still looked at him askance.

"Well, I've ... passed some time with Lady Luck at the poker table. It ain't a fortune, but it'll get us by."

"Mama!"

Abbie spun at the cry, and Cole watched the small, dark-haired boy spring through the door and down the steps. Abbie rushed to meet him. That was all right. Cole could share. Jenny followed more slowly and stood with that big-eyed look both wary and pleading. What surprised him was that she had it turned on him instead of Abbie.

Jenny caught her hands behind her back, which made her skirts stick out in front. It was a defensive pose that tugged his heart. "Did you really marry Aunt Abbie like your wire said?"

"I did. Twice."

She puzzled that a moment. "Why twice?"

"Your Aunt Abbie wanted a church weddin', which Father O'Brien performed when we came through." He didn't need to explain the doctrinal dictates Abbie had cited, nor the fact that her vows had been much more forthcoming the second time.

Jenny looked over her shoulder at Elliot, still wrapped tightly in his mama's arms with her tears falling in his hair.

Cole waited for Jenny to turn back, then squatted down. "Come 'ere."

She came. "Are you . . . mad at what I said?"

"What you said?"

"In my note."

He reached out and cupped her thin elbows in his hands. "No, I ain't."

She bit her lip. "Then you don't mind if I pretend you're my pa?"

"I don't mind."

She came closer until she was right between his knees. "May I call you Pa?"

Cole looked into the dark depths of her eyes, eyes that had no right to be so yearning. "Unless your Aunt Abbie says otherwise, I cain't think what I'd like better."

Jenny pressed in and wrapped his neck in her arms. He held her snug against him. It nearly made him soft, the way she burrowed into his heart. But then, he'd been a hard-riding cowboy a long time. He reckoned a little tenderness might just be in order.

Abbie squeezed Elliot as though making sure he was truly there, real and solid in her arms. The burned house was nothing if her children were safe.

"You were gone too long, Mama. You won't leave again, will you?"

She felt his need and answered it with her own. "No, I won't. If I have to leave I'll tie you to my back and take you right along."

"Me too?" Jenny left Cole's embrace, and he stood up.

Abbie reached and pulled her close. "You too. Absolutely." She looked up at Cole. She hoped he knew she meant him, too, hoped he knew how she loved him. The intensity still surprised her. She hadn't looked for it, hadn't expected it, hadn't believed she could love again.

It wasn't the same star-swept love she'd had for Monte. It was a love born of risking their lives for each other and of Cole's faithfulness. He hadn't given up on her, even when she'd sent him away. Had Monte known when he put her in Cole's charge? Had it been his final blessing to them both?

And now Cole's faithfulness belonged to God, as well. He had told Father O'Brien he'd been baptized by Brother Lewis in the Rio Grande. She could scarcely picture it. But her heart swelled as she stood and took Cole's hands. "I can't think what could be better than a hot bath, a good meal, and a soft bed."

He gave her a crooked smile. "I can. But I cain't say it in front of the young'uns."

Abbie's heart jumped and she felt fire in her cheeks. As long as she lived, she'd never get over loving Cole Jasper.

He bent and kissed her cheek with a low chuckle. "What's the matter, Abbie? You're blushin' like a bride."

Acknowledgments

Special thanks and blessings to my new sisters in the Lord, Patty Deakin and Betty Busekrus, for your support and encouragement, and Betty, for your unfailing eagerness. Thanks to Dorothy Ranaghan for kind words, to Al Heitzmann for your warm notes and helpful comments, and to Mary Jane Heitzmann for your unflagging promotion. And always, thanks to my family for your love and belief, to Barb Lilland, my editor, who makes it better, and to all those at Bethany who make a dream reality.

All thanksgiving to the Lord our God who dwells with and within us and makes all things possible.